Be Afraid

James Bellis

Take a Peek Publishing—Conway SC
Paperback ISBN: 979-8-9859469-1-8
eBook ISBN: 979-8-9859469-4-9
Library of Congress Control Number:
Title: *Be Afraid*
Author: James Bellis
Digital distribution | 2023
Paperback | 2023

This is a work of fiction. The characters, names, incidents, places, and dialogue are products of the author's imagination, and are not to be construed as real.

Dedication

To my fabulous daughter Isobeil with love.
Special thanks to Susan Benade, Margaret Sweetnam.
To my wife and soulmate Philippa thanks for putting up with me.

Chapter 1
Thursday December 30 2021, 4.30 pm

Almost time to call it a day. The detective's room on the third floor of New York Police Department's 35th precinct was deserted, apart from two homicide detectives quietly packing up their personal belongings, savoring the thought of a cold brew at O'Hagan's Bar. The peace and quiet was interrupted by the office door being kicked open. They turned towards the door, fearing the worst.

'We've got another one.' Detective First Grade Mike Garcia walked into the team room, with a cup of steaming coffee in his hand. He waved the note in his other hand.

'Fuck it!' Detective Second Grade Dave Shaw swore under his breath. 'Sorry Mills, I…'

Detective Third Grade Linda Mills waved a hand, cutting him off. 'Seriously, Shaw, you think it's my first day listening to you idiots?' She shot him a sideways glance over the top of her paper.

'Still, I'm sorry. My mama taught me better,' Dave apologized.

Mills rolled her eyes at him; he'd apologized to her for every cuss word he'd ever uttered in her presence. It would be cute if it wasn't so damn annoying. 'You might want to take a refresher course, Shaw.'

'You both done jibber jabbering over Shaw's potty mouth? We have another one, right here. This is where I need your attention.' Garcia slammed his coffee mug onto his desk. He'd broken so many mugs that the team had clubbed in to buy him an indestructible refillable mug because cleaning up his coffee stains was almost a full-time job. It had been meant as a gag gift, but Garcia never went anywhere without it. At this rate, his desk would break before the mug did.

'What have we got?' Shaw asked, moving over to Garcia's desk.

Mills sat back in her chair, arms crossed and put her feet up on her desk, getting ready for the briefing. If the guys could do it, so would she. Garcia raised an eyebrow at her, smiled and turned his attention to the white board.

'This one is technically two. Double homicide. It looks like our perp was mid-assault on the Mrs. when Mr. walked in. He slaughtered them both.' Garcia rattled off the facts like it was another Thursday at the zoo.

'How can we be sure it's the same guy? Up to now it's been robberies, rapes and assaults; murder is a huge next step. You saying he's escalating?' Mills dropped her feet to the ground and leaned forward, frowning at the implications of what Garcia was saying.

'We think it's the same perp. CSI guys sent over a snapshot of this.' Garcia passed his phone to Shaw, who passed it on to Mills.

'Well, fuck me,' Shaw said, immediately glancing over at Mills, who had a hand raised in his direction. He took the hint.

Mills zoomed in on the picture and caught sight of the small zodiac symbol on the woman's forehead.

'Sagittarius this time?' she asked, even though the answer was obvious.

'Yep, back to Sagittarius. Last one was Gemini, so next one was Sagittarius. It has to be him.' Shaw rubbed his hands over this face, the strain of the day clearly showing. Mills passed the phone back to Garcia.

'I don't get it. There are twelve zodiac signs, but this guy is only using two; Gemini and Sagittarius.'

'Yeah, looks like those are the only ones that get his motor running. We have to be missing something obvious here. I mean, come on, what links those two signs? None of the victims have been Gemini or Sagittarius so what is the significance?'

Shaw pulled out the files on the ongoing cases they had credited to their mystery perp; four so far. 'Do we know what star signs the victims are on this one?' Shaw asked while Garcia scrolled through his phone.

'Hold on, checking that now. Mrs. was born in early Jan, so Capricorn and Mr. was born in early March, so Pisces. Other than Capricorn being one on from Sagittarius and Gemini being 2 from Pisces we got nada. So, unless this mofo is going Fibonacci on this, I'm going to say there's no link between the victims and the symbols he's leaving behind.'

'It's the escalation in violence that is concerning me more right now. Up to now it's been robbery, rape and assault. Murder is a big jump,' Mills said and Garcia nodded.

'I agree. Maybe it was Mr. walking in on him that necessitated the murder. So far none of the victims have been able to ID this guy, not a single feature to go on. Maybe Mr. saw him clearly, so he had to die? And if you're killing one, may as well go balls to the wall and whack them both?' Garcia suggested. Mills winced at his crass description of the situation but couldn't argue with his logic.

'I sincerely hope we don't have another Zodiac killer problem,' Mills muttered to herself.

Garcia glanced down at her. 'I highly doubt it. We have four cases so far, all sexual assaults. Today makes victims five and six but the first murders. The CSI guys are still on the scene finishing up. They'll send over their report as soon as they have one, but in the meantime, we need to head over there and get some eyes on the situation,' Garcia said, turning to grab his coffee mug and keys.

Mills and Shaw followed behind him, not looking forward to whatever carnage awaited. The challenge of solving cases was exciting but neither Mills nor Shaw had yet gotten used to the gore that often accompanied those cases.

They had barely reached the office door when Garcia's phone pinged, he swiped to answer. 'Garcia.' He held up a hand to stop the others while he listened intently to whoever was on the other side. 'But Sir, I…' He was obviously cut off because his sentence died in midair. 'Yes Sir. Fine. Thanks Sir.' He jabbed the end call button and rammed his phone into his back pocket.

'Sir?' Mills asked.

'That was the Lieutenant. Looks like we won a prize in some competition we didn't enter and we're getting another body assigned to our group. Some kid who just can't wait be a detective. Fan-fucking-tastic. Like I have time for this shit,' Garcia grumbled.

'Wow, were you this happy when we got assigned to you?' Mills teased.

Garcia shot her a glance and smiled. 'Damn straight I was, but you turned out half decent. What are the odds of that happening twice?'

'Uh… I'm right here. You saying I'm no good?' Shaw interjected.

Garcia laughed and replied, 'My comment stands. Right, let's go we'll pick the Rookie on our way out. Hope he hasn't had anything to eat recently. I am not cleaning up his last meal.'

Shaw rolled his eyes, grabbed his gear and followed Mills and Garcia out of the room.

Chapter 2
Crime Scene

Mike Garcia, followed by detectives Dave Shaw and Linda Mills, headed for the stairs, three flights down, the damn elevator not working as usual. He cursed silently under his breath, this was going to fuck up his New Year plans, he could see it coming. His plan to sneak himself and his team out and avoid his boss Lieutenant Grover Johnston were ruined as they reached the second-floor landing.

'Garcia, hold up. I told you to report to me immediately, just where do you think you are going?'

'Double homicide, Boss. Two more stiffs, it looks like the work of our Zodiac man, I reckon he has graduated to homicide now. I'll keep you posted, gotta run.'

'Not so fast, the bodies will keep, and CSI will secure the scene. I want you to take our new recruit with you.' Johnston stepped aside and called a tall dark-haired man forward. 'This is Ethan O'Connell, he has just transferred in from the 10th. O'Connell, this here is Detective First Grade, Mike Garcia.'

O'Connell stepped forward confidently and extended his hand. 'I look forward to working with you, Boss, I have heard good things about you and your team.'

Taken aback Garcia took the proffered hand and shook it. Looking over his shoulder he said, 'This here is Dave Shaw and Linda Mills, the rest of the team, welcome aboard. You can ride with me; Dave and Linda can follow in the other car. Let's move.'

The four of them made their way down to the basement parking area. The two vehicles assigned to homicide were parked near the exit. With Garcia in the lead, they drove up the exit ramp and turned left. The snow was heavy and pelting down, the fourteen block drive to the crime scene was going to be a bitch. Garcia hit the siren button, best way to clear New York Traffic during rush hour on a Thursday.

Although the sirens helped, progress was still slow. Garcia took the opportunity to question his new recruit.

'So, what did you do at the 10th? Don't tell me that miserable bastard, Lieutenant Marcus "Hollywood" Thomas, drove you out?'

'No, fortunately I had nothing to do with him. He still heads up homicide, I was working on "White Collar" crimes, riding a desk.'

'And you requested a transfer. How come you ended up at the 35th?'

'I want to be a real cop, not a paper pusher, I asked for the 35th as they had a vacancy. There was no way I could work for Hollywood Thomas. So here I am.'

'I haven't read your sheet yet. You look a little young to have made detective, how old are you?'

'I am 31, made detective five years ago.'

'Shit, that is young, you a college boy?'

'No, I dropped out during my last semester, almost ten years ago.'

'In your last semester? Why would you do that? What were you studying?'

'I was studying criminal law and forensic science. I had a traumatic experience which changed my perspective on life, so I dropped out and joined the academy.'

The conversation in the following vehicle centered around the new recruit.

'O'Connell looks a bit young to have made detective; must be a college boy or know someone in high places. What do you make of him, Mills?'

'I don't know about his credentials, but he can slip his shoes under my bed any time. He really is a hunk.'

'A bit too much of a pretty boy for you, too clean.'

'I know. I like them rough and ready but with a bit of guidance, he could do just fine for me.'

'We will have to call him Floyd, as in Pretty Boy Floyd. Hopefully he doesn't turn out to be an asshole. Shit, look at the mob; every mother and their son is here. Let's go.'

Further conversation was halted as they reached the outer perimeter of the crime scene. A large crowd was being held back by uniformed police; it looked like a scene from a disaster movie. Emergency vehicles blocked any further progress, at least two ambulances and a New York Fire Department engine. Garcia pulled over his car and switched off the engine killing the siren, the two detectives stepped out into the snowy chaos.

Followed by Mills and Shaw; the four of them pushed their way past the throng of people. When stopped by the uniformed cop; they produced their credentials and were allowed through.

The building was a typical New York brownstone, the middle unit of three, consisting of a basement, ground floor and two upper floors. They were stopped by a nervous looking patrolman at the front door.

Reading his name tag, Garcia addressed him. 'Nunez what have we got here?'

'Two victims on the second floor, both dead. CSI and the medical examiner are with the bodies. It's a fucking blood bath.'

'Who was the first on the scene?'

'I was, along with my partner, Silvia DuPont, that's her over there. She managed to make it back downstairs before she threw up. We got a call from Dispatch saying there was a possible domestic disturbance. The guy standing next to DuPont lives in the house on the left. He heard a racket next door and went to investigate and found the front door open; he called 911.

'We entered the premises, announced our presence and got no reply. We did a search of the ground floor and found no one, we then went up the stairs. The first room we went into we found two bodies, one male and one female. He was on the floor, and she was on the bed. Both were obviously dead, there was blood everywhere.'

'Did you touch anything?'

'No. Silvia took one look at the carnage and ran for the exit. I called it in, and we waited for CSI and the medical examiner. I have seen some shit in my time on the job but nothing like this.'

'Ok, Nunez, stay on post and don't let anyone in, no family, neighbors, no one. Got it?'

'Sure thing, Sir. What sort of animal could do this to another human?'

'O'Connell, Mills, it looks like there is a basement, check it out. When you are done with that do a cursory check on the other rooms on this floor. Shaw, you're with me.'

Leaving the two detectives, Garcia and Shaw headed up the stairs. There was no need to guess where all the action was. They were met at the door by the departing medical examiner, Doctor Matt Jarvis.

'Doc, what's the status?'

'It will be in my report, but I can tell you both victims are dead and have been for about 3 hours. The female was raped, and her throat was slit. Both her eyes were gouged out, her left nipple is missing, bitten off I would say. Looks like she was still alive when both happened.

'The male had his throat slit; he would have died in less than a minute. In all my years doing this job I have never seen so much blood. Whichever sick bastard did this must be covered in it and should have left a trail. Talk to the CSI blokes, they should be able to give you more information. Good night. I'm out of here, what a way to end the fucking year.'

Jarvis headed down the stairs muttering to no one in particular. Garcia and Shaw edged their way into the main bedroom, the scene of the slaughter. The CSI team were hard at work dusting for prints, taking photos from every conceivable angle, trying their best not to disturb the crime scene. Garcia spotted the CSI lead, Barry Hughes and walked over.

'What have we got here, Barry?'

'A fucking slaughter is what we have. The female, Christine Marx, 55, Caucasian, the male her husband, Colin Marx, 57, Caucasian. Both reside at this address. Christine was found naked, both wrists tied to the headboard. She had been strangled and her throat slit, both eyes gouged out. Jarvis reckons she had been raped, we found no semen present in her vagina or anus. Colin was found on his knees with his ankles and wrists secured, his throat slit from ear to ear.

'We should be done collecting forensic data in the next twenty minutes or so. Make yourself at home and try not to lose your lunch.'

'Thanks Barry, we will stay out of your way. What do you think, Dave, first impression?'

'Jesus, Boss. If this is our guy he has moved on big time. Previously robbery and rape. This one maybe he was busy with the wife and got interrupted unexpectedly by the husband. But shit this looks like he lost it, a total overkill. The Sagittarius symbol. I don't know. There have been several Zodiac killings over the years.'

'Yeah, the one out in California was never caught, they thought it was a guy named Gary Francis Poste, but it can't be him on our one; he died in August 2018. I hope this isn't some copycat bastard looking to make a name for himself.'

Their brief conversation was interrupted by the arrival of Mills and O'Connell.

'You two find anything in the basement?'

'No Boss, just normal stuff; nothing of value. Jesus, what a mess,

I'm glad I skipped lunch or you would be cleaning that up as well,' spluttered Mills, turning away momentarily as she addressed her colleague. 'I hope you have a strong stomach, O'Connell, this one is a blood bath.'

Ethan O'Connell craned his neck and looked over Mills' shoulder, getting his first look at the results of the murder scene. Confident in his ability to process a murder scene dispassionately, he stepped into the master bedroom. He stopped as though he had walked into a brick wall, his face went as white as a sheet. He staggered to his right and grabbed hold of a dresser to prevent himself from falling.

His reaction to the scene did not go unnoticed, 'Whoa there, Rookie, take it easy big fella. The first one is always the worst, take a deep breath and hold on to your lunch,' called out Garcia. 'Step out of the room and get some fresh air, come back in when you feel okay.'

Regaining his composure slightly, but still deathly pale he answered, 'No Boss, I am okay. It's just that I have seen the almost identical scene, exactly ten years ago to the day.'

'What do you mean "identical scene?"'

'Ten years ago today my parents were murdered in very similar circumstances. I would have to do a piece by piece comparison to be able to say it was identical, but it looks like it could be. Too close to be a coincidence.'

The discussion was interrupted by Barry Hughes calling out. 'What have we here? A pair of female panties stuffed in the male victim's mouth. There is a second Zodiac symbol, wedged in behind the panties, Gemini. That's the symbol for the twins, right?'

'Jesus, maybe there were two of them involved. Check for prints and bag them both. Dave, get the uniforms to canvass the area. Knock on every door, someone may have seen something. Get them to report their findings back to the precinct.'

'Sure thing, Boss.'

'Barry, it goes without saying, we need your evidence asap. We are heading back to the precinct.'

'Mike, we will transmit the photographic evidence as soon as we are done. It will probably beat you back to the precinct. Swabs and prints will be processed as top priority. You need to catch the sick bastards who did this.'

Chapter 3
December 30, 2011

Twenty-one year old Ethan O'Connell had just completed the penultimate semester of his Bachelor of Science degree. He was majoring in criminal law and forensic science and hoped to use his degree in landing a position with the FBI. The initial interviews had been positive but he had yet to receive any formal offers of employment.

Although Ethan had a number of colleges to choose from when he graduated from High School, he selected Cornell as his university of choice. Offers of scholarship had been in both academic and sporting. At six foot three inches, he was an accomplished basketball player and an All State wide receiver. He had set his mind on achieving his goals using his intelligence and not his sporting prowess. He was approximately 250 miles away from home, far enough to feel independent and close enough to go home when he needed to.

With three and a half weeks to kill before the start of the next semester, he decided to have one last blast with his three roommates before heading home for Christmas and New Year. Living off campus in a shared apartment was an upgrade to the first two years he had spent in a dormitory. Their local, O'Hagan's, was within walking distance so no worries about drinking and driving.

Ethan woke up early, a little worse for wear, on Friday 23. Depending on the traffic he had a five to six hour drive home to Greenpoint. The I81 and I80 would be a nightmare, given that it was a Friday and the last business day before Christmas.

A quick shower and a cup of black coffee and he was ready to go. His red 2006 Honda Civic, a present for his sixteenth birthday, was fully fueled and traffic permitting would get him home without the need for refueling. His only stop would be for a McDonald's breakfast of two sausage egg McMuffins.

His initial fears of the traffic on the I81 were realized. Just south of Binghamton a fully loaded car transporter had rear ended a Ford T150 truck. The two vehicles had completely blocked two lanes and partially blocked the third lane. With emergency vehicles and cop cars on the scene, traffic was at a standstill. It took nearly an hour to travel past the accident.

The next problem occurred on the I80 at the Delaware Water Gap. Three vehicles had run into the back of fourth, which had braked for no apparent reason. Another thirty minutes wasted.

It was then plain sailing, he joined the I280 and until he reached the I95 junction traffic ran smoothly. The I95 led him in towards central New York, the traffic became heavy, typical of a mid-afternoon flow. Taking the 495, the Lincoln and Queens Midtown tunnels, his last bottleneck was the Pulaski Bridge.

His five to six hour drive had taken him almost eight hours. He pulled up outside his parent's Greenpoint home at 3.15 pm. He miraculously found parking just fifty feet to the right of their front door. He switched off the engine, grabbed his bag and locked the car.

His mother was waiting at the front door and flung her arms around her son's neck and whispered, 'Welcome home, Son, we have missed you terribly. Come on in, your Dad isn't home yet, that will give us time to chat.'

Mother and son spent the next hour and a half chatting about university life, both excited that in the next five months he would be fully qualified. Ethan, at this stage, was still totally unaware that he had been adopted at birth. Mary and Dennis had discussed telling him and had settled on waiting until he had graduated before broaching the subject, they wanted their son to have no distractions with his studies.

Their conversation was interrupted by Dennis' arrival, 'I see Ethan's car outside. Where is that young man?'

'In the kitchen with Mom. It's great to see you, Dad, come over here and have a beer with me. I am now of legal age so you don't have to feel like you are breaking the law.'

The three of them talked late into the night. There was much to catch up on, it had been a long six months since their last get together. Ethan was quizzed about his future plans; he had already had a few offers but had not committed to any. After three and a half years of study. he felt that he might take some time off and do a bit of traveling. A summer in Europe sounded appealing.

The following day, December 24, Ethan spent the afternoon buying presents for his parents and helping his mother prepare for the

Christmas Day lunch. As a practicing Catholic family, December 25 was an important religious day in their calendar. Lunch was a typical 'English' affair that they had started during their time in Ireland.

On Friday morning, December 30, Ethan got a call from one of his high school buddies whom he hadn't seen in nearly four years.

'Ethan, you old reprobate! I heard you were back in town. It's time we caught up. A group of us are heading out tonight to celebrate the New Year and I hope you will join us.'

'Mack, is that you?'

'Sure is, so what do you say?' asked Graham Mackintosh.

'I would love to, what's the plan?'

'I know it's a day early but no one in their right mind wants to be out and about on the 31st, too many nutters. So, we will do it tonight, a real piss up. I will pick you up at 6.30. We have hired a bus to take us around, no DUI's tonight!'

With the plans set, he called to his Mom, 'Ma, I am going out with some old school buddies tonight and will probably be home a bit late. If I remember them, we will be a bit worse for wear as well.'

'That's nice, Son, just be careful. Your Dad should be home around 7.'

On the dot 6.30 a refurbished school bus pulled up outside the O'Connell brownstone. Aboard were fifteen of his old school mates, there were going to be two more stops before hitting the first of the local watering holes. Ethan boarded to a mixed chorus of cheers and boos, all in good nature.

Robert "Sparrow" Watkins, had been appointed in charge of the cash, his job was to settle the bar tabs as they progressed through each establishment. The buy in was an initial $50, if that was exhausted, there would be another collection. To get everyone in the mood, two cases of ice-cold Corona Extra had been loaded aboard the bus.

The rules for the evening were simple; drink as much as you can, no females aboard the bus, no puking on the bus, the bus will leave each bar after two drinks anyone not on board will be left behind, walk away from arguments but if unavoidable, it's everyone in.

No sooner had Ethan left the house, Mary realized she had not made anything for hers and her husband's supper. She decided a quick trip to the local deli would be the best option. Donning her overcoat, she picked up her purse and headed out. Ever conscious of cost, she turned off the downstairs lights, leaving only the front door light on. She closed the door behind her but forgot to engage the lock.

As she hurried out, she failed to notice a man standing directly opposite her front door. As she had turned off all the lights, the man assumed she would be out for some time. As soon as she was out of sight he walked casually across the road. He walked up the three steps and tried the door, to his utter surprise he found it unlocked. He pocketed his lock picks, opened the door and slipped inside.

Fully expecting to spend time picking the front door lock, he was elated. This would give him more time to spend stealing the good stuff without rushing. Figuring all the small valuable stuff would be in the bedrooms, he headed up the stairs.

He opened the door to the first room on the right at the top of the stairs. Scanning the room with his flashlight it was obvious that this room belonged to a son. Trophies, pennants, medals, football and basketball shirts adorned the walls. Impressive but nothing of any real value. He shut the door and moved on to the next room, directly across the hall on the left.

First pass of his flashlight confirmed that this was indeed the master bedroom. Spacious and well furnished, a dressing table with mostly female paraphernalia took up most of the left wall. On the far side was a walk-in closet and adjacent to that was the master bathroom. He immediately began a search of the dressing table looking for jewelry, cash or anything that could be converted into cash.

Satisfied he had all the valuables, he moved onto the bedside tables. Here he hoped to find more cash and hopefully a firearm. Many New Yorkers had a firearm with handy access near the bed, always good to fetch a couple of bucks. Having no success on what must have been the woman's side of the bed, he made his way around to the other side.

He opened the top drawer and there it was a Glock 19, probably never used. He picked it up, checked the magazine and found it loaded. He slipped the gun into his pocket. As he opened the second drawer, he heard a sound downstairs.

Mary, armed with cold cuts and bread rolls, had returned in double quick time. She hurried up the stairs, inserted her key into the lock and turned it. To her surprise she found the door already unlocked.

'Strange' she thought 'I am sure I locked up before I left. Dennis must be home, but why hasn't he switched on any lights?'

She opened the door to total darkness, instantly realizing her husband wasn't home and she must have forgotten to lock up. Cursing to herself she took off her overcoat, hung it up and headed for the kitchen to deposit her purchases. It was 6.50 pm; her husband would be home soon, she had just enough time to change. She always liked to be well dressed to welcome Dennis home after a long hard day's work. She was old fashioned that way. She headed up the stairs turning the lights on as she went.

In the master bedroom Mary's arrival had not gone unnoticed, the burglar panicked. Having seen the house unoccupied, he had failed to don his balaclava, he dashed across to the walk-in closet and attempted to conceal himself among the many hanging coats and dresses.

Mary walked into the bedroom switching the lights on as she entered. With time of the essence, she hurriedly started disrobing. Off came the grey sweat shirt followed by the matching sweat pants. Clad only in her bra and panties, she glanced at her profile in the dressing table mirror; *not bad for a fifty-four year old.* She could easily pass for someone at least ten years younger. She reached over and sprayed a dash of Chanel No5 on her neck and wrists, Dennis' favorite. Fluffing up her hair she stepped into the walk-in closet.

Flicking on the light she turned to her right and reached for her favorite blue dress, it really did her figure justice. As she lifted the hanger a hand reached out and pushed a gun into her right cheek.

'Make any noise and you are dead. Do what I tell you and no one gets hurt. Do you understand?'

Unable to talk, Mary just nodded.

'Turn around and walk slowly back into the bedroom.'

Mary turned and walked into the bedroom; she was barely able to comprehend what was happening.

'Just take whatever you want, my husband will be here soon. Please leave, I won't call the police if you just go.'

'Your husband is going to be here soon? That changes the whole thing. Take off the rest of your clothes and lie down on the bed on your back. Any noise and I will shoot you.'

'Why must I take off my clothes?'

'Because I said so, it will make it less likely that you will run away naked. Now do it!'

Mary turned her back to him, unhooked her bra and dropped in to the floor. Bending slightly forward she slid her panties down to below her knees and stepped out of them.

'Good, now lie down on the bed and do not move or make a sound.'

Picking up Mary's underwear, the man moved to the edge of the bed. Pointing the gun at Mary, he told her to raise her head, she complied. He opened her mouth and stuffed her panties in. Laying the gun on the bed, he picked up her discarded bra, threading it across her open mouth he tied the two ends together behind her head, effectively gagging her.

He picked up the gun and told her to lie down and not move. Mary lay back, staring at the ceiling wondering what was going to become of her. She had taken a good look at the man and was sure that she would be able to identify him again if he was captured.

The man stepped back into the dressing room and emerged almost immediately carrying two of Dennis' neckties. Using the red necktie, he secured her right hand to the brass headboard, he repeated the same using the blue tie to her left hand. She was now securely tied and gagged, absolutely helpless. No sooner had he tied her up he heard the front door open.

'Hi Mary, I am home,' a male voice called out. He could be heard taking off his heavy overcoat and placing what was likely a briefcase on the floor. The burglar, knowing he was cornered, moved quickly and positioned himself behind the bedroom door. Anyone entering the room would walk past the door on their left and the first thing they would see would be Mary, naked and tied to the bed. This would give him the element of surprise.

Dennis, not finding Mary downstairs, called out, 'Mary, are you up there?'

Getting no response, he looked up the stairs and noticed their bedroom light was on, he decided to check up. He called again, 'Mary are you okay?'

Again, no response, he became a little frantic and started to run up the remaining steps.

Reaching the landing he turned into their bedroom. His first sight was of his wife, stark naked and tied to the bed. She was shaking her head vigorously trying to warn him. He started to rush towards her but was stopped by a gruff sounding voice directly behind him.

'Do not move another step and do not turn around.'

Dennis instinctively turned to see who was behind him. He was met by a gun aimed at his head, stopping him dead in his tracks.

'Now look what you have done, you fucking idiot. Keep your hands where I can see them, any sudden moves I will shoot you in the face.

Now turn around and walk slowly to the foot of the bed.'

Dennis realized he had to comply; he would have to look for an opportunity to disarm the man. It was going to be difficult as the man was at least six foot tall and of medium build. He was white with a scraggy beard, long dark brown hair and Dennis estimated him to be somewhere between mid-twenties to mid-thirties. All this would be important for future identification.

He reached the foot of the bed and gave Mary a reassuring smile, it was going to be okay.

'Now take off all of your clothes and throw them behind you. Do not turn around.'

'Why do you want me to take off all of my clothes, what is the purpose?'

'It will stop you running away and give me time to get out of here.'

Okay, thought Dennis, he just wants to tie us up and get out of here, so he means no harm. Stupid fool, doesn't he realize I can identify him. I better just play along.'

Dennis disrobed and tossed his shirt, necktie, pants, belt, underwear, shoes and socks behind him, all the time nodding reassuringly to his wife. This would all be over soon.

'Get on your knees, face the bed and put your feet together, ankles touching.'

As soon as he knelt down, he felt his feet being pulled together and securely bound. The burglar had used Dennis' leather belt to secure his legs. Next, he ordered Dennis to put his hands behind his back, these were tied together with his own blue and silver striped necktie. The necktie was then looped through the belt and tied. He was now unable to move.

'What is it that you want?'

'What do I want? I want to take anything of value and leave. You have a safe? Where is it?'

'If I tell you, will you leave?'

'Yes, where is it?'

'It is in the small room under the staircase. The keys are in my bedside table, there is no combination.'

The man retrieved the bunch of keys from the bedside table. As he passed by Dennis he said, 'Don't do anything stupid, stay as you are. I do not want to hurt you.'

The man left the room heading down the stairs, Dennis looked over at his still gagged wife.

'Don't worry my dear, he will take what he wants and leave. It's just money and things, we will recover.' Mary, unable to speak, gave her husband a hopeful smile but her eyes told another story, one of fear.

The downstairs safe yielded $2,500 in cash, two high end wrist watches, a small diamond pendant, a pearl necklace and a beautifully decorated Japanese Tanto short twenty-inch sword. All easily disposable, not bad for a couple of hours work. Gathering up his bounty, he headed for the kitchen where he secured a large black garbage bag. He loaded the items from the safe and those he had taken from the bedroom into the bag.

With his adrenaline pumping, he slung the bag over his shoulder and headed back up the stairs. His captives were where he had left them. Both avoided eye contact with him. Dennis broke the silence.

'You have got what you came for, please remove the gag from my wife when you leave, she is struggling to breath.'

'No need to worry, she won't have to struggle much longer,' said the man who was standing directly behind Dennis.

Visible only to Mary, he began to undress. He piled his clothes neatly just inside the walk-in closet. When he was completely naked, he walked back into the bedroom and stood at the left side of the bed in full view of both Dennis and Mary. Stroking his rapidly growing penis he leaned in and removed Mary's panties from her mouth. He turned to his right and forced the panties into Dennis' mouth, effectively gagging him.

Mary, finally able to speak, pleaded with the man, 'Please stop this madness and leave us alone. You have all of our valuables, take them and go. We are both helpless, you will have plenty of time to make your escape.' Her voice breaking in a sob.

'Oh no, sweet lady, the fun is just beginning and your dear husband will have the prime viewing position.' Dennis gave a guttural scream through his gag and the burglar just smiled. *This was going to be so much fun.*

He climbed onto the bed and positioned himself, standing between Mary's legs. He knelt down and forced her legs wide apart. Now fully erect he lifted her hips slightly off the bed and with a vicious thrust he penetrated her. She gasped in pain but fully aware of Dennis being unable to help her, did not cry out. Dennis was straining against his restraints, determined to get loose to help his wife, never taking his eyes off her. *I should be saving her!*

Pounding away viciously the man took the time to look at Mary's expressionless face, she stared back determined not to show any fear, she would not give him the satisfaction. This seemed to drive him on, but getting no reaction he leaned forward and took the nipple of her left breast in his mouth. At first, he gently sucked on it causing it to become erect, then without warning he bit it. Mary cried out in pain, finally giving him the reaction he was looking for. He clamped his teeth into the skin and bit the nipple off. With blood dripping from his mouth, he lifted his head, stared at Mary and then swallowed the severed nipple. Dennis pained scream was just background noise to him. A pleasant soundtrack to the show.

Mary again cried out both in pain and fear. This was the trigger her assailant was looking for, with a manic look on his face he ejaculated instantly. Satisfied with his dominance over his victim, he withdrew his penis and knelt over her. He looked down to survey his handiwork expecting to see Mary cowering in fear, she just stared back at him with a blank look in her eyes. Infuriated, he lost what little control he had left, he reached over her and with both of his thumbs he covered her eyes.

He looked over his shoulder at Dennis and said, 'What did you think of my performance old man?'

Dennis, who had helplessly watched the violation of his wife, was unable to answer due to the gag in his mouth. His face was contorted in shear hatred, his whole body shaking with anger but there was no fear. He stared back at the man who didn't need a verbal answer, he saw it in Dennis' eyes.

Enraged, he pressed down with both thumbs pushing her eyeballs hard into their sockets. Mary let out a loud, frightened shriek as her eyeballs were ripped from their sockets, the pain was unbearable, mercifully she passed out. He leapt off the bed and ran to the walk-in closet, opened the garbage bag and withdrew the Tanto short sword.

Brandishing the weapon, he jumped back on the bed and lifted Mary's head making sure she was facing her husband. Allowing Dennis to see every detail of his wife's battered face, he pulled her head slightly backwards and with a flourish, drew the blade of the sword across her neck, almost severing the head. Blood gushed everywhere drenching all three of them.

Covered in blood, he leapt off the bed and ran around behind the helpless Dennis. He grabbed him by the hair and pulled back his head exposing his unprotected neck. He pulled the gag out of his mouth.

'This is all your fault, if you had listened and not looked at me this would never have happened. Time to join your wife.'

Not giving Dennis a chance to respond, he drew the sword blade across his neck, cutting all the main arteries and almost severing his spine. Blood squirted everywhere; Dennis was dead within seconds. The man, drenched in blood, pushed Dennis forward balancing him neatly against the bed. It looked like Dennis was staring blankly at his dead wife.

Satisfied with his handiwork, it was time for him to leave the building. Still naked and carrying his sword, he walked towards the bathroom, leaving bloodstained footsteps as he went. He turned on the water in the walk-in shower and when the water temperature was perfect, he stepped into the cubicle still carrying his sword. Satisfied he was clean of his victims' blood, he switched off the water, stepped out and went about drying himself and his weapon.

Returning to the walk-in closet he placed the sword back in the garbage bag and dressed himself back into his unstained clothing. He hefted the garbage bag onto his shoulder, walked out of the room, down the stairs and out of the front door. What had started out as a simple robbery had turned into a frenzied bloodbath. Unseen, he walked down to the corner of the road, turned right and left the area.

Chapter 4
December 31, 2011

At 1.15 am the converted school bus pulled up outside the O'Connell residence with only three passengers left on board, Mack, Sparrow and Ethan. Only Sparrow Watkins was in any state of awareness. With Mack's limited assistance, he helped Ethan off the bus, pointed him in the direction of his front door and waved him goodbye.

The minute Ethan got to the front door the bus left the scene. Ethan fumbled with his keys finding it difficult to get the key into the keyhole. He took a firm grip of the door handle to balance himself. To his surprise the handle turned, the door was unlocked. He assumed that his parents had expected him to be a little drunk and left the door unlocked.

He opened the front door and quietly stepped into the lobby. He shrugged off his overcoat and looked up the stairs to see the light was on in his folks' bedroom. Realizing they were probably still awake and waiting to see that he got home safely, he took a deep breath and walked up the stairs, stopping on the landing to compose himself. He knocked lightly and stepped into the bedroom.

'Hi folks, I am home safe and sound, you shouldn't have stayed up waiting for me, I'm a big boy now.'

He stopped dead in his tracks. At first, he couldn't comprehend what he was seeing. His father was naked and on his knees at the base of their bed, his mother naked tied up lying on the bed, neither moving. After the initial shock, he noticed that there was blood everywhere; unable to help himself, he vomited, spewing up the contents of a heavy night of drinking.

Turning around he staggered out of the room. Instantly sober he groped for his cellphone and dialed 911.

'911, what is your emergency?'

'My parents have been murdered, please send someone immediately.' He struggled to keep his voice steady.

'Are you sure they are dead, what is your name?'

'Absolutely sure, no one could have survived. I haven't touched anything, there is blood everywhere. My name is Ethan O'Connell, my parents are Dennis and Mary.' His head was swimming with images of his parents covered in blood. *This can't be real.*

'What is your address?'

Ethan rattled off the address in a daze and was told that the police would be there within five minutes. He made his way downstairs, white-knuckling the hand rail to keep himself upright. He stumbled to the front door, wanting to get out of the house but not wanting to leave his parents. The wait felt like forever but in reality, the cops arrived in only three minutes. The patrol car pulled up in front of the house and two cops, one male and the other female stepped out of the vehicle.

'Are you Ethan O'Connell?' Ethan nodded. 'I am Officer George Logan and this is my partner, Officer June Hayes, we are from the 94th precinct. Can you show us where the victims are?'

Finding it difficult to speak, Ethan indicated that the officers follow him. He stepped back and pointed up the stairs, without saying a word. The officers drew their weapons and instructed him to wait while they investigated the scene. It didn't take more than a few seconds for Logan to emerge from the bedroom, his hand covering his mouth. He rushed down the stairs, pushed past Ethan and ran out the open front door, stopped and left his last three meals in the flower box.

Hayes followed Logan down the stairs at a more pedestrian pace and a whole lot more composed. She pressed the call button on her radio and said, 'Hayes here, we need forensic and homicide, it's a blood bath here. Two victims one male, one female both in their mid-fifties. No, no need for a bus.'

She turned to Ethan. 'Excuse my partner, he has a weak stomach. I am sorry for your loss but I need to ask you a few questions while we wait for the experts. I know this is a difficult time so I'll keep it as brief as I can. Have you touched anything since you found the bodies and after you called 911?'

'No.'

'Good. I assume the vomit just inside the bedroom door is yours, correct?'

'Yes, it is. Sorry, but seeing them there like that I couldn't help it. Who the fuck does something like that? They were good people nobody deserves that.' Ethan ran his hands through his hair, struggling to comprehend that any of this was real.

'Can you tell me your movements up until you found them?' Hayes had her notebook in hand, scribbling his responses. Her calmness both reassured and infuriated him. *Did she not see the same thing he had? How could she be so calm right now?*

'I had been out with a bunch of old high school friends who I hadn't seen in a couple of years. We went out to celebrate an early New Year, eighteen of us. We hired a party bus and driver to drive us around from bar to bar. They picked me up at about 6.30 and I was dropped off just after 1.00. We had all drunk a large amount of alcohol.

'I found the front door unlocked and assumed my folks had left it unlocked for me, I don't know why I assumed that. I saw their bedroom lights on and went up to let them know I had got home safely. I saw the carnage; I knew they were dead. I threw up and called 911.'

'The call to 911 came through at exactly 01.18. Can anyone verify what time you arrived home, any witnesses?' *Seriously?* Some part of his brain knew this was standard procedure but the idea that he could be a suspect made him irrationally angry.

'Why are you asking me this? Do you think I had anything to do with this?' Ethan asked, incredulously.

'No, just making sure that the details can be verified, the detectives will ask the same question.' Hayes remained unflappable and dispassionate, waiting for his response.

'Yes, my two buddies and the bus driver can corroborate my story. Well, one buddy and the bus driver, Mack was in no condition to verify anything much.'

'Thank you, Sir, the forensics and detectives are on their way. Again, I am sorry for your loss. Please take a seat in the living room; the detectives will want to talk to you as soon as they get here.' She pocketed her notebook and gestured towards the living room.

Ethan, still reeling from the shock, just nodded and trudged sadly into the living room. He looked around the room, it was filled with photographs of him and his parents. The enormity of what he had witnessed finally caught up with him, he sat down, put his face in his hands and began sobbing uncontrollably.

Fifteen minutes after the two patrol cops had arrived, two detectives pulled up outside the building. Both had been off duty and had managed to get dressed and be onsite in record time. Micky Cairns and his partner Brian Robinson, both hardened homicide detectives in their mid-forties, had seen just about every type of murder there was.

They were in for a shock.

'Hayes, what do we have here? And what the fuck is wrong with Logan? He looks like he just shit himself,' asked Cairns.

'He just lost his supper, lunch and breakfast, he'll be okay. Inside is a fucking blood bath, two dead, husband and wife mid-fifties I reckon. Both still bound, almost decapitated, the female looks like her eyes have been gouged out.'

'Who found the bodies?' Cairns looked around, taking in the scene.

'The son, Ethan O'Connell. He is in the living room. He says he returned home sometime after 1.00 am, had been out with a bunch of buddies, all of whom had consumed a copious amount of alcohol. He says he touched nothing but he did throw up his night's alcohol consumption just inside the bedroom. I think he is genuine.'

'Logan, secure the front door, no unauthorized persons allowed in. Hayes, have a look around, see if you can spot anything out of the ordinary, check with the son. Okay Brian, you and me, let's see what we have.'

With Cairns leading the way, the two detectives made their way up the stairs and onto the landing. Ethan's vomit clearly visible at the bedroom door. Neither man was ready for what they saw the minute they stepped into the room.

'Jesus Christ, what a fucking mess, there's blood everywhere. The forensics are gonna have some job on their hands with this one. What do you make of it, Brian?' Cairns surveyed the scene, his eyes scanning for immediate clues out of habit.

'Whoever did this must be a psycho, this was done in a fit of rage by the looks of it. Killing for the sake of it, it's a fucking slaughter.' Robinson stepped closer to the bed, drawn in to the scene in front of him.

'The wife looks like she was raped, just the way the body is positioned. I reckon the husband was forced to watch. Her eyes have been gouged out, I hope the coroner can establish if that was done while she was alive or postmortem.

'The bastard must have been covered in blood. Look at the footprints leading around the bed and into the bathroom. If we catch the bastard, we will have all the forensic evidence we need.'

Their conversation was interrupted by the arrival of the forensic team and the coroner. This group had seen everything they thought possible at a murder scene but even they took a step back in horror.

The forensics team of five stepped aside for the coroner as the first order of business was to confirm both victims were in fact dead, cause and time of death. The hardest part of this investigation was going to be avoiding stepping in blood. They had suited up, ready to sift through the bloodbath for evidence.

The coroner got to work. 'Well, they're definitely dead. Both died from severed carotid arteries, would have been almost instantaneous. Time of death looks to be 7:30 pm and 8:30 pm, give or take. She was alive when her eyes were gouged out, see the blood from the sockets? There's evidence of recent sexual activity with ejaculate left in the vagina. Assuming it was not the husband, there's a good chance of DNA from the perp. I'll have a better idea after the postmortem once I clean up the blood and can get a better visual on internal injuries, to confirm if this was rape or consensual. That's about all I can confirm right now.' Cairns and Robinson nodded, and the coroner grabbed his kit.

'I'll get the report over to you as soon as I have it. Man, this shit doesn't get easier, does it?' The coroner shook his head sadly, and turned to leave.

'It certainly doesn't,' Cairns muttered and Robinson nodded in agreement.

The coroner left and the CSI team descended on the crime scene dressed in full white jumpsuits, hoodies, masks, gloves and protective footwear. Everything would be dusted for fingerprints, the bodies photographed from every conceivable angle and blood spatters documented. The two detectives decided to leave the team to get on with their work and headed downstairs to interview the son.

They were met by Hayes, who gave them a brief rundown of her conversation with Ethan.

'According to the son, Ethan O'Connell, there seems to be nothing missing on the surface. There is a small safe in the area under the stairs, I haven't inspected it as I did not want to contaminate the area. The son says that there is usually cash, watches, jewelry and a valuable Japanese short sword in the safe. He thinks his father may have kept a gun in there or maybe next to his bed.'

'Good work, Hayes, we will have a word with him. In the meantime, can you go upstairs and ask the CSI team to check in the bedside table for a gun? Thanks.' She nodded and headed back upstairs.

'Right, Robinson, let's see what young Mr. O'Connell has to say. You take notes, I'll ask the questions but as usual chip in whenever you feel it necessary. We need to find out if he had anything to do with this.'

'Mr. O'Connell, I am Detective Michael Cairns and this is my partner Brian Robertson, I am sorry for your loss. We have some question for you, are you up to it?'

'Yes Sir. I can't believe they are both gone, you have to catch the bastards who did this.'

'You say "bastards" plural, do you think there was more than one?'

'I don't know, maybe just a figure of speech. I am sure my dad would have put up a fight if there was only one.' Ethan couldn't imagine his dad standing meekly by while his mother was harmed.

'Alright, let's just go through the time line from when you left home until you called 911.'

Ethan repeated what he had told Officer Hayes.

'Will we be able to verify this?'

'Yes Sir.'

'Do you know if your parents had any enemies that may have done this to them?'

'I doubt very much. They kept to themselves, living a very private life. They were model citizens and lived well within their means. Dad worked as an accountant and Mom was a homebody.'

'We will need to see what, if anything, has been stolen. Do you think you could check around downstairs without disturbing anything? When the CSI team have completed their investigations and the bodies have been removed, can you do the upstairs rooms?' Ethan nodded. *Bodies. His parents were now just bodies.* 'Now, let's look at the safe, do you know the combination?'

'No combination; it's secured by a key lock. The safe is under the stairs.' Ethan gestured towards the stairs.

'Okay Robinson, let's have a look at the safe.' Hayes had returned from upstairs. 'Hayes, see if you can rustle up a glass or bottle of water for me. Thanks. Oh, any news on the gun in the bedside table?' Hayes shook her head indicating no gun and headed off to grab some water.

The detectives found the door to the small room under the stairs, it was open and the light was on. The safe door was ajar with the key still in the lock. Cairns, using a handkerchief pulled the safe door open. It looked pretty empty, just two passports and a bunch of documents.

'Well, nothing of salable value just documents. No cash or jewels, definitely no gun or sword. I wonder if the perp broke in down here found the sword and gun and then was disturbed.' Cairns mused out loud.

'No way, Mickey. There was no forced entry through the front door. I doubt the keys were left in the safe. I reckon he was busy upstairs when he was disturbed either by the wife and or the husband.'

'You could be right, maybe just a robbery gone wrong. We will get the CSI boys down here to check for prints. Yeah, what you got there Hayes?'

'I found this in the kitchen, it was on the counter next to a packet from Mo's Deli. The packet has bread rolls, meat cuts, tomato and mustard, probably meant for tonight's supper. Mary O'Connell paid for it with a credit card, date and time stamp – today at 6.46 pm.'

'Hey O'Connell, what time does your father normally get home from work?' asked Cairns.

'Usually around 7.00 pm.'

'Was your mother home when you left at 6.30 pm?' continued Cairns.

'Yes, Sir.'

'So, she left to the Deli, bought food, paid for it by 6.46 pm, based on that she was probably back before 7.00 pm. What do you think, Brian?'

'Seems possible. So, the perp may have seen her leave, tried the door found it open and went in. Probably assumed she would be out for some time,' replied Brian.

'So, her returning early may have disturbed him and a simple robbery turned into mass slaughter. There is not much more we can do here. CSI need to do their job and get the results to us pronto. Go up and tell them we are leaving for the precinct.' Robinson nodded and headed back upstairs.

'Hayes, take O'Connell up to his room, let him check if anything is missing. Get CSI to take a copy of his fingerprints so we can eliminate any of his found. O'Connell, you will need to come down to the precinct and make an official statement. You will also have to make a formal identification of the bodies; you can do that when the bodies get down to the morgue. Doesn't have to be right now, but the sooner the better. I know this has been an incredibly difficult evening for you.

'As this is now a crime scene you will have to find alternate accommodation until everything is sorted. Pack a bag and come down to the station when you're ready.'

Cairns waited until Ethan was out of earshot, looked over at Robertson, shook his head and said, 'It's 4.00 am on the last day of the year and we have this shit on our hands. I am going home to shower and change into some clean clothes and then I'll head back to the precinct, I suggest you do the same.'

'Sure thing, Mickey, I will pick up some coffee and breakfast. Hey, Hayes, what time does your shift end?'

'Two hours – 6.00 am. I will call dispatch to send replacements and I will stay on until they arrive. Will you organize the troops for canvassing the area, or should I?'

'You go ahead. Make sure they knock on every door on the whole block, maybe somebody saw something. By the way, good job Hayes, pity about your partner's weak stomach.'

'Yeah, other than that he is a good man. See you all later'

Chapter 5
Situation Room 94th Precinct

It was a few minutes after 8.00 am when Detective First Grade Michael 'Mickie' Cairns made it up to the third-floor detective's office. He was surprised to see Officer June Hayes waiting for him.

'Hayes, I'm surprised to see you here, I thought your shift was over at 6, and you would have headed home.' Mickie tossed his keys onto his desk.

'No Mickie, after witnessing that slaughter, I wouldn't have been able to sleep so I want to stay on and help in any way I can. Logan took the sensible route and went home, he still looked ill.' She rolled her eyes.

'Can you check if O'Connell is in yet? If so, bring him up to Interview Room #1 and get him started on his statement.'

Hayes passed Robertson on the stairs.

'You still on duty, Hayes? Is Mickie up there?'

'Not officially, but I want to help, anything to catch that bastard. Yes, he is. In the situation room.'

'You coming back up? I have breakfast and coffee.'

'Yes, just going to collect O'Connell for his statement.'

Robertson walked into the Detective's office, nodded to Cairns, put down the breakfast bagels, donuts and coffee and asked, 'Where we at, Mickie?'

'I have called the Lieutenant and brought him up to speed. He has mobilized a team of boots and got them canvassing the neighborhood, hopefully somebody saw something. I hope you got enough grub and coffee; Hayes is going to be helping out.

'Deeks and Cooke are on their way in, it's all balls to the wall. The Boss says anything we need, we get; this one is top priority.'

The two detectives retired to the 'Situation Room,' a fancy title for a very drab room. Two rows of tables and chairs, all facing the front wall. Along the entire wall were a series of pin and white boards. Colored pins, marker pens, area maps and tape filled one of the tables.

It was going to be a working breakfast.

Hayes returned to inform them O'Connell was in the interview room, ready and waiting.

'Sit down, Hayes, get some food and coffee down your neck. Deeks and Cooke can take O'Connell's statement when they get in. Where are those lazy bastards? It's after 8.30 am, they should be in by now. Talk of the devil.'

'Great, breakfast, what's the occasion?' asked Deeks.

'We have a big one, boys. Middle aged white couple murdered in the Greenpoint neighborhood, an absolute blood bath. Got the son in the interview room, you and Cooke can get his statement. We don't think he is the perp.'

'So, we get to eat first?' asked Cooke.

'Not for you, but you can watch us or go get the statement done.'

Deeks and Cooke left the room muttering obscenities, Cairns, Robertson and Hayes settled down to breakfast. Cairns was first to break the sound of eating.

'Hayes, what's your handwriting like?' he asked, some crumbs spluttering out of his mouth.

'Pretty good, why?'

'You can be our official documentation person, if you okay with that. I will get you reassigned for the duration.'

'I would like that very much.'

'Right, let's get going: Hayes, start on the left white board with the victims.'

Male – Dennis O'Connell – age 57

Female – Mary O'Connell – age 54

Estimated time of death between 7.30 to 8.30 pm on 12/30/2011

Victims found by son Ethan O'Connell – age 21

911 call at 01.18 am on 12/31/2011

Officers on the scene Logan and Hayes at 01.21 am on 12/31/2011

Detectives Cairns and Robertson on the scene at 01.36 am on 12/31/2011

CSI and coroner arrived on the scene at 02.05 am on 12/31/2011

'Do we agree on the timeline so far?'

Robertson and Hayes both nodded in agreement.

'Okay, let's document the son, we will need to get corroboration on this. He states he left with seventeen friends and the bus driver at 6.30 pm on 12/30/2011, arriving back at around 01.00 am on 12/31/2011. Three witnesses to be contacted for verification. He enters the building finding the front door unlocked, sees the parents' bedroom light on, goes up to investigate. Finds parents dead, throws up and then calls 911 at 01.18 am.

'Mary O'Connell purchased goods from Mo's Deli and paid for them at 6.46 pm. Assuming she left shortly after her son did, she managed to walk to the shop, buy goods and pay for them in less than sixteen minutes. If she returned home immediately, she would have got there by no later than 7.00 pm. Check the distance between the house and the deli.

'We know that Dennis O'Connell was not home when Ethan left but he usually was back from work around 7.00 pm most days. So, by the time Mary left the building and returned within at the most 30 minutes, the perp or perps entered the house. As there was no forced entry, they either picked the lock or the door was left unlocked.'

'She must have left it unlocked or she knew the perps and let them it,' offered Robertson.

'Okay, but what are the chances that somebody just happened to try the door, found it unlocked and went in? I think whoever it was, was probably lurking around the area looking for opportunity. They saw Mary leave, maybe she turned off the lights giving the impression she would be away for some time, so they took a chance.'

'So, you reckon this was just a burglary gone wrong?' suggested Hayes.

'Yes, I do. I think Mary disturbed them and then moments later Dennis arrived and that's when things got out of hand and escalated into what we found.'

'So, you think more than one perpetrator, all male hence the rape?' asked Hayes.

'I do indeed. I think their faces were seen by Mary and or Dennis and would be identifiable so they were killed.'

'Jesus, Mickie, but they weren't just killed; they were slaughtered. And gouging her eyes out while she was still alive. If she was going to die why the eyes?'

'Well, Brian, we'll have to ask the shrinks about that one, but I guess maybe she looked at him in a bad way while he was raping her. Maybe she knew him. It will be interesting to find out if there was more than one sample of semen in her.'

'Only one set of bloody footprints that I saw. Let's hope CSI hurry up with whatever evidence they have found. Based on the fact that someone raped Mary without a condom leaving their DNA, I reckon there is a good chance we find fingerprints as well. This does not seem like a well-planned robbery, just a fuck up that turned into a blood bath.'

'Good point Hayes. See if Deeks and Cooke have finished taking O'Connell's statement, make sure they get his prints, get them to take a swab for a DNA check. Also, get a contact number for him. Brian, the son mentioned a Japanese Tanto sword that should have been in the safe: see if you can find a picture of one on the internet, it could be the murder weapon.'

With Robertson and Hayes going about their assigned duties, Cairns decided to bring his boss, Lieutenant Constance Wyatt, up to speed. Affectionately known as Connie, Wyatt was a single white female, never married, other than to the force. She was eighteen months away from retirement and this case was not going to be the one that besmirched her legacy.

'Good morning, Mickie, what have we got going here? Sounds like it could be a bad one. No doubt the Captain, Police Commissioner and the Mayor will be all over our asses. We need a quick resolution. Anything you need, you got it.'

Mickie brought Wyatt up to date, believing there could have been two perps, and also eliminating the son as a suspect. He secured Hayes' service for as long as needed and she approved any overtime that he thought necessary. He returned to the Situation Room to find the whole team present. Deeks and Cooke had polished off what was remaining of the breakfast.

He addressed the team, 'Connie has given us the go ahead on this one, she wants it done ASAP. Deeks, Cooke you up to speed on this?'

'Sure are, Boss, but what's with the boot? She now a detective?' Deeks pointed his thumb at Hayes, as if she wasn't there.

'Deeks, watch your mouth. Hayes is part of this team for as long as I need her. Hayes, don't take any shit from either of them. Deeks, you and Cooke get over to the crime scene and see how the canvassing is going. If they have the slightest lead, personally investigate and report back here. We will analyze the data coming in from forensics, Hayes and I will go down to the morgue and see what the Doc has for us.'

Cairns and Hayes made the short trip to the morgue where they found Doctor Gareth Edwards busy with the corpse of Dennis O'Connell.

'What can you tell us, Doc?' inquired Cairns.

'I can tell you the female had sexual intercourse; I found a large amount of semen present in her vagina. I doubt whether it was consensual as there is clear bruising and some tearing. Her left nipple was bitten off while she was still alive. I found black synthetic strands in both eye sockets, probably means the killer was wearing gloves. The eyes were removed while she was alive.

'Her death was caused by slicing across her neck from left to right. It would suggest that the killer was behind her, which is consistent with the blood spatter, making him right-handed. She would have died instantly. Forensics should be able confirm positioning based on the blood spatters.'

'Any idea on the type of knife,' asked Cairns.

'A long smooth and very sharp blade did this. You can see no jagged edges, one clean cut end to end.'

'Time of death?'

'I stand by my initial estimate between 7.30 and 8.30 pm.'

'What can you tell us about the male victim?'

'Cause of death the same as the female, also from behind, perfect cut almost decapitating him. Time of death, same window as his wife. No other signs of violence other than bruising around his wrists where he was bound up. He must have been straining against the restraints given the position he was in.

'I don't normally get emotionally involved in my cases but this one's got me going. I hope you catch the sick bastards who did this.'

'Do you think there was more than one involved?' Cairns asked.

'I don't know, you are the detective so get detecting. I have sent the semen and the fibers up to the lab with a rush order.'

Cairns and Hayes returned to the Situation Room where they found Robertson waving a picture at them.

'Here you are, Mickie, a Japanese Tanto sword. Found it on the internet. Anything from ten to twenty inches long, sharp as fuck. Nasty weapon, could have been used to slice the vics' heads almost off.'

'Okay, Hayes, let's update the timeline. Murder weapon – Japanese Tanto sword, see if we can get an approximate value. Time of death 7.30 to 8.30 pm.

'Missing gun – Glock 19, see if you can find out where it was registered and get the serial number. They may try and hock the thing along with the sword, watches and jewels.

'Missing watches and jewels, we need descriptions and values, see if the son can give us any information, if he has any photos, that would help. Check if they are insured; maybe they are itemized.'

The office phone rang, Hayes answered, 'Homicide, Hayes speaking, yes sure.' She handed the phone to Cairns. 'It's Deeks.'

'Boss, forensics have left, the site is secure and every house on the block has been canvassed. Nada, not a sausage, nobody seen a damn thing. The neighborhood is out in force rubbernecking and the press have just arrived. We are heading back to the precinct before we get accosted for comments.'

'Okay, just stay clear of them, let the top brass do the commenting.'

The first set of results from forensics arrived just after lunch, photographs of the crime scene. Hayes plugged the flash dive into a laptop which was hooked up to a projector. The first one was of the whole scene taken from the bedroom door. Deeks and Cooke got their first look at the carnage.

'Jesus, Mary and Joseph. You weren't kidding, Boss, when you said it was a slaughter,' exclaimed Deeks. Cooke remained silent but visibly blanched.

'Don't worry boys, it gets worse close up. Hayes, document each photo as they come up. The rest of us will look at each one in great detail. Any immediate observations?' Cairns got closer to the projector screen, scrutinizing the picture.

Deeks: 'All the blood spatter seems centered between the two corpses. Husband killed from behind while facing the bed, I reckon.'

Cairns: 'Agreed, next we have the dresser, clearly been ransacked. Must have done this immediately on entry and then been disturbed. Hopefully forensics find some prints. Next, the female from above. Brian, what do you see?'

Robertson: 'Head almost severed; eyes gouged out both left on the bed. Left nipple missing looks like it was bitten off, I wonder if they have found it?'

Hayes: 'It looks like semen leaking out of her vagina. Both wrists secured to the bed's headboard, looks like neckties were used, one red and one blue. Must belong to her husband, difficult to find fingerprints on cloth. Maybe they'll find prints on the brass headboard.'

Cairns: 'Next, we have the male front on. His face is covered in blood, probably that of his wife. Head almost severed, blood spatters left, right and front. Shit, so much blood it's going to be difficult to separate his and hers.'

Getting no additional comment he projected the next photo, male from the left side.

Cooke: 'Maybe one of them was a cowboy, he sure looks hog tied. Leather belt secures the feet, hands tied with what looks like a striped necktie and then looped though the belt. That man was going nowhere.'

Cairns: 'Cowboy, really? May not be as dumb as it sounds. He is well secured, even when his throat was cut, he never fell over just forward to the edge of the bed. Hopefully they get some prints off the leather belt. Next slide: bloody footprints leading to the bathroom.'

Hayes: 'Only a single set leading from behind the male victim directly to the bathroom and none exiting. He was barefoot, did he go and wash off the blood in the bathroom?'

Cairns: 'That must be it. Why was he barefoot? If there were two of them, both must have been covered in blood, yet only one set of bloody footprints. Makes me think this might have been a solo.'

Deeks: 'I understand why the female was naked but why her husband? Do we know if he was butt fucked or not?'

Hayes: 'Jesus Deeks, show a little respect. I am sure if he was the Doc would have said so, after all he has examined him.'

Robertson: 'I reckon they were both stripped naked for easier control, less likely to make a run for it.'

Cairns: 'Makes sense. The way he is positioned he would have to watch his wife get raped, assaulted and then murdered. Nothing he could do except watch, fucking psychopath. Next photo – bathroom shower, small traces of blood. What looks like a wet towel on the floor. The bastard showered before leaving.' Cairns ran his hand over his face.

Robertson: 'Hayes, can you zoom in on the towel?' Hayes zoomed in. 'Thanks. It looks like a hair in the corner.'

Hayes zoomed in more and sure enough there was a single curly black hair.

Robertson: 'That's gotta be a pube and can only be the perp's.'

Next slide was of a close up of the towel confirming a pubic hair. The final photograph was of a pile of vomit just inside the bedroom door, confirming what Ethan O'Connell had stated.

Cairns: 'I am leaning towards a single perp. We have his semen, a pubic hair, footprints and hopefully a finger print or two. If this bastard is in any of our databases, we have him. We need forensics to give us their final report on fingerprints, any DNA and fibers from the eye sockets.'

Hayes: 'Boss, I didn't see any pics of her left nipple. Do you think he took it as a trophy?'

Deeks: 'Savage bastard probably swallowed it, sick fuck.'

Cairns: 'You are probably right, Deeks. While we are waiting on forensics can you and Cooke go back to the crime scene and retrieve any documents still in the safe? Brian, get hold of the son and arrange to show him the picture of the sword. Maybe he can give us a better idea of colors etc.

'Brian, you, me and Hayes will work on putting the word out that anyone making a deal with buying a Tanto sword or a Glock 19 will be charged with accessory to murder. The murder charge won't stick but should scare the "fences" off.'

By the end of day, the team had an exact picture of the Tanto sword and its valuation was put somewhere between $3,000 and $5,000. The purchase of the Glock 19 was traced and its serial number recorded. The two watches, a male and female matching pair of Rolex Datejust watches, valued in excess of $25,000. Pearls and diamond necklace and earrings combination insured for $5,500.

Cairns: 'We don't know the exact amount of cash but the son reckons around two grand. Anyone with any additional thoughts?'

Hayes: 'It has been nagging at me, the barefoot blood-soaked footprints. He must have been covered in blood; his clothes soaked in it so why was he barefoot? I think he may very well have been naked. Taken all his clothes off, put them out of range for blood spatters. After showering he simply got dressed in his still clean clothes and left the building. Could be why nobody noticed anything.'

Cairns: 'I think you hit the nail on the head. Our only hope is finding a DNA or fingerprint match. I don't think forensics will have that done until tomorrow. Let's pack up for the day, go home get some sleep, it's been a long day, especially for you, Hayes. I reckon tomorrow's gonna be a busy day.'

Deeks: 'Tomorrow's Sunday, Boss, New Year's Day in case you forgot. There's no way the labs are going to be working. I doubt we'll see anything before Monday or Tuesday, do you really want us in?'

Cairns: 'It totally slipped my mind. What a way to usher in the new year. Take it easy tomorrow, relax and recharge I think we are in for a rough ride. I'll be working tomorrow, so if anything pops, I will call you if needed, otherwise, see you Monday bright and early. Happy New Year.'

Chapter 6
Aftermath

According to Mayan legend, the world was due to end on 12/12/2012. To Ethan O'Connell it felt like the world had ended the day before the start of 2012. Still numb from the shock of finding his beloved parents slaughtered, he had managed to complete his police statement and officially identified his parents. He had given his fingerprints and a swab for DNA testing and was now free to leave the precinct.

His first order of business was to find some temporary accommodation. He was due back at Cornell on January 9 to start his final semester. He thought of contacting Mack or Sparrow but decided he needed to be alone, so a cheap hotel for eight days would be the best solution. As he left the precinct, he noticed that the YMCA building was directly across the road, he decided that was a perfect solution.

Hoping that the family house would be released from being a crime scene in a few days, he took a room at the YMCA on a day-to-day basis.

The first thing he did once he was settled in his private room was to call first Mack and then Sparrow to let them know what had happened and that they were likely to be called to corroborate his alibi. Both expressed their condolences and let him know if he needed anything to just call.

Alone with his thoughts, he tried to process exactly what had happened. His mother had apparently left the house directly after he had left. Either she'd forgotten to lock the door or she knew the perpetrators. Whichever scenario, if she was alone she would not have stood a chance. If it was after his father had arrived home from work, then there had to be more than one of them. No way a single person would have been able to overpower his father without a struggle. There seemed to be no signs of a struggle, so in his opinion his mother was alone at first.

The persons had to be in the house when she returned from the deli.

Did she disturb an ongoing robbery? Surely the robbers were masked but if not, did she see their faces? The only logical explanation was that either or both parents had seen their assailant's face and that's why they were murdered. There is killing and then there is slaughter, what triggered the violence?

From what he saw from the position of the bodies, his father must have been forced to watch his wife get raped and then murdered. Knowing how much his parents loved each other, it must have been devastating for his father being helpless and unable to help his beloved wife.

Unable to get the images out of his mind, he vowed that he would not rest until the killers were brought to justice. The cops better find them first because if he did, he knew he would exact revenge, an eye for an eye. Literally in this case.

The following day, New Year's Day 2012, he took the ten-block walk back to the family home. On arrival he noticed a uniformed police officer on duty at the front door. He walked up to the man who immediately recognized him.

'Sorry, Mr. O'Connell, you can't enter the premises yet, it is still a crime scene.' The officer looked genuinely sorry.

'I just need my college books and a few changes of clothes I won't disturb or touch anything.'

'Sorry, just following orders, try the precinct and see if you can get permission.'

Ethan just shrugged his shoulders, turned around and walked over to his car. His car keys were in his bedroom but he always had access to a spare set. He walked around the rear of the car, pressed down on the trunk and at the same time bumped the lock with his fist. The trunk popped open, he reached in, lifted the cover of the spare wheel and retrieved his spare set of keys.

He made the short trip back to the YMCA, parked his car and returned to the solace of his room. With the first day of the year 2012 being a federal holiday, everything was closed. Having time to contemplate his future, he went through his options. First, he realized, he would have to plan a dual funeral. His parents had made it clear on a number of occasions that they both wanted to be cremated. What about their house, car and other belongings? There was surely a will, his father would have made certain of that.

Then there was his final semester of university concluding four years of hard work. He would put his degree to good use.

Not having slept for almost two days, he decided to hit the sack and recharge his batteries. He was asleep the second his head hit the pillow. Within minutes he jolted awake, images of his dead parents' bloodied bodies haunting him. This would be the pattern every time he fell asleep for the foreseeable future. January 1, 2012 would be the start of four very long weeks ahead for Ethan O'Connell.

January 2, the team reassembled in the situation room, the excesses of the previous day evident on Deeks, Cooke and Robertson. Cairns brought the group to order.

'We can expect the first of any forensic evidence to start coming in early this afternoon. Hayes, get on their case and try and speed things up. None of us feel the son is the perp here but let's follow up on him.

'Deeks, get ahold of his cell phone records, check in detail all calls in and out from December 30 through today. See if you can place his whereabouts throughout the period.

'Cooke, get onto his bank records, look for any red flags there. Any abnormal outgoings, big cash withdrawals and the like.

'Brian, Hayes and me will go back to the scene of the crime and do a thorough, top to bottom search of the house. We will look for anything that could be construed as a reason for the killings.

'Any questions? No, okay let's meet back here by 2.00 pm.' Everyone got started on their assigned tasks.

With Hayes at the wheel, the trio took the short drive back to the scene of the crime. They were met by a young police officer who barred their way. Cairns, impressed by the young man following protocol, congratulated him and flashed his gold shield to identify himself. Slightly embarrassed, the police officer stepped aside and allowed them entry.

'Brian, you take the basement, Hayes, you do the ground floor and I'll take upstairs. Look for anything out of the ordinary, documents, bills, any computer equipment. You find anything relevant, take a photo and bag it. Right, let's get at it.'

Robertson made his way down the steps to the basement, and switched on the light. As basements go, this one was probably the neatest and most organized he had ever seen. There was a folded-up table tennis set in the far left corner, right up against it was an exercise treadmill. Two lazy boy recliners were in the middle of the floor facing the far wall, where a flat screen TV was mounted.

The walls were liberally decked with family photos. Against the right-hand wall were two filing cabinets, each with three drawers. A small bar fridge was located at the rear of the room. Robertson tried the door, it opened only to show the fridge was completely empty and not switched on.

He tried the first filing cabinet – top drawer. It opened to reveal hanging files meticulously arranged A through Z. He pulled the first file and found invoices relating to a vehicle covering services and repairs. These went back to 1996 and covered at least five different cars.

He paged through each file; whoever did the record keeping at the O'Connell residence had kept everything. Utility bills, phone bills, tax records all filed chronologically by date all starting in 1996. He wondered what was significant about that year. He wasn't about to read through each set of files.

He moved to the middle drawer. This drawer contained three remote controls, Robertson matched them to the TV, a DVD and a satellite box. The bottom drawer was packed with DVD movies, all stacked in alphabetical order. He wondered if it was the mother or father who liked everything in order. He moved over to the second cabinet.

The top drawer held photo albums starting in 1991. He opened the first one and found photos of baby Ethan, mother and father in various poses. Halfway through the album, he found photos of the baby and parents together and separately marked – Ireland. By the end of the album, the pictures showed they had arrived and settled in Kerry, Republic of Ireland.

The albums 1991 through 1995 documented the O'Connells' life in Kerry. The 1996 version documented their arrival back in the USA and their move back into their current abode. The drawer held photo albums 1991 to 1999. He opened the second drawer and found albums 2000 through 2010. All meticulously captioned, a pictorial view of their life.

The third drawer held two cameras, one film based and the other digital. It also contained envelopes filled with photos and negatives, all filed by month. It was the year 2011, not yet assembled into an album. He wondered if they ever would be.

It would take a great deal of time and effort to go through the contents of both cabinets. With the unlikelihood of finding anything relevant, it would probably be a waste of time, but that was not his call. Deciding there was nothing more to see in the basement, he made his way up to the ground floor.

Hayes, in the meantime, had also found nothing relevant. Everything was in its place, cutlery, plates, cups and saucers all neatly stored. The pantry was the same; everything had its place. It was obvious that the thieves had not touched anything downstairs other than the safe.

'You find anything of interest, Hayes?' Robertson asked.

'Nah, and you?'

'Lots of stuff but nothing of interest. Whoever did the filing here was meticulous. Let's go and see how the Boss got on.'

They met Cairns on the stairway coming down, he was carrying two laptops.

'What did you find, anything interesting?' ask Robertson.

'Everything was still pretty neat and tidy. They obviously went through the bedside drawers; nothing of use in what was left. The various jewelry boxes are almost empty, just a few cheap earrings scattered about. The walk-in closet seemed undisturbed apart from a small gap in the clothes hanging on the right at the entrance of the closet. Maybe someone was hiding there when the female came home.

'I found two laptops, both in the son's bedroom. We can have the forensic team have a look at them.

'Let's get back to the precinct and see if anything has come in from forensics.'

The team assembled back in the situation room just after 1.30 pm. Deeks was first to report.

'With the help of the cellphone company, I managed to get a clear picture of Ethan O'Connell's movements. His phone was switched on for the entire period that we are looking at. On December 30, at 10.17 am there was a single inbound call from a Michael Morrison lasting just on three minutes. The caller was also the person O'Connell referred to as being one of the people on the bus.

'No other calls inbound or outbound were made until the 911 call at 01.18 am on December 31. This tallies with O'Connell's statement. The cellphone company were able to provide a list of "pings" from various towers over the period 6.45 pm through to 12.55 am. The pattern indicated that none of them were in the vicinity of the crime.'

'Boss, I went through the financial records of the three family members. Absolutely nothing out of the ordinary, no red flags, no large deposits or withdrawals.' reported Cooke

'Well, it looks like we can eliminate Ethan as a suspect. Searching the house nothing stood out, seemed like a normal robbery. We must get the kid to do an inventory and see if he can tell us exactly what is missing.

'It seems to me that our theory of a robbery gone wrong is the likely scenario. Hopefully forensics can give us something to work on. Talk of the devil, what have got for us, Sinclair?'

Dave Sinclair, the lead forensics officer, greeted the assembled team and plonked a pile of sealed evidence bags on the main table.

'I will give you an overview of our findings, everything is categorized and clearly marked; you can document the details later. It was impossible to check all of the blood types but what we did check we found only two. Doc Edwards has a copy of both, I am sure they belong to the deceased.

'Fresh fingerprints were found on the door frame of the bedroom, we confirmed those belong to the son. Fresh prints were found on the belt securing the male, we confirmed they belong to him. The only other prints in the room belong to the deceased.

'The black fibers found in the eye sockets of the female told us nothing. The rapist must have been wearing gloves. The bloodied footprints were made by the blood of the male victim.

'The only DNA found not belonging to the two victims was a black pubic hair and the semen from the female victim's vagina. Both were sent for DNA testing and good readings were obtained; the samples were confirmed as being from the same person. We ran it through all of our databases but no match was found. We are in the process of getting permission to run it through all agency databases.

'I don't hold out much hope as I don't think this person was a mastermind but just some burglar who got caught and then lost it. Without fingerprints, I don't think we will get a match. If he has a record we will have his prints on file but unlikely to have his DNA.

'Sorry folks, but that's all we have. I hope you catch whoever did this, in all my time on the job it is the worst I have ever seen.'

'Thanks Dave, we appreciate your effort,' said Cairns.

Now began the onerous task of documenting the scene and updating the timeline. The only confirmation they had was who the victims were, cause and time of death. No eye witnesses and no suspects. The consensus was a single perpetrator, an unplanned robbery that turned into murder.

A list of the stolen items was circulated to all the local pawn shops and known fences. The word was clear that if anyone tried to pawn any of the items, the police were to be notified immediately. Any deviation found would result in prosecution as an accessory.

The two laptops were analyzed and found that one belonged to the son and the other to his parents. Nothing was found to indicate any connection to the robbery and subsequent murders. Both were returned to Ethan.

Although an appeal to the public to come forward with any information was held, none were forthcoming. Only the basic details of what had occurred was released to the public.

The house was no longer a crime scene and was released to Ethan O'Connell on January 7. His first task was to rip up the blood-stained carpets in his parents' bedroom. He removed the bedding and dumped it in the garbage. The blood stains on the walls were covered up by repainting the entire room, walls and ceiling.

No matter how hard he tried, he couldn't remove the scene of the murders from his mind. Every time he looked into or stepped into the room the scene flashed before his eyes. He decided he had to move out of the house and put it up for sale.

The terms of his parents will left everything to their son. The house was mortgage free and its market value was in the mid $400,000's. A 2009 Lexis SUV had an outstanding loan of $11,000 on the vehicle valuation of $41,000. There were two life insurance policies, one on each parent for an amount of $500,000 each. Savings and checking accounts added almost $159,000. All in all, it left Ethan as a wealthy young man.

The finalization of the will, the sale of the house and the transfer of all of the assets took him into early March. He had missed the start of his final semester and it seemed unlikely that he would be able to graduate with the rest of his class. The university had been sympathetic to his situation and promised a plan would be made for him to do the final three credits needed for graduation at a convenient time.

No progress had been made in tracking down his parents' murderers. He was in regular contact with Detective Cairns and as time passed it was obvious that unless the murderers made a silly mistake, there was little chance of apprehending them. The case remained open but had been relegated to the back burner until a useful lead turned up.

By early April, Ethan made the decision to forego his university obligations, at least for the interim period, and join the New York Police department. He joined the academy intake of April 23, 2012 and graduated in the top three of his class on October 19, 2012. He was now a New York Policeman, serving a twenty-four month probationary period.

He never did complete his university degree and the case of his parents' murders became an open cold case.

Chapter 7
Situation Room 35th Precinct - December 2021

It was after 7 pm by the time the four detectives arrived back at the newly set up "situation room" on the third floor at the 35th Precinct. Lieutenant Grover Johnston was nowhere to be seen, obviously left for home. He had left a note for Garcia, ordering him to have a report on his desk by 8.00 am the next morning. *Typical.*

'Okay folks, it looks like our boss has left for the day which is a bit surprising as the press are going to be all over this by the morning. I don't think we are going to make any significant progress tonight. Why don't you all head home, get some rest and be back here first thing tomorrow O'Connell, before you leave, I want a word with you.'

Shaw and Mills looked at each other, shrugged their shoulders and left.

As soon as they had left the office, Garcia addressed O'Connell.

'What exactly did you mean by your statement *"that I have seen the almost identical scene, exactly ten years ago to the day"*?'

'My folks were murdered on December 30, 2011. Today's crime scene looked like an exact copy of how my folks got murdered. The way my Mom was killed, her exact positioning, my Dad bound up on his knees facing my Mom with his throat cut. I fully expect there to be blood-stained footprints leading from the bed to the bathroom. The forensics pictures will probably confirm that.'

'Shit. I can see why you reacted the way you did. Do you think we have a copycat killing? If so, why ten years later?'

'Boss, I can't answer that until we have seen all the crime scene photos and any fingerprints or DNA the forensic team have collected. If it is how I saw it, I am sure it is an exact duplicate of my folks' murder. The only exception so far is there were no zodiac signs found at their murder.'

'A personal question, did you join the force because of what you saw back then?'

'Yes, I was unable to get the picture out of my mind, couldn't think of anything else. I hoped to help find their killers.'

'I don't recall the case but did the killers ever get caught?' Garcia asked, already knowing the answer.

'Nobody was apprehended, the case is still open but obviously not active. I feel that maybe this one might lead to catching my folks' killers. It seems like too much of a coincidence that this happens on the day I transfer to the 35th and exactly ten years later.'

'If your instincts are true, then we have a situation. Someone knows you and your movements, plus has intimate knowledge of your parents' murder. We need to follow that trail. It's getting late, the forensics data will only be here tomorrow, I suggest you go home and think of any possible connections you can. I have a report to write for Johnston so head off home. By the way, welcome to the 35th. When did you learn of your transfer?'

'Lieutenant Thomas told me three weeks ago but said I should keep quiet about it as there were others who might cause a stink over it. You know length of service and all that. Thomas said he would inform the rest of the precinct today that I had transferred, so it was pretty much a secret.'

'Okay, O'Connell, take off; we have a big day ahead of us tomorrow.' Garcia patted his shoulder and Ethan turned to leave.

All alone, Garcia sat down at desk and started a report for his boss. Not wanting to theorize just yet, he stated the facts as they were known. There would be plenty of time later to attempt to get into the perp's mindset. It was a big leap from robbery and rape to murder, but that would be one for the shrinks to explain. He chose not to mention O'Connell's observations, as detailed comparisons of the two scenes would be needed. He was pretty sure Lieutenant Johnston wouldn't want to scare up the notion of a serial killer on the loose in the city. *Just the facts, he decided.*

As Johnston had left him a note instructing him only to have the report on his desk by 8.00 am, he decided against a phone call. He dumped the report on his boss's desk and headed home.

Back in the office by 7.30 am, Garcia was joined minutes later by O'Connell. Mills and Shaw made it just before 8.00 am. If was funny how the two of them always seemed to arrive together, Garcia wondered if there was anything going on between the two of them. His thoughts were interrupted by his office phone ringing, it was Johnston demanding his presence. He took the short walk down to the second floor.

'Morning Boss, I hope you had a pleasant evening.'

'No need to be sarcastic, Garcia. I have read your report, no mention of the zodiac signs or previous connections, why is that?'

'I figured that if there is any suggestion of a 'Zodiac Killer' there will be wide spread panic and the press will make a meal of it. I suggest we, meaning you, just report a robbery gone wrong that ended up in the murder of two innocent people. Normal spiel – we are following leads and are confident in apprehending the perpetrators.

Don't give out any details of how we found the bodies, nothing about the female being raped or how they were killed.' Garcia suggested.

'I reckon you are right. I will bump this up the line and if there is a press conference, keep yourself available.'

'Boss, you know I hate those fucking things. Can't you handle it? You are so good at it.' Johnston raised an eyebrow at the blatant refusal but relented.

'Okay. Get back to work and keep me posted.' Garcia happily took the dismissal and left the office.

He dragged himself back up to the third-floor, muttering that it was about time they fixed the *fucking elevator*. He walked into the situation room to find the other three detectives drinking coffee and sharing a box of donuts. Jesus, talk about stereotypical cops.

'Okay people, let's get to work on a timeline. We probably won't get all the forensics until much later today so let's work with what we know. O'Connell, you can man the white board.

We have four instances of rape and robbery that we can tie to, for want of a name, the Zodiac man. Mills, you have the details of the first one. O'Connell, you document these.'

'Yes, Boss. The first one: January, 13 this year, it was a Wednesday. The victim, a thirty-four-year old single white woman – Sandra Williamson. She came home from work at 6.30 pm and found a man wearing a ski mask, busy rummaging through her bedroom drawers. She panicked and froze. She stated the man was white, tall and well built. He produced a knife and told her if she made any noise, he would kill her.

She was ordered to undress completely and lie on the bed. He secured her hands to the bed headrest, dropped his trousers and in her words flashed a well-endowed penis in her direction. He produced a condom which he rolled onto his penis and proceeded to rape her.

He was in no way violent, he reached a climax, rolled off her, stood up without saying a word. He flushed the condom down the toilet. He pulled up his trousers, leaned over her and stuffed her panties in her mouth. He gathered up his stolen bounty and left without saying another word.

Thirty minutes later, the precinct received a call that there was a woman in distress at 435 West 46th Street. Two beat cops were dispatched where they found Ms. Williamson. She was freed and taken to the local hospital where she was examined and a rape kit taken. No semen was found, there was no bruising and the only clue was a zodiac card for Sagittarius which had been inserted in her vagina.

She made her statement and was allowed to leave. She took great pains to tell everyone that she had not had an orgasm. She was distressed that a lot her valuables had been stolen.'

Garcia: 'So what do we think? Just an interrupted robbery turned into a rape?'

Mills: 'Could be, but he had at least one condom in his possession. Maybe planned the rape or maybe just a boy scout, "always be prepared."

Shaw: 'And what about the zodiac card? Did he just have that handy? First time we had seen that."

Garcia: 'Mills, check if there have been any other robberies where a zodiac card was left behind. Just check any NYPD cases. Maybe he has been active elsewhere and this was his first rape. Shaw, you've got the second one.'

'April 12, Monday: Lola Estes, 28 years old, single Hispanic female. She arrived home 4.30 pm after spending the day with her family. This one is similar but just slightly different. She did not disturb her assailant; he was waiting just inside the front door. There was no forced entry, the door lock must have been picked.

She was caught by surprise and a masked man of the same description as the first guy grabbed her from behind and placed his hand over her mouth. He forced her into her bedroom and from there on in the events were exactly the same as for Williamson. No violence, just fucked her, came and left.'

Mills: 'Seriously, Shaw, what the fuck is wrong with you? Don't be so crude!'

Shaw: 'Chill out, Mills. Anyway, the same process – a phone call made to the precinct, cops arrived on the scene, freed the victim and took her to the hospital. She was examined, no damage and a zodiac card found in the vagina: this time Gemini.'

Garcia: 'So what else connects these two? We have rape and robbery, one white, one Hispanic. The two have no common features. See if we can link them by work or friends, something. Next, Shaw, what about number three?'

Shaw: 'July 10, a Saturday. Heather Smith 41, single white female. Been out shopping with friends, returned home around 7.15 pm. Virtually identical to the previous two situations. Again, no overt violence, the Sagittarius zodiac card found in her vagina. Flip flopping between Gemini and Sagittarius. No obvious connection to the other two.'

Garcia: 'Mills, you've got number four.'

Mills: 'October 6, a Wednesday. Denise Todd 52, divorced white female. Returned home from Buster's Gym, where she is a personal trainer, at around 8.15 pm. Same story, she unlocked her front door stepped in and was accosted by a tall well-built white male wearing a black ski mask.

Taken by surprise, she was overcome by her assailant who brandished a knife, told her to remain silent or he would kill her. From there on it was the same as the other three. He made off with a number of her valuables, leaving her tied to the bed with her panties stuffed in her mouth.

As with the others a call was made, two beat cops arrived and freed her. The examination at the hospital showed no violence from the rape and a Gemini zodiac card was found. Other than the method of the rapes, there seems to be no connection between the victims.'

Garcia: 'And with all four no fingerprints, DNA or identification was recorded. Smacks of planned attacks to me, we need to find a connection other than the zodiac cards. Any ideas?'

O'Connell: 'Each incident is roughly three months apart. Originally the day of the month and the day of the week seemed random. I just did a quick check of the lunar chart – each incident was on the new moon – might be significant.'

Garcia: 'Good work there, O'Connell, maybe the man is guided by the moon. All of these attacks were done by a single white male. The victims' descriptions all tie in. Is our latest situation linked or not? The press has made a big deal about this so called "serial zodiac rapist," has he turned to murder as well, or is this just a copycat?'

Shaw: 'These were all done by one man, our murder could have been done by two. We have to find some connection to link them. He has almost been a 'caring' rapist, yes raping but without any violence other than threatening them to comply.'

Mills: 'Boss, based on what O'Connell reckons about the new moon and the three-month gaps between robberies, if he stays true to form the next one should be on Sunday January 2, two days away.'

Garcia: 'Jesus, you are right. There is no way we can predict where that might happen or if it happens at all. If ours is the same guy I think he has moved on from the new moon scenario. Sunday will tell. In the meantime, we need a profile on the guy. We may have to involve a shrink on this one, find out what makes him tick.

'O'Connell, in the meantime while we wait for forensics' help, work with Mills to track down any other reported robbery/rapes in the area. There may be others with a similar MO but without the zodiac cards.

'Dave, you with me, we need to set up interviews with the four females he raped. It may be difficult given the holidays. I'll contact the first two, you get ahold of the second two. I'll let Johnston know our plan of attack.'

O'Connell: 'Boss, what about the possible link between this murder and the murder of my folks? There are too many similarities for us to just ignore them. Can I do anything in that regard?'

Garcia: 'Let's wait for the forensic evidence before we go down that road. Your suspicions must remain in this room until we find a link, I don't want a panicked reaction that there may be a serial killer out there. Let's get to work.'

Chapter 8
Forensics

While waiting for forensics data, Garcia and Shaw got busy with trying to contact the four rape victims. Garcia suggested that they attempt to get all four victims together as maybe they would be more forthcoming as a group with additional evidence. The basic message to each victim would be '*We have a new lead on your attacker and would appreciate you coming down to the precinct to discuss your original testimony. We hope that interviewing you and the other victims will lead to an arrest.*'

Hill and O'Connell were dispatched to the records department to gather all logged evidence from the four rapes.

Garcia's first call was to Sandra Williamson, the first victim. The number was no longer in service, he made a note and dialed victim #2 – Lola Estes. He had two numbers, the first was her home landline number. The phone rang but was not answered, the answering machine kicked in. Garcia left a detailed message requesting her to call him at her earliest convenience. He dialed the second number, a cellphone, it too went unanswered so he left the same message.

Shaw's first call was to victim #3 – Heather Smith. The call went directly to voicemail, the detective left a detailed message requesting she call him back as soon as possible

Shaw was the first to get lucky. He called Buster's Gym and asked for Denise Todd – victim #4. She had just finished a session with one of her regular clients and had a few minutes before her next one.

'Ms. Todd, I am Detective Dave Shaw from the 35th Precinct. We are following up on your case of October 6 of last year as we have some new leads. I wonder if you could come into the precinct and spend some time with us reviewing your case? As you may know, there were three other women who had the same experience as yourself. If possible, we would like to interview you all as a group. We think that doing so will maybe highlight something that was missed in your original statements. How do you feel about that?'

'I am happy to do anything that leads to the arrest of that asshole. Count me in.'

'Excellent. We are in the process of contacting the other three. I will call you to set up a time, what time of the day would be best for you?'

'I work very flexible hours so it shouldn't be a problem even after normal working hours. I live very close to the precinct, so no problem.'

'Thank you, Ms. Todd. I will be in contact soon.' Shaw hung up.

Garcia: 'Only one out of the four and one of them has a number no longer in service. We have an address. I will send Mills and O'Connell around to her house and see if they can get ahold of her.

I will give the other two until 5 pm to respond before calling them again. It's New Year's Eve; who knows where they could be. Well, here's hoping.'

Mills and O'Connell returned with a large box filled with the logged evidence covering the four cases.

Garcia: 'Mills, you and O'Connell get yourselves around to this address and see if you can make contact with Sandra Williamson. Her number is no longer in service. Try and get her to agree to come in for an interview and get a new contact number. She may very well have disconnected her original number to avoid unsolicited crank calls. We want to try and get them all in together.'

At 3.15 pm, Garcia's office phone rang; it was Lola Estes. She had received the message and was eager to join the other victims in an interview. She felt as a group they would achieve two things; one: maybe some additional information may come out of the interview and two: there would be an affinity between the four of them. She was currently visiting her sister in Boston and would be back in the city on January 4 and would be available at any time.

Twenty minutes later Shaw's phone rang; it was Heather Smith. She listened to the detective's plan and agreed that January 4, any time after 5.00 pm would be agreeable. He promised to call her back as soon as he had a fixed time. He then called Denise Todd and locked her in for January 4, time to be confirmed.

In the meantime, Mills and O'Connell had reached the address for Sandra Williamson. She answered the front door, opening only as far as the chain lock would allow. 'What do you want?' she asked nervously, looking them up and down.

'I am Detective Linda Mills from the 35th Precinct and this is my partner, Detective Ethan O'Connell. We are investigating your rape and robbery case from January 13, can we come in and ask you a few questions?' They held up their IDs for her to scrutinize them. Sandra stared at their badges, silently.

'Why? I answered all of your questions months ago and I have heard nothing, I am trying to move on.'

'We have new evidence and would like to clarify a few points. If you could let us in, we can bring you up to date.' Mills said gently, understanding the victim's reluctance.

The door closed, the sound of the chain being removed and then it opened fully. They were met by a short dark-haired woman, with a very nervous look on her face, she directed them to follow her. She led them into a neat living room and indicated they should take a seat.

Mills: 'We noticed your telephone number is no longer in service, is there any connection to what happened to you?'

'Yes, I got a few crank calls shortly after my attack and felt very nervous about them so I changed phone numbers.' Sandra crossed her arms, as if hugging herself, and Mills smiled reassuringly.

Mills: 'Were you threatened and did you report them to the police?'

'No on both accounts. They were just sick and disgusting.' She shuddered at the memory, turning to look out of the window.

'I'm sorry you went through that. We believe we have new leads on your attacker. As you may be aware, there were three other women attacked in the same way as you. We have contacted them and they have agreed to come into the precinct and be interviewed as a group. This way we hope that some clues emerge that may have otherwise been missed when you were all interviewed separately. How do you feel about that?' Mills asked, gently.

'I am not sure that I am comfortable rehashing that whole experience in front of others. Would it be confidential?' Sandra turned back to look at Mills, fear clearly evident on her face.

Mills: 'Yes, completely. If anything leads to capturing this freak, we will make sure we apprehend the bastard that did this to you and the other three. We hope to do this on January 4 after 5.00 pm. It will be held at the precinct. I hope you will agree.'

'Okay, I'll go. If you do catch him, I will sleep a lot easier at night, I have not had a good night's sleep since it happened.'

Mills: 'Thank you very much, Sandra. If you give me a contact number, I will call you to confirm the exact time. Here's my card as well. If you need anything, please call me. We are here to help you, okay?'

Sandra Williamson gave her new number, a cellphone, to Mills who thanked her. They waited outside until they heard her lock and chain the door and then left to return to the precinct.

Mills reported on their meeting with Williamson and her agreement to be interviewed. O'Connell was tasked with calling all four of them to inform them that the meeting would be on January 4 at 6.30 pm.

At 5.10 pm there was a knock on the situation room door. A uniformed cop stood nervously in the doorway; he was holding a large evidence bag.

'This is for Detective Garcia from Barry Hughes and his team.'

'Thanks officer, I'll take that', turning to his assembled team, 'Well, folks, looks like our work is just starting. I know it's New Year's Eve but the Lieutenant has authorized whatever overtime we think we need so it's up to us. Are you up for working tonight and the weekend?' Garcia had a habit of giving them the illusion of choice when it was clearly evident that they would all be working, one way or another.

Shaw: 'I have plans for tonight with some chick I met online. Signs are good I might just get lucky, but I am good for working the weekend.'

Mills: 'I agree with Shaw, a night off and hit it tomorrow.'

O'Connell: 'I could work tonight if you need me, but maybe a fresh start tomorrow is best.'

Garcia: 'Okay, let's lock the place up. I will see you all tomorrow bright and early. Have a good evening but try not to drink too much. Tomorrow is going to be a long day' There was a collective groan from the group but Garcia knew that Mills and Shaw would be in it for the long haul, no matter what. O'Connell may only have joined the crew but he had a vested interest in this case. Garcia didn't doubt for a second that O'Connell would be here for as long as it took.

January 1, 2022

Garcia was the first to arrive at 8.15 am, he was followed by O'Connell. Both men looked refreshed and relaxed. The same couldn't be said about Mills and Shaw, who arrived minutes apart shortly after 8.30 am

Mills was puffy eyed and nursing a mild hangover, Shaw on the other hand was a different story. He arrived carrying coffee and donuts and looked in dire need of both. He was disheveled and appeared to be wearing the same clothes as the previous day.

Garcia: 'Jesus Dave, you look like shit, did you have a bad night?'

Shaw: 'No Boss, I had a pretty damn good fucking night, well almost. Sorry, Mills.' *Again with the pointless apology and Mills shrugged it off for the millionth time.* 'I mentioned yesterday I was meeting up with this chick I met online. First off, let me tell you she looked nothing like her profile picture but I figured the bar was reasonably dark and no one I know would see me, so I reckoned why not.'

Mills: 'Jesus, Shaw, I bet you looked nothing like your profile picture either, she was probably just as happy to meet in a dark bar.'

Shaw: 'Well, what started as a couple of drinks turned into a whole lot of drinks. As each beer went down, she started to look better and better. By the time the clock struck 12 we were both well on the way. Anyway, as the New Year dawned, she grabbed me and put her tongue down my throat. She wanted us to go back to her place and well, I was past giving a shit at that point, so we grabbed a cab back to her place. She Houdini'd out of her clothes so damn fast and well, you know how it goes. That was the best damn workout I've had in forever.

We eventually both passed out. I woke up around 3.00 am and she was lying across my arm, I was unable to shift her and was scared to wake her so I just lay there, while my arm went dead. I tried to save my arm at around 5 am but she woke up and let's just say that she gave me another pounding. They say that all cats are grey in the dark but this one proved that saying wrong. Her makeup was all smudged, her hair was wild and I was sober. I swear I will never drink again; she was scary.'

Mills: 'What a load of crap, it's not like you are an oil painting. Maybe she also got a fright when she saw you in the cold light of day.'

Shaw: 'By the time she finished with me I barely had time for a shower and definitely no time to go home and change.'

Garcia: 'Enough bullshitting about your sex life, let's get to work. At least you can put that one down to experience, Shaw, you got out with your life. I suggest we start with Doc. Jarvis' report.

He puts their deaths at around 2.00 pm to 3.00 pm. Both dead within minutes of each other, cause of death severing of the carotid artery, death instantaneous. Female raped but no semen found in either vagina or anus, but traces of a lubricant, probably from a condom, found in victim's vagina.

O'Connell, check the evidence boxes of the rape victims and see if there is anything on condom lubricant. It's unlikely but you never know, maybe we can get a match.' O'Connell nodded and headed for the box of evidence while Garcia continued.

'Female victim had both eyes gouged out while still alive, traces of black fibers found in both eye sockets, Perp wore gloves. Her left nipple was missing, probably bitten off while she was still alive. The Sagittarius symbol is the same as those found on our four rape victims, but was found on her forehead not in her vagina. A deviation of his normal MO? According to his cycle the next sign should have been Gemini and then Sagittarius. Did that mean the male who has the Gemini sign died before the female?'

Mills: 'Maybe, or in the frenzy of the situation he got confused.'

Shaw: 'Boss, how confident are we that all of this is the work of one guy? We know the four rapes were done by a single person in each case but there is a good chance our murder may have been done by two people.'

Garcia: 'To be honest, I don't know. So far, the only connection we have is the zodiac cards. If it was one person, he would have had to subdue either the male or female first. Either that or he had a gun, the rapist threatened his victims with a knife. So, this is all speculation. O'Connell, you got anything on the condom lubrication?'

O'Connell: 'Nothing mentioned in the reports. We still have the swabs maybe they can still do a test checking for any lubrication.'

Garcia: 'Good idea. Right, let's go through the hard evidence. There were no foreign fingerprints found, only those of the two victims. Fingerprints on the leather belt are those of the deceased male. No foreign DNA found. Wait, there was some, a single pubic hair found in the bathroom, which was unmatched in any of our known databases. It was found on a wet towel.'

O'Connell: 'Jesus, Boss, the same thing was found in the murder of my folks. It's got to be the same guy.'

Garcia: 'Don't be jumping to conclusions, but it does suggest the perp took a shower. Probably to clean off any blood splatters. Let's go on in sequence.

First photo taken from the bedroom door entrance. Male, naked on his knees facing inwards from the bottom of the bed. Ankles secured with a leather belt, hands secured behind his back with a red and blue striped necktie which is looped through the ankle restraints. He definitely looks posed, a full view of what was happening to his wife. Wife, naked, hands secured to the bed headboard with what appears to be neckties.

Second photo from behind the male. He has direct view of his wife's splayed legs. Slight bruising on the wife's upper thighs, probably because she resisted somewhat and her legs had to be forced apart.

Third photo from the front of the male. Neck sliced open almost severing his head from his body. Blood splattered forward so the killer was behind him. Doc says the cut was from left to right meaning the killer is probably right-handed. The cut is clean no jagged edges so the knife had to be extremely sharp.

Fourth photo taken directly from above the female. Her left nipple is missing, Doc's report says it was bitten off, maybe we can get some match from the teeth marks. Her throat was cut in exactly the same way as her husband, from behind. He must have lifted her up before slicing her throat, most of the blood is in front of her.

Fifth photo showing her hands secured to the headboard, Left one with a blue necktie and the right with a red one.

Photo number six, blood-stained footprints leading from the base of the bed into the bathroom. The killer was barefoot, possibly naked and walked from behind the male into the bathroom. By Barry Hughes' estimate he puts the foot size as about a fifteen, that's a fucking huge pair of feet.'

O'Connell: 'I wear a size fifteen, it's quite common.'

Shaw: 'Not so common, how tall are you?'

O'Connell: 'Six three.'

Mills: 'Six three and size fifteens, it is true what they say that you can tell the size of a man's dick by the size of his feet. You must be a really big boy.'

Garcia: 'Come on Mills, get your mind out of the gutter and back on the case.'

Mills: 'Just kidding, Boss, but I wouldn't mind finding out if it is true. What do you say O'Connell? Care to show us?'

O'Connell: 'I have never had any complaints but I am not hauling my Johnson out for your benefit.

Boss, the more I see of this the more it looks exactly the same as when my folks were murdered. I think we should get the records out for their case and do a side by side. Most of the details of their killing were not released to the press. If this murder matches up, it has to be the same person or persons. Can I get permission to review their case alongside this one?'

Garcia: 'I think we should. If there is no match up then we can disprove the connection and concentrate on this case alone. But if there is a match, why the ten-year gap?'

Mills: 'Maybe he was incarcerated, recently released and couldn't resist the urge. O'Connell, what zodiac card was found at your folks' murder?'

O'Connell: 'None were found. Semen and a pubic hair were found but no DNA match found in any database. If he has been recently released from prison a DNA sample may have been taken and is now on file. Boss, we have to get all the evidence from my folks' case.'

Garcia: 'You are right; it is best we check. Where was the case logged?'

O'Connell: '94th Boss.'

Garcia: 'I don't know anyone there so it will have to go through official channels. I'll get the lieutenant to put in the request, I doubt if he'll do it before Monday at the earliest.

So here we have no fingerprints, seems he was very careful with that, but then he leaves a single pubic hair. According to Barry Hughes it was left in plain sight. This does not strike me as a robbery gone wrong, it looks very staged and well planned out. Any thoughts?'

Shaw: 'You could be right, everything neat and tidy if you ignore all the blood. Almost looks like he wanted to leave certain clues but none that could incriminate him.'

Mills: 'Doesn't make sense to me. Why would you set up something like this?'

Garcia: 'He is sending us a message, maybe even taunting us – look how smart I am; you are too stupid to catch me.'

O'Connell: 'It is too much of a coincidence, he knows things about my folk's murder that were not made public. It is either him or he had access to secured evidence.'

Mills: 'Do you think it could be a cop?'

Garcia: 'No, don't go down that road just yet, let's wait until we do a side by side. In the meantime, we look at what was found during a canvass of the neighborhood. What we got, Mills?'

Mills: 'Not much; we have the next-door neighbor's statement. He says he heard what sounded like an argument coming from the Marx's house. That was around 2.15 pm, he heard a further noise at about 3.00 pm, he waited about ten minutes and then went to investigate, he found their front door open: that's when he called it in. That ties in with the 911 call. The rest of the neighborhood – nothing.'

Garcia: 'So a man or men break into a house in broad daylight in the middle of the day, slaughter two people and then leave and nobody saw a thing. Let's stay with the theory of a single man. He must have showered otherwise he would have been covered in blood, not conducive to walking around a New York neighborhood.

If we tie this in with our serial rapist, what do we see? He raped three white woman and one Hispanic. Christine Marx is also white, if he likes white woman how did he choose Estes, the Hispanic?'

Mills: 'Looking at Lola Estes, you would never say she is Hispanic, she is whiter than white.'

Shaw: 'I wonder how much planning went into the rapes. It's possible he just picked them at random, there is no apparent link other than they were seen as white and female.'

Garcia: 'The first one, Sandra Williamson, said she came home and disturbed the man who was busy robbing the place. He turned a robbery into rape. The next three were all accosted the minute they stepped into their houses. They were tied up, raped and then the perp robbed them so I reckon the first rape wasn't planned.

O'Connell, get the four women's details up on the timeline. Date, time and location: let's see if there is any connection other than the new moon once every three months.'

Mills: 'The Zodiac cards for all the rapes and the murders are from the same manufacturer but then there are thousands of outlets selling them. Gemini is the sign of the twins and Sagittarius is half man, half beast, I wonder what the connection is there.'

Working on the theory that the ten-year gap between O'Connell's family murders and the latest ones if the perpetrator is the same maybe he has been in prison and recently released. Mills did a search of NYPD databases of any white male aged 30 to 50 having served a 5-to-10 year sentence for rape and or robbery released in the six months prior to the first rape.

First returns were 1,826, she changed the search to only include rapes – 412. Robberies returned 615, rapes and robberies 162. These were only NYPD cases, if the perp had been caught and released, then he could be from out of the city or even out of state. Tracking him down this way would be a last resort.'

With the time line updated with dates, names, photographs and locations there wasn't much more they could do. None of the evidence rooms were open as it was New Year's Day and with tomorrow being a Sunday, they would remain closed until Monday January 3.

Garcia: 'I am going to get ahold of Lieutenant Johnston and bring him up to date. I will get him to put in a request to the 94th as a priority. We are not going to be hassled by the press, as no connections have yet been made to the Zodiac rapist. We need to keep this in-house otherwise we will have City Hall all over us.

Let's pack up here for the day, go home and recharge our batteries. Take tomorrow off and be back on Monday morning.'

Getting no argument from his fellow detectives, the team covered up the white board to keep it away from prying eyes, switched off the lights and locked the room. Each went their separate ways.

Chapter 9
January 2, 2022

Sunday, January 2, 2022 was a surprisingly mild day for a New York winter. The previous day there had been a light snow shower which didn't stick. By mid-morning the temperature was a cool 55°C and the sun was shining.

Shirley Richardson a 39-year old white woman was on her way home after attending the morning service at the non-denominational Harvest Christian Fellowship Church. She was walking down West 37th Street heading home to Baxter Apartments on the corner of Dyer and West 34th Streets. At most it was a twenty-minute walk.

Having sat through an inspiring sermon from the Church Pastor, she was full of the joys of life. On Friday night she had reluctantly agreed to join some of her work colleagues and watch the Ball drop in Times Square. During the evening the group had visited several bars in the area, consuming a fair amount of liquor. It was the first time she had been out socially in just over two years, the COVID19 pandemic had seen to that.

Shirley had had a tough adulthood. She married her high-school sweetheart Bobby directly after graduation. They were seen as the perfect couple, he was a football star and she was a pretty and intelligent student. In hindsight they married too young.

The plan was that Bobby would attend Ohio State University on a full football scholarship and she would work and study part-time to get her Bachelor of Science degree. Initially things went well. Although not starting in his freshman year, he was encouraged by the head coach that his time would come. Shirley was working at Firestone in the accounts department and had made great strides with her part-time studies.

The trouble started in Bobby's second year. At the preseason training camp, he was late tackled and suffered a season-ending knee injury. Shirley spent all her waking hours working, studying and consoling her husband. The strain started to tell. Bobby was depressed and started to miss his rehabilitation sessions; his knee was not mending at the required rate for him to resume playing

By the end of the football season in December 2004, the beatings started. Bobby's scholarship was canceled as it was unlikely that he would ever play football again. Depressed, he began drinking heavily and taking out his frustrations on his wife. After each beating, he would break down in tears and beg forgiveness.

March 16, 2005, Shirley's twenty third birthday, was the final straw when she ended up in hospital. Interviewed by the police as to the source of her injuries, she was forced to admit that it was her husband. Charges were laid against Bobby but Shirley refused to testify against him. She was discharged from hospital on March 18. She returned to their Akron apartment, packed her clothing and left. She purchased a one-way ticket to New York on a Greyhound bus and that was the last she saw of him.

The marriage was ended by mutual consent and Shirley settled down to life in New York. She completed her Bachelor of Science degree in June of 2008. She joined a software company – Titan Inc. where she worked as a computer analyst/programmer.

Over the next several years she dated sporadically, had a few one night stands but nothing seemed to stick. It was not for lack of opportunities, she remained very attractive and in great shape but she always seemed reluctant to get involved.

During the New Year's Eve festivities, she was approached by a very handsome man who asked if he could buy her a drink. Taken aback she said yes. It wasn't the most well-lit of bars but she could see him clearly. Her first impression was he seemed a bit younger than her, maybe early thirties or late twenties, tall towering over her 5'8" frame. She put him well over 6'.

He returned with their drinks and introduced himself as Maurice Turner and said he worked on Wall Street. The bar noise was quite loud, making conversation difficult. They traded rounds until it was time for the Official Ball Drop in Times Square. Slightly tipsy, Shirley looked up to Maurice who leaned down and kissed her gently on the lips.

When they eventually ended the kiss Shirley looked up at him and made an instant decision. She took him by the hand and led him out of the bar. They picked up their checked coats and without a word left the building. It was only a three block walk to Shirley's apartment.

Seven minutes later they were in the elevator heading for the 6th floor of her building.

Having barely spoken since leaving the bar they entered her apartment and Shirley led him to her bedroom. The first coupling was frenzied, both sated within a few minutes. Half an hour later round two was slower and gentler. Neither slept that night.

Maurice was the first to make a move. He got out of bed to use the bathroom. When he returned, he began picking up his discarded clothes, Shirley watched him hoping he would say something, he did.

'Shirley, I had an amazing night, you are absolutely stunning. I am afraid I have to leave. I have a big meeting tomorrow and I need to do a lot of planning before then. I would really like to see you again, if that is okay with you.'

'Yes please, I had a wonderful time. I don't normally bring strange men home with me but it just seemed so right.'

'Give me your cellphone, I will put my number in it, then I will send myself a message so I have your number.' Shirley handed him her phone.

Maurice entered his details in Shirley's cellphone and then sent himself a message.

'I've gotta go, thank you for a wonderful evening and a fabulous night, I will call you Sunday morning, maybe we can do something together in the afternoon.'

True to his word Maurice had called her early that morning and it was with these thoughts running through her head she entered the ground floor of her apartment building. The elevator was waiting, she stepped in and pressed the number 6 button. There were four apartments on her floor, hers was the far one on the right.

The front door was double locked, she methodically unlocked the top lock and then the bottom one. She turned the door handle, opened the door and stepped into the hallway. As she was shrugging out of her jacket, a gloved hand reached around and covered her mouth.

'Do not attempt to turn around or struggle. I have a very sharp knife and will not hesitate to use it. Walk forward slowly and do not talk or look at me.'

She was guided towards her bedroom and was made to stand facing the right side of her bed; she was ordered to remove all of her clothes. Terrified, she struggled, she unbuttoned her blouse and dropped it to the floor, next she unfastened her bra. Before she could drop it to the floor the man snatched it from her. She unzipped her skirt and stepped out of it, she bent forward and with some difficulty pulled down her pantyhose. Lastly, she removed her panties.

Standing totally naked with her back to him she made no attempt to move. The man bent down and retrieved her pantyhose and panties. She felt her mouth being forced open and her panties stuffed into it. She was turned around to face her attacker, given a firm push in the chest forcing her onto the bed. She closed her eyes not wanting to see her assailant and give him a reason to kill her.

She was pulled up to the top of the bed and using her pantyhose her hands were secured to the headboard. He lifted her head and by pulling her bra across her mouth and tying it behind her head ensured she was unable to spit out her panties.

The man took up a position at the foot of the bed. He unbuckled his belt, unbuttoned his pants and dropped them to the floor, he was not wearing underwear. He was already erect as he unpeeled a condom and with slow deliberation, rolled it onto his penis.

He climbed on the bed, knelt down and forced Shirley's legs apart, she gasped and involuntary opened her eyes. He was wearing a black balaclava with just his blue eyes showing, he was white. Judging by his height kneeling she judged him to be over six feet tall. His penis was huge, she had never experienced anything of that size before, she braced herself.

With no preamble the man leaned over her and thrust his penis into her vagina and she gasped in pain. He sensed her pain and this seemed to drive him on as he thrust in and out violently. Within thirty seconds he stiffened, ejaculated and with a groan fell forward almost crushing her. He lay there for less than a minute, then pushed himself off her and rolled off the bed.

Without a word he peeled off the condom, walked into the bathroom and flushed it down the toilet. He returned to the bedroom pulled on his trousers, buckled his belt and silently turned away from the bed. He walked over to the dresser and picked up a bag of items he had stolen and left the room. Shirley, unable to free herself or shout for help, struggled frantically.

Thirty minutes later the desk sergeant at the 35th precinct answered the telephone, '35th Precinct, Sergeant Blake, what can I do for you?'

'I am calling to report a disturbance in the Baxter Apartments building on the corner of Dyer and West 34th Street. It sounds like it's coming from the 6th floor, apartment #63.'

'Who is this?'

'Just a concerned citizen. I don't want to get involved, just send somebody to check on it.' the caller hung up.

Blake, thinking it might be a crank caller, debated whether to send a patrol car to the address, and finally erring on the side of caution he called it in.

Officers Custer and Kendall answered the call as they were only one block away. They parked their cruiser in the no parking zone directly in front of the building and made their way up to the 6th floor, found apartment #63 and knocked on the door. Receiving no response, they identified themselves as police officers, still no reaction.

They tried the door and found it unlocked. Opening it slowly, first Kendall and then Custer entered the apartment with their weapons drawn.

Kendall called out, 'NYPD – is there anyone here?'

No reply. The two policemen moved cautiously down the hallway. Glancing first into the living room and then the kitchen they found no one. Custer was first to reach the bedroom. He peered in and saw a naked women tied to the bed; she had something stuffed in her mouth which was preventing her from talking. Without thinking, he rushed into the room and removed her gag.

'I've been raped and robbed, please help me,' the woman sobbed.

'Okay lady, I am going to free you, just keep calm.' said Custer.

His police training kicked in. Before touching anything further he donned a pair of surgical gloves and instructed Kendall to do the same. Once gloved up, he moved to the head of the bed and untied her hands. She immediately sat up and tried to cover her nakedness.

'911, this is Officer Kendall of 35th, we need an ambulance and paramedics at 63 Baxter Apartments, corner Dyer and West 34th. We have a female, she has been raped and appears in reasonable condition. Please ensure female officer accompanies the bus.'

He then radioed 35th duty desk. 'Sarge, Kendall here, we have a rape victim, she looks like she is in good condition. I have called for a bus; can you get the forensics team out here to dust the place.'

Receiving confirmation from the Sergeant he ended the call. By this time, Shirley Richardson had covered herself with a robe and was sitting quietly on the edge of her bed, shaking uncontrollably.

'Ma'am, my name is Officer Kendall, I realize that this as a traumatic situation for you but I need to ask you some questions, can you tell us what happened, what is your name?'

'My name is Shirley Richardson and this is my apartment. I had just returned from church, when I unlocked my front door, both locks were still in place. I stepped into the hall and started to take off my coat and this man grabbed me from behind. He covered my mouth and put a knife to my throat. He told me not to talk or turn around.' Her voice hitched as she recounted her ordeal.

Kendall: 'Can you describe him?'

'He was wearing a black balaclava with only his eyes showing, they were blue. He was very tall I am sure over six foot and strongly built. He was also wearing long sleeves and black gloves; he was fully covered. He was white.'

Kendall: 'How can you say he was white if he was fully covered.'

'He had a white penis, very large.'

Kendall: 'What happened next?'

'He walked me to my bedroom, made me take off all my clothes. He stuffed my panties into my mouth, secured by my bra and then tied me to the bed. He then put on a condom and forced himself on me. It was very painful'

Kendall: 'Did he say anything?'

'Not a word other than the warning at the front door.'

Kendall: 'Anything else you can tell me?'

'I think he got turned on by my fear. He put on a condom; he had a very large penis. From the time he forced himself into me and him coming it couldn't have been more than one minute. He got off me, took off his condom and flushed it down the toilet, pulled up his trousers and left. He had cleaned out my jewelry boxes and maybe something else in the apartment, I will have to check.'

Kendall: 'I have called for medical assistance; they will probably take to Mount Sinai Hospital for a check-up and to get a rape kit done. Don't use the bathroom or attempt to wash yourself. Hopefully he left some of his DNA on you. Anything else you want to add before the forensics people and the detectives arrive?'

'No. Thank you, you have been very kind. I am expecting a friend later this afternoon, is it okay if I call him and tell him what happened?'

Kendall: 'No, that is not a good idea. If he arrives after you have left, I will talk to him. What is his name?'

'Maurice Turner.'

Kendall: 'Thank you, just relax and take it easy the paramedics will be here shortly, they will take care of you.'

The paramedics arrived first. They proceeded to give Shirley a cursory examination before relocating her to the hospital. The female paramedic asked for privacy so as she could check for any bleeding of the vagina. She gently parted Shirley's legs and opened the entrance to her vagina. Spotting some foreign object, she reached in with tweezers and pulled out what looked like a small business card.

'Jesus, there's a zodiac card here, it's Gemini.'

Custer was first to react, 'Here, put it in this evidence bag. Kendall, call the Sarge and let him know the Zodiac Rapist has struck again.'

While Kendall was on the phone with Sergeant Barry Hughes, the forensic team arrived and got down to business. The first thing they did was finger print Shirley Richardson after which they released her to the paramedics who immediately left with her for the hospital.

Next they began the onerous task of checking for fresh fingerprints, blood and semen stains. They scanned the bed with a black light and it lit up like a pinball machine. Semen stains were found in the middle and left hand side of the bed.

'Looks like we hit the jackpot here, take samples and bag them,' ordered Hughes. 'This could be what we need to nail the bastard.'.

Two distinct sets of fingerprints were found. Barry Hughes felt there was good possibility that they finally had something on the Zodiac Rapist. His euphoria was briefly interrupted as detectives Garcia and O'Connell arrived on the scene.

The two police officers brought the detectives up to speed on the situation and their conversations with Shirley Richardson.

'Fuck it! We even talked about his cycle and thought he would strike again on this date. How did we lose sight of that?' fumed Garcia.

'Boss, there was nothing we could have done to prevent this. At least with the forensics we may have our first lead in catching this bastard,' replied O'Connell.

'You are probably right. Barry, can you let us have your findings asap? We are going to head to the hospital and talk to the lady. Happy New Year, what a way to start it. Come on O'Connell, let's go.' Garcia nodded to the door and O'Connell followed him out.

They found Shirley in one of the curtained off cubicles in the Emergency Room at Mount Sinai. She had been examined by a doctor and was just waiting for a police release. Garcia conferred with the ER doctor who confirmed that no semen had been found and other than some bruising consistent with a rape, there was no damage to the vagina. Two swabs were taken, one of which was handed over to Garcia.

'Ms. Richardson, I am Detective Garcia and this is Detective O'Connell. I would just like to ask you a few questions, if you are up for it.'

'Yes Sir, I am, please go ahead.' She was visibly shaken but was trying to be brave.

Garcia went through virtually the same line of questioning that Kendall and Custer had asked, the responses were noted by O'Connell.

'Thank you for your cooperation, Ms. Richardson. With your help I am sure we will apprehend this monster and put him out of business very soon. As you may be aware, there have been at least four other instances that we know of which are almost exactly the same as yours. The four victims involved have agreed to a joint interview with us as we hope it will lead to more clues. Something one says will hopefully trigger a memory or clue for the rest of the group.

We have scheduled this for January 4 at 6.30 pm down at the 35th Precinct. If you are up to it, we hope you would agree to join them. The more we know, the better chance of catching this bastard,' Garcia spoke gently. She had been through a traumatic event, and he knew it was a huge ask of her.

'I will be there. I want this bastard caught!' Shirley broke down and cried.

'We promise you, Shirley, we will do everything in our power to make sure that happens. This case is top priority,' Garcia promised. He only hoped that he could make good on that promise.

Chapter 10
Side by Side

Bright and early on Monday morning the team assembled in the situation room at the 35th. As usual, Shaw brought the coffee and donuts, though strangely arriving well after Mills. Garcia brought the meeting to order.

'By now, Shaw, you and Mills are aware of the latest Zodiac rape. Yes, the one we predicted and back on the Gemini track. O'Connell has the details up on the time line. If it is true to his MO, then the Marx murders don't make sense. I got the Lieutenant contacting the 94th Precinct for the files on O'Connell's parents' murders; he should have an answer shortly. Any thoughts?' Garcia had filled his usual mug to the brim with coffee and took a huge swig.

O'Connell: 'Boss, maybe the killer has been following the Zodiac rapes and decided to have a try himself or themselves. If it is the same perp, then why the deviation? Why would he de-escalate back to rape after escalating up to murder?'

Mills: 'I agree with O'Connell. Maybe we need a profiler to help us on this. You know as soon as the Richardson rape hits the press, the shit is going to hit the fan. If someone else works out the lunar cycle, they would have expected us to have done the same. What does the Lieutenant have to say?'

Garcia: 'I have no idea. I think he is worried about his pension and too scared to make any announcements.'

The conversation was interrupted by Garcia's phone ringing, he answered, grunted his thanks and turned to O'Connell.

'That was the desk sergeant from the 94th; the evidence box from your folks' murder is available. I suggest you get yourself over there and pick it up. His name is Dickerson.' O'Connell nodded and grabbed his keys, heading out.

Although the 94th was only 7 miles away, a round trip was going to take O'Connell at least an hour, although at this time of the morning maybe a whole lot longer. NYC traffic was a bitch every day of the week.

He arrived at the precinct and introduced himself to the desk sergeant. 'Hey sarge, I'm O'Connell from the 35th and have come for the evidence box for the O'Connell murders of December 2011.'

'Jesus, are you related to these folks?' Dickerson asked, noticing the surnames.

'Yes, my parents,' O'Connell answered, trying to keep it clinical.

'Sorry for your loss. It seems there has been a recent request for this evidence; you are the second person to request it,' Dickerson noted.

'A second request when?'

'Yes. When the request came in from your Lieutenant, I personally went to collect the box. Sammy, our evidence custodian mentioned that it had been checked out on March 8 and returned on March 19,' Dickerson read off his notes to get the dates right.

'That's strange. I was informed that this was considered a cold case and if it was ever reopened, they would contact me as a courtesy. Do you think I could have a word with Sammy?'

'Sure, he is down in the basement, I'll let him know you are coming. Stairs are that way; it's the only thing down there so you can't miss it,' Dickerson nodded in the direction of the stairs.

O'Connell thanked Dickerson and made his way down the stairs to the basement. The evidence room at the 94th was typical, a caged off area manned by a uniformed man of indeterminable age. Almost like the person lived down below and never saw the light of day.

'Dickerson said you were on your way, what can I do for you, young man?'

'I was told that this evidence was logged out for two weeks back in March. Can you supply the details on who logged this out?'

'Right here. it is in the log, which you might as well countersign with Sarge Dickerson while you are here.' Sammy pointed to the spot on the form, handing O'Connell the pen. 'As you can see, it was logged out to Detective Ronald MacDonald from the 69th on March 8 at 8.55 am and returned on March 19 at 5.30 pm by Sarge Dickerson himself. They must have dropped it at the front desk.'

'Really… Ronald MacDonald, did you check his credentials?'

Not seeing the obvious connection, Sammy replied, 'Sure did, as we do with everyone. I have his shield number – 84431 and I verified his ID.'

'Did you check with the 69th?'

'Don't have to, once his ID and badge have been presented to my satisfaction, I release the evidence.'

'Sammy, you ever had a Big Mac?' O'Connell felt his irritation rising.

'What the hell is a Big Mac?' *Did this guy ever go above ground? How could anyone living in NYC not know what a Big Mac was?*

'Just joking around, thanks for your help.'

'Jesus. Detective Ronald MacDonald. I'll check with the 69th but if there is a detective with that name, I'll eat my hat,' thought O'Connell.

The trip back to the 35th took a lot longer than the outward journey, putting O'Connell back at the precinct just after 11.30 am. He carried the evidence box up the three floors to the situation room. First thing he noticed was a second woman present.

'O'Connell, welcome back, first things first. Let me introduce Detective June Hayes; she is on assignment with us from the 94th. Pity we didn't know ahead of time; it would have saved you a trip. Hayes, this is Detective Ethan O'Connell, he has a close interest in this case as you know.' O'Connell dumped the evidence box on the closest desk.

'I remember you from the crime scene at my folks murder. You were one of the first officers to arrive. If I am not mistaken, you weren't a detective at the time. Nice to see you again.'

'Yep, I was just a regular beat cop, Detective Mickie Cairns had me assigned to the case for as long as I was needed. The bug bit and I tried for the Detective's Exam, got lucky and passed. Three years ago I made detective, it only took seven years.'

Garcia: 'We are glad to have her help. Your parents' case is still technically owned by the 94th but if we find a connection to our case, we will have it officially transferred to us. Hayes being here will help but it is also so that the 94th can keep tabs on what is going on. She will keep them in the loop.

I see you have the evidence box. I suggest you and Hayes work together and do a side by side. The rest of us will continue with the Richardson rape and also try to find about any recently released rapists/robbers.' Garcia turned away from them, his hand still welded to his coffee mug.

O'Connell checked out Hayes. He remembered her from the night of the murders; she looked quite different. Most noticeably she was not dressed in police blues but in jeans, blouse and a short jacket, typical female detective attire. Working from her statement that it took her seven years to make detective, he calculated he had around two years seniority on her, so he would take the lead.

'What do I call you? June or Hayes?'

'Hayes is good.'

'Okay, Hayes, here's what I suggest. I unpack the evidence from the 94th and we both line it up as close as possible to our timeline on the Marx murders.'

Hayes nodded and the task began. First up were the pictures of the victims, Colin Marx, 57 Caucasian, pinned to the timeline under Dennis O'Connell, 57 Caucasian. Next up Christine Marx, 55 Caucasian pinned under Mary O'Connell, 54 Caucasian.

Hayes: 'Similar ages, not too dissimilar looking. Do you think the Marxs' were scouted and targeted?'

O'Connell: 'Sure looks like they were specifically selected; way too close in looks and age to be a coincidence. The dates are exactly ten years apart to the day. My folks were murdered sometime after 7.00 pm, the Marxs' were around mid-afternoon. Let's get the crime scene photos up,' O'Connell lingered a moment, looking at his parents. He'd never get used to seeing them that way. Photos on a white-board. Dead. Another unsolved murder.

First up was the shot taken side on of Dennis O'Connell kneeling at the foot of the bed, hog tied. Absolutely identical to that of Colin Marx, same color striped necktie looped around his wrists through a leather belt securing his ankles. Both of the men's heads fallen forward, chin on their breast bone.

Hayes: 'Exactly the same right down to the way they have been tied. This has to be the same killer or killers. I remember the scene so clearly. None of these details were released to the press.'

O'Connell: 'Shit, I forgot to tell you all. The evidence custodian at the 94th told me that a detective from the 69th signed out this box back on March 8 this year. Hayes, you know the guy, Sammy, I didn't get his last name?'

Hayes: 'Sure do, he is a harmless old feller, lives in a world of his own but knows exactly where everything is located. Did you get the detective's name?'

O'Connell: 'Yes, but I need to check it out as I think it's bogus. Really, Detective Ronald MacDonald but he said he checked his credentials. I'm going to call the 69th now before we go any further. Put up the next photo in the meantime.'

O'Connell looked up the number for the 69th precinct and dialed it, it was answered on the first ring.

'69th Precinct, Sergeant De Rosin speaking what can I do for you?'

'I'd like to speak to Detective Ronald MacDonald please, this is Detective Ethan O'Connell from the 35th.'

'Are you fucking with me? You know I can trace this call it's a felony to make hoax calls or impersonate a police officer.'

'Not a hoax call just checking up. A detective from your precinct checked out an evidence box from the 94th and his credentials were supposedly checked. The ID showed name as Ronald MacDonald with shield number 84431. I figured it was bogus but I had to check. So, no one of that name at your precinct?'

'Damn sure. Any idea what is going on?'

'Working on it. Thanks for your help.'

O'Connell hung up the phone and walked over to where Garcia was sitting.

'Boss, I have just confirmed that a bogus detective checked out the evidence box way back on March 8 and brought it back on March 19. There has to be a connection to the Marx murders. That would explain how the killer was able to match the details so closely'

'I don't suppose they have CCTV video in their evidence room. You carry on with the side by side and I will follow up.'

O'Connell rejoined Hayes, who now had the side by side of the two female victims. You could overlay one photo over the other, they were identical. Both tied with a blue necktie on the left wrist and a red one on the right. Both missing their left nipple. Both women had their eyes gouged out. One by one the photos were laid out; all exact copies of each other.

Hayes: 'Looks like this is an exact replica right down to the positions, the way the necks were sliced. This could only have been done by the same person or persons.'

O'Connell; 'It's unreal. Even the exact number of blood-stained footprints leading to the bathroom. Wait a minute, look at the size of the prints. The Marx murderer's feet must be at least three sizes bigger. What do you think?'

Hayes: 'I think you are right. We should get forensics to do an estimate on the sizes. Last piece of the puzzle is the single pubic hair.

The item was logged on the check sheet but seems to be missing. We do have the DNA record but no hair in the box, what do you make of that.'

O'Connell: 'This is just a wild guess but I think the perp took the pubic hair when he checked out the evidence and then planted it after killing the Marxs'. We need to compare the DNA records of both, put them side by side.'

Hayes laid the two sheets next to each other and the two detectives did a visual check.

O'Connell: 'They are identical but I am pretty sure they have been taken from the same pubic hair. I reckon this is a copy-cat killing, not done by the same person. Look at the cut marks on each neck. My folks had very straight clean cuts, obviously from the very sharp Japanese Tanto sword. The Marxs' cuts are little more jagged, not as clean cut, so probably a much shorter knife.' He pointed to the marks on the two photos and Hayes leaned in to get a closer look.

Hayes: 'None of this was released to the press. This perp must have planned the whole thing based on what he saw in the evidence box. The question is why. What possible reason could he have to duplicate a ten-year old murder?'

O'Connell: 'Why was this done on this specific day, the same day I joined the 35th? Supposedly nobody knew I was being transferred other than me and Hollywood Thomas. This perp is sending a message and I believe it is aimed at me. He has been planning this since at least March but to have set it up to happen on the anniversary on my folks' death, it has to be an inside job.'

Hayes: 'Sure looks like it but for what purpose? You know anyone that has a big grudge against you? Maybe the perp was at the scene of your folks' murder. We need to check everyone who was canvassed that day.'

Their discussion was interrupted by Garcia's phone, he picked it up and listened carefully. He hung up the phone and turned to his team with a big grin on his face.

'We've got the bastard. The fingerprints and semen stains on the bed at the Richardson rape have been matched. The zodiac rapist is Maurice Turner; he has a pretty long rap sheet. Strangely no rape collars but is a con artist who specializes in ripping off single women. He befriends them, gets all cozy and they fall for him. Next thing you know he disappears with any valuables and cleans out their bank accounts. He was also suspect in a number of burglaries, all targeting single women.

He was serving an eight-year stretch and got released on probation in November 2020. He seems to have been quiet since then, never missed a scheduled meeting with his probation officer.

The first rape, Sandra Williamson, was the only one where the perp was busy robbing the place and was interrupted. She ended up getting raped, so maybe he got a taste for it.

I have his current address. Shaw, you and Mills take a couple of uniforms with you and go pick him up. Gotcha, you bastard!'

Chapter 11
January 4 2022

Garcia, elated with the news of the upcoming apprehension of the Zodiac Rapist, hurried down to tell his boss the good news face to face. Lieutenant Grover Johnston had been sweating bullets since December 31, three full days of uncertainty. A serial rapist was one thing, but when that turned into murder of such horrendous brutality, that was a whole new ball game. A pessimist by nature, he could see a huge ball of shit rolling down the hill, ultimately landing on his head.

Garcia knocked on Johnston's door and entered with a big grin on his face, 'Boss, I am here to make your day.'

'Make my day! Put me two years in the future on the day after I have retired, that will make my day.'

'We got him, the Zodiac Rapist, stone cold and we like him for the killings as well. Shaw, Mills and couple of uniforms are on their way to pick him up.'

You could see the strain lift off Johnston's shoulders, 'You better not be shitting me, Garcia. There is a God, praise Jesus. I have to get the good news to the Captain and I'm sure he will bump it to the Chief and him to the Mayor. There will be a press conference; I will need to get into my Blues.' He was jabbering a mile a minute. It wasn't like Johnston to get ahead of himself and Garcia needed to reign him in.

'Hold on, Boss, let's get him booked. We have his DNA and fingerprints all over the bed at the crime scene. Also, the five rape victims are coming into the precinct at 5.30 pm. If we can get them to identify him in a lineup, it'll be a slam dunk. You can bump it up the line with one hundred percent confidence. Let's not rush it and fuck it up,' Garcia cautioned.

'Maybe you are right. Shit, I could use a drink right now. Let me know when he is in the system, I want to see this bastard that has made my life so fucking miserable. Good work by you and your team; it's going to be epic to get this one off the books. I am sure commendations all around.'

Shaw, Mills and the two uniforms headed out to an address in the 800 block of East 150th Street in The Bronx. They found the building, run down almost derelict, Shaw knocked on the door. After repeated banging, the door was eventually opened by a bleary-eyed woman of indeterminable age. Shaw waved his badge under her nose.

'I'm looking for Maurice Turner, is he in?'

The woman looked the badge over like she had seen a number of them before, no surprise to Shaw. She grunted one word – Basement and pointed to the entrance down one level from the street and closed the door.

The four cops stepped down the few steps and knocked on the basement door, it was answered immediately. A tall good-looking man who fit the description opened the door. He was well dressed and smiling.

'What can I do for you officers?'

'Maurice Turner, I am arresting you for the rape of five woman and the associated robberies. Put your hands behind your back and turn around. Mills, read him his rights.'

'Sir, you are making a big mistake, I have not raped and robbed anyone. I had in the past but I served my time, I am innocent!' Maurice protested as he was man-handled into cuffs.

'Yeah, sure you are. We have enough evidence to arrest and convict you on these charges. We are taking you to the 35th Precinct where you will be formally charged. I'm sure you know your rights; not your first rodeo, right? Okay boys, put him in the van, let's go home.'

Turner continued to proclaim his innocence throughout the drive to the 35th. Mills observed his demeanor and couldn't help but see just why women allowed this conman into their homes. He was good looking, well dressed and had the gift of the gab. She hoped the bastard got life.

Back in the situation room as O'Connell and Hayes continued to match the two timelines, it became glaringly obvious that the Marx murders were a replica of the ten-year old O'Connell murders. The small differences, the addition of the zodiac cards and the possible larger bloodstained footprints were the only notable differences.

Both agreed that it was very unlikely that Turner was the killer. They figured that adding the zodiac cards to the murder was just to muddy the waters and send the cops on a wild goose chase. Time would tell.

Shaw and Mills arrived with Turner in tow and handed him over to the booking officer. Every cop not out on duty turned up to get a look at the famous Zodiac Rapist/Killer. The general consensus was that he was not that impressive, good looking, yes, but not a stand out in the crowd good looks. Neatly dressed, a bit preppy if anything, so who knew, maybe that was why he could move around so easily without being a suspect. He'd blend into a crowd anywhere.

Mug shots were taken; height 6'1" weight 193lbs. No discernible scars, no tattoos. He was booked and charged with the rape of five women, along with the murders of Colin and Christine Marx. He was led away to holding cell #2 and locked up as the sole occupant. The cell door had hardly clicked shut when Lieutenant Johnston, Mike Garcia and Ethan O'Connell arrived.

'Maurice Turner, we have got you at last, you sick bastard. I am going to throw the book at you, when we are finished with you I will make sure you never see the light of day,   ' ranted Johnston.

'Sir, I don't know what you are accusing me of, I haven't raped or killed anyone. I'll admit in my past life that I did rape one woman and stole from a few, but I was caught, charged and served my time.'

'I know about your past. I can read a Rap sheet. You are a piece of shit, preying on unsuspecting, vulnerable single women. You got out in November 2020 and were at it again in less than two months. Did you think you were taunting us with the zodiac cards – *look at me I am invincible you dumb cops won't catch me*". Well we have. Mike get his statement.'

'I want a call to my lawyer, it's my right.'

'You will get a call when I say you get a call.'

'O'Connell, get Shaw down here. I want him in the interview room with me.'

'Boss, I want to be in on the interview with you. I have vested interest in this piece of shit.'

'Exactly why you shouldn't be in on it, too close. Go get Shaw. You, Mills and Hayes can use the viewing room but stay out of the interview room. I can't have you going nuts and attacking the prisoner'

Turner was securely shackled to the single desk in Interview Room 2. Facing the desk were two chairs and a one-way mirror. Garcia let him stew for thirty minutes before he and Shaw entered the room. Both cops sat down and locked eyes with the prisoner, who was surprisingly calm with a grin on his face.

'Is this the old good cop/ bad cop routine? How stereotypical.'

Garcia: 'Nope. This is the bad cop/ bad cop routine. You have been arrested for the rape and robbery of five women. An additional charge for the murder of Colin and Christine Marx will be added. A further charge for the murder of Dennis and Mary O'Connell is also being considered. Do you have anything to say?'

'I am not saying anything until I call my lawyer.'

Garcia: 'Give me his name and telephone number and I will call him for you.'

After hesitating for a few seconds, Turner replied, 'I don't have his number with me.'

Garcia: 'With your rap sheet I am surprised his number isn't burnt into your brain. You don't have a lawyer, do you?'

'I am entitled to one so get me one.'

Garcia: 'Sure, we will get you one when the time is right. This interview will be recorded. I am going to ask you some questions. Shaw, you got anything to say before we start?'

Shaw: 'Sure Boss, why don't we not record the interview then we will have only his word against ours about what goes down in here.'

Garcia: 'You know you are right. He does look like he would get aggressive, become uncooperative and any injuries he sustains we could put down to that. Good idea.'

Turner was not so cocky any more 'No! I will cooperate one hundred percent, you must record the interview.'

Garcia hit the record button and stated for the record, *The time is 3.23 pm on January 4,2022; present are detectives Michael Garcia and David Shaw who are conducting the interview of Maurice Turner. Turner has been charged with the rape of five women and the associated robberies.'*

Garcia: 'Maurice Turner, Caucasian male, age 37, resident of The Bronx, New York, do you understand these charges?'

'I hear them but I do not understand why you are accusing me, I did not commit these crimes. I am innocent.'

Shaw: 'Boss, switch off the recorder he is not going to cooperate.'

'No, no, I am going to cooperate I just don't understand what is going on. Please continue with the recording.'

Garcia: 'On January 13, 2021 you broke into the residence of one Sandra Williamson, a 34 year old white female. She arrived home unexpectedly and caught you in the act. You overpowered her and proceeded to sexually assault her. Can you account for your movements on the day in question?'

Turner: 'It is almost a year ago! I can't even account for my movements last week. I did not break into anyone's home. I am a conman not a burglar, I did not rape that woman.'

Garcia: 'Moving on. After you raped her, you inserted a zodiac card into her vagina, you chose Sagittarius. What was the purpose of this?'

Turner: 'Jesus! You think I am the Zodiac Rapist? You have got the wrong man.' The blood drained from his face as he realized the implication of the charges.

Garcia: 'You collected the valuables you had stolen and left the unfortunate woman gagged and tied to the bed's headboard. Thirty minutes later, you called 911 to report a disturbance and gave them the address of your victim. Did you think this was clever? Rubbing it our faces?'

Turner: 'I did not do this.' Maurice looked around frantically, as if looking for someone to back him up.

Garcia: 'On April 11, 2021 you entered the property of Lola Estes, a 28-year old Hispanic woman. You overpowered her as she entered her apartment, stripped her naked, tied her to her bed and proceeded to rape her. This time after you raped her, you inserted a Gemini card in her vagina, what is the significance of this?'

Turner was now visibly sweating: 'This was not me. I am not a rapist!'

Garcia: 'Can you verify your whereabouts for this day?'

Turner: 'I don't know where I was on that day.'

Shaw: 'Boss, he is fucking us around, I say stop the tape and erase it and let me beat the truth out of him. There are no witnesses, the whole of New York wants this Zodiac Rapist off the streets, no one is gonna call "police brutality".

Garcia: 'I am starting to think along the same lines but we need him alive to answer for the O'Connell and Marx murders as well. Look, I am going to take a break. I need the bathroom. Turner, Detective Shaw will take care of you while I am away.'

Turner shouted, 'No! Don't leave me alone with him. I am innocent I want a lawyer now!'

Garcia winked to Shaw, he switched off the recorder stood up and made ready to leave. He was interrupted by a knock on the door.

Mills leaned in to whisper to Garcia, out of earshot of the accused: 'Boss, the victims have all arrived. I am putting them in the conference room.'

Garcia: 'Thanks, get them some refreshments and I will be there in a minute. Dave, take this piece of shit back to his cell; we will deal with him later,' leaning in closer to Shaw, 'Make sure none of the victims see him as I am sure that five angry women will do far more damage to him than you ever could. Also, don't let O'Connell anywhere near him.' Shaw nodded.

Garcia picked up the Turner files and left the room. He was followed by Shaw who dragged Turner to his feet and roughly shoved him towards the door where he handed him over to a uniformed officer with the instructions to return him to the holding cell. O'Connell, Hayes and Mills had observed the entire process from behind a one-way mirror.

Garcia had reasoned that due to the sensitivity of the upcoming interview, that it should be conducted by Mills and Hayes. He would attend if all the victims agreed, O'Connell and Shaw would observe from the adjoining room.

Garcia: 'Dave, see if you can round up seven or eight guys roughly the same size as Turner for a lineup. Get hold of black balaclava's, all the same if you can. We can do a line up after we speak to the vics. We have his fingerprints and DNA but a positive ID would be a bonus.'

Shaw nodded and left to complete his task, Garcia was on his way to the interview room when he was accosted by Lieutenant Johnston.

'You got an update for me, Mike? I'm itching to get the good news out to the Captain. We need to tell the City it's now safe because we've got the Zodiac Rapist.'

'Hold your horses, Boss, let us do the interviews with the vics, get a line up done then go for it. I am going there now I will let you know the instant we have a lock.'

'Okay, but don't drag it out, we can still make the evening news. You know how much the Mayor likes the limelight.'

Chapter 12
The Interviews

Garcia walked up one flight of stairs and entered the observation room adjoining the conference room. There he found O'Connell and Shaw. Looking through the one-way mirror he saw Mills and Hayes chatting casually to the five rape victims.

'Good afternoon, ladies, my name is Detective Mike Garcia, I am leading the investigation into the case of the so called "Zodiac Rapist." I would like to thank you all for agreeing to come in and help us with our investigation.

I realize it has been a traumatic experience for you all and we don't want you to suffer through reliving the events any more than is absolutely necessary. I also hope you will speak freely about what you can remember. Maybe as a group, a memory gets triggered and provides us with another key piece of information.

My two detectives here, Linda Mills and June Hayes, will conduct the interviews. If it is acceptable to you all, I would like to sit in on the discussions but fully understand if it is better for you that I don't.'

The five women looked at each other, mostly shrugging, but no one offered an opinion until Sandra Williamson spoke up.

'I can't talk for all of us but I would prefer if you didn't sit in. Some of the things that happened to me are very embarrassing, I would feel more comfortable expressing myself if it was just us girls. I apologize, but that's how I feel.'

There was a unanimous nodding of heads and a muted muttering of agreement.

'No apologies necessary. I fully understand. I will leave Linda and June to guide you through the interview. Again, I greatly appreciate your agreeing to do this, you are all very brave. I will speak to you all again when you are finished.'

Garcia left the room and joined Shaw and O'Connell in adjacent observation room. The three men watched Mills take charge.

Mills: 'I think the best way we can go about this is start at the beginning with Sandra. Your statement said you arrived home and found the man in your bedroom. What can you remember about him and what he said, if anything?'

'He was very tall; I think at least 6-foot. He had on a black balaclava or ski mask and wore black gloves. The only thing showing were his eyes, I am pretty sure they were blue. He said very little and I would say he had a bit of a Bronx accent.

He was white, I could tell as soon as I saw his penis. He was not fully erect at first but as he saw my fear he seemed to get very turned on. His penis was huge. I have never seen a bigger one in real life. I am pretty sure he was uncircumcised. Once he had on the condom and was inside of me, he became quite rough. He had an orgasm, I did not. He finished, removed the condom and flushed it down the toilet.

Without a single word he zipped up his pants, collected what he had stolen and left,' Sandra recounted her ordeal in a steady voice, her fingers twisting and untwisting a thread on her dress the only visible evidence of the strain of reliving the event.

Mills: 'Thank you, Sandra. I know this is very difficult to relive but we appreciate it. What about you, Lola?'

Lola clutched a bottle of water as she started her account: 'Much the same as Sandra, except he was waiting for me as soon as I entered my apartment. He grabbed me from behind, told me he would kill me if I didn't obey him. I think Sandra was right; he did have a bit of a Bronx accent.

I don't remember the color of his eyes but yes, I agree he was white. Apart from his eyes, the only part of his body that was uncovered was his penis, which was huge. I couldn't tell if he was circumcised or not as he had a huge erection. He put on a condom and jammed that thing into me so hard, it hurt.' Her hands trembled at the remembered violation. She squeezed her eyes shut and continued.

'He didn't last long before he came. I don't know, maybe two minutes tops? He grunted, rolled off and got rid of the condom. Based on the color of the hairs around his junk, I would say he had dark brown hair. As he walked away, I could see he was very tall.'

Mills: 'Thanks Lola. So far, we have a tall white man with a very large, possibly uncircumcised penis. He may have blue eyes and dark brown hair. How did you remember it, Heather?'

Heather inhaled deeply to steady her nerves: 'It was the same for me as Lola. A tall man surprised me from behind. He had an enormous penis, it was fully erect when I saw it but I think he was uncircumcised. I didn't get to see the color of his eyes but he was definitely white. Jesus, I have never seen anything that large before.' She shuddered and rubbed her hands over her crossed arms.

Mills: 'Thank you, Heather. What about you, Denise, anything more you can add?'

Denise: 'I am a bit older than the rest of you girls, so I may have been around the block a few more times. He was definitely uncircumcised. But yes, a tall white male with an enormous penis. Can't be sure of the color of his eyes. A Bronx accent for sure.

I think he gets his kicks from the fear his victims show; that's why it's all over in a very short time. I refused to be cowed by him and I think it made it hard for him to ejaculate as it seemed to go on an awful long time.'

Mills: 'Okay Shirley, I know it must be still fresh in your mind; are you up to talking about it?'

Richardson: 'Oh yes. I feel violated but I will do anything to get this bastard locked up and the key thrown away. I concur with everything the rest of you have said. I do think his eyes were blue and I know his penis was huge but not sure if he was uncircumcised.

It was interesting what Denise said, I think she is right. He gets off on us showing fear. I was scared to death and it showed, it was all over in about a minute.'

Mills: 'Ladies, thank you very much you have been a great help and we applaud your bravery.

You all agree on the race, height and size of his penis. Pretty unanimous that he is uncircumcised, we are not sure of the color of his eyes but they could be blue. Well, I have some good news. We have apprehended a suspect and if you are up to it, we can put him in an identity lineup. You need not be afraid; he will not be able to see you. How do you all feel about that?'

The response from the group was unanimous "yesses" all round. Mills sighed with relief.

'It will take about ten minutes to get it all setup, so relax in here until we come and get you. Hopefully your ordeal is almost over and we can get the bastard who did this to you.' Mills stood up to leave, picking up her notes.

Mills and Hayes left the five women alone and joined Garcia and O'Connell in the observation room. Shaw had been dispatched to organize the lineup.

Garcia: 'Good job Mills. So, we have a consensus on a number of things – tall, white, huge penis and talks like he is from the The Bronx. In doubt are the color of his eyes and whether he is circumcised or not. It's a pity we can't get the line up to haul out their dicks it would make identifying a whole lot easier.

Go back into the room and wait, Shaw will call you when the lineup is set then bring the ladies downstairs. O'Connell, you and I will go and give Shaw a hand if he needs one.'

The lineup assembly took a little longer than ten minutes as it wasn't easy to find nine other men at 6 foot or more. As a last-ditch effort, Garcia convinced O'Connell to act as one of the "suspects", so he reluctantly agreed to be #9.

Ten men varying in height from 6 foot to two men at 6'3". Turner at 6'1" was at number 5. All had their faces covered by identical black balaclavas showing only their eyes. Shaw buzzed the conference room and told Mills the lineup was ready for them.

The observation room was a little more crowded than normal with the five victims and four detectives plus a neutral observer. Ten in a room where five is a crowd. Garcia addressed the victims.

'Behind this curtain there is a room with a one-way mirror. You will be able to see them but they cannot see or hear you. The door to the left of the room will open and ten men will enter and turn and face us. They will be holding a number in front of their chest – numbers 1 to 10.

I want you each to look through all ten but make no comment until all of you have had an opportunity to carefully look at each man. If you are sure that you recognize your assailant, please remember his number. When you are all as sure as you can be, they will be escorted out and hopefully you all agree on who the rapist is. Understood?'

Unanimous agreement. Garcia picked up the intercom and instructed the lineup to be allowed into the room. Numbers 10 through 1 entered, number 1 on the left and 10 on the right. They were instructed to stand still and face the wall. O'Connell and the other 6'3" were at #9 and #3 respectively with Turner at #5.

Garcia: 'Okay, I am going to turn on the lights and you will now be able to see them all. Take your time and be sure.'

For the next five minutes there was silence in the observation room. There seemed to be some doubts among the women. Finally, Denise

Todd spoke up.

'It is very difficult only seeing the height and the eyes. Do you think it possible that each of them could say a particular sentence? We all heard him speak. For example, if they could just say *"Do as I say or I will kill you."*

Garcia: 'That is a great idea.' He pressed the intercom button. 'Listen up I want you to step forward one a time and say the following in your normal voice *"Do as I say or I will kill you,"* number 1 you are first.'

One by one each man stepped forward and uttered the required phrase, Garcia and Mills were tasked with watching the women's faces. The voices of #1, #3, #5 and #7 seemed to get their attention.

Garcia: 'Okay, ladies, did that help or are there any other requests?'

Denise Todd: 'If we could see their dicks, it would make it easier.'

Garcia: 'I am with you there, but unfortunately, they have rights and even though it would give a positive ID, it would never pass in court. Do you think you can identify your assailant?'

Denise Todd: 'Can we have a few minutes on our own to discuss this before we go any further?'

Garcia: 'Sure you can. Mills, take them all back to the conference room and give them the privacy they need. Call me when they are ready.'

Back in the conference room Denise Todd took charge.

'Okay girls, what do we think? The height thing is difficult #3 and #9 were the tallest, but #1 and #5 were also pretty tall.'

Williamson: '#9 had really blue eyes and #7's eyes were bluish. I would lean towards #9.'

Richardson: 'I agree with you about #9, Sandra, but his accent was no way from The Bronx. I like #3, tall and the right voice.'

Todd: 'I am sure that he would have tried to change his accent so as not to incriminate himself. I agree about the height thing it's difficult to tell as I was lying down on the bed which made everybody look really tall.'

Estes: 'I am looking at #7, tall, blue eyes and has a real Bronx accent.'

Smith: 'I am with Lola #7 but #3 could be him.'

Richardson: 'Wait, I think I recognize the voice. I am now certain it was #5 it's just come to me.'

Todd: 'Why are you so sure all of a sudden?'

Richardson: 'It only happened a few days ago and I keep having little flashbacks. That was his voice one hundred percent.'

Unbeknownst to the group, Garcia and his team were listening in. The moment Shirley Richardson picked Turner with such conviction they knew they had their man. After 'high fives' all around he made the call to the Lieutenant informing him they had a positive ID.

Todd: 'Okay, he is tall and has the right voice. I didn't notice the color of his eyes but they weren't blue. Should we tell the cops we have an answer?'

With everyone nodding in unison, Denise Todd pressed the intercom buzzer to let the detectives know they had a winner. Mills arrived and escorted them back to the lineup room. The ten men were marched back in and turned to face the wall.

Garcia: 'Are you one hundred percent certain you have the right man?'

Getting a positive response Garcia pressed the intercom button. 'All of you except #5 and #9 please exit to your right. Thank you for your help. #9 remove your balaclava and move behind #5.'

O'Connell removed his balaclava and stepped in behind Turner. On Garcia's nod he reached forward and removed Turner's balaclava. The reaction from behind the one-way mirror was shocking.

Richardson: 'But that's Maurice Turner! He was at my apartment on Friday night, he slept over and left on Saturday morning, it can't be him.'

Garcia: 'We found his fingerprints and DNA all over your bed. That's how we knew it was him. Is he a friend of yours?'

Richardson: 'No, not really, we hooked up on New Year's Eve and went back to my place and had sex. I don't normally do that kind of thing but it just felt right.'

Garcia: 'Well, he probably picked you out and had the opportunity to case your place. He knew of your movements he came back on Sunday and robbed and raped you.'

Richardson: 'No, it wasn't him.'

Garcia: 'How can you be so sure?'

Richardson: 'His penis wasn't that big and he is circumcised. Whoever raped me, it wasn't him. This is so embarrassing. He never wore a condom so his DNA would be all over my bed, as would his fingerprints. I am sorry, I have screwed this up.'

Garcia: 'No, you haven't. All of the others in the lineup were cops.

We had Turner figured as the rapist. Ladies, I apologize we really thought we had him. You are free to leave and thanks again for your help. We will do everything we can to make sure we get the guy who did this.

Ms. Richardson, can you stay back please? I would like to pass some information to you about Maurice Turner.'

Garcia turned back to the viewing window and pressed the intercom button. 'O'Connell, take the piece of garbage back to his cell. We will book him on parole violation.'

After consoling Shirley, the other four women left the precinct vowing to keep in touch. Shirley followed Garcia up to his third-floor office. He closed the door and indicated for her to take a seat. He walked around his desk and sat down facing her.

'Am I in trouble Detective? I am so sorry.'

'No Shirley, you are not in trouble; you did a fine job. The reason I want to speak to you is to give you a warning about Maurice Turner. He has many aliases; it's what he does. He picks out who he considers as vulnerable single women. He finds them usually in a crowded environment where the first contact could be accidental.'

'Yes, now that you mention it. He bumped into me at a New Year's gathering in a crowded bar. He apologized and offered to buy me a drink.'

'Yes, that's one of his methods. He hopes to get your confidence, he is charming and knows all the right things to say and do. Once into your life, usually through your bed, he will spin you a story of working in big finance. He will offer you great investment opportunities but will ultimately clean out your life savings.

He has fleeced dozens of women this way, although I am sure not everyone has come forward to report him but he made one fatal mistake. He ended up raping one of his victims. When that happened, a number of other victims came forward to report that he had conned them. He was only charged with the single rape added to fifteen charges of fraud.

He was sentenced to twelve years, he served eight and was released on parole last November. I think you were his first target since then. His parole obviously prohibits him from doing this type of activity, so we will bust him for breaking his parole. He will go back and serve the rest of his sentence.

You may not have put the Zodiac Rapist behind bars but you have saved yourself and probably a number of other women a whole bunch of grief. I thank you on their behalf, you have been a very brave lady and I wish you all the best. If you have any issues, or if there is anything you need, you just call me.'

An emotional Shirley Richardson got up from her seat walked around the desk and hugged Garcia.

Chapter 13
The Press Conference

A disappointed and disconsolate group of detectives regrouped in the situation room. Garcia addressed them.

'Team, I thought we had the bastard, everything pointed to him. In a way we are probably lucky that we didn't book him for it. If Shirley Richardson hadn't recognized his voice and known the size of his dick, we would have spent a lot of time going down the wrong road.'

Mills: 'So what do we do now, Boss, back to square one? We have nothing.'

O'Connell: 'No, we do have something. We have a pattern in the behavior of the rapist. If we look at where each rape occurred there is a definite area he operates in and if he stays true to his MO, then we know when he will strike again.'

Shaw: 'Yes, but look at the area and the population. There is no way we have a hope in hell in catching the guy in the act.'

Garcia: 'I am just going down to tell the Lieutenant the bad news, better to do it face to face. I am sure he's going to chew off my balls. Carry on. I'll be back, hopefully, in a couple of minutes.'

Garcia made his way down the stairs and knocked on Lieutenant Johnston's office door. Getting no answer, he opened the door and stepped into an empty office. He thought maybe Johnston had left for home as it was after all past 5.00 pm. He put his head out of the office door and called out.

'Anyone know where Johnston is, has he left for home already?'

'Nah, he has got himself dressed up in his "blues" and has left for the press conference,' called out the desk sergeant.

'What press conference?'

'The one with the Captain, the Chief and the Mayor. To celebrate the capture of the Zodiac Rapist,' answered the sergeant.

The realization hit Garcia like a freight train; he had told Johnston that they had him. Johnston had taken this as a done deal and gone ahead and bumped the news up the line. Those up the line just loved a press conference where they could extol a very public case that had been resolved.

'What time is the press conference?'

'Ten minutes at City Hall.'

Garcia's heart sank, there was no way he could get to City Hall in ten minutes. He grabbed the nearest telephone and dialed Johnston's cellphone; the call went directly to voice mail. He tried the Captain's cellphone with the same result, he had no way of contacting the Chief or the Mayor. In a panic he thought of calling in a bomb threat to try and halt the press conference, but sanity prevailed. He took a slow walk back up to the situation room.

Hayes was first to see him, "Jesus, Boss, you look like you just lost your best friend, what the Lieutenant say?'

'Nothing. He is probably already at the press conference at City Hall. Him the Captain, the Chief and the Mayor, the whole fucking mob. I'm fucked. Switch on the TV local news and you'll see what I mean.'

Shaw: 'You mean the poor dumb bastard went ahead and handed out the good news before we charged the perp. Who the fuck does that?'

Garcia: 'I told him we had Zodiac Rapist, a slam dunk. I didn't think he would spread the news all the way to the top. We have to get message to them to stop the press conference. Any ideas?'

Hayes: I have a contact in the Mayor's office, I'll call her and see if she can get to them before it's too late.'

Garcia: 'Do it.'

Hayes pulled up her contacts list on her cell and picked the required number, she put it on speaker phone. The call was answered almost immediately, 'June, what a lovely surprise! It's good of you to call. I was just thinking about you.'

'Mags, no time to chat, we have a huge problem and need to get an immediate message to the Mayor. Are you able to contact him?'

'We are all on the way to a press conference, he is stepping onto the podium at this exact minute.'

'We need to halt the press conference; he has bad information. Can you get to him?'

'I'll try; what is the bad information?'

'We do not have the Zodiac Rapist in custody, tell him.'

The TV in the room was tuned to the local news channel. You could see the Mayor, Chief, Captain and Lieutenant Johnston lined up waiting for the signal to start. In the background Hayes spotted her friend Mags valiantly trying to get to the men in the front of the podium. She was frantically waving her hands in the air trying to get the Mayor's attention.

She was being held back by two large security men who had no intention of letting her onto the stage. If one could lip read, she was obviously explaining that the Mayor had been given incorrect information about the arrest of the Zodiac Rapist. Just as she was about to be let through the press conference started.

In an election year this was a coup for the Mayor, making the streets of New York safer by getting a dangerous rapist off the street. He didn't hold back and those watching in the situation room watched as the train smash unfolded. The press conference was strategically scheduled for 7.05 pm so as to headline the evening news. All the channels had reporters in the audience.

'Ladies and gentlemen and members of the press. I would firstly like to thank you for attending at such short notice. As you are all no doubt aware. I have run my reelection campaign on cleaning up crime in our great city. Unlike other major cities, I have not succumbed to outside pressure to "defund the police". If anything, we have increased the police budget and it is paying us back in decreased crime statistics.

So, with that in mind I am very happy to announce due to diligent police work by the detectives of the 35th precinct, we have managed to take a dangerous rapist off our streets.

The low-life known as the 'Zodiac Rapist' is now safely behind bars. We have enough evidence to put him away for life. The Chief and I want to commend Captain Bruce Andrews and Lieutenant Grover Johnston for their excellent work on this case. I think a word from Bruce is in order.'

'Thank you, Mr. Mayor. I accept your commendation on behalf of the 35th, but the real heroes in this case are the men and women of our homicide squad led by Detective First class Michael Garcia.'

Back in the situation room the team cringed; they knew that the shit would hit the fan when the truth came out. They also knew that shit rolled down hill.

Back at the press conference things were wrapping up. Mayor Rodney H. Harmon, smiling and basking in the moment, handled a few questions before announcing the end of the session. His final words before walking off the stage were: 'I will continue the fight to clean up our streets and make them safe for all New York citizens.'

The press announcements were carried by all local and state news casts. The message was one of relief as a very dangerous rapist was finally locked up and off the streets. Single women could feel a whole lot safer due to his capture.

The five detectives in the situation room were so deflated that they just sat down with their thoughts. All of them knew there would be consequences; they just didn't know what those consequence would be. The silence was interrupted by the shrill ringing of Garcia's phone. *It has begun* he thought as he lifted the receiver and hit the speaker button.

'35th precinct, Detective Garcia speaking, how can I assist you?'

'Detective, I have just watched the press conference all about my arrest.'

'Your arrest. Who are you?'

'I am the one who you have supposedly arrested, but we both know that you haven't arrested the Zodiac Rapist. By the way, I hate that name.' Garcia sat upright in an instant, and everyone's head spun around to stare at his phone.

'Who are you? Is this some bullshit call?'

'No, I am the so-called 'Zodiac Rapist' and you have the wrong man in your cells but you already know that, don't you?' the voice mocked through the speaker.

Garcia knew any person calling in to claim to be the Zodiac Rapist could be a crank caller but this one knew that the person in the cells was not the rapist. How did he know that?

'Got you thinking, Garcia, you are not sure about this call. That's okay. When I am done with you, I am going to call one of the TV news outlets and let them know I am still in business. Do you have any preferences? Maybe you have a favorite station?' the taunting continued.

'Call whoever you want, you sick bastard, they won't believe you and they definitely won't broadcast it.' Garcia was furious that there was no way to trace this call.

'Oh, but they will. I have proof. There are things that were not released in the press that only the perp would know. While we are chatting, let me ask how you are getting on with the Marx family investigation? How is Detective Ethan O'Connell taking it? A bit close to home I think.' Garcia looked up at O'Connell, who never took his eyes from Garcia's phone.

'What are you talking about?' *This guy likes to talk; keep him talking.*

'Ethan O'Connell, I went to a whole lot of trouble to make that special just for him. Memories are important in life; we should embrace them. I hope he appreciates my effort.

Look, it's been fun chatting to you but I've gotta get my call into the TV station. It's too late for tonight's news but what better way to wake up in the morning than to stick one to our Mayor and Chief of Police. I hope it fucks up his reelection campaign. I think I will call one of the newspapers as well, might as well get the total coverage.

According to your timeline board, you have worked out the rape cycle so I may have to change that to make it a bit more fun for all. We don't want to be too predictable; it'll give the profiler something to think about.'

'You sick bastard! You think you can call me up and talk shit to me. If you are who you say you are, I will catch you and I hope you resist as I will make sure we save the taxpayers a chunk of money.' Garcia's knuckles had turned white as he slammed his fist into his desk.

'Bye bye, Detective, and to your team as I know they are all listening. When this breaks, I reckon you will all be in the crapper. I personally hope not as I am enjoying watching you run around like headless chickens.' *Click.*

The call ended and Garcia slammed down the receiver.

'Jesus! How the FUCK did he know about our timeline board?! Who the fuck is this guy?!' Garcia slapped his coffee mug off his desk in an uncharacteristic fit of rage and it slammed into the wall, landing on the floor without a scratch. The gift that kept on giving.

O'Connell: 'Boss, it's good that he called it's going to make our job a whole lot easier.'

Garcia: 'How do you figure?'

O'Connell: 'I think he gave it away either on purpose or by accident. He is the Zodiac Rapist and he also murdered the Marxs. We are no longer looking for two people; just one, him.'

Hayes: 'Why do you think he mentioned you in that way?'

O'Connell: 'I don't know exactly why, but he clearly has some beef with me. We need to follow that line of reasoning. I don't think I have ever pissed anyone off to the extent that they would resort to murder.'

Garcia: 'Guys, I am going to try and get hold of the Lieutenant and give him a heads up of this shitstorm that's about to bury us all. I suggest the rest of you head home and try and get some sleep, I feel tomorrow's going to be a tough day for all.'

Chapter 14
The Next Day

Try as he might, Garcia was unable to reach Johnston by phone. He briefly thought of calling the Captain, but decided if he did that Johnston would be even more pissed off with him. He eventually decided to go home and pour himself a large Bourbon followed by a few more. He finally fell asleep at 1.30 am, his alarm went off three and a half hours later.

By 5.30 am he was on his way to the precinct, stopping only to buy copies of the morning edition of the newspapers. His worst fears were confirmed by the New York Post led with the story: ***"Mayor Rodney H. Harmon jumps the gun – The Zodiac Rapist remains at large."*** The story detailed that the real perpetrator called the Newspaper and with indisputable evidence proved he was, in fact, the rapist. The article ridiculed all of the law enforcement teams involved but took real delight in showing up the Mayor. The newspaper, being very anti-Harmon, held nothing back in criticizing him and his administration. Garcia read the article with trepidation it would definitely be hitting the fan within the hour.

Garcia arrived at the precinct at 6.35 am where he was met by the night duty desk sergeant who had a copy of the Post in his hands.

'Jesus, Mickey, who the fuck decided that the press conference was a good idea? Someone is going to get their balls chewed off in the next hour or so. What happened?'

'Probably my fault. I told the Lieutenant that we had the bastard locked up and it was a slam dunk. I didn't think he would do anything before we booked the perp but he bumped the good news up the line. Mayor Harmon saw the opportunity to gain some reelection points and the rest is history.

Worse than all of this is that the sick bastard called me up on the phone to tell me we had the wrong man. I am going up to get ready to face the shit storm.' Garcia rubbed his hands over his face, already exhausted and the day hadn't even begun.

'O'Connell and Hayes are up there already, been in about ten minutes. They arrived together, something going on there, Mickey?' the sarge prodded, hoping for some juicy gossip.

'Who knows, that would be the least of my worries. Don't let any of the press into the building, whatever you do.'

Garcia trudged up the two flights of stairs silently cursing that the elevator was still not working. It was better to bitch about something than think about yesterday's events and those that would be on their way shortly. He stepped into the situation room to find O'Connell and Hayes working diligently on the timeline.

Hayes: 'Any news from above? We have been watching the news feed and it seems like there are many outlets that have little or no time for our esteemed Mayor.'

Garcia: 'You are right there, and he is going to react badly over that in the only way he knows – blame someone else. I would love to know if it was his idea to do the news conference. Either way, a pile of shit is sure to be on its way downstream so we may as well assume the brace position.'

At exactly 8.01 am Garcia's phone rang, it was Lieutenant Johnston, who did not sound happy with his instruction that *Garcia get his ass down here immediately*. He rolled his eyes, hung up the phone and went to face the music. He passed Shaw and Mills on the way down, both knew exactly where he was going and they gave him a sympathetic smile.

Taking a deep breath, he knocked on Johnston's door and without waiting for a reply opened the door, walked in, closing the door behind him, Johnston was standing behind his desk waving a copy of the Post at him.

'Just what the fuck were you thinking by telling me you had the perp? Slam dunk you said. I have had the Captain on the phone chewing off my balls, the Chief chewed his balls off and I would imagine the Mayor did the same to him. The Chief is on his way to City Hall and wants answers, so what do you have to say?' Johnston slammed his copy of the Post down on the desk in front of Garcia.

Garcia decided to go on the offensive. 'Boss, when I told you we had the perp locked up and it was a slam dunk, we were damn sure it was. We had his prints, his DNA all over the crime scene, he was picked out of a lineup.

I called you to tell you this, but we hadn't booked him at that point in time. What possessed you to bump the news up the line? You know it's police procedure not to release any statements until we have booked the perp and allowed him legal representation.

Christ, within minutes you were dressed in your "blues" and on your way to a press conference. When I found out that the man we had wasn't the Zodiac Rapist, but just some schmuck who happened to screw victim #5 the previous day, which was why his prints and DNA were all over the place, I tried calling you. Maybe if you had answered your cell, this whole train smash could have been avoided.' It was a ballsy move to chew out his boss, but Garcia wasn't going to be the only one going down with the ship.

Johnston, realizing he was at fault, countered, 'If you hadn't booked him, why the fuck would you call me about having a slam dunk result?'

'Boss, you know any booking of a major crime must be signed off by the officer in charge, in this case you. I don't get it, this has dropped us all in the shit, but I am not taking the rap on this one. You need to deal with the Captain because if I get pulled in, I will just quote "Police Procedure". So how you do this is up to you, although I do see the Mayor's fingerprints all over the press release. I hope his reelection hopes take a beating as he is so anti the police, useless bastard.

We have work to do tracking down this fucking rapist, so if it is okay with you, I will be getting back to work.'

Without waiting for an answer Garcia turned around and left the office. Half expecting Johnston to call him back, he hesitated, but hearing no response he made for the stairs. He walked back into a silent situation room and to the nervous stares of his four detectives. Ignoring all of them, he walked over to his desk, sat down, and put both his feet up on the desk.

Shaw: 'Come on, Boss, what happened?' Garcia ignored him.

Mills: 'Are we still on the case? Are you still leading us?'

Garcia: 'As of right this minute, Mills, the answer is yes to both of your questions. What happens in the next half hour will determine my future. I questioned Johnston as to why he would bump up the news about us catching the rapist. Basic police procedure means he would have had to sign off on the case and complete the booking.

It may be an out for me, but I think he could face a boat load of crap. I think the mayor got a hard on when he heard the news; he could see all the voters clamoring to reelect him. He sure fucked himself there, it will be interesting to see how he spins it.'

O'Connell: 'Boss, I traced last night's call from the perp, it was from a call box on the corner of 35th and 9th Avenue. There is a call box right next to the bus stop; maybe we can pick up a print or some DNA.'

Garcia: 'Good idea. I'll get someone from forensics over there sharpish. It's a long shot but we are scratching.'

Shaw: 'Are you telling us that the bastard was maybe one hundred yards away from us when he made that call?'

Garcia had no sooner put down the phone receiver after calling Forensics than it rang, he answered uttered a few grunts and hung up.

'That was Johnston. I have been summoned to 1PP (One Police Plaza – NYPD headquarters). I will be joining him and Captain Andrews for a meeting with Commissioner Rodgers, no doubt to have our balls chewed off. If I am still employed, I will see you later.' He grabbed his phone, keys and coffee mug and headed out.

With Garcia's departure the team turned their attention to the events of the previous day. Hayes was first to speak up.

'There are a couple of things that bother me about yesterday. All of the women were adamant that number 5 was the perp, that is until Shirley Richardson recognized him as her hookup from New Year's Eve. According to her it was the size of his dick that eliminated him from suspicion.

The other thing that bothers me is the call Garcia got from the perp. It was to his private direct line, not through our switchboard, how did he know that number? And then what about his reference to Ethan? What the hell is that all about? There must be some connection.'

O'Connell: 'I must admit it has got me confused, I cannot think of any reason that someone would go to all that trouble just to set up a murder scene that copied my folks' deaths exactly. He has to have something personal against me.'

Mills: 'The only positive thing to come out of this is we now know that the rapist and the murderer are one and the same person. So, we can concentrate our efforts on one man. We find the connections and we find our perp.'

Shaw: 'There are always people hanging around that phone box area. Directly opposite is a Deli and that smoke and vape shop; maybe they have CCTV. O'Connell and Hayes take a walk over there and see if they have anything. Also, if there is anyone just hanging about, check if they saw anything last night.'

Mills looked over at Shaw with a frown on her face. What was he doing pairing up O'Connell and Hayes? That was surely Garcia's job. Normally you never paired up two rookies as partners. What should have happened was she should have been paired up with O'Connell and Hayes would team up with Shaw. She decided she would have a word with Garcia at an opportune moment.

The two rookie detectives took the short walk over to the corner of West 35th Street and 9th Avenue. They decided to try the Deli first. The Italian owner, Mario Zola, told them he only had CCTV inside the store but one of the views centered on the front door of the store. Yes, he did have backup, the files get overwritten every 48 hours.

Hayes, showing some initiative, had brought along a flash drive and with the owner's permission copied the files off the CCTV hard drive. They would peruse them back at the precinct. When questioned, Zola did not recall seeing any tall white man with blue eyes enter his deli on the night in question. The two detectives thanked him and left to check up on the Smoke and Vape shop.

Here they had better success. The owner, Scott Wilkins, had CCTV coverage in the entire shop from all angles plus coverage of the surrounding area. The shop had been robbed a number of times in the past, which was strange given its close proximity to the 35th. Hayes again copied the files off the CCTV hard drive. Wilkins, as with Zola, had no recollection of seeing a tall white man with blue eyes.

As Hayes and O'Connell walked back into the precinct, they were halted by the desk Sergeant who handed them a brown envelope, courtesy of Barry Hughes from the CSI division. It contained the results of the fingerprints and DNA lifted from the call box opposite the deli. They decided to wait for Garcia and let him open the envelope.

Trudging up the two flights of stairs to the third floor, O'Connell stopped at the closed door. There was a heated discussion going on inside. He opened the door and stood back to let Hayes enter first. As Hayes stepped into the room the discussion ended abruptly as Garcia, Shaw and Mills turned to see who had entered; there was an uncomfortable silence. No guessing who the discussion was about. Garcia broke the silence.

'Good that you are both back. I have decided to pair each of you up with a more senior detective. Hayes, you will partner with Shaw, O'Connell you are with Mills. This will be in force for the duration of this case. What do you have there, Hayes?'

'Looks like the results of the forensics on the call box Boss.'

Garcia took the offered envelope and ripped it open. He studied it for a few minutes and then tossed it aside in disgust.

'Nothing of any damn use. What did you get from the two shops?'

Hayes: 'CCTV from the deli all inside the store and maybe something around the front door. The smoke shop could have something going for it; we just need to search through it. What happened at 1PP, Boss?'

'Turns out when Captain Andrews told the Commissioner, he called Mayor Harmon and told him we had a suspect in custody who could very well be the Zodiac Rapist but to keep it confidential. The Commissioner said Harmon ignored his comment and seeing the publicity for his reelection campaign, went ahead and called a press conference.

I was questioned about the Police Procedure as far as booking the perp was concerned but before I could answer, the Lieutenant butted in and said he was at fault for not completing the procedure before calling the Captain. I was surprised but impressed that he stood up and took the blame.'

Shaw: 'What did the Commissioner say to that?'

Garcia: 'Surprisingly, he barely reprimanded Johnston. We did hear that he had recorded his conversation with Harmon advising him to keep the information confidential until all due process was complete. I think he quite enjoyed seeing Harmon squirm as there is no love lost there.

Anyway, enough of that, lessons learned all around. Shaw, you, and Hayes take the smoke shop recordings and Mills, you and O'Connell do the deli. I want you to look in detail fifteen minutes either side of the phone call. I want this bastard so bad I can taste it. Right get to work.'

Chapter 15
CCTV

The call to Garcia's phone was made at 7.53 pm so it was decided to search the CCTV footage from 7.30 pm through to 8.10 pm. It was unlikely that the perpetrator would have hung around much after the call but may have been in the area sometime before making the call.

Hayes booted up her laptop and uploaded the footage from the smoke shop files, she then passed the flash drive to Mills who uploaded the deli files onto her laptop. The two groups then relocated to different ends of the room to work in peace.

The first observation from each of the files was that, due to the inclement weather the previous day, the background was quite dark, and all foot traffic was heavily clothed against the cold.

With Hayes working the smoke shop CCTV footage, the screen showed five different concurrent views. One at the check-out showing the clerk and a second face on of any customers checking out. A third, a wide view covered the inside of the shop. View four was centered on the door from inside and the fifth a wide view from the outside of the door.

With such a "busy" screen, Hayes suggested that they deactivate views one, two and three concentrating on the two views of the door. Of those two views, Hayes enlarged the outside view and moved the inside view to the top right of the screen. It would be easy enough to recall the other views if needed as they ran concurrently.

On the other laptop Mills showed her expertise and took control of the deli files. There were three concurrent views available. The view of the customer check-out, a wide view of the inside of the store and a view directed on the door from the inside. They decided to scrutinize the view of the door only, if they found anything suspicious, they would focus the other views as needed.

It was a painstaking effort. Due to the time of the evening, there was a lot of traffic in and out of the deli. Almost all of the people entering the shop were wearing a heavy coat and many had either a hoodie, a hat or a balaclava covering most of their faces. Given the angle of the cameras, it was difficult to judge a person's height.

By the 7.53 pm time stamp, no likely candidates had been identified. Even with the difficult angle, it would be easy to spot someone who was well over six foot in height. The two that they thought qualified by height were both black.

At the 7.57 pm mark a man appeared at the front door, wearing a black balaclava. He stopped but did not enter but from the angle it was obvious that he was tall. Staring directly at the CCTV camera he appeared to give a double "thumbs up" sign. After holding the pose for exactly five seconds, he turned and walked away.

Mills marked the position on the video and the two of them continued to the 8.10 pm mark without finding anything else of use.

In the meantime, Hayes and Shaw, concentrating solely on the bus stop and call box area, were progressing much slower than the other two. Each time there was some movement they would pause the video and zoom in. As with the deli traffic, almost everyone was heavily clothed, most wearing headgear of some sort. They were hoping to catch a view of someone unaware of the CCTV cameras and exposing their face.

At precisely 7.50 pm they spotted a likely candidate approaching from 35th Street. He appeared to be of the right height, wearing a balaclava covering all but his eyes and mouth. They zoomed in to find that he was smoking a cigarette. The fingers on both his hands were bare, the gloves only covering his palms. As he neared the call box he flicked the lit cigarette through the fence, he then walked up to the call box and lifted the receiver. He dialed a number at exactly 7.53 pm, this was their man.

All the time the man spoke on the phone, he kept his back towards the smoke shop's CCTV. As he finished the call, still facing away from the smoke shop, he waved the receiver above his head holding it in his left hand. His fingers still bare. With a flourish, he pulled a white handkerchief out of his right coat pocket and proceeded to wipe the receiver clean, he then did the same to the call box. He then turned around and looking directly into the CCTV camera, did an elaborate bow.

Unconcerned, he started to walk towards the smoke shop. Parked just in view was a precinct patrol car. The man extracted a cigarette from his coat pocket and walked up to the police officer standing next to the patrol car. He engaged the officer by asking for a light, he lit his cigarette, took a long pull and blew out the smoke directly at the camera. He turned left and headed back towards 35th Street.

'Jesus, the bastard knew we would get around to checking the CCTV and now he is just fucking with us,' exclaimed Shaw.

'We need to get hold of that cop who gave him a light. If that is his ride, I can just make out the number, it looks like 1416 or 1418,' said Hayes.

Garcia: 'O'Connell, get down to the duty sergeant and find out whose patrol car that is and get them in here asap. I want this bastard; I want to bring him in. I hope he resists so we can save the taxpayer a whole lot of money.

Hayes, can you get the view of him just before he blows the smoke at the camera? Zoom in as best you can and see if we can find any characteristics that would help identifying him.' Hayes turned back to the screen.

Hayes zoomed in on the man's face, the closer it got the less clear it looked. The colors, not clear at the best of times, just blurred into a grey mess. Yes, it was definitely their man, but the image was of no help.

Shaw: 'Boss, maybe we can send this in to the computer geeks, see if they can work some magic and we could get a better image.' Garcia nodded.

Garcia: 'Hayes, you and Mills make a copy of the files and note the exact frames we want enhanced. When you've done that, put it in an envelope and send it over to Barry Hughes. I will call him and see if we can get a priority on it. I'm sure he owes me a favor for something.

The arrogant bastard stopped in front of both cameras just to show us he knew we would be looking for him. Can we get someone out to see if they can find the cigarette butt he flicked away before making the phone call? It's unlikely but maybe we get lucky and pick up his DNA.'

Garcia picked up his phone and called Lieutenant Johnston. He explained that he needed some cops to search the area around the 35th Street side of the call box on 9th Avenue looking for a cigarette butt that the rapist discarded. He also gave a brief account of what the team had found on video surveillance. Johnston gave his assurance that whatever manpower and overtime needed had his blessing.

With little else to go on, the detectives got back to the timeline to see if there was some pattern that they had missed. Garcia's direct line rang, breaking the stony silence. It was an external call. He walked over, picked it up and hit the speaker phone button.

'Garcia here,'

'Detective Garcia, are you having fun yet? I know I am. It's been a real treat watching your detectives tracking down obvious leads, you are all so predictable, just like sheep. It's like watching someone reading the "Police Procedure Manual – following leads 101".

I am going to have to make this a bit more interesting, but I will keep you in suspense about my plans. Follow the dots to see where I will pop up next. Goodbye for now.'

Before Garcia could say anything, the phone went dead.

'O'Connell, see if you can trace that call. Hopefully the bastard used the same call box.'

Within seven minutes O'Connell had traced the phone number.

'Call box, corner of West 39th Street and 8th Avenue, next to the bus stop. He will be long gone. Do you want me to send a patrol car to the area, maybe they can look to see if any CCTV cameras in operation?'

'Nah. I am pretty sure there are cameras and he wants us to run over there and search through more CCTV footage. We won't find anything; he is just fucking with us. I think it may just piss him off if we ignore this call, kind of get under his skin. Maybe he will end up doing something stupid.'

O'Connell: 'What do you think he meant by "follow the dots?"'

Shaw: 'Probably just screwing with us again.'

Hayes: 'No. I don't think so, but he is taunting us; there is a pattern here, we just haven't found it yet. It must be there somewhere. I bet it is staring us in the face,' Hayes turned back to the board. Somewhere in that jumble of facts was the clue they needed to crack this thing.

Mills: 'The only thing he has done more than once so far are the rapes. The only constants are single women and new moon days.'

All of a sudden, Garcia shouted out, 'It's the addresses, look!

Victim #1 Williamson – 435 West 46th Street

Victim #2 Estes – 411 West 43rd Street

Victim #3 Smith – 405 West 40th Street

Victim #4 Todd – 466 West 37th Street

Victim #5 Richardson 430 West 34th Street

Every single one of them is in the 400 block and each subsequent rape is three blocks south of the previous rape.'

Shaw shook his head in awe: 'Boss, I think you've cracked it!'

Hayes: 'One thing we know about serial criminals is they like to stay true to some sort of a pattern. It is almost as big a thrill as the actual crime, showing just how clever they are. Based on this logic, the next victim will be a single white female living in the 400 block of West 31st Street. When is the next new moon?'

O'Connell quickly looked up the lunar calendar for 2022 and replied, 'Next one is February 1, then March 2 and if he sticks to his MO it will be April 1, April Fool's Day. I bet that's the one, make fools of the dumb cops again.'

Garcia: 'Right, we have a plan. I want a team of cops to canvass the entire 400 block of West 31st, I want a list of every single white woman who lives alone. Actually, make it every single woman, immaterial of color, just to be safe.'

Hayes: 'Boss, I understand the plan, but won't we attract undue attention? People are going to ask questions; we surely don't want to cause a panic and absolutely don't want this to get into the press.'

Garcia: 'Good point. Mills, we must come up with a believable reason for the canvass. I will speak to Johnston and see what we can come up with. It's going to be difficult to keep our discovery under wraps until April 1, we don't want to spook him or the residents in the area. This does not leave the room and this room remains locked, unless at least one of us is present. Is that clear?' Everyone nodded their agreement.

"Okay, that's it for the day, tomorrow we hit it hard, be in bright and early.'

'Boss, we are heading out for a couple of drinks at Murphy's, why don't you join us?'

'Thanks Dave but I have some work to do here, you folks go ahead, I'll see you in the morning.' Garcia waved them off.

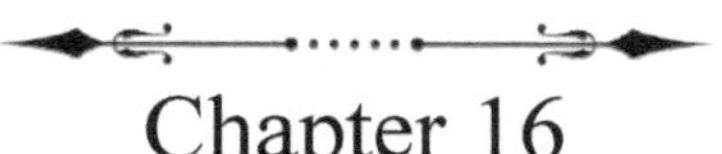

Chapter 16
Hooking up in more ways than one

The four detectives took the short walk over to Murphy's Irish Bar on West 33rd Street, it was a regular meeting place for cops from two different precincts. The closest other precinct is the 10th, just a couple of blocks to the south of the 35th.

Led by Shaw, Mills, Hayes and O'Connell stepped into the crowded bar and looked around for a table with close access to the very busy barmen. They had barely sat down when Shaw was recognized as two detectives from the 10th wandered over.

'Hey Shaw, I see your team finally put the Zodiac Rapist away for good. Seems your Boss couldn't wait to get the news out. I suppose he's locked up and already signed a full confession.'

'Fuck off, Cruz, we are just having a quiet drink here, go back to your cronies and continue your riveting discussion on how many parking tickets your precinct has handed out already this year and leave the detective work to real detectives.'

Cruz turned around and shouted over his shoulder, 'Hey boys, come on over and hear how real detectives do their job. The whole female population of New York are all feeling safe again, thanks to the 35th. Oh no, wait, they fucked up and nabbed the wrong man.' Cruz taunted.

Shaw, where's Mickey Garcia? Still looking for his chewed off balls, poor bastard. Well, at least you lot made the Mayor look like a real asshole, we should thank you for that,' Cruz raised his pint in mock salute, to cheers from his mates.

The banter went back and forth for a few more minutes and was finally interrupted by O'Connell carrying a round of four Buds. Losing interest, Cruz and his partner rejoined the cops from the 10th.

Shaw: 'Cheers guys, let's hope tomorrow is a better day than today. So, Hayes, what do you do with yourself when not on the job?'

Hayes: 'Well, I follow baseball, I'm a huge Mets fan. I try to get to the game as often as I can but it's becoming damn expensive, and parking is a bitch.'

Mills: 'I can't see that parking should be a problem with that little toy car that you drive. What is that thing?'

'It's a Mini Cooper and it will run rings around that tank that you drive. So, what do you do with your spare time, any hot number that we don't know about?'

'I also follow baseball but support a real team, Go Yankees! As for any *hot numbers,* I am afraid the available talent pool is very shallow. They are either married looking for a bit on the side, divorced and still hankering for their ex or gay. As soon as they know you are a cop, they seem to back away. Getting laid is a tough ask but it doesn't stop me trying. What about you?'

'Pretty much the same, the job does seem to get in the way a lot. The most success I get is with another cop but it still difficult to have any long-term relationships.'

Shaw: 'Okay ladies, enough of your struggling sex lives, but I am sure if you need an itch to be scratched, O'Connell and I could help you out.'

Mills winked with a sly grin: 'What do you say, Ethan, can I rely on you?'

'Well, I thought I had a line into your pants, that is until Mike paired us up. You know the rule; no sex between partners as it could cloud your judgment in a critical situation.' replied O'Connell jokingly.

Glancing over to Shaw, Mills said, 'Bad luck, Dave, that rules you out with June, so I guess it's back to the drawing board.'

For the next ninety minutes and three beers, the conversation centered around their case. All were angry by the way that the top brass had handled the news, adding additional pressure for them to nail the perp. As if they didn't already feel that pressure. Finally, the party started to break up.

Mills: 'Anyone need a ride? How about you, Ethan?'

'I am fixed up; June will drop me off thanks.'

Shaw: 'June will drop you off? Behave yourself with my new partner, I don't want you corrupting her.'

Hayes: 'Give it a break, Shaw. We take turns driving in, today was my turn, Ethan gets tomorrow.'

Mills: 'Sounds like a nice convenient arrangement, how did that come about? You've only been with us for a minute.'

'Ethan lives about two miles away from my place. We both live in Brooklyn, me in Ridgewood, and him in Greenpoint. It would have been better if we had been paired as partners, but hey we'll play it by ear. It saves us on gas and we can discuss the case while we drive in to the precinct.'

O'Connell: 'Okay June, I am ready if you are, we'll see you bright and early tomorrow.'

The two junior detectives stood up, pulled on their warm overcoats, nodded to their colleagues and left. Mills turned to Shaw and said, 'My place?' He nodded in agreement, and they got up to leave.

As each couple left the bar, they were observed by a tall man standing in the shadows in the opposite corner. He was dressed in a heavy overcoat and his face was partly obscured by a scarf wrapped around his head to shield against the cold weather. He had a backpack across his left shoulder and was wearing gloves. As soon as he saw Mills and Shaw leave, he turned to his left and began the short walk to the 35th precinct.

Timing his arrival to coincide with the 10 pm shift change at the precinct, he walked into temporary chaos. Those leaving at the end of their shift were eager to get home, those starting the third shift were in no rush to start work. The normal efficiency that would greet anyone entering the precinct was not in evidence.

Still covered up against the cold, the man walked past the reception desk, nodded at the sergeant on duty who barely looked up, and made his way towards the stairs. He was not logged in by the duty sergeant, so no record of his arrival was ever noted.

He alighted the stairs to the second floor which was in darkness, all the offices locked. The third floor was also in darkness but the only locked door was the one to the situation room.

The man lowered his backpack to the floor and extracted a headband that contained a small but powerful flashlight. He donned the device and switched on the light. Next, he opened a zipped wallet containing his lock pick set. Using two metal handles he went to work on the door lock. In less than thirty seconds he had the door open.

He entered the room closing the door behind him. Using only his flashlight, he surveyed the room and made his choices. Across one wall was the timeline, a single lockable office belonging to Garcia was on the left side of the room. Four desks were spread out, all set up to get the best view of the timeline. Placing his backpack on the closest desk, he began to unpack the equipment he would need.

A previous trip to Radio Shack had provided him with all the equipment he needed. Three micro cameras with a lens a bit smaller than a dime, a central controller used to network the cameras and a tablet to view the camera output. In addition, he had two small bugs perfect for hiding in a telephone.

He removed his thick leather gloves and replaced them with a pair of much thinner surgical gloves. Picking up the battery powered drill, he walked over to the wall facing the timeline board. He unscrewed a framed poster extolling the benefits of joining the NYPD and placed it on the nearest desk. Carefully he drilled a small hole in the top of its frame, he then turned the frame over and drilled a slightly larger hole in the rear.

The micro camera was then inserted into the frame from the rear, once it was secure, he then attached a small but powerful long-lasting battery. Once satisfied that everything was in place, he activated it using the controller. He checked the footage being recorded using the tablet, everything was clear. He deactivated the camera, replaced the framed poster and securely reattached it to the wall. Unless you were looking for it, the camera wasn't visible at a casual glance...

He located a suitable position on the right wall facing across the room towards Garcia's office. Here, he unscrewed a framed poster of the president of the United States and proceeded to do the same as he had done to the previous poster. Once he was satisfied, he checked the connectivity and finding all in order, he replaced the poster.

His next stop was Garcia's office, the locked door proved no deterrent as he picked the lock in seconds. He decided to install the third camera on the wall directly facing Garcia's desk. The office walls were adorned with certificates and awards for service, he selected one and planted the camera.

With all three cameras in place, he did a network check, all were functioning correctly and had a guaranteed battery life of one hundred hours. The cameras would stay inactive and only start recording when triggered by motion or sound. The cameras could also be activated or deactivated from his controller or tablet. He now had a live feed directly into the situation room.

His next step was to add the small bugs to the two telephones in the rooms. One in Garcia's office and the other on the general telephone in the situation room. Neither bug was connected to anything, but it would send a signal as though it was connected. The idea was that if the cops got suspicious and started looking for recording devices, they would find the bugs quite easily. Having found the two bugs and nothing else they would likely give up the search for any more devices.

Checking his watch, he found that he had accomplished what he set out to do in just short of two hours. He did a final sweep of the areas he had worked in to ensure no tell-tale evidence had been left behind. He locked Garcia's office door and left the situation room, locking that door behind him.

Instead of turning right to the staircase, he went left towards the emergency exit. The door was self-locking from the inside, careful not to make any noise, he slowly opened the door out onto the external fire escape. With his dark clothes blending into his surroundings, he made his way silently down the metal stairs to the ground. Unobserved, he smiled to himself, a job well done, time to head off home.

Hayes made good time on the drive to O'Connell's Greenpoint apartment. She pulled up to an empty parking spot right in front of 595 Morgan Avenue and stopped the Mini and turned towards O'Connell.

'Thanks for the ride, you must be a good luck charm; there is never an available street parking spot outside my building. Drive carefully. I'll pick you up in the morning same time as usual.'

'Seems a pity to waste a perfectly good parking sport, don't you think?'

O'Connell looked across at Hayes and thought for a few seconds before answering, 'You are right, it would be a waste. Do you want to come on in for a nightcap?'

Without answering, Hayes switched off the Mini's engine and opened the car door, both of them exited at the same time. With O'Connell leading the way, they walked up the five steps to the front door of the building, he unlocked the door and opened it. Stepping back, he ushered Hayes into hallway, he took her coat and hung it up, then shrugged out of his coat and hung it up next to hers.

She followed him down the hallway into the living room. In the far corner was a bar with three stools, he went behind the bar and she took the middle stool.

'What can I get you to drink? I am full of beer and am ready for a single malt scotch, I have got just about every type of liquor you can think of.'

'I'll join you with the scotch.'

'Drink it slowly, you don't want to drive home over the limit.'

He poured two glasses of Glenlivet neat and passed one to her. Raising the glass he proposed a toast, 'To catching the real Zodiac Rapist, let's get the bastard before he causes anymore damage – cheers.'

Hayes, ignoring his advice to sip her drink, knocked it back in one swallow. She downed her glass and looked over at him, he got the hint and followed suit; the whiskey was down his throat in a single gulp.

'Aren't you concerned about driving home over the limit?'

'I will be under the limit by morning, I'll need the bathroom first if you will show me the way.'

He stepped out from behind the bar and taking her by the hand led her out of the living room and up the stairs. He turned right into his bedroom and without a word pointed to the en suite bathroom. He turned towards the bed and pulled down the duvet and top sheet. He was busy removing his tie when the bathroom door opened, he turned to see June Hayes naked.

At 33-years old, she was nearly two years older than him. Having only seen her in her "work clothes" of jeans, blouse, and short jacket, he knew she had a good body. Naked she was quite spectacular, not an ounce of fat on her body, her slim waist and flat stomach extended down to well-shaped legs. Her breasts were on the small side but beautifully shaped with dark pointed nipples. At about 5'9" and 140lbs she was in fantastic shape, a well-toned body.

Seeing him standing there still fully dressed staring at her, she thought for a moment she had read the signs wrong.

'Still dressed I see, have I made a fool of myself here?'

'No, I am just flabbergasted, you are absolutely stunning.'

Not waiting anymore, she walked over to him and began unbuttoning his shirt, finding that she was getting in the way of him disrobing she stepped away and watched him get undressed. At 31 years old, 6'3" and a muscular 210lbs he was in great shape. She admired his strong chest, just enough hair to make it attractive, tapered body down to his waist, chiseled six pack abs. He dropped his trousers and stepped out of his underwear, she looked down at his semi erect penis and gasped.

'Oh my God. You are lucky that the guys in the lineup weren't allowed to show their dicks. Over six foot – check, blue eyes – check, large penis – check. You would have been screwed, definitely picked as the Zodiac Rapist, locked up immediately.'

Ignoring the look on his face she walked over to him, put her arms around his neck and pulled him towards her. He leaned down and kissed her passionately, she responded. They could both feel his penis becoming erect, without a further word she pushed him onto the bed. Straddling him, she lowered herself onto his penis and with a gasp of pleasure began slowly moving up and down.

With all thoughts of foreplay out of the question, they spent the next hour exploring each other's body, taking pleasure in their lovemaking. Hayes had two mind blowing orgasms before O'Connell joined her. Exhausted, they lay in each other's arms trying to catch their breath. Hayes was first to break the silence.

'Wow, I needed that big time.'

'Me too, I am finished. You are magnificent, this can't be a one off, can it?'

'Hell no, but we are going to have to keep it secret. Once we get the Zodiac Rapist, I will be sent back to the 94th and it will be much easier then. They know we commute together so if we plan it right, we can do this on a regular basis. If that is okay with you, right?'

'Works for me. Now I need to sleep, you have worked me over and I am done.'

Hayes got up and went to the bathroom to freshen up. By the time she got back into bed, O'Connell was already fast asleep. *Typical male*, she thought. She set the alarm on her watch for 5.00 am, climbed back into bed and was asleep within a minute.

5.00 am she was woken up by the alarm vibrating on her watch. Initially she was confused as to where she was, strange surroundings, it took her a few seconds to get her bearings. O'Connell's shallow, even breathing brought her to full consciousness, she leaned her arm across his chest taking in his manly smell, he was in a deep sleep. She cheekily reached down and gently gave his penis a tug. He was instantly awake, he sat up, looked around and then noticed her.

'What time is it? I must have fallen asleep.'

'Fallen asleep? You were unconscious within minutes. I didn't mean to wake you, but I have to go now, otherwise I will be late for work.'

'No time for a quickie, then?'

'It better be real quick, think you can manage that?' she teased.

Not bothering to answer, he rolled her on her back and without ceremony was inside her immediately. She responded and the frantic coupling was brought to a shuddering climax in under three minutes.

June rolled out of bed, scouring the room for her clothes. 'Okay, I am off. I just need to use the bathroom before I go. I will see you in a few hours. Thank you for a wonderful night; I hope I can stop smiling at work today.'

She leaned over and kissed him on the cheek. Climbing out of bed, she made her way to the bathroom. By the time she emerged fully dressed, O'Connell was fast asleep again.

Chapter 17
Under Observation

As usual, Garcia was first into the situation room, carrying his trademark coffee mug, he made his way to his office, unlocked the door and walked over to his desk. The camera in his office automatically activated. Sitting in his two roomed apartment sixteen miles away in the East Bronx, the man watched Garcia stare thoughtfully directly at the camera.

Suddenly there were voices coming from the room outside of his office, and the two cameras in the room burst into action. Garcia stood up and walked out of his office to find Hayes and O'Connell.

'I hope you two are ready to start planning how we will canvass the four hundred block of West 31st Street. We need a plan that will not spook the area or attract any undue attention to what we are doing.'

The man watching smiled, this was going to be interesting and possibly fun.

Hayes: 'Boss, we were just talking about it on the drive in.'

'You two drive in together every day, how's that work?'

'I live about two miles away from O'Connell, we take it in turns to drive in, saves on gas. Today it was his turn, tomorrow mine.'

'Oh, I see, maybe I should pair you two back up as partners, it would make sense given your transport arrangement. Let me think about that. When Shaw and Mills get in, I want to have a strategy meeting, so gather your thoughts.'

Garcia returned to his office leaving Hayes and O'Connell staring at each other. They walked over to their two adjoining desks and sat down facing each other.

Talking in a low voice, Hayes whispered, 'Crap, if he partners us up again then we cannot have sex, what do you think?'

'Oh man, that would not be a good situation. If they do transfer you back to the 94th we can pick it up again then. Shit, we better catch this bastard soon as he is now affecting my sex life.'

'So, these two are fucking each other… that's going to make this

interesting. Should be easy enough to find their addresses.'

Their conversation was interrupted by Mills and Shaw arriving together.

Hayes whispered to O'Connell, 'Is Shaw wearing the same clothes that he had on yesterday?'

'It sure looks like it', replied O'Connell, with a knowing smile.

'The two of them are sleeping together, I'm sure of it. They often arrive together, they must be, maybe because they are not partners now. I wonder if they were doing it all the while.'

'Just because they are, doesn't mean we should risk it, we could lose our jobs.'

'Screw that, no one cares and anyway, we will keep it a secret and be damn careful. I don't know if I can wait until we catch the bastard.'

Garcia heard the rest of his team arriving and got up from his desk, making his way into the general office. 'Okay folks, we need to formalize a plan to catch this bastard. We know where he will strike next and what day it is likely to be. Given his track record of moving south three blocks at a time, it's going to be April 1 in the 400 block of West 31st Street. Any comments?'

Mills: 'Nope, I think you've got it Boss. Three blocks south every three months. Just wonder why "three", there must be a connection. Do you think we need a profiler on the team?'

So, they think I am obsessed with the number 3, I will have to change it up a bit for the next time just to screw up their theory. It will also give me time to implement the next phase of my plan.

Garcia: 'What we don't know is whether the murders of Mr. & Mrs. Marx was just a deviation from his rape and robbery routine or will he strike again.'

No, the Marxs' were killed to send a message to O'Connell to get his attention, I have a big plan in store for him, but I want him to sweat a bit first.

Shaw: 'Difficult to say. These psychos can't be judged like normal people. Once they have a taste for it, they can't stop.'

You are right there, Fatso, I do have a taste for it but it has to be just right.

Garcia: 'Hayes, I want you and O'Connell to partner up again. Your first task is to check all the accommodation available in the 400 block of West 31st. Get a list of all residents, check for any single women of any race.

The age range of his victims so far is 28 to 52, all have been reasonably attractive and in good physical shape. Try and find if they have a driver's license and if so' get a photo, height, and weight although the photo often looks nothing like the person in real life.

Shaw you and Mills follow up on the evidence box that was checked out back in March at the 94th taken out by a so-called cop. Re-interview the custodian again, put a bit of pressure on him for not following police procedure. I will call up the Lieutenant there and tell him you are coming.'

Get the team busy, Detective Garcia, a lot of work is going to go to waste. I have a trip to Greenpoint in Brooklyn scheduled. Don't worry. I will keep an eye on all of you while I am traveling.

Deciding against taking a taxi, he went for public transport, cheaper and less chance of being remembered. He plugged his headphones into the tablet, put on his heavy overcoat and slung his backpack over his left shoulder. Looking like any one of thousands of New York commuters, he took the short walk from his apartment to the Gun Hill Subway station.

With the morning rush over, the crowds had thinned out considerably. He caught the first southbound #5 train and found a seat in the rear of the second coach. Being a big guy and carrying a backpack, he made sure he had the seat to himself. Constantly monitoring the action at the 35th precinct, he started the ninety-minute trip to Greenpoint, Brooklyn.

At the 14th Street Union Square station, he alighted the train and made the short walk to connect with the Canarsie-Rockaway Parkway line. The short eight-minute trip saw him alight at Lorimer Street. A short walk to the corner of Union and Metropolitan Avenues, there he boarded the number B48 Greenpoint/Meeker Avenue bus service.

Ten minutes later he got off the bus at the corner of Nassau and Morgan Avenues. A short walk later he found himself standing outside of 595 Morgan Avenue. Leaning against a tree directly opposite the front door, he lit a cigarette. Taking a long satisfying draw, he casually surveyed the scene.

There was virtually no one moving around outside in the immediate vicinity. The front door to the building was slightly recessed giving him almost perfect cover. He took a second pull of the cigarette, nipped off the burning end and completely ground the rest of it under his shoe. There would be no DNA to be found on that cigarette, he was not really a smoker but lighting up a cigarette was a natural occurrence, and it gave him time to survey his surroundings.

Satisfied, he crossed the street, walked up the five steps to the front door. With two of his metal lock picking handles at the ready, he began the task of opening the front door. The door had two locks, the upper one, a heavy bolt action, was the easier of the two, he had that open in less than half a minute. He turned his attention to the lower lock; this proved a little more difficult but ninety seconds later he turned the door knob and was inside.

The first thing he noticed was a small rack on the wall, the kind used for hanging up bunches of keys. Part of his skill set as a burglar was his ability to recognize key types. Lifting off the larger of the three sets of keys, he selected two that he was sure were for the front door. Trying them both confirmed this. Ever prepared, he searched in his backpack and extracted two small metal tins. Each tin contained a smooth thick layer of clay. Taking each key one at a time he gently pressed it into the clay creating a perfect image of each key. He would get copies of the keys made for easier future access to the building.

He walked slowly down the short hallway to the living room. The first thing that caught his eye was a large, framed photograph secured to the wall above the fireplace. It was a photograph of Ethan O'Connell and another police officer taken at their graduation from the Police Academy. He had seen the exact photograph before, when doing a robbery back in October of 2020. It was this photograph that had set him on the path he was on.

Being able to see exactly where O'Connell was on his tablet, he knew he had plenty of time to accomplish the tasks he needed to.

He removed the photograph above the fireplace and turned it face down on the coffee table. As with the cameras at the precinct, he proceeded to install a camera in the upper frame of the photograph. He thought it ironic; O'Connell would be keeping an eye on O'Connell. He extracted a second controller and his tablet from his backpack and tested out the camera. It gave a perfect wide angled view of the entire living room, including the corner bar.

Satisfied that the camera was working correctly and undetectable, he took the stairs to the upper level of the apartment. There were two bedrooms, it was clear which was the main one. He looked around, a typical single male's bedroom with no unnecessary knickknacks on the walls.

Above the bed was an "Art of War" by Sun Tzu poster mounted in a wooden frame. On the right-hand wall was a large framed photograph of O'Connell, flanked by his parents. *What a happy family, pity they are no more,* he thought sarcastically. On the left side wall was the iconic poster of Bruce Brown's movie "The Endless Summer". None of the three items gave a perfect wide angled view of the bedroom.

The wall facing the foot of the bed proved to be the best location for the camera. There were three shelves, each holding some sporting memorabilia, either his personally or those of well-known sports franchises. Right in the middle of the middle shelf was a wooden plaque from his Alma Mater. It was securely screwed to the wooden shelf at the perfect position for the second camera.

Fifteen minutes later the camera was perfectly hidden in the Cornell University coat of arms plaque. He tested it and found it working perfectly. He sat on the edge of the bed and, even knowing where it was hidden, he couldn't see any trace of the camera.

He had two more cameras and he needed to find useful spots for them. He decided the en-suite bathroom wouldn't have any additional benefit, neither would the spare room. Leaving the upper floor, he returned downstairs and continued his exploration. He thought about the kitchen but after looking around, he decided no benefit would be found having a camera installed there.

As he left the kitchen area, he saw a door, he tried it but found it locked. Remembering the bunch of keys on the rack at the front door he decided to try them rather than pick the lock. He retrieved the keys and the second one he tried opened the door. He found a staircase leading down into a basement, he flicked the light switch and headed on down.

At the very bottom of the stairs was another door, this one was not locked so he opened it. He flicked the light switch and found that the basement was completely finished. To the left of the basement, extending the full length of the building was a furnished lounge. Two Lazy-boy leather recliners, both facing a large 64" flat screen TV.

On the right, a wall ran the full length of the building, there were three doors evenly spaced. The first door led into a small bathroom containing shower, toilet and hand basin. The middle door led into a bedroom where he found a closet and a Queen-sized double bed. The third door opened into a kitchen, complete with a glass top oven, microwave, small refrigerator and a double basin sink. In the center of the kitchen was a small table and four chairs.

The setup was perfect for a self-contained apartment or the ideal man cave. Based on all the sport and movie posters spread evenly around the lounge, he deduced that it was probably a man cave. Looking around he spotted the perfect place for the third camera. In the middle of the wall facing the TV screen was a mounted poster of the Arnold Schwarzenegger and Danny De Vito movie *Twins*.

He carefully removed the poster, turned it over and drilled a hole just big enough to insert the camera. After the battery was attached, he remounted the poster and activated the camera. The wide-angle view from the camera gave perfect coverage of the entire lounge.

Satisfied that he had a view into all the key areas of the apartment, he performed a concurrent test of all three cameras, all were in perfect working order. Less than two hours after he walked into the apartment, he left via the front door, remembering to reset the two door locks.

A short walk to the corner of Meeker Avenue and Hausman Street brought him to the bus stop for the northbound B24 bus. The uneventful return journey took eighty-five minutes. He made a quick check on the activities at the 35th precinct, O'Connell and Hayes were working on the resident's list for 400 block of West 31st Street. Garcia was in his office staring into space and Mills and Shaw were nowhere to be seen.

All in all, a very successful day, now for the next phase of his plan. He now had full viewing access to the 35th precincts situation room, Garcia's office and the key areas of O'Connell's apartment.

Chapter 18
Chasing Leads

Shaw and Mills left the situation room and headed for their police vehicle for the trip to the precinct. A short seven-mile trip through the Queens Midtown tunnel into Brooklyn could take anything from half an hour upwards.

Shaw: 'What do you think about Garcia pairing us back up again? Just when I thought I had traded up getting Hayes in your place.'

Mills: 'Trading up? Huh, as if you have any chance of getting into her pants. I am the one who lost out getting you back as a partner and losing out on a stud like O'Connell. At 6'3" and huge feet, I bet he is hung like a horse.'

Shaw: 'I wonder if the two of them are fucking, they always arrive together and leave together. She looked disappointed when Micky put them back together. I reckon O'Connell is probably a bit of a "by the book" kind of guy. No screwing with your partner, so that leaves her available, I should try and get her out for a few drinks.'

Mills: 'Good luck with that, I'll let you know what O'Connell's like in the sack.'

By the time the two of them arrived at the 94th they had gone back and forth about the Hayes/O'Connell possibilities and had twenty bucks on which of them scored first. Deep down both thought their chances of collecting were very remote.

Parking directly in front of the precinct, they walked up to the reception desk and asked for Lieutenant Dickerson. As they were expected the desk sergeant ushered them to his office.

'Detectives, good to see you both, Johnston called me about your visit. I must admit it struck me as strange, as you folks already have the evidence you required.'

Shaw: 'Thanks for seeing us; yes, we do have the physical evidence but it's the request you had back in March last year that we're interested in. As you may know, we have two cases open and feel they are related. The cold case evidence you have is very similar to the murder case we have on the Marx family.

The ongoing Zodiac Rapist cases now seem to have a link to Marx murders because of the use of the Zodiac cards and also to your cold case, due to the number of similarities in the crime scenes. We think there may be a cop involved in the two murder cases and then by association, all of the rapes.'

'Jesus, how is a ten-year old murder case linked to current murder and rape cases? I watched the news conference where that asshole Mayor was waxing lyrical about your precinct solving the Zodiac Rapist, I bet you someone took a load of shit for that fuck up,' replied Dickerson.

'You are dead right there, but if any good came out of that it's that Mayor Harmon probably screwed up his reelection chances. Anyway, as we think a cop may be involved, we want to have a further chat with your Evidence Custodian and see if he can shed any further light on the cop who asked for the evidence on the O'Connell murders.'

'Sure thing, the man's name is Sammy Colby, he may look a bit simple, but he knows exactly where everything is filed. We overlook a lot of what and how he does things but would be completely screwed without him. I am working to get a more organized setup down there but like all other precincts, we have manpower restrictions. Come on, I'll take you down.'

Shaw and Mills followed Dickerson down the two flights of stairs into the basement and into Sammy Colby's world.

'Hey Sammy, I've got two detectives here from the 35th. they would like to ask you a couple of questions, so give them all the help you can. I'll leave you folks to it. I will be in my office if you need me,' Dickerson took his leave.

'Hi Sammy, I am Detective Shaw and this is my partner, Detective Mills. I would like you to think back to March 8 last year and the evidence box for the O'Connell murders.'

'Yes, Detective Ronald MacDonald from the 69th, badge number 84431. I already told one of your detectives about him and showed where he signed out the evidence on March 8 and returned it March 19. What else do you want to know?'

Shaw: 'Did you check his ID?'

'He showed me his shield, I recorded the details, and he signed out the evidence. I did not check a photo ID.'

'Why not? Isn't it police procedure to check a photo ID?'

'Yes, but a shield verification is also allowed.'

Seeing he wasn't going to get anywhere while harping on about the photo ID, Shaw tried a different approach. 'I know it is almost a year ago, but could you tell us anything about the man's appearance, height, weight anything?'

'Yes, he was well over six feet, well-built, not fat, brown hair and blue eyes.'

'Are you not getting confused with our detective from a couple of days back?'

'No, but the two of them looked very much alike, could have been related, brothers maybe.'

Shaw turned to Mills and shrugged his shoulders, she just gave him a look that said *we are wasting our time here*.

'The only big difference was that the cop from March 8 had a heavy Bronx accent and your guy spoke real posh, like a college boy.'

'Jesus, did you tell this to our detective when he came in?'

'No.'

'Why not?'

'He never asked for a physical description, so I didn't waste his time babbling on.'

Shaw just shook his head, 'Sammy, thanks for your time and help, we'll be leaving now.'

The two detectives left Sammy to his devices and headed up the stairs, they waved to Dickerson on the way out and didn't speak until they were in the car heading back to the 35th.

'Jesus, Dave, what the hell is he telling us? I reckon he just got confused and mixed the two up. We can't take anything he said seriously.'

'Maybe we can. Just think about the lineup we did. They picked O'Connell and the only thing they all agreed on was the accent. They all said the rapist was tall and more than one remarked on the blue eyes. Our guy could very well be of the same size and build as O'Connell, that gives us something to work on.'

'Maybe we can ask O'Connell to show us his dick, as all the victims were adamant about that,' Shaw deadpanned.

Meanwhile, back at the 35th, Hayes and O'Connell were busy with the odious task of identifying all single women living alone residing in the 400 block of West 31st Street. The area in question was mostly made up of high-rise buildings catering to various businesses. Several buildings did have apartment facilities, the difficulty would be finding who lived in those company type apartments.

There were 88 apartments in 4 listed apartment blocks, the number of registered companies that had one or more floors in any building that could potentially have an apartment located in them numbered 23. A further complication was that in many cases, the apartments were not occupied by the owners but rented out.

Progress was very slow; at the rate they were going it was going to take several days to comb through the lists. Even with complete diligence there was a very strong chance that they would miss some. They decided to take on the apartments in the 4 apartments blocks first.

'Ethan, you take 414 and 428, I'll take the other two. I suggest we use the city database to establish the apartment owners first.'

'Sure thing. If we can establish if the owners actually reside there, then we should be able to narrow down our list considerably.'

Watching from his apartment in The Bronx, the man chuckled to himself, *keep busy, little piggies, wasting your time, I have other plans for my next step.*

Shaw and Mills returned to the precinct and went to report to Garcia.

Shaw: 'Boss, we interviewed the custodian at the 94th, his name is Sammy Colby. He looks like he is on another planet, but he sure knows his inventory. We asked about the cop who withdrew the O'Connell evidence, and he remembered the date and what went down without us even asking.

He admitted to not checking a photo ID but suggested that once he saw the shield, he was okay with the person. I asked for a description, and he basically told us the man was over six foot, well built, brown hair and blue eyes. He also told us he looked a lot like O'Connell but spoke with a heavy Bronx accent.

I reckon he got confused and was remembering O'Connell, not our perp. We have no CCTV of the person from back in March, so I don't think we have anything to go on.'

Observing from The Bronx the man just smiled. *Good, they don't think it was me and they surely don't suspect it was O'Connell both times. This is working out just perfectly.*

Chapter 19
A Mugging

Having spent the previous ten days working on the occupancy of all residents living in the 400 block of West 31st Street, Hayes and O'Connell had arrived at seven persons possibly fitting the search criteria. The problem now became how to protect these women without them being aware of it for the next two and a half months until April 1.

With no further leads on either the Marx murders or the five rape victims, the team's best chances would be capturing the rapist in action. The problem they faced was how they could be certain that there would be no changes to his routine or the potential victims. No further communications from the rapist had been received.

Pressure from above had lessened. The Mayor, having made a fool of himself, was more than happy to keep the investigation going but also keeping a low profile in the press. Like most sensational stories, it had run its course and the hullabaloo had died down.

All the while, the team were being observed in the office and O'Connell was being observed both in the office and at home. He was content to let them waste their time trying to track down his potential next victims. He needed the time to make a detailed study of O'Connell, his habits, mannerisms, and his normal routine.

Having originally thought that O'Connell and Hayes had a sexual relationship, his observations indicated that they did not. O'Connell had slept at home alone every night since he began his observations, which would make his task a whole lot easier.

The New York weather during the month had varied quite considerably. From daytime highs of 45° to lows of 18° and nighttime lows of 15° to highs of 34° it was common to see most people well wrapped up when outside.

With the cameras placed in O'Connell's apartment, he had a good idea of his movements and routines. Once in the apartment after work, he was a creature of habit. He seldom left the building, either cooking a meal himself or getting delivery. Most evenings he would spend down in his basement watching TV, sports, or Netflix. Up until this point, he had not had any female company.

Between observing the office and O'Connell's apartment, he had discovered that Hayes and O'Connell traveled into the office together. One day he drove, the next she did, the routine never varied. When it was his turn to drive, he left the apartment at precisely 7.15 am, when he was being picked up, he left at 7.30 am. What he didn't know was what O'Connell's movements were from the apartment to his car and where he waited to be picked up by Hayes.

He decided the only way to get the full picture of O'Connell's movements would be to watch him as he left the building. It would mean a very early rise and a long cold trip to Greenpoint in Brooklyn. According to the cycle, on Monday January 17th, O'Connell would be driving.

Stationed on the opposite side of the street about fifty feet to the right of the front door, he watched O'Connell on his tablet. Right on cue he put on his thick overcoat, unlocked the front door, and exited the apartment. He turned to his right walking away from his observer, who followed him. About two hundred feet up the road O'Connell stopped next to a blue Honda Civic and unlocked the door with a remote. He placed his bag onto the back seat, climbed in and closed the door. Turned on the car's ignition and pulled out and drove off in a northerly direction. The time 7.17 am.

The following day' Tuesday January 18th, he watched O'Connell get up, shower, get dressed and walk down the stairs. He put on his heavy overcoat, picked up his bag and opened the front door. After locking the door, he turned north on Morgan Avenue, he walked up to the intersection of Nassau Avenue where he turned left. Crossing the road he walked into The Coffee Shop, it was 7.33 am.

Closely following, the man observed him walking up to the counter, where he exchanged a few words with the barista. He was immediately handed two cups of coffee, he paid, turned around and left the shop. He made the return journey to 595 Morgan Avenue just in time to greet Hayes, driving her Mini Cooper, it was 7.36 am. He watched them drive past going north on Morgan Avenue.

Satisfied that they were on their way to the precinct, he walked south on Morgan looking for O'Connell's blue Honda. He found it parked about one hundred or so feet south of his apartment. He deduced the only variable was where O'Connell parked. New York street parking was a bitch.

Looking around, he walked up to the car and using his lock picking skills had the driver's side door open in seconds. He climbed in and looked around. The glove box held nothing of interest other than a parking permit disk allowing him to park in front of the 35th precinct or any other place normal parking was not allowed, when on Police business.

He climbed out of the car and locked the doors. So far, he had not found the ideal spot where he could implement the next part of his scheme.

The following day, he arrived and located the Blue Honda, moving further south he waited for O'Connell. Right on cue he followed the same routine as he had on Monday, truly a creature of habit.

Thursday was an exact repeat of Tuesday, the only difference was that Hayes arrived two minutes later at 7.38 am. Friday was an exact repeat of Monday. With all the action happening between 7.15 am and 7.40 am, sunrise made the risk of being observed by someone too high; another plan would have to be made.

During this time, Hayes and O'Connell had documented the next seven possible victims of the Zodiac Rapist. Their names, addresses, age, race, and driver's license photographs had been added to the timeline on the white board. The seven women were spread over three different buildings. All of this was being observed by the strategically placed cameras.

On Monday January 24th, Garcia called the team together to formulate a plan to protect the potential victims.

'Okay, we have identified where we think the rapist will strike next. If he stays to his normal MO, it will be on April 1 which is a Friday. We have just over two months to get this setup, we cannot let this bastard get away this time. I am open to suggestions.'

Hayes: 'I think because we have time on our side, we should do a reconnaissance of the three buildings. We have each person's address, two at 410, three at 435 and two at 466. I think we could probably have a couple of undercover cops knock on each of the apartment doors in the three buildings. They could pretend they are with the gas or electric company or something such like, checking for leakage.'

Shaw: 'Great, but for what purpose?'

Hayes: 'Get the layout of the seven specific apartments, check the lock types but the main task would be to see how best to observe them on April 1.'

Garcia: 'Good idea, but we need a cast iron cover in case any of the occupants call the utility company. What I suggest we do is check each of the addresses and find out which utility company services that apartment. We can mockup an official looking document with their name and address showing that they had been selected for a free examination of their electrical/gas installation. Most people like free stuff.

I will speak with the Lieutenant and see if he agrees with this approach. We've gotta make sure we don't spook these women. If it gets out what we are doing our whole plan would be compromised. We cannot let this get into the press; it must stay in this office if we have any chance of catching him in the act.'

Garcia left the situation room to go and have a talk with Johnston, leaving the other four to get started on the planning.

Hayes: 'Ethan and I will pull together the utilities data for the various apartments. Dave, you and Linda can set up a stakeout rotation that we would need for April 1.'

Shaw: 'Who the fuck died and put you in charge?'

Hayes: 'It was my idea, if you think you can do better, have at it.'

Mills: 'No, we go ahead with your plan.'

Hayes: 'Okay, then let's see if we can get this put together by Wednesday.'

Watching from afar the man just grinned to himself, are you all in for a big shock.

Garcia returned with the news that Johnston had given his permission to continue with their proposed plan and reiterated that this was not to be discussed outside of this office. With their assignments allocated, the team got work on the plan.

At 5.30 pm, Garcia called time and invited the team down to Murphy's for a couple of beers, the first round on him. The detectives needed no second invitation. Two rounds of drinks later, Hayes, concerned that she had to drive, called time for her and O'Connell.

Leaving the other three to continue drinking, the two of them headed back towards the precinct and Hayes' Mini Cooper. As it was nearly 7.00 pm, the traffic had subsided slightly and the drive to O'Connell's apartment only took twenty-nine minutes. Hayes pulled up outside the apartment to let O'Connell out, she looked across at him and their eyes locked. Without saying a word, she turned off the engine, got out of the car, locked the doors and followed O'Connell up the stairs and into the apartment.

Hanging up their coats in the hallway they headed into the sitting room and made their way over to the corner bar. The movement activated the camera and at the same time alerted the man in his apartment. He picked up his tablet expecting to see O'Connell alone, but to his surprise Hayes was also visible.

What do we have here? This is a deviation from his normal routine. Things could get interesting.

Without asking, O'Connell poured two whiskeys and handed one to Hayes.

'I can't drink this. I am already on the limit and I sure as hell don't want a DUI. I better make myself a coffee, but don't let me stop you having a drink.'

'Forget about the coffee, drink the scotch.'

'I thought you were going to follow the rules, "no cohabitation amongst partners".'

'Screw the regulations, I want you tonight. If you don't want to risk it, go and make a coffee. I will understand.'

Hayes looked him straight in the eye, picked up the whiskey glass and tossed the drink down her throat in one gulp. Without a word, she placed the empty glass on the bar counter, turned around, crossed the room and went up the stairs, O'Connell followed suit seconds later.

So, they are fucking each other, this should be fun.

By the time O'Connell got up to the bedroom Hayes was almost naked, there was going to be no preamble tonight. Within minutes they were both naked and under the blankets, not a word had been spoken. They started out slowly but the tempo increased rapidly, the blankets were thrown off the bed giving the observer a perfect view of what was going on.

Finally, with both of them exhausted, Hayes rolled off O'Connell and flopped onto the bed and lay on her back. She was first to say something.

'Jesus, I needed that. I don't care about the regs. I want this to continue. We must just be discreet.'

'Damn, that was something. I am with you on this,' he said turning towards her.

She was already asleep.

The entire session was observed and recorded. A visibly turned-on observer thought to himself, *I am definitely going to enjoy having her, I better get the next phase of plan implemented. I think Wednesday is the day.*

At 5.00 am Hayes' alarm on her watch buzzed, instantly awake she sat upright in the bed and surveyed her surroundings. As she became more aware she looked over to her right to see O'Connell still fast asleep. She quietly slid off the bed and began collecting her discarded clothes, she dressed silently not wanting to wake her partner. By 5.15 am she was on the road on her way home.

Tuesday was spent fine tuning their plans for protecting the female residents of the 400 block of West 31st Street. O'Connell drove Hayes home; both having decided that it was better for them to sleep in their own beds that night but made no plans for their next encounter. O'Connell dropped her off and she confirmed that she would pick him up the next day at the same time.

Wednesday morning dawned to find the sidewalks covered with a light dusting of snow. O'Connell, true to his routine, left his apartment on schedule and headed north on Morgan Avenue on his way to The Coffee Shop. With his backpack secured across his left shoulder and carrying a cup of hot coffee in each hand, he began the short walk back down Morgan Avenue.

Well covered up to keep out the cold weather, a tall man wearing a balaclava and heavy coat walked towards him, nothing seemed out of the ordinary. The narrow sidewalk didn't lend itself to walking two abreast, both men move slightly to their respective rights to allow easy passing.

As they passed, the oncoming man swiveled and with the precision of someone trained in the martial arts, he chopped O'Connell using his right hand, connecting him on the right side of his neck. The force of the blow on his carotid artery staggered him, before he could take any evasive action he was struck with the same force across the left side of his neck, again hitting his carotid artery.

O'Connell fell forward dropping the two cups of coffee, he was unconscious by the time he hit the sidewalk. His assailant rolled him onto his back, reached under his overcoat and relieved him of his weapon, a Glock 19, his detective shield and his wallet. Hardly breaking stride, he stood up and continued at a normal pace towards Nassau Avenue where he turned right. Two minutes later he entered the subway and was out of sight.

Hayes arrived on time and double-parked outside O'Connell's apartment. She checked her watch and confirmed she was on time; he was never late. She put the car into Park, turned off the engine and walked over to the sidewalk. Looking to her left she saw a body lying in the snow, she knew instantly it was her partner.

Drawing her weapon, she ran towards the inert body, there was no one else in the immediate vicinity. As she got to the body she recognized her partner, she leaned down to check his pulse, he was alive. Her touch to his neck revived him, he sat up stared at her with a confused look on his face.

'What the hell happened, why am I lying in the snow, coffee everywhere? I remember walking down towards my place carrying the coffee, I passed someone coming the other way. I think he must have hit me, how the hell did I let that happen?'

'You've been mugged, is there anything missing? Your backpack seems intact.'

O'Connell stood up and brushed the snow off his coat. He instinctively felt for his weapon, it was missing, as was his detective's shield. He checked his wallet, also gone. 'Fuck it. They got my weapon and shield. FUCK!'

'Don't you think you should get to the hospital and get checked out; you may have concussion? I'll call the mugging in.'

'No, I am fine, just get me to the precinct asap.'

Chapter 20
Taunting

Hayes, concerned for her partner's welfare, made the trip to the precinct in record time, but not without a few near misses. O'Connell saw a side of her she had until now kept well hidden. He had heard all the curse words before but never out of her mouth. He was sure if someone had taken exception to being cursed at and wanted to confront her, she probably would have just shot them.

She parked her car right outside the front door and told O'Connell to get out and to report to Lieutenant Johnston immediately; he needed no second invitation. He barely greeted the desk sergeant on his way to the Lieutenant's office on the second floor. It was a little after 8.00 am and to no one's surprise, Johnston's office was unoccupied. It was way too early for the Lieutenant, so he decided to report the mugging to Garcia instead.

He trudged up the stairs to the third floor, his head pounding, reached for the door handle and tried to turn it, but it was still locked; he was the first one in. By the time he managed to get his key inserted into the lock, Hayes had joined him. He opened the door and the two of them stepped into the room activating the hidden cameras.

The man watched as his tablet came to life. 'So, you have made it into the precinct but you look very stressed out. I would love to be a fly on the wall when you have to explain to Internal Affairs (IA). Time for a bit of fun for all of us.'

'Jesus, Hayes, how could I be so unaware to have let this happen?' O'Connell sank into a chair and laid his pounding head into his hands.

'Stop beating yourself up, let me have a look at your neck. Sit down and lean forward.' He complied and she loosened his shirt and pulled back the collar. 'Shit, he must have hit you very hard, there is a colossal bruise on your neck right over where your carotid artery runs. Let me see the other side.'

She maneuvered around to his left side. "Damn, exactly the same as the right side. This guy clobbered you well and truly; he must have some martial arts expertise at the very least. I still think you should get checked out for concussion.'

'No, I am fine. I need to report the incident but neither Johnston nor Garcia are in yet.'

Hayes inspection of O'Connell's neck was interrupted by Garcia's arrival.

'Hey, you two, break it up. No fraternization between partners, you know the rules.'

'You got the wrong impression, Boss, O'Connell got mugged.'

'What the hell happened? How did you manage to get mugged? Were you robbed?'

'I got blindsided, the guy was walking towards me and just after we passed, he knocked me out with two blows to the neck. I don't remember anything until Hayes helped me up. Yes, I was robbed, my weapon, badge and wallet were taken.'

'Your badge and weapon, fuck, we need to get this reported to IA immediately. Let's go through to my office. They are going to shit themselves.'

'Boss, I need to get my credit cards canceled before this asshole starts cleaning me out.'

That's gonna have to wait. IA is a priority. If he starts using your badge and weapon and IA doesn't know you have lost it, your life won't be worth living. Come on, I will call them. Hayes, see if the Lieutenant has arrived yet and if so, bring him up to date.'

O'Connell followed Garcia to his office, he closed the door behind him.

'Did you get any kind of look at him, some description we can work with?'

'Not really, he was wrapped up against the cold, he was wearing some sort of face covering, a balaclava, I think. Tall, about my height, I think he was white.'

'All right let me call IA, take a seat.'

Garcia took a deep breath and called IA. The call was answered on the second ring.

'Good morning, I need to report a mugging and robbery of one of my detectives. Yes, that's right, a mugging, his name is Detective Ethan O'Connell, 35th precinct. His weapon, a Glock 19, his badge, and his personal wallet all taken.'

There was a slight pause, Garcia nodded and looked over at

O'Connell, 'Where and when was this?'

'This morning, around 7.40 am, outside my apartment in the 500 block of Morgan Avenue in Greenpoint, Brooklyn.'

Garcia relayed the information and then listened for a few seconds and then looked surprised, 'You can't be serious.' IA disconnected the call.

'What did they say, Boss?'

'They will send someone over to take your full statement and they will decide on whether to suspend you or not. In the meantime, I suggest you get those bruises on your neck checked. No no, this is not a suggestion, it's an order. It will be on record that you were attacked and not just bullshitting because you lost your weapon and badge. Go now, get Hayes to drive you.'

O'Connell met Hayes on the way back from Johnston's office, he had still not made it into work.

'Boss said you should drive me to the nearest hospital for me to be checked out.'

'I told you so, the Mount Sinai Beth Israel Hospital a mile away on East 34th Street is the closest. Let's go.'

For some reason, Hayes decided that this was a medical emergency. No sooner than they buckled up in her Mini she opened her window and placed her siren on the roof. She lit it up and floored the accelerator, they covered the distance to the hospital in less than two minutes. She pulled up just short of the entrance to the Emergency Rooms, put her "Police" parking tag on the dashboard and hustled O'Connell into the ER.

Walking up to reception she flashed her badge and addressed the receptionist.

'We have an emergency here,' pointing to O'Connell, 'Police officer attacked and suffering from possible concussion and other injuries, I need a doctor to do a thorough examination immediately.'

The nurse, overwhelmed by Hayes, just nodded, and said to follow her. She led them to the first available examination room, told them to wait. Two minutes later a young doctor appeared, he looked the two detectives up and down and sneeringly said, 'The nurse told me there was an emergency in here, I don't see anything of the sort.'

'Listen Doc, my partner here was assaulted. I need you to examine him for any lasting effects.'

'No, you listen to me. I am too busy for this, just because you are a cop doesn't mean I should drop everything on a whim.'

'You heard of the Zodiac Rapist? Yes? I see you have; well, this man was on the track of said person when he was assaulted. I see your wedding ring, you okay with that maniac walking the streets, maybe your wife is his next victim? So, do your damn job so we can get out of here and do ours.'

The doctor stared at Hayes, sheepishly shrugged his shoulders, and started his examination. Twenty minutes later he announced his findings.

'Detective O'Connell, you have two large bruises, one on each side of your neck, these mostly likely caused you to lose unconsciousness within seconds of being struck. You have contusions to your forehead because of landing face first onto the ground. You have a mild concussion, also probably from your head striking the ground. I see no reason for these issues to stop you from doing your job.'

'Thanks Doc, now just put that in writing and we will be out of your hair. Glad you are okay, Ethan, let's get back to the precinct and face the music.'

As they walked into the precinct the desk sergeant called out, 'O'Connell, the lieutenant wants you to report to his office right away. Shit, what's going on? The IA bastards came striding in here five minutes ago and went straight up to Johnston's office.'

Ignoring the sergeant, they headed for the stairs. Hayes continued up to the third floor leaving her partner to make his way to Johnston's office. Johnston saw him coming before he made it to his office, he got out of his chair and walked to the door, leaving his two IA visitors behind.

'Jesus, O'Connell, what happened? I have those two goons looking for blood,' he whispered.

'Got mugged, Boss, weapon, badge, and wallet taken. Here's the doctor's report,' he replied, handing Johnston the piece of paper.

Johnston escorted him into the office and introduced him to the IA officers, who immediately read him his rights, like he was being accused of something. Johnston got up and closed his office door.

Half an hour later, he emerged from the office and headed for the third floor where he found the rest of the team waiting anxiously.

'What happened?' asked Garcia.

'Chewed my balls off, suspended me with pay pending a fuller investigation. I had to make a detailed statement of what happened.'

'Shit, man, that's not right, it's not like you went looking to get mugged.'

'Damn right, Boss, but right now I need to make some phone calls and get my credit cards canceled.'

'Sure, you go ahead, if you need any help just shout.'

Fortunately, O'Connell kept an up-to-date list of his credit card details in his desk drawer. He had six active credit cards but normally only carried four in his wallet at any one time. He was not sure which four were in his wallet that morning, so he decided to suspend all six.

His first call was to American Express, who asked the standard questions ending with could he remember when he last used the card and what was purchased. He replied he hadn't used the card for at least three days and couldn't remember what he had paid with it.

'The most recent purchase was at 10.14 am this morning at Best Buy in Greenpoint. The item was a 65" 4K television set for $2,475.'

'That was not me, can you reverse the transaction?'

'I am sorry, Sir, but no. We can suspend the transaction and create a query with the store to see if the correct rules on ID and signature were followed.'

O'Connell thanked the lady and hung up the phone. 'Hayes, can you see if there is a patrol car in the vicinity of Best Buy, Greenpoint, tell them to look for someone carrying a 65" TV set. Thanks'

Next call was to Bank of America. Here he was told that a top end Citizen wristwatch had been purchased at 11.05 am that morning, value $1,650. The Kay Jewelers store was one block away from the Best Buy store. He passed the information onto Hayes.

The call to Capital One had a similar story, 11.55 am barely one block away from the jewelers a second 65" 4K TV set for $2,800 had been bought at Target. 'Why the hell would someone buy two large TV sets from two different stores within a couple of blocks of each other?' he said to himself.

The next three cards had not yet been used for any purchases. With all six cards now suspended, he turned to Hayes.

'Jesus, he wasted no time getting into my credit cards. But why two TV sets? They are difficult to transport, the watch I understand. Who is responding?'

'Car 628 is in the area they have just arrived at Best Buy. I have Jackson on the phone.'

'O'Connell here, what can you tell me?'

'We haven't got into the store yet, but we have apprehended a homeless man trying to sell a 65" TV. He says some guy came out of the store and handed him the TV and told him he should sell it for cash. The guy just gave him the TV and the receipt and left. The poor fool was trying to sell it for a hundred bucks.'

'Did he give you a description of the guy?'

'Yes, tall and white, nothing else. He said he just walked away in the direction that we think would have led him towards Kay Jewelers. What do you want us to do?'

'Take the TV and receipt back into the store and find out as much detail about the person who the bought the TV as you can. Hayes, can we get over to Kay Jewelers? Okay with you, Boss?'

Garcia nodded his agreement, 'Do you want a car to check up on the Target purchase?'

'Yes please, get them to call me when they have anything. Let's go Hayes.'

The two detectives got into Hayes' Mini and headed off to Kay's Jewelers in Greenpoint. Driving like she was on an emergency call; Hayes made the trip in record time. She pulled into a "No Parking" bay, stuck her permit on the dashboard and got out of the car. They walked into the store, and she flashed her badge at the same time introducing themselves.

'A few hours ago, you sold a Citizen watch to a customer who used a Bank of America card in the name of Ethan O'Connell. That was my card and it had been stolen.'

'I remember the sale. He came in, pointed at the watch he wanted, wasted no time. I rung the item up $1,650 and nice quick sale, he tapped his credit card against the reader, it was accepted, and he left.'

'What can you tell me about the man?'

'Tall, about your height, white. He was wearing sunglasses, had a heavy overcoat on and a scarf around his neck covering most of his lower face, he wore thin leather gloves. Didn't say much.'

'I see you have CCTV; we need to look at it urgently.''

'Do you have a warrant?'

'Oh my God, no we don't. I can go and get one and will be back within the hour. We will shut down your store and check each and every piece of merchandise for fingerprints, it will probably take about two days. We'll be back.'

'No, wait. I will take you to the CCTV console.'

'See, that was easy. Come on Ethan, let's see who this bastard is.'

The store clerk set up the CCTV to start from 9.00 am when the store opened. As soon as the store's doors were first opened you could see a tall man enter and walk up to the counter. No clear view of his face or features could be seen, he obviously knew exactly where the cameras were. The entire transaction took exactly 5 minutes from the time he walked in until the purchase was rung up. Keeping his head down the man left the store at 9.07 am, no clear views of his face could be seen.

'Shit, we can see nothing. The only thing we have is he looks about the same height as you, but then we knew that already. Let's see if they have anything from the sale at Target.'

'In less than two hours in a five-block radius, he makes three big ticket purchases running up around $8,000 for my account. He gives away one of the TVs, what's that about? Can we see who took the call to Target? The store is two blocks down.'

Hayes called the cops from car 628, 'Do you guys have anything for me?'

'Not much. We took the TV back into the store, and they credited O'Connell's credit card. I found the clerk who rang up the sale to try and get a description. He told me the guy was tall, well over 6', white, he was wearing sunglasses and a black scarf. Not much to go on. He paid for the TV with a credit card in the name of Ethan O'Connell by tapping the card on the reader, it was accepted, and he left.'

'Thanks, can you meet us at Target?'

'Car 638 is there already do you still need us?'

'No. Can you do a detailed report back at the precinct? Thanks'

Hayes drove up to the Target parking lot, spotted Car 638, and pulled up next to them.

'What do you have for us?' asked O'Connell.

'Guy walks into the store, picks a big screen TV, puts it on a flatbed cart, goes to the check out and pays for it with a Capital One credit card, he declined insurance and left. The clerk reckons he was over 6' and white. He had dark sunglasses and a scarf covering his mouth area.

We have one witness who said he saw the guy leave the store pushing the cart. He was spotted approaching two teenage black boys. There was some sort of conversation, the man left the TV with the two kids, and it looked like he gave them the sales slip. They apparently headed off in a northerly direction, I alerted any cars in the area to look out for them, nothing so far.'

'Shit, how far could they have got pushing a cart with a big screen TV on it. If they are found, apprehend them but don't arrest them; they didn't steal the TV, it was given to them. Thanks for your help, please make a statement when you get back to the precinct. Hayes, let's get back to the precinct. I am supposed to be suspended so I need to find out exactly what that means.'

Back at the precinct, Garcia, Shaw and Mills had discussed the morning's events. All agreed that there was very little one could do when unexpectedly attacked, they all had sympathy for O'Connell. He was lucky that IA had only suspended him as he was still on full pay; maybe they had a soul after all.

The two detectives arrived back in the situation room and O'Connell gave an update on their findings.

'Good news and bad news, I'm afraid. The TV bought at Best Buy was recovered by the cops in car 628, Jackson took it into the store and got a refund. No clear description of the perp, why would he buy a TV then give it to a homeless man to sell? Does he think he is fucking Robin Hood – rob the rich and give it to the poor?

The watch bought at Kay's is a lost cause, the perp's description was the same as the other one. Found nothing on the CCTV, he knew where the cameras were. That's $1,650 down the tubes.

The second TV he bought from Target he gave to two teenage kids. As of now they haven't been found so I am probably in for $2,800, total $4,850.'

Shaw: 'Do you reckon this was just a chance mugging, it does seem like you were targeted?'

'Why would I be targeted and then he buys stuff on my credit cards and gives it away? Doesn't make sense.'

Mills: 'Maybe you pissed someone off and they are getting back at you.'

Watching from afar the man smiled. 'Oh no, it's more than just someone being pissed off; it is so much more. Payback is coming, watch this space.'

Garcia: 'The bigger concern is your weapon, badge and ID has been stolen. I think the credit card purchases are just to throw us off the scent. I have had a word with the Lieutenant, we agree that you can still be a part of the ongoing investigation but will be office bound.

Without your credentials and weapon, you will not be allowed to go to any crime scenes or the like. Sorry, but at least it's better than you sitting at home pissed off.'

'Thanks Boss. I will spend my time tracking down the movements of the seven women we have identified as potential targets.'

The conversations were interrupted by the situation room telephone ringing. Garcia picked up the receiver and hit the speaker button, 'Garcia here, what can I do for you?'

'Detective Garcia, you sound a bit tense. A little birdie told me that you have had a bit of unexpected drama. I hear one of your detectives had the misfortune of losing his weapon, badge and wallet very clumsy of him.'

'Where did you get that information from? It's a load of bullshit'

'No it's not, and you know it. It would be really embarrassing to the department if his weapon, a Glock 19 I believe, were used in some criminal activity. I will keep in touch from time to time, don't bother trying to trace the call, it's a burner. Have a good day.'

Garcia slammed down the phone and cursed loudly, 'Fucking bastard! He is taunting us. How the hell did he know about the mugging?'

'Maybe he is the one who mugged O'Connell.' said Hayes.

'That would make sense, otherwise we have a huge leak in the precinct. Just what we need - someone running off at the mouth.'

Chapter 21
Internal Affairs

Thursday morning Ethan O'Connell was called to report to 1PP (One Police Plaza) to answer more questions about the loss of his weapon and detective's shield. Having driven into work that morning, he decided that due to parking issues, it would be easier to take a cab to 1PP. The six-mile trip to Lower Manhattan took him almost half an hour.

His appointment with Internal Affairs was set at 10.30 am on the sixth floor of 1PP. It was not a welcoming sight to any New York cop. IA had a reputation of going after cops with relish, almost getting a hard on if they could "convict" one of their own. He reported to reception, signed in and was told to take a seat, it was 10.25 am.

He was made to wait until 10.55 am when a female officer approached where he was sitting and asked him to follow her. She led him down a passage to the far north side of the building. She knocked on the door and without waiting for an answer, opened it and indicated O'Connell should enter.

He walked into the room where he was faced by two men and one woman, all seated behind a large conference room desk. He was shown to the single seat facing his "interrogators" and told to sit. The officer seated in the middle spoke first.

'I am Captain Sparks, on my left is Captain Jacobs and on the right is Lieutenant Bergman. You are here today to answer questions on what occurred yesterday, January 26th, that led to you losing possession of your service weapon, a Glock 19, your detective's shield and your personal identification documents.

Lieutenant Bergman is your Union Representative and legal counsel. She will ensure that any questions we ask you will be solely focused on the incident in question. If, at any stage, she feels we are overstepping any boundaries she may terminate the interview. Do you understand?'

'Yes Sir, I do.'

'Okay let us begin. Tell us in your own words exactly what occurred.'

O'Connell thought to himself, *'I have already detailed this in the first interview and supplied a written statement, what is the purpose of doing this again? Are they trying to see if my story will change? Fuck it, here goes.'*

'I share a ride into the precinct with Detective June Hayes, we alternate. Yesterday was her turn to drive. I had walked up to The Coffee Shop on Nassau Avenue, a three-minute walk, there I picked up two coffees and began the return trip back to my apartment on Morgan Avenue.'

'Was this a regular occurrence or just for this day?' asked Captain Sparks.

'It was a regular thing, every time she drove, I supplied the coffee.'

'So, you are a creature of habit then?'

'Yes Sir.'

'Presumably if someone was watching you as a potential victim, they knew exactly what your routine is?'

'Yes Sir, I suppose so.'

'Alright, continue.'

'I was carrying the two cups of coffee, one in each hand and was walking south on Morgan. The sidewalk is quite narrow, not enough room for two people walking side by side, particularly when there is snow on the ground. Because of the snow I was looking down at the ground as I didn't want to slip and fall. I noticed a man walking towards me, tall, white, dressed to keep out the cold. He had on a type of balaclava and a scarf around his neck.

I moved to the right of the sidewalk as I saw it and he did the same from his side. As we passed, I felt a blow to the right of my neck. Before I could react, he struck me on the left side of my neck. Both blows were expertly placed right across my carotid arteries.

I don't remember anything else until Detective Hayes rolled me over onto my back. I must have fallen face first into the sidewalk, probably unconscious before I hit the ground.'

'You say you were carrying coffee cups in both hands. Wouldn't that make you vulnerable to an attack?'

'Yes, it would and in this case it did. The attack was so unexpected that I did not have a chance to defend myself.'

'So, Detective Hayes brought you around, then what did you do?'

'I stood up and started to brush off the snow. I felt for my weapon, found it missing, I then checked for my shield and my wallet both were gone. I realized I had been mugged and told Hayes we should get to the precinct asap to report the incident to my Lieutenant.'

'You said it was Hayes who assisted you, did she see anything?'

'No Sir.'

'How did she find you, what made her come to your aid? Don't you find that a bit suspicious?'

'Hayes is a stickler for being on time. When I wasn't waiting for her, she got out of her car to go and knock on my apartment door. Before she got there, she saw me lying on the ground and came to see if I was alive.'

'What, if anything, did Hayes witness?'

'She said she never saw the actual incident; my attacker was nowhere to be seen.'

'Okay, so let's look at the timeline of the incident. As you agree that you are a creature of habit, you must have a very good idea about what time the incident occurred.'

'I left my apartment at exactly 7.30 am, the walk to the Coffee Shop takes me around 3 minutes, so I estimate I arrived there at approximately 7.33 am. My coffee is a standing order so there was no wait time. I paid the barista and started the return journey immediately. Normally Hayes arrives at between 7.35 am and 7.40 am.

My return trip from the Coffee Shop puts me in front of my apartment at about 7.36 am. Anyone following my routine would be aware of that timeline.'

'So, one would think that this was not a crime of opportunity but one that was meticulously planned. Do you agree?'

'It would appear so.'

'Your assailant would have to have known you were a cop and carrying your weapon and credentials. For him to assail you, remove your weapon, credentials and wallet and disappear within seconds, doesn't this seem strange to you? How far away from the corner of Morgan and Nassau were you attacked?'

'I was maybe fifty to one hundred feet from the corner.'

' In the space of probably less than one minute, you were knocked unconscious, robbed, found by your partner and your assailant had disappeared. Are you sure there is nothing you want to change about your description of events?'

'No Sir, to the best that I can recall, it happened as I have stated.'

'Once Hayes had got you to your feet and realized what had happened, did you make any effort to track down your assailant?'

'No Sir. He had to have got away to the north towards Nassau. There was no sign of him, my first concern was to get back to the precinct to report the incident to my Lieutenant.'

'What was his reaction?'

'He had not arrived at the precinct yet, so I went up to our incident room to report it to Detective Garcia. He had not arrived either so Hayes made a cursory examination of my neck. Detective Garcia arrived while this was in progress and he insisted I be taken to the nearest hospital to be examined for concussion and any other possible injuries.'

'I see the doctor's report confirming this. Do you have anything else to add to your testimony before we end this interview?'

'No Sir.'

'Okay can you step outside the room while I confer with Captain Jacobs,

Less than five minutes later O'Connell was called back into the room by Lieutenant Bergman, she was smiling.

Captain Sparks with no preamble addressed him. We have decided to lift your suspension but you will be confined to the precinct until further notice. Thank you for your cooperation; you are free to leave.'

O'Connell stood up, turned around and without saying a word left the room. He took the elevator from the sixth floor down to the ground level and exited the building where he took his first breath since leaving the interview room. Relieved, he looked for a cab, unaware he was being observed from across Madison Street.

The man smiled to himself, O'Connell had a relieved look on his face, *'Good, it looks like he hasn't been suspended it; that would've interfered with my plans.'*

O'Connell hailed a cab and was back at the 35th just in time for lunch. He stopped at the food vendor truck stationed just before the corner of 35th Street and 9th Avenue. He ordered five bagels with cream cheese and jelly, four coffees and one orange juice.

Loaded with his purchases he made the short walk back to the precinct. He walked past the desk sergeant, ignoring his question about "what happened with IA" and headed up to the third floor. His timing was perfect as his four colleagues were making plans for lunch.

'Hey O'Connell, you're back, how did it go? You brought food for us. You are the man,' exclaimed Shaw.

'Went well, I am no longer suspended but I've gotta ride a desk until further notice. I have bagels and coffee, and a juice for you Mills'

The activity was monitored on the man's tablet. 'As I thought. He is no longer suspended, just what I needed. I now know where he will be at all times giving me the time I need to study his voice and mannerisms. After all, I need to be perfect if I'm going to implement my plan.'

'Normal procedure when confined to desk duty is that you will only get a new set of credentials when you have served your time, same goes for a new weapon. Did they say how long you've got?' asked Garcia.

'No Boss, I hope it's not too long.'

Their conversations were interrupted by the office phone ringing, Mills picked up the receiver and hit the speaker button, '35th precinct Mills speaking.'

'Ah by the sound of it you must be Detective Linda Mills; you don't sound like Detective June Hayes.'

'Who are you and what do you want?' barked Mills.

'I have reason to believe that Detective Ethan O'Connell has been cleared of all wrong-doing regarding his carelessness of losing his gun and his credentials.'

Garcia strode over to the phone and shouted directly into the speaker. 'Who the fuck are you and where did you get this information?'

'Come on Mickey, don't tell me you have forgotten my voice already. As for the information, my little bird let me know the minute it happened. Ethan, sorry to hear you will be riding a desk for the foreseeable future, it will do you good, make you more careful in future. Sorry, but I gotta go, lots of things to do. Bye.'

Before Garcia could react, the line went dead. 'I want that bastard! I will cut his balls off. How the fuck does he know what has happened so quickly? Somebody in the department is feeding him information, we have to find that piece of shit. This bastard seems to know our every move. O'Connell, since you are desk-bound, I am tasking you to track down this mole and put a stop to the leaks.'

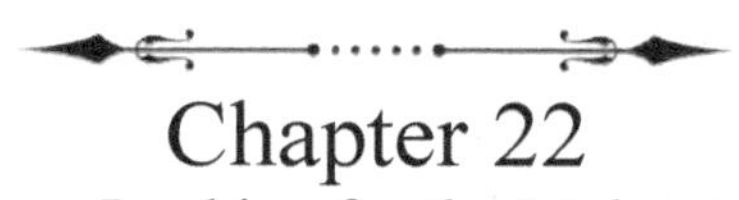

Chapter 22
Looking for the Mole

Friday morning, January 28, Hayes arrived outside O'Connell's apartment at exactly 7.38 am, he was waiting as usual with two cups of coffee. A light snow was falling and the morning temperature was hovering around 32°. She popped the door open, O'Connell got in and put the two coffees in their designated cup holders.

'Morning June, on time as usual.'

'You know me Ethan, I hate to be late. How are you doing today? Looking forward to a day of riding the desk?' she laughed.

'I am fine, not too excited about the desk work but I think I got off lightly, they could have suspended me without pay. This feeling that we have a mole in the precinct has got me bothered, I can't see it.'

'Yeah, I think it is unlikely but he is getting his information very quickly, someone must be blabbing. Good luck with the search.'

'The thing that bothers me is that this asshole seems to have it in for me. I would love to know what I have done to him to piss him off. I wonder if he is also the mugger.'

'I am sure you are onto something; he does seem to direct his insults toward you. He obviously would have known about your attack if he was the mugger, he may have worked out that IA would call you in. I wonder if he followed you to 1PP, and as you returned to the precinct, he would have worked out you were probably only suspended not terminated.'

'But it still doesn't account for him knowing everything else that is going on. We need to nail this piece of shit and put him out of business.'

They arrived at the precinct to find Garcia already present. Mills and Shaw arrived separately, five minutes apart. Once all were present Garcia called a meeting.

'Okay team, today we hit the plans for April 1. I want a detailed hour by hour of what we need to cover for all the potential apartments. We need to get the plan approved by the Lieutenant, so as to be sure that there will be men and funds available for this task. The other thing is we need to keep this confidential, which goes without saying, but we don't want to warn this bastard.'

Watching from afar, the man just chuckled. He concentrated his observations on O'Connell, watching his every move, each nuance, the way he continually stretched his fingers, his posture and the balance and tone of his voice.

O'Connell settled down to gather his thoughts. He figured the best way to start the process would be to chronologically list the times that the rapist had contacted the precinct with information that only a cop would have privy to. He needed to find a connection to each instance.

"After each of the five rapes the call to the police came via an anonymous phone call. It was possible, in fact most likely, from the rapist himself, but he did not identify himself as such. All of the calls came in to the 35th precinct desk sergeant not to the situation room.

The telephone call about the murder of Mr. and Mrs. Marx came in via a 911 call. The caller identified themselves as a "concerned neighbor". The Zodiac Rapist did not claim the murders directly after they occurred.

The first call we received directly to our phones was on the day of the Mayor's disastrous press conference. Not only did he claim to be the Zodiac Rapist but he also claimed an involvement in the Marx murders. He taunted Garcia and asked how I was coping, hinting that the murders "were a bit close to home". A definite reference to their similarity to the murders of my folks.

He also referred to our timeline board, how did he know about that? Had he seen the actual white board? If he had, was he in the situation room as a cop? The room is always locked when none of us are present, cleaners only come in during normal hours. If he isn't a cop, maybe he was just guessing we had a timeline board, seen how we do it from a TV show.

He said our timeline board indicated that we had worked out his rape cycle and maybe he would have to change it to make it a bit more interesting. How would he know this unless he had seen the white board? And what did he mean by changing it up?

So many questions, but it keeps coming back to the link between the rapes and the murders. He said he staged the Marx murders for my benefit, why would he do that? He must know me or at least of me, he knew about the murder of my folks, but that was ten years ago so why now? Why did he murder the Marx's on the exact tenth year anniversary of my folks' murder? How did he know I would be transferred to the 35th on the same day? Nobody other than a handful of people knew exactly when I was joining the 35th. None of this makes any sense unless he is a cop or has a direct line to a cop.' Ethan pinched the bridge of his nose, trying to collect his thoughts. The others didn't want to interrupt his train of thought.

Then there is the mugging; he knew of my exact movements. He knew I had to report to IA and was then subsequently suspended. It's almost like he knows our every move. Jesus, maybe he has the office bugged, that's got to be it!"

O'Connell's first thought was to check the phones. He picked up the receiver on his phone and unscrewed the mouthpiece, there was nothing out of the ordinary. Undeterred he got up from his desk and walked over towards the office phone.

Putting his finger up to his lips he indicated for the others to remain silent. He walked up to the phone and unscrewed the mouthpiece, directly underneath was an electronic device. Never having seen an actual bugging device before, he could only surmise this was one. Without saying a word, he screwed the mouthpiece back together and replaced the receiver.

He signaled for his colleagues to follow him, the five of them left the office.

Observing from afar the man chuckled. They have found one of the bugs. It will be interesting to watch what they do next. I must be ready to deactivate the cameras if they call in their technical people.

With all of the detectives out of the office and hopefully out of range of the telephone bug, O'Connell spoke softly.

'I think I have found a bug, probably a listening device on the office phone, there may be others. I think this is how the perp has been following our progress. What do you reckon, Boss?'

'Good catch. There has to be something. I think we should get the techies in to do a sweep and find if there are more. In the meantime, leave everything as is, we don't want him to know we are onto him. Just be careful what we talk about, maybe we can send him false information to mislead him. I will put in a call and let's get this sorted.'

O'Connell: 'Boss, if it is a listening device then he knows we have plans for April 1. We are going to have to change them, maybe he already has changed his plans.'

Garcia: 'Let's wait and see if it is a listening device before we make any decisions. We can relocate to the interview room if necessary.'

Mills: 'If he has bugged the phones then it raises a number of issues. Firstly, how the hell did he get access to our office? He talked about our timeline and the whiteboard; if he planted the bugs then he saw the evidence we have collected. Our plans for April 1 are screwed.'

Garcia: 'You are right Mills, but let's wait for the techies', Garcia pulled his cell out of his pocket.

Garcia locked the door to the situation room and relocated the team to interview room #1. He put in a call to the technical office and was told two experts would be on their way immediately. He warned the desk sergeant of their impending arrival and instructed him to send them to the interview room.

Right on cue, the two techies arrived at the 35th, Garcia was informed and he and the team escorted them up to the third floor. He unlocked the door and ushered everyone into the room, not a word was spoken but the cameras were instantly activated.

Watching from his apartment the man worked out what was happening. He watched the proceedings with interest, ready to deactivate the cameras the second there was any chance of them being detected.

Having briefed the techies, they began checking all of the telephones. In addition to the one in the general office, a bug was also found in Garcia's office. The two bugs were isolated by covering them with a signal blocking device. The next step would be to scan the rest of the two rooms for any other recording or transmitting devices.

'The telephone bugs are active all the time, not just when the phone is in use. It is hard to say for sure but I think that any normal conversation in the two rooms will be picked up and transmitted.'

The minute he saw that the rooms were going to be scanned, he deactivated the cameras. No signal either in or out so the cameras would now be undetectable by scanning. There was always the possibility that they would be found by careful examination. He planned to reactivate them in two hours.

The detectives watched as the technical duo went about their scanning. All the furniture, desks, chairs were scanned but no additional bugs were found. Next the walls, pictures, posters and light fittings were examined, nothing was detected.

Satisfied that other than the two telephone bugs the room was clear, the lead technician turned to Garcia.

'We are done here, Detective, what do you want us to do about the two bugs we found? We can try and track where the signals are being sent, that process is likely to warn the persons bugging the place that we are onto them.'

'No. I think we should leave them in place. If we remove them then he will know we are onto him and he may just disappear. This way we can send him misinformation which may help in apprehending him. We will just have to be very careful with what we say.'

'Sure thing, I will remove the blockers and we will be on our way. We hope you catch this bastard soon.'

The team got back to work, conscious of the bugs, they tried their best to carry on as normal. Anything that needed discussing on their April 1 plans was done by writing the questions on a sheet of paper and passing that to whoever needed to provide an answer. When a person-to-person discussion was needed, they adjourned to one of the interview rooms.

At 3.30 pm, unknown to anyone in the room, the cameras were reactivated. The man, unsure whether they had been discovered or not, was wary. His observation told him that the detectives were very conscious of what they were discussing, concerned about the telephone bugs. The irony of the situation was that the signals from the bugs were actually going nowhere. He was confident that the cameras had not been discovered.

By 5.00 pm the tension had got to the team, the constant concern that the bugs were recording everything they said was taking its toll.

Shaw: 'Come on guys, it is time to knock off for the day, and for that matter the whole fucking week. I don't know about the rest of you but I need a drink. What do you say?'

Mills: 'Count me in.' She stood up and grabbed her purse, ready to leave.

Garcia: 'I'll join you for a couple.'

Hayes: 'I'm driving today and need to get home. But O'Connell, if you want to go, I can wait for you.'

O'Connell: 'No, I am ready to head home but thanks for the offer.'

The drive back to O'Connell's apartment was a somber one. Both were deflated by the possibility that their plans for April 1 were likely compromised. Hayes pulled up in front of the O'Connell's apartment and turned towards him.

'Do you feel like some company?'

'Not tonight June, I am wiped out. The frustration is getting to me.' He put his head against the headrest, blankly staring out of the windscreen.

'Okay, maybe some time over the weekend then?' she asked, hopefully.

'I have to take care of something that has been bothering me for a while now. My folks left a large box of various correspondence when they died. I need to finally go through it, I am hoping there is something in there that may give me an indication why this bastard is targeting me.

I don't know where I have wronged him in some way, maybe my folks had a run in with him. There has to be something.'

'If you need any help, give me a call, I am not busy at all.'

'Sure thing, June, you take care.' He leaned over and pecked her on the cheek and then got out of the car.

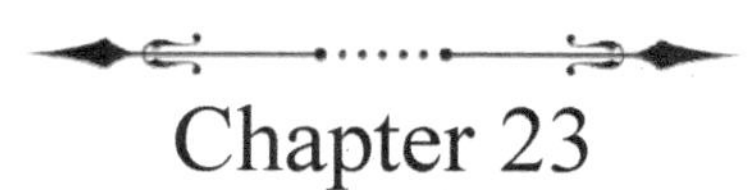

Chapter 23
Looking for Clues in the Past

June having left, Ethan decided on an early night. The past week had been very stressful and he felt the need to switch off. There were so many things bothering him, the mugging, the taunting by the rapist but mostly the nagging question: *did this person murder his parents?* There had to be a reason why someone whom he did not know would go to so much trouble to replicate a ten-year old murder.

In an apartment across town, the man could sense the frustration and confusion that his victim was suffering. 'Don't worry… it will be over soon.'

Ethan woke early on Saturday morning; he had not slept well. The recurring dream of discovering his parents murdered had turned into a nightmare where the two murders had blended into one. He decided a walk to The Coffee Shop for breakfast would be in order.

Returning from breakfast he immediately went down into the basement to begin a task he had put off for over ten years. Stored in the far corner were two large plastic containers, both almost full of all the personal correspondence belonging to his late parents.

A third container held photo albums starting in 1991 right through to 2010; a meticulously captioned pictorial view of their life. It also contained envelopes filled with photos and negatives, all filed by month. It was labeled 2011; they had not yet assembled those into an album. There were also two cameras, one with film and the other digital. He decided that he would search through all of these at a later date.

He picked up the first of the plastic containers and carried it over to the basement kitchen and set it down on the table. He lifted the lid and looked into the container. Meticulously filed in date sequence were large brown envelopes, they were clearly marked by month from August 1995 right through to December 2003. His father had been an accountant and his mother a teacher; either one of them could have set up this filing system as they were both meticulously organized.

With no idea of what he was looking for, he decided to go through each of the envelopes and see if there was anything that could hint at a reason someone could have held a grudge against him or his parents.

August 1995 coincided with the family's return to the USA from Ireland. In what was to be a pattern throughout the monthly files, every single bit of correspondence, however insignificant, would be filed. Any receipt paid or monies received was documented. Ethan's school registration, deposits paid for lights, water and telephone. A copy of the letter Dennis sent out to his old clients and a list of their names and addresses.

It was a tedious process, his parents saved everything, it gave a paper trail of their lives. The only really interesting finds were his school reports. If there was one consistent thing about Ethan, it was his ability to regularly get glowing reports from his school teachers. Clippings documenting his sporting achievements appeared often, either clippings from a school magazine or in two cases, an article from a local newspaper.

It took him an hour and a half to work his way through the last five months of 1995. Based on the time it was taking, he figured it would take him more than the whole weekend to get through both boxes if he was to check every envelope and every document. He was going to need some help.

June picked up the call on the second ring. 'Ethan, I'm surprised you called, how are you doing?'

'I can't believe my folks, they kept and filed everything. If the car got an oil change – filed, a plumber fixed a faucet and provided an invoice – filed. I know you said to call if I needed help, so if that offer still stands, I need help.'

'Sure thing, I am on my way over.'

'Bring your toothbrush if you have no other plans.'

'What about my PJ's?' she teased.

'You won't need them. I'll leave the front door unlocked, I am in the basement so let yourself in.'

Not only will I watch him searching for something that won't tie him to me but I'll get to watch him and the delicious June Hayes perform. I am going to enjoy her very soon.

June arrived armed with two subs and two coffees from the local deli. She was dressed in black tights, with a low-cut T-shirt and her hair untied. This was the first time Ethan had seen her dressed outside of her normal work clothes.

'Wow, you look good! A sight for sore eyes, dressed like that and carrying food and coffee. What more for a guy ask for? Thanks for coming over, but you might regret your offer once you see all the stuff we have to go through.'

'Anytime! I'm really glad you called; we have had very little alone time with everything happening on the case. Exactly what are we looking for here?' she put the coffees and sandwiches down on the nearest table and walked over to the open tote, filled with envelopes.

'I am looking for anything that might lead to finding out who it is that seems to have it in for me or my family. Maybe my folks had a run in with someone who has now exacted their revenge and murdered them. There has to be some connection to their murder and me being targeted. I don't know if we will find anything but I have to look.'

'Let's eat first and then I will help you,' Ethan nodded and walked to the table to grab a coffee and a sandwich.

For the next ten minutes there was little conversation as they consumed their Italian subs and drank coffee. Ethan was first to finish.

'This container has stuff filed from August 1995, which is around the time we returned from Ireland, right through to December 2003.'

'I didn't know you lived in Ireland, were you born there?'

'No, we moved there when I was a couple of weeks or months old and returned when I was five. I never knew why we did that; I should have asked my folks.'

'I am sure they had a good reason, where do you want me to start?'

'Take that other container; it's got documents filed from January 2003 up until November 2010. There are a whole bunch of loose documents which are probably for December 2010 which they never had a chance to file.'

By 5.30 pm Ethan had got through December 2000 and June had managed March 2006. Apart from a few letters between Dennis and clients of his, where strong words had been exchanged, they had found nothing that could be construed as a threat.

'I don't know about you but I have had enough for one day. What do you say we call it a day?' June suggested, stretching her neck.

'I agree, let's go out and have a couple of beers. We can walk over to Goldie's Bar over on Nassau Avenue, it is as close to being my local as any other around here,' Ethan suggested.

'It's your stomping ground. As long as I don't have to drive, I am good.'

Dressed against the cold weather, the two of them made the short walk to Goldie's. 6.00 pm on a Saturday and the place was pretty much full. Ethan showed June to a booth near the jukebox while he made his way to the bar. Carrying two Goldie's Lager drafts he wormed his way through the crowd and joined June.

'I hope you like this beer, it's a bit different. Anyway, cheers! Let's hope we find the link that leads us to this bastard,' he raised a glass and she clinked hers against his.

'Let's hope so. Going through your folks' filing, apart from every invoice, letter and warranty, there sure is a lot of stuff about you and your achievements. They sure were proud of you, you must miss them terribly.'

'Yes, to both of those. We never did find out why they were murdered and by whom. It was so senseless. I doubt our rapist/killer has anything to do with it, which makes it so weird why he should have committed the Marx murders.

You're finding out all about me, thanks to my mother keeping everything she could lay her hands on, but I know nothing about you, so come on. Spill the beans.' He took a swig of his beer, his eyes never leaving her face.

'Oh, my growing up was so boring compared to yours.'

'No excuses, let's have it.'

'I was born and grew up in Naperville, Illinois. I was the second of three kids. We were a typical Midwest middle-class family. My dad was an insurance agent and my mom was a dental nurse. My younger sister Meredith, is a year younger than me and is the brains of the group. She is now an attorney with a large well-known Chicago law firm.

My older brother, Ben, who was two years older than me, was killed in a carjacking, on his way to a White Sox game. They never caught the culprits, he was twenty-one years old. I left Naperville six months after that and joined the New York Police Academy.'

'I am sorry for your loss. It seems like we both joined the force after a devastating family loss.'

'Why didn't you finish your degree? Are you ever going to?'

'I couldn't think of anything other than finding out who murdered my folks. It seemed so insignificant going back to university when their killer was walking free. I might finish the degree one day but right now I need to take care of this fucking Zodiac Rapist.

I want this done for a number of reasons; one of the most important is getting you back to the 94th so as we can be together without breaking any regulations,' June smiled at his admission.

'You say the sweetest things. Let's get something to eat and a bottle of wine. After that I'll take you back to your place and remind you what you can look forward to on a regular basis when I am back at the 94th,' she winked suggestively and he laughed.

Back at the apartment the two of them headed straight up the stairs and into the bedroom. Within minutes they were naked. Now more relaxed with each other, their lovemaking was slow and sensual.

That's right, Ethan, take your time and savor her, enjoy it while you can. It won't be for much longer though, but don't worry I will take good care of her. She won't miss you when you are gone.

The following morning Ethan woke up first, it was almost 8.00 am. The Coffee Shop opened at eight on Sundays; coffee, Danish pastries and a scrambled egg and chives roll would really hit the spot. He dressed quietly so as not to disturb June, but his movement activated the bedroom cameras.

Returning armed with breakfast, he opened the front door and headed straight up the stairs, he was halted by a voice from the living room.

'Hey there, Sailor, I'm in here. That better be breakfast or I will be complaining to management.' June teased.

'Don't be cheeky. Let's eat, we still have a pile of stuff to get through.' He walked through to the kitchen and she followed him. She wrapped her arms around his waist from behind as he plated up their food.

With breakfast over, they made their way down to the basement to continue the job of trolling through the O'Connell's life history. It was much of the same as the previous day until June found a sealed brown envelope with the words "For Ethan's Eyes only". She passed it over to him. 'Have you seen this?'

Ethan looked at the envelope and turned it around to look at the back. 'No, I haven't, let's see what we have here.' He carefully opened envelope and took out two typed sheets of paper. He started to read the top page, he went white and sank down into a chair. 'Oh my God. I don't believe this.'

'What is it, Ethan?' she sat down beside him.

'It's from my folks addressed to me, listen to this.'

Dearest Ethan, if you are reading this letter then we are probably dead. It is with a heavy heart I am writing this. We had planned to talk to you face to face many times over the years. Your father had said it would be best to wait until you were in a position to understand why we did what we did. Our plan was to tell you on January 1, 2012 by which time your university would be almost complete.

We are not your biological parents. You were adopted at birth. Your Dad and I couldn't have children, we tried everything possible without any luck. When we admitted failure, we tried the adoption route. The authorities deemed us unsuitable to adopt, for reasons that are insignificant, so we took the risk of doing so out of the normal process.

While we acknowledge that what we did was completely illegal and could have landed us in prison, I was desperate. Your father found a contact that assured us that they could provide us with a healthy baby. The baby's biological parents were unable to provide for their upcoming child and were prepared to come to some arrangement for us to "adopt" you.

When we received the call that the baby was due within a few hours, we drove to an address in Prospect Heights, Brooklyn. We were met there by a "Baby Broker". Your father paid the man a fee and we left with you. We did not meet anyone else connected to your birth.

Your birth was registered through all the normal legal channels. To avoid anyone becoming suspicious about your sudden appearance, we left for Ireland when you were just a month old. By the time we returned home, you were five and we felt safe that there would be no connection to your actual birth.

We realize that this will come as a shock but please believe us that we have always had your very best interests at heart. We both love you more than you could ever know. We are both deeply sorry to have not had the opportunity to talk to you directly about this situation.

I realize you may want to try and track down your biological parents. Dad revisited the place where you were given to us to see if we could find out anything about your parents. He was there in May of 1999 just before your eighteenth birthday. He found the building had been demolished and small single storey houses had been built in its place. He found no trace of the previous owners. You may have more success, the address is 81 Prospect Place, Prospect Heights in

Brooklyn.
We so very sorry, please forgive us.
We love you very much.
Mom and Dad.

'Oh my God, Ethan, how terrible. From everything I have seen in these documents you were the center of their universe,' June put her hand over his.

'I know, but this comes as a shock. For all of my life they have been the one constant I could hold onto. I am lost for words,' Ethan sat back in the chair and stared at the ceiling. Everything he thought he knew was suddenly wrong.

'This may be a shot in the dark but do you think the rapist may have found out about you and this is his way of extracting revenge?'

'A bit of a long shot indeed, how would anyone else know? Also, revenge for what?'

'Unless he was in some way connected to the whole adoption situation. Maybe there is more to the adoption than what your parents have said.'

Clever girl, June, you hit the nail on the head. He thinks finding out he was adopted was a shock; he ain't seen nothing yet. The fun has only just started.

'They said they were going to talk to me about all of this on January 1, 2012. That's two days after they were killed. Just two fucking days and I could have told them I don't care that I was adopted. They were my Mom and Dad, and I want them to know that. What stress and tension they must have been under, just two days before, two days and I could have told them how much I loved them.'

'Do you think there is any significance in them being killed on that particular day? Did somebody connected with the adoption set up their murder?' June suggested.

'I just don't know. I need some time to process this.'

Chapter 24
June 15, 1990

Dennis O'Connell's deep sleep was interrupted by the jangling sound of an incoming phone call. He switched on the bedside lamp and checked his watch: 3.45 am. Instantly awake he picked up the phone and answered, 'O'Connell here.'

The voice on the other end simply said, 'It's almost time, you know the address, bring the cash as agreed. You have about an hour to get here.' The caller waited for O'Connell's confirmation before ending the call.

Dennis ended the call and turned to his wife, Mary, who was now fully awake. 'It is time, we must hurry.'

The couple got out of bed, dressing hurriedly. They made their way to the front door, picking up a briefcase and a small prepacked suitcase on the way out. They had been waiting for this call, knowing that it could have come at any time. It was almost 4.00 am by the time they exited the building and got in their car. Even at this time of the morning, New York was not totally asleep and the journey would take them fifty five minutes.

Leaving their Greenpoint home, they traveled south and picked up the 278 Brooklyn Queens Expressway. Taking the exit at Tillary Street they entered downtown Brooklyn. Following Flatbush Avenue Extension in a southerly direction, they arrived at their destination, a small nondescript building in Prospect Heights.

Dennis checked his car's GPS to confirm he had the correct address, and instructed Mary to wait in the car. He would take care of the transaction himself. He picked up the briefcase and small suitcase and alighted the vehicle, walked up to the front door of the building and knocked loudly. The door opened immediately.

'O'Connell?' Dennis nodded. 'Follow me.'

As he followed the man, Dennis tried to assess his guide. About five foot six inches, very dark complexion, possibly Middle Eastern or Italian. His left arm was covered in tattoos as was the back of his neck. He noticed a bulge in the middle rear of his waistband, covered by his over-hanging shirt. Given the shape, Dennis surmised it was a gun, he would have to be careful of this one. He just hoped that he wasn't walking into a trap.

He followed the man down a long corridor. Just before the end of the passage, the man stopped and knocked on the door on the right. A voice was heard instructing him to enter, he opened the door and stepped back indicating that Dennis should enter first, which he did. The room was lit by a dim single light bulb hanging from the ceiling. The furniture consisted of a single wooden table, no chairs or cupboards. The only other occupant was a short stocky man who looked like he could be a relative of the one who had escorted him to the room.

'Do you have the money?' he asked in a thick accent.

'Yes, as agreed, $100,000 in used notes. Where is the child?' Dennis asked, eager to get this over with.

'All in good time, my friend. Pass me the briefcase I need to check the amount.'

'I want to see the child first.' Dennis insisted.

'That is not an option. You will be given the child as soon as I verify the amount. You will dress the child and then leave the building immediately. What we are doing here is not legal, the sooner we all disappear, the better. Give me the briefcase.'

Dennis handed over the briefcase, worried that the whole thing was one big con. He and Mary had tried everything to have a child of their own, to no avail. The legal process to adopt was slow and fraught with red tape and petty bureaucracy. They understood the risk they were taking but decided it would be worth it if they succeeded. Everything had been done through intermediaries so no face-to-face contact had been made. The price was $100,000 in cash, used $100 bills.

Dennis' thoughts were interrupted when the door opened behind him. A man dressed in a white doctor's coat entered carrying a baby wrapped in a white birthing blanket. He looked like he could be a brother to the two other men he had met. Maybe it was a family business.

'Your son is healthy and has no obvious defects, all the toes and fingers are present. I suggest you dress him and leave this building as soon as possible. I am sure your wife has all the necessary feeding instructions. My colleague has an official New York State birth certificate. All you need to do is fill in the parents' names and that of the child. This is the last time we will be in contact. Good luck and goodbye.'

The doctor handed Dennis the baby, turned around and left the room. His colleague, satisfied that the money was correct, handed Dennis a birth certificate. Picking up the briefcase he left the room only to be replaced by the man who had initially answered the door.

Dennis laid the baby on the table and unwrapped the birthing blanket. Still showing traces of blood, the baby freed from the restraints of the birthing blanket kicked his legs vigorously. Dennis stared at his new son unable to move, he was struck by the innocent beauty of the baby boy. Brought back to reality by the gruff voice of the man watching him, he began to dress the baby as carefully as he could. It was his first time dressing a newborn and he wanted to do it properly.

He picked up the baby and turned to leave the room. His guard followed him back down the long passage. When they reached the door, he paused while the door was unlocked and opened. The man stepped aside to allow Dennis to exit, the door was immediately closed behind him and Dennis heard the bolt slide back into place. Not a word had been spoken between them.

Dennis walked around to the passenger side of his car and opened the rear door. Mary, who had been waiting nervously, had already moved in to the back seat. Dennis passed the baby to her and closed the car door. He hurried around to the driver's side, got in and started the car. He glanced at his watch, it was 05.01 am, June 15, 1990. The whole saga has taken one hour and sixteen minutes since the original phone call.

Dennis, with adrenaline still pumping through his veins, took a deep breath and calmed himself. New York morning traffic was starting to build and there was no need to rush home. It would be senseless to attract the attention of a random cop by speeding.

The O'Connell's had agreed that if the baby was a boy, he would be named Ethan Liam O'Connell. The Liam was in deference to his great, great grandfather.

They were two blocks away before Mary uttered her first words. 'Dennis, he is perfect, the most beautiful child I have ever seen. So peaceful, he is just staring at me with his beautiful blue eyes, gripping my finger. He knows he is safe with us.'

'I have his birth certificate signed and stamped by Dr. William Smith. He definitely didn't look like a Smith to me. We must fill in our names as parents and get him registered later today and apply for a passport.'

It took them and hour and twenty minutes for the return journey to their Greenpoint home. Dennis parked the car and rushed around to the rear passenger side to assist his wife and their son. They made it into the house without attracting any attention. The second they closed the front door behind them, Ethan started wailing, he was hungry. It was almost as if he knew he was home and could let them know it was feeding time.

While Mary was feeding Ethan, Dennis filled in their names as parents on the birth certificate. His first order of business was to have the baby registered at the Vital Records Office. He completed the application forms for a child passport and a Social Security Number.

With Ethan fed and cleaned up, Dennis took a photograph that would be acceptable for the issuance of a passport. Armed with all the necessary documents he left Mary to attend to their son while he went about getting the child registered.

His first stop was at the local Vital Records Office. Being that it was a Friday and most of the staff had one eye on the weekend, he hoped there wouldn't be too many questions asked. By the time he got to the front of the line he lucked out. The gum-chewing female clerk attending to him could not have looked more bored if she was asleep.

'Good morning, I would like to register the birth of my son please.'

'You could have done this at the hospital you know.'

'I realize I could have but we will be traveling for the next few weeks and I wanted to be sure that it reached here before we left.'

The clerk gave him a dirty look, extended her hand and almost snatched the form from him. She reluctantly keyed the necessary information into her computer terminal. Once complete she asked for the $45 processing fee and preempted Dennis by saying that it would take three to four weeks to be processed. She printed a receipt noting that the application was in process.

Dennis left the building and headed for the nearest Social Security office, two blocks away. As per usual, there was always a waiting list.

He was told it could take up to three hours to be attended to so he took a seat.

It was one of the better days at the office as he was called after just two hours and five minutes. The friendly Latina lady who attended to him was highly efficient and had him processed and out of the office in under ten minutes armed with a brand-new Social Security Card in the name of Ethan Liam O'Connell.

Last stop was the local Post Office where he handed in the passport application accompanied by the photograph and $100. He was informed it should take no longer than three weeks.

It was now time to implement the next phase of their plan. Working through the intermediaries they had been aware of the potential due date of their baby. They realized that for Mary to suddenly appear with a baby would be a major problem.

Mary, an eighth-grade school teacher at Greenpoint Middle school, was currently on summer break and not due back at school for another six weeks. Dennis, a qualified CPA, ran his own business as a financial consultant. For the past three months he had not taken on any new clients and was finalizing the needs of those still on his books.

His final task of the day was to contact Ronda Realty and confirm that they were ready to list their townhouse as a rental property. They had previously discussed the possibility with the owner, Ronda Townsend, of renting the accommodation on a long lease. It would be available fully furnished. Townsend had assured them that the property would not stay unoccupied for long. Townsend offered to bring the lease agreement around to the house but Dennis declined and said he would visit her office the following day.

The couple kept a very low profile for the next few weeks. Only Dennis left the house and only to restock essential supplies. Ethan's passport and birth certificate arrived a day apart on July 5 & 6. With all the documentation they needed in hand, it was time to take their final step in securing their family's immediate future. Dennis called the local office of United Airlines and booked three one-way tickets to Dublin, Ireland.

On the evening of July 15, Dennis, Mary and one-month old Ethan left JFK airport aboard United flight UA47. It would be five full years before they returned to New York

Chapter 25
Ethan O'Connell

July 16, 1990 the O'Connell family landed at Dublin Airport in the Republic of Ireland. It had been an uneventful six-and-a half hour flight from JFK, landing at 7.15 am. This was just the first leg of their journey.

After clearing immigration, the family made their way to the Avis Car Rentals counter. Dennis had pre-booked a Toyota minivan for the trip to Cork in the south west of the country. It was almost 9.00 am by the time they were loaded up and ready to make the 259km (161 miles) to 14 Pearse Road in Cork. This would be their new home for the next five years.

The decision to leave the USA with their new baby was to avoid any possibility of someone asking awkward questions about the sudden appearance of a newborn baby. There was also the small chance of the birth parents changing their minds over the adoption. There was no way Dennis and Mary were handing that baby back.

Cork is the second largest city in Ireland and is located in the province of Munster. The largest county, Cork, is bordered by the Atlantic Ocean in the south and by the counties of Waterford and Tipperary in the east. Limerick is on the north boundary and Kerry to the west.

Dennis had chosen Cork, as the O'Connell family had been residents in the area since before the Great Famine of 1845-51. His great, great, great grandfather, Brendan, had left the Irish shores with his wife, Margaret, and six-year old Ethan. They had landed at Ellis Island on February 9, 1848. Dennis was a fourth generation Irish/American. While on a self-imposed exile he would take the time to trace his roots.

The drive from the airport to Cork took them through some of the most fertile and green countryside in the whole of Ireland. It's not called the Emerald Isle for nothing. Four and a half hours later they arrived at their new home. The house was a single-story brick structure. Three bedrooms, two bathrooms, a separate lounge, dining room and a neat functional kitchen. There was no covered garage but there was a parking space on the property. A low three-foot wall marked the property boundaries. Dennis had bought the property fully furnished.

On the opposite side of the road, 150 meters to the right, was the Church of the Assumption. In the opposite direction a little further away, was the Maria Assumpta Catholic preschool. Very handy when Ethan was of the required age. The first thing they noticed, being a Sunday and also 2.00 pm, was that there was a great deal of foot and bicycle traffic in and around the church. Just in time for Mass. First thing Monday they would visit the church and introduce themselves to the local priest.

With their hasty departure from New York and the time spent organizing it, they had not yet had their son baptized. It was their strong Catholic beliefs that made it a priority. On Monday morning they presented themselves to the parish priest, Father John O'Shea. As with any new parishioners, they were welcomed with open arms. Baby Ethan was baptized the same day.

It didn't take long for the O'Connells to settle into the Irish way of life. Being staunch Catholics, the church introduced them to parish life. The Irish as a people are probably the friendliest and most accepting people in the world. The O'Connell name was well known in the area and Dennis was able to find several distant long forgotten relatives.

Once it became known that Mary was a qualified teacher, she was offered a part time job at the Maria Assumpta preschool. She took up the job on the condition that she could bring Ethan with her. The head nun readily agreed and Mary started at the beginning of the new term at the end of the summer holidays.

For the first six months Dennis spent his time getting to know the area around Cork County. He spent many hours researching his family tree and their history in the area. His direct branch of the family ended with Brendan's emigration to the United States. Many of the O'Connells on that side of the family had perished during the Great Famine. The British and their government at the time had a lot to answer for.

By the Christmas of 1990, the O'Connells were well entrenched into Cork life. Dennis thought it was about time for him to find some gainful employment. As a USA qualified public accountant, he had no officially recognized qualification in Ireland. It was quite by chance that an opportunity arose.

As a property owner, he was obliged to pay council taxes based on occupancy and value of property. He sought the advice of a local accountant and made an appointment with one of the parishioners. Darragh Keane. Keane, on the wrong side of sixty, ran his own business taking care of mainly family financial matters but he did have a few local businesses on his books as well.

'Mr. O'Connell, come in come in, take a seat and make yourself comfortable. I hear you are settling into our wonderful city, your lovely wife and wee lad are very popular at the Assumpta. What is it I can do for you today?'

'Good of you to see me, Mr. Keane. We are loving it in this beautiful part of the world, everyone is so gracious and friendly. I am in a bit of a quandary as far as my tax obligations are concerned. I don't want to get on the wrong side of the tax man. Back home in the States if you misstate your taxes and they call you on it, you never hear the end of it for the rest of your life. I would very much like to avoid that here.'

'Well, I am here to help you with that. What did you do for a living back in the States?'

'I am qualified Public Accountant. I ran my own business, probably something very similar to what you do here I would imagine.'

'Ah a CPA, well you should have no problems with our tax systems. If you don't mind me asking, are you currently working at anything here in Ireland?'

'Not at the moment. I am considering looking around. There is only so much exploring one can do before becoming a little tired of it,' Dennis joked.

'Young man, if I may be so bold, I have a proposition to put to you. I will be sixty-three next birthday and could really use the assistance of a knowledgeable person such as yourself to take on some of the load.'

'Mr. Keane, I am not licensed to practice in your country. As much as I would like to help, I am not sure if I am authorized.'

'Please call me Darragh. If you are truly bored why not come and join me on a trial basis? I have a spare office all set up, I was hoping my son Robbie would have had the calling and join his old Dad, but no. I am sure given a couple of weeks' study you would have no trouble passing the Irish accounting requirements. In the meantime, I would give you only what you are comfortable handling. It would help me no end, please agree in principle. We can work out the financial arrangements over a couple of whiskeys.'

Dennis contemplated for a few seconds then stood up to shake his new bosses' hand, 'Darragh, thank you for the offer, I accept.'

Dennis started what would turn out to be four and a half years of working within the Irish accounting system. He and Mary formed a lifelong friendship with Darragh and his wife Cara.

Every weekend, weather permitting, the three of them would pack the Ford Escape and head out into the countryside. Life went on for the family; Mary and Dennis enjoyed the adult company that their jobs provided them. The church and its community accepted them as they would any local.

It was Ethan who flourished the most. The staff and children at the Assumpta adored him. He was an amiable young boy who made everyone smile. As his vocabulary expanded, his parents noticed a distinct Southern Irish Brogue.

At the beginning of 1995 Dennis and Mary discussed the possibility of returning to their home in New York. The current tenants had given notice that they wished to end their lease as of the end of February 1995. As much as they loved the life they had built in Ireland, both had been feeling a little homesick.

Mary decided that she would see out the school year that would end June 16 and Dennis would tender his resignation with Darragh Keane effective the same date. Although their various employers were disappointed by their decision, they understood. The house was put up for sale and a buyer was found very quickly.

The O'Connells all packed up, left the beautiful city of Cork behind them and flew back to JFK on July 31, 1995. They moved back into their Greenpoint home. Within a week, Dennis reopened his accounting business and Mary registered Ethan at a local school, Saint Stanislaus Kostka Catholic Academy. He would start in PK1 on August 2.

Having spent a number of years in and around the classroom while his mother taught had given Ethan an advantage over his fellow classmates. It became obvious very quickly that he was way ahead of PK1 so he was moved up to PK2 with his parents' permission. Throughout his school career he was always the youngest in his class.

He may have always been the youngest but he was never the smallest. By the age of ten he was as tall as his mother. When it was time for him to attend high school, he was registered at The Loyola School – a Jesuit run institution. His daily commute to school took him to Park Avenue on the upper east side. Barely twelve years old he could easily pass for fifteen, 5'10" and a solid 140lbs.

Aside from excelling academically, given his 6'3" frame, he was a first-choice member of the school soccer team, an avid cross-country runner and when given the opportunity, a more than useful basketball player. The school did not offer football or baseball but he turned out most weekends during the season for the local Greenpoint Boys' baseball team.

The next five years for the O'Connell family could not have been more perfect. Dennis' accounting practice was flourishing, Mary was teaching high school English and Ethan was getting top grades at school. Ethan was voted "most likely to succeed" in his senior year, and was in line to be voted as most popular.

Dennis and Mary had made the decision that at some point they would tell Ethan that he had been adopted at birth. The question was always when exactly to do that; they didn't want to upset or distract him in his school work, but they knew that they would have to do it one day.

After his graduation the talk got around to what college he would like to attend and what degree he would study for. He said he would like to do a Bachelor of Science degree specializing in criminal law and forensic sciences. He decided on applying at Cornell University in the city of Ithaca, upstate New York. It was far enough away from home for him to experience the whole college life and close enough to home that he could visit on a regular basis.

Ethan aced his studies at Cornell. Throughout his three years and six months he was never out of the top three in his class. A bright future was predicted for him.

Full of the joys of life he headed home for the Christmas and New Year festivities. He would return for his last semester and graduate in June of 2012.

Dennis and Mary were thrilled that their son would be home for just about a week had decided to sit down with him on New Year's Day and tell him that he had been adopted at birth. Both were very nervous but knew it had to be done. He would graduate in a few months and they wanted him to know who he was as he stepped into his future.

Chapter 26
February 1, 2022

Monday morning Ethan picked up June at her apartment on the way to work. He thought to himself that it was strange that they had spent so much time together, but he hadn't even seen the inside of her apartment. *Was that her choice?*

'How are you feeling, Ethan, have you come to terms with your parent's note?'

'Still shocked and saddened that they never got to explain the situation to me before they were murdered. I want to keep this between us and not make it public at the precinct. There could be a connection with the Zodiac Rapist but until we establish that, I don't want anyone knowing the situation.'

'I fully agree with you,' June agreed.

With Ethan still desk bound, he was given the task of going through the list of reported burglaries in the Manhattan area since January 2020. It was a long shot but there was a chance that a connection could be made. He was also to check on any known burglars that had been released from prison around November of 2020.

June Hayes' job was to revisit all the rapist's victims' statements. It seemed like a pointless process to her, but Garcia insisted that somewhere along the line, something must tie the victims together.

Garcia, Shaw, and Mills relocated to the downstairs interview room. They decided that the rapist probably knew of their plans to counteract him for April 1. They were going to put together a plan to send him misleading information on what their next steps were to be.

Ethan, still reeling from finding out he was adopted, decided to put his task on hold and concentrate on trying to track down the "Baby Brokers". All he had was his date of birth and the physical address where his parents took delivery.

His first step was to trace the current owners of the property. This was very simple, he accessed the property tax records for 81 Prospect Place, Prospect Heights in Brooklyn. He found that the property had been purchased in February of 1994 and the house was constructed two months later April 15, 1994.

The property had changed hands four times since it was built. The original construction company was listed as National Builders and the Realtor who now listed the property was Midtown Property Brokers. He decided to try the Realtor first, looking up their address he found their sales office located in Brooklyn.

He left the confines of the situation room and dialed the number. The call was answered by a receptionist whose sole function in life seemed to be attaching all inbound calls to a salesperson. He explained that he was a police officer and would like to speak to someone about the property at 81 Prospect Place, Prospect Heights.

'Hold the line, I will put you through to Alfred Harmon; he is the salesman for that area.'

Before he could stop her, his call was transferred. 'Good morning, you are speaking to Alfred Harmon, to whom do I have the pleasure of speaking to?'

'Mr. Harmon, my name is Detective Ethan O'Connell from the 35th precinct here in New York. I am looking for some information on 81 Prospect Place, Prospect Heights.'

'Detective, thank you for your service. Let me look up that property for you. Are you ready to purchase or just looking?'

'Neither. I need to find out where the previous owners were. We are following up on a criminal investigation. How far back can you trace all the previous owners?'

'I think you may have been put through to the wrong person, I am strictly in the selling business. I can pull up the property on our computer system and see what we have.'

'I would appreciate that, thank you.'

Ethan could hear Harmon tapping away on his keyboard. Ninety seconds later he picked up the phone and spoke.

'Okay, what I can tell you is the property was constructed April 15, 1994, by National Builders. Our system shows two sales of the property – the first in November 2011 and the second March 2015.'

'Can you tell me who the seller and the buyers were on the November sale?'

'Yes, I can. The seller was Mohammad Yousef who sold the property to Brian and Sharon Miller. The property was listed again in December 2014 and eventually sold to the current owners in March

2015. Do you need their details as well?'

'No thanks. Do you have an address for Mohammad Yousef?'

'We do, the one on file is eleven years old, but at the time his address was listed as 2615 Avenue U in Brooklyn. The telephone number on file is 347-555-1989.'

'Thank you, Mr. Harmon, you have been very helpful,' Ethan hung up the telephone and dialed the number for Mohammad Yousef.

The telephone rang three times before automatically going to a voicemail message *'You have reached the number for Persian Rug Importers. We are unable to take your call as our offices are temporarily closed for refurbishment. Please leave your name and number and we will return your call as soon as we reopen.'*

Not wanting to wait for a return call Ethan decided to try the original builders. He looked up the number for National Builders. The call was answered by a very cheerful lady who asked how she could help.

'I am Detective Ethan O'Connell from the 35th precinct and I am trying to find out about the ownership of a particular piece of property that your company built back in 1994.'

'I'll put you through to Mr. Samuel Mulligan; he runs the company so maybe he can help you.'

The call was transferred and answered immediately, 'Mulligan here, how may I be of assistance?'

Ethan explained his situation and what he was looking for.

'April 1994, you say, in Prospect Heights. My late father was still running the company then. I had joined the previous year and being the boss's son I was given all the crappy jobs that needed doing. I do recall a large development in that area.

A property broker had bought up a large swath of land there to be used for redevelopment to build affordable housing. We tendered for several of the units and were successful in quite a few as far as I remember. What are you looking for exactly?'

'I need to find out who owned 81 Prospect Place on June 15, 1990.'

'Well, I can't help you there, the property broker would have that information as they bought up the whole area in sometime around 1992.'

'Do you have a record of who the property broker was who bought the property?'

'Yes, I do but they no longer exist. They went to the wall in 2008 during that whole financial fiasco. Your best bet is City Hall's records archive. Don't waste your time phoning them, go see them in person. Also, go as a private citizen. If you go as a cop, then they will want warrants. Crazy hey!'

'Thanks for your help, I'll take your advice.'

Ethan hung up the phone and went looking for Garcia, who he found in interview room #2.

'Boss, I need some personal time tomorrow, if that is okay with you.'

'Sure thing. You are desk bound anyway so no problem, take all the time you need.'

He thanked Garcia and took the short walk back to the situation room where he found Hayes.

'June, I need to take some time off tomorrow, so you won't need to pick me up. If I finish up before the end of workday, I will come into the precinct for a ride home. Maybe we could get a meal together afterwards.'

'Anything I can help you with?'

'Not really. I just need to follow up on what I found out yesterday.'

Ah, so Ethan you are on track. This suits me very well with you not being in the office, I think I will add a little twist to tomorrow's fun.

The following morning bright and early, Ethan walked the short distance to the bus stop at Meeker Ave/Hausman Street where he caught the B24 bus to the subway stop at Metropolitan Ave/Graham Ave. There he boarded the M line to 14 street and Union Square. From there he took the R line to the City Hall stop. End to end the trip him just five minutes short of the hour.

He joined the throng of crowds winding their way up from the subway to ground level, silently thanking the lord above that he didn't have to do this daily. He reached the front doors of City Hall at 8.55 am, there were already at least fifty people ahead of him waiting for the 9.00 am opening.

The doors opened on the dot at 9.00 am. Ethan was taken into the building with the surge of the crowd ahead and behind him. Facing them were two security scanners, the crowds funneled into two semi orderly lines and the process began. As with all security scanners, there were inevitable problems, people not emptying metals from their person, metal joints, language issues and personal scans. It was 9.35 am before he made it through the scanner.

Not sure where he needed to go, he joined the line at the Inquiries counter. Half an hour later, after explaining what he needed, he was directed to room number 107 in Hall B. He entered the room and was given a ticket showing number 16 and told to take a seat. His number was eventually called at 11.02 am. He again explained what he was searching for, the clerk handed him a form to be filled in. The search carried a fee of $20.00, he was instructed to fill in the form, take it to the cashier in room 100, pay the fee and return with the receipt.

The line in room 100 was long and moved very slowly, he paid his fee at 12.15 am. He made the return trip to room 107 where he was given a new number 73 and told to take a seat. His new number was called at 1.08 pm.

He stepped up to the counter and presented his completed search request form and the receipt for $20.00. The clerk inspected the form, tapped a few strings of data into his computer screen and printed out a ticket which he handed to Ethan.

'Take this up to the second-floor, room 212, where property records are located.'

Ethan thanked the man, left the room and taking the stairs walked up one floor to find room 212. He walked up to the closed door and tried the door handle, it was locked. He took a step backwards and read the "Hours of Business" board on the door. *Open 9.00 am to 1.00 pm, Closed for Lunch 1.00 pm to 2.00 pm, Open 2.00 pm to 4.00 pm.*

Ethan just shook his head and was grateful he did not have his weapon with him as he would surely have shot someone.

Four miles to the north of City Hall, thirty-three-year-old Louise Martin had just finished the early morning shift at the local Target Store on West 45th Street. Her apartment was a short four block walk to 426 W 49th Street. She was looking forward to spending the afternoon relaxing and getting ready for her date later that evening.

With no elevator in the building, she trudged up the stairs to her fourth-floor apartment. The door to 4B was double locked, she struggled juggling her two parcels with her set of keys, eventually getting both locks opened. Using her right elbow, she pushed the door open and reversed into the apartment.

Before she knew what was happening, she felt an arm around her neck and a strong hand over her mouth.

'Don't make a sound and you won't get hurt, cry out and I will slash your throat. Drop your parcels and turn around very slowly.'

Louise Martin dropped her parcels and turned around as instructed. She was faced by a tall man, at least a foot taller than her 5'4", he was dressed in black and wearing a black balaclava. He brandished a large knife in her face reasserting his threat that he would slash her throat if she cried out.

He pulled her by her hair and dragged her down the short passage to the bedroom. Realizing she was about to be sexually assaulted, Martin, although terrified, decided to remain passive and not fight the man. He pushed her towards the bed and instructed her to get undressed. She turned her back to him and complied.

As soon as she was naked the man spun her around and pushed her roughly on the bed, she lay there on her back trembling. He picked up her discarded panties, shoved them into her mouth and secured them by tying her bra around her head. She was now unable to talk or spit out her panties.

Next, he produced two pairs of her pantyhose. He secured both her hands around the wrists and tied them to the headboard. Fearing the worst, she tightly closed her eyes and braced for what she knew was coming.

The man stood back to admire his handiwork, he could feel the excitement, he was ready. He unzipped his fly, pulled out his rapidly hardening penis and carefully rolled on a condom. He knelt on the bed, forcefully pushed her legs apart, lifted her knees up and entered her. He could see in her eyes the pain she felt as he thrust into her. It was the victim's fear that turned him on, it was all over in less than a minute.

He lifted himself off her and rolled off the bed. As he walked towards the bathroom, he removed the condom and flushed it down the toilet. Zipping up his fly he walked over to the bed and looked down on Louise Martin. She was lying quietly sobbing with her eyes tightly closed. Deviating from his normal modus operandi he leaned over her and hit her with a short sharp right hook square on her jaw. She went out like a light and would stay that way for at least the next hour.

He moved around to the foot of the bed and removed two cards from his pocket which he inserted in her vagina. He then pulled out a Ziploc baggie from which he extracted two strands of brown hair, placing them in the middle of her stomach. A single dark pubic hair was taken out of the baggie and carefully placed at the top end of her vagina.

Satisfied that everything was set up to his satisfaction, he picked up the bag of valuables he had stolen and left the room. He walked down to the ground floor unobserved and turned right on 49th Street. Two blocks north he found the payphone he was looking for, lifted the receiver, put two quarters in the slot and dialed the number.

Back in the situation room at the 35th precinct the call was answered by June Hayes. It was 1.22 pm.

'35th precinct'

'Ah, I was really hoping to get Garcia, who do I have? Is it the delectable June Hayes or the unfortunate Linda Mills?' the voice taunted down the line.

'Who is this, what do you want?' June was on full alert.

'Don't tell me you don't recognize my voice? How disappointing. I won't keep you on the phone so please pass this message on to Detective Garcia.

I have left a present for your team at 426 W 49th Street apartment 4B. Tell your boss *"All things may seem the same, but they are also different."* Have fun, but do hurry along, goodbye.'

He hung up the phone, leaving Hayes stunned. Gathering her composure, she dropped the phone and ran downstairs to Interview room 2. Breathlessly she related her conversation with the caller.

'Jesus, Hayes, are sure it was him?' asked Garcia, white-knuckling his coffee mug.

'The voice was a little different, but I think it was him.'

'Okay, we need to get over there, right now. Hayes, you are with me. Shaw, call the forensics team and then you and Mills follow us.'

Chapter 27
Apartment 4B

Garcia and Hayes were the first on the scene, they parked the car and went into the building. They found the door to apartment 4B closed but unlocked. With guns drawn and Garcia in the lead, the two detectives entered the apartment, checking each room as they went. Hayes was first into the bedroom.

'In here, Boss! There is a naked Caucasian female tied up on the bed, she looks unconscious,' she stepped into the room; gun still drawn.

Garcia brushed past her and headed for the bathroom, while Hayes checked inside the walk-in closet. Both rooms were empty. Garcia walked over to the bed careful not to disturb anything, he leaned in to check the woman's pulse. Satisfied she was alive and not in any immediate danger, he decided not to try and revive her.

'Hayes, see if you can find another blanket and cover her up. I don't want to use anything currently in the room.'

Hayes went into the closet and emerged with a bed sheet which she used to cover up the woman. No sooner than she was covered, the forensics team led by Barry Hughes arrived, followed seconds later by Shaw and Mills.

'Hi Barry, I covered her up, she is naked under the sheet. It looks like she has been smacked on the jaw but seems okay. Hayes took the call at 1.22 pm and we got here at 2.02 pm. The call was from a payphone, so she must have been unconscious for at least forty minutes, maybe a bit longer. The crime scene is all yours,' Garcia stepped aside and Barry moved to take his place.

'Thanks Mike, hopefully we find something this time. The smack on the jaw differs from the Zodiac normal modus, let's hope this isn't an amateur copycat,' speaking to his team. 'Okay guys, remove that sheet and shoot photos of the victim, once you are done remove the gag and replace the sheet.

Grace, I assume she has been sexually assaulted. Medics are on the way; they can apply a rape kit and examination once she has been revived. Right, get to work. You know what to do.' Everyone silently went about their assigned duties with the efficiency of a well-oiled team.

To make space for the forensics team, the four detectives left the bedroom and walked over to the living room.

Garcia: 'Hayes, can you tell us anything further about the person on the call? You said his voice sounded different, maybe it was because he wasn't on speaker.'

Hayes: 'No I don't think that was the reason. He just sounded less 'Bronx' than before. I can't quite put my finger on it, I am sure I have heard that voice before.'

Garcia: 'If it is our man, he must have heard our plans for April 1. Is he accelerating?'

Mills: 'I have just checked the date on the internet, today is the New Moon. So, he hasn't waited until April 1. He has also changed direction. We figured his next victim to be in the 400 block of West 31st Street.'

Shaw: 'Well, this one is in the 400 block but in West 49th Street.'

Mills: 'Shit! He hasn't gone three blocks south; he's gone three blocks north from the first one. What was that thing he said to you, Hayes?'

Hayes: '"*All things may seem the same but they are also different.*" The New Moon is the same as is 400 block, the difference is the street number although it is similar in that it is three blocks from a previous attack.'

Mills: 'The other difference is that he knocked this one unconscious. Also, he called this one directly into the situation room. Do we know who she is?'

Garcia: 'I have her purse here. Her name is Louise Martin, age 33. She fits his victim profile. He is fucking with us. Hey Barry, what do you have for us?'

'She is awake but a bit shaky. She agreed to let Grace give her a cursory vaginal examination, this is what she found,' waving three evidence bags he continued. 'This one contains a Gemini Zodiac card, same print and type as all of the others so no surprise. The second one however is a bit of a shocker, what we have here is the American Express credit card for one Ethan L. O'Connell. How the hell would that have got in there? Where is he by the way?'

Garcia: 'I can explain than one. He was mugged a few days ago, his weapon, shield and wallet were taken. We suspected the rapist did it and this confirms it. IA has temporarily suspended O'Connell so he's riding a desk back at the precinct.'

Hayes: 'Actually, he has the day off today for some personal business.'

Garcia: 'See if you can contact him. You got anything else there Barry?'

'Oh yes, I do. What I have here are two light brown hairs that do not belong to the victim, she has jet black hair. They were found stuck to her stomach, they must belong to the perp. I also have a single pubic hair.'

Shaw: 'That could be hers, couldn't it.'

'No, it couldn't. She is completely shaved.' Barry noted.

Garcia: 'Has the bastard made his first mistake? Can we get a rush job on the DNA? Lieutenant Johnston has told me that anything to do with the Zodiac Rapist will take precedence.'

'I have authorized Grace to escort Ms. Martin to the hospital where she will get a full examination and an official rape kit will be taken. My team will continue to dust for prints and look for any other evidence. I suggest you interview Ms. Martin after she has been to the hospital.'

'Thanks Barry, we will do that. Mills, you and Hayes follow Martin to the hospital and take her statement there. Shaw, you and I will head back to the precinct. Hayes, any luck raising O'Connell?'

'Nothing Boss. His cell goes straight to voice mail. I have left him a message to call me.'

'Okay, it's 2.17 pm, we are going to head back to the precinct. If O'Connell returns your call tell him about the situation and to call me immediately,' Garcia instructed.

Back at City Hall the doors to room 212 opened on the dot at 2.00 pm. A single clerk was in attendance, there were two people in front of him, both had their prepaid tickets. The clerk perused each ticket and after a brief conversation the holder was directed to a computer screen.

Ethan stepped forward and presented his ticket, the clerk checked the request, looked up at him and said, 'You are looking to trace the ownership of the property 81 Prospect Place, Prospect Heights from June 15, 1991, to present day?'

'Yes Ma'am, that is correct.'

'That may be a bit of a problem. We have computerized all our property records from January 1, 1998, through until the present day. All records prior to that are filed on microfiche. There are two available computer screens for the records on file and a single microfiche reader.

The microfiche records can be found by entering the address of the property. All relevant documents should be filed in date sequence. Let me know if you have questions.'

As there was only one microfiche reader, he decided to grab it while he had the chance. He sat down in front of the screen and switched it on, it took about thirty seconds to warm up and become usable. From the menu he selected property records. When presented with the address screen he entered "81 Prospect Place, Prospect Heights". There was a whirring sound while the system searched the records file.

Eventually the master record for the property was displayed. It showed the property was first established in May of 1934, it was a subdivision of 80 – 89 Prospect Place, one whole block. The original owners were William Stockton Holdings. The entire block was divided into twenty subdivisions.

Ethan began scrolling through the records on file. Throughout the years the property changed hands several times. It was used mainly as storage and office space. In August 1987 the section identified as 81 Prospect place was sold to Ahmed Khan and registered as offices for Persian Rug Importers. That name rang a bell, so he referred to his notes from when Mohammad Yousef sold the property in November 2011.

In 1992 the whole block was bought by an investment company – Urban Renewal Inc. who demolished the entire block and then sold off units to various construction companies.

So, at the time of his birth on June 15, 1991, Ahmed Khan owned the property under the name of Persian Rug Importers. After rebuilding, Mohammad Yousef bought the property also under the name of Persian Rug Importers and they held it until November 2011.

Ethan decided a visit to Persian Rug Importers would be his next stop. He shut down the microfiche viewer and left the building. Having obeyed the sign to switch off all cellphones while in the building, he switched his back on. Immediately it buzzed indicating missed calls and voice messages waiting. There were four missed calls and two voice messages waiting, both from June Hayes.

He dialed his voicemail and the first one was 2.05 pm; it was Hayes asking where he was and to return her call as soon as possible. The second call was at 2.13 pm again from Hayes, this one was repeating the message but to call urgently as there had been an incident.

Hayes answered the call on the first ring, 'Ethan, we have been trying to get hold of you, where have you been and why didn't you answer your phone?'

'I have the day off today and so far; I have spent it at City Hall trying to track down information on my parents. You must switch off your cellphones while in the building. What is the panic about?'

'The Zodiac Rapist has stuck again. Garcia wants you to come into the office immediately.'

'I'll take a cab and be there soonest,' Ethan disconnected the call and hailed a cab.

Chapter 28
October 2020

2020 had been a good year so far for Matthew Livingstone. Always on the hustle and ever on the lookout for his next big score, he had found a profitable line of income in burglarizing. Back in his East Bronx apartment his one wall held a large map of New York City. Highlighted on the map was the location of every police precinct in the greater Brooklyn area, there were 21 in total. Across the East River in Manhattan there were a further 20 precincts.

Livingstone, who had turned thirty that year, was a single white male, six foot three, bright blue eyes and considered attractive by the opposite sex. Although he had had many short-term relationships, none ever seemed to stick. One of the bugbears was that he had no discernible steady employment.

His mother had died when he was ten years old, and his father died just after his 16th birthday. He had been living off his wits ever since. To avoid being picked up by Child Services when his father was murdered, he had left New York and headed for San Francisco. He returned to the Bronx in July 2009 when he was 19 years old.

Still concerned that his father's murderers, the notorious Point Crowns gang, may still be looking for him, he kept a very low profile. He took work wherever he could find it, mostly low paying, off the books' jobs, strictly cash. He left a very small footprint, no official record, no close friends, and no lasting romantic relationships.

Throughout his life he had always felt something was missing. Life had dealt him a shitty hand which had led him not to trust anyone or anything. He kept to himself, not giving away any personal information to anyone. He moved from one menial job to the next, never hanging around long enough to become well known. In November of 2017 things changed for him.

Needing to change the locks on his apartment's front door, due to being unable to get rid of a persistent female acquaintance, he found his way to Key In Locksmiths in the 900 block of East Gun Hill Road.

It was a small shop owned and run by 63-year-old Spencer Turner. Livingstone opened the door to the shop and a small bell announced his arrival. Turner looked up from his counter and greeted his potential customer.

'Good morning young man, what can I do for you today?'

'I need to change the two locks on my apartment's front door.'

'Do you have the keys with you? Good, let me have a look at them.'

Turner carefully examined both keys, recognizing them immediately. He looked up at Livingstone and asked, 'The easiest way to change the locks is not to replace the whole mechanism but just the actual case and tumblers. If I show you how to do that on this lock, do you think you could manage? It will save you a few bucks and a lot less hassle if you can.'

'Sure, why don't you show me how.'

Turner proceeded to walk him through the process. It took Matthew just two attempts to successfully change the case on a lock.

'That'll be $4.50 for two cases and two sets of duplicate keys. Saves you $14.00.'

'It is strange that you would show me something that actually loses you money.'

'Son, I am 63 years old. I have been doing this for all my life. My wife is long gone, and our two kids left home years ago. I make enough to get by and when I die this place will die with me. A skilled locksmith is a dying breed in this generation's throw away society, I wish I could have passed my skills on to my own son, but no such luck.'

'I noticed you have a "Help Wanted" sign in the window, what would that entail?'

'Most of my business consists of answering calls for people who have locked themselves out of their homes or their cars. This means I must leave the shop unattended while I go out on a call. I am getting too old for that, so I turn down a lot of business. I need someone much younger to do these calls, it's a lucrative part of the business,' Turner explained.

'What skills are you looking for?' Matthew asked.

'Ideally someone with locksmith experience, or someone who could be trained in the art of changing, installing and opening of locked doors. Why, are you interested?'

'I have none of those skills, but I reckon I could learn, what's the pay like?'

'Working in the store I can only pay you minimum wage - $14.50 per hour. But if you are trainable, based on how quickly you learned to replace a lock, I'd say you have the ability to learn quickly, then that is different. For a callout to unlock a door there is a minimum charge of $50. Add to that the cost of any parts.

So, if you can handle the callouts I will split the fee, $40 to you and $10 to me. I am currently turning down five or six of these calls per week, and that is without advertising.

If you are interested, I will teach you everything you need to know to open any lock. You will also know how to cut keys, install completely new locks, and replace existing ones. What do you say?'

'When do I start?'

'That's my boy! As soon as you want to. Do you have a valid driver's license? You need one to drive the van.'

'Yes Sir, I do. How about I start on Monday morning? It will give me time to end up my current job on a good footing, never want to burn any bridges.'

So began Matthew Livingstone's career as a locksmith. Spencer Turner taught him well and it didn't take long for him to be the go-to man for callouts. By the beginning of 2018 there weren't many locks that he couldn't open within thirty seconds.

He and his van became a common sight around The Bronx. He was taking calls as far north as 242nd Street and south as far as Hunt's Point. Turner had advised him not to venture into Brooklyn or Manhattan, as he would almost certainly attract attention from Union workers.

As with most things in Matthew Livingstone's life, the good times never lasted. Spencer Turner's health began to deteriorate to such an extent that Matthew was virtually running the business. The first thing Turner did was to transfer the title of the van into Matthew's name, to preserve the callout business.

On April 15, 2019, Spencer Turner had a severe stroke, Matthew called 911. Turner was transported to nearby Wentworth Hospital just one mile up the road. His condition was listed as serious but not immediately life threatening. The attending doctor suggested Matthew contact any family members and update them on Turner's condition.

He returned to the shop and found Turner's contact file. On a list of contacts, he found the phone number for Spencer Turner Junior, it was a Manhattan area code 212-555-1367 so he dialed the number. It was answered on the third ring.

'Yes Dad, what do you want now? I am very busy.'

'This is not your dad. I am Matthew Livingstone; I work for him. I am calling to tell you that he has had a serious stroke and the attending doctor said I should call immediate family just in case.'

'Which hospital?' Spencer Junior wasn't one for pleasantries.

'Wentworth in the Bronx. You should call anyone else who needs to know.'

'From the phone number you are calling from, I know you are in the shop. Please lock up and leave the premises. I will speak directly to my father. Do not remove anything that is not yours.'

'Wow. You seem really concerned about your father's health. I will see you at the hospital,' Matthew replied sarcastically and hung up the phone.

Matthew complied with Junior's instructions; he emptied the cash register putting the meager proceeds into a bank bag. He double locked the front door and pocketed the two keys. Climbing into the shop's van he made the short trip to Wentworth Hospital. There he was met by Spencer Turner Junior.

Junior was a short, fat balding man with a mean look about him. Matthew surmised he must have taken after his mother, as he looked nothing like his father. He confronted Matthew immediately.

'You must be Livingstone; you better not have taken anything out of the shop that doesn't belong to you. We will be taking a full inventory of anything missing and I will lay a charge of theft against you. Give me the keys.'

Matthew handed him a bunch of keys, there were around thirty of them of various sizes. He also handed him the bank bag.

'These are all the shop's keys and this is the contents of the cash register. I emptied it in case someone broke in. Good luck with the shop, I am going to see how your father is doing.'

'You will go nowhere near my father. Which of these keys are for the van?'

'None of them; the van belongs to me.'

'The van is the property of the shop, hand me the keys or I will lay a charge of theft,' Spencer barked.

'Lay all the charges you want. I have the legal title,' Matthew replied, icily.

Matthew turned around and left Junior holding the keys and the money. As he left the building, he threw the two front door keys in the trash. He never saw Spencer Turner again. He died two days later without ever fully regaining his senses. The irony of the whole thing was that Junior, unable to find the front door keys, had to call out a locksmith to open the shop and change the locks.

Key In Locksmiths ceased to exist two months later. Matthew had the van repainted removing the company name. With no base of operations, callouts stopped, leaving him unemployed but now with a specific skill.

As part of the mobile business, he had kept a detailed log of every call he had made. He listed the name and addresses, the date and time and what specific function he had performed. It was for his benefit and that of his boss in case of any complaints.

One thing he had noticed on his calls was that many people had no alarm systems and many of them had left valuables lying around. With no prospects of opening and stocking a locksmith business, he needed a new source of income. He had a van stocked with everything he needed for handling callouts but no way of getting his name "out there".

Trying to look like a legitimate business, he had 1,000 business cards printed. They were very simple – *Mobile Locksmith – telephone 212-555-2323. For all your lock requirements 24/7.* The back of the card listed all his services.

His plan was two-fold; he would case a possible "victim" and once he was sure the residence was unattended, he would walk up to the front door and knock. If by any chance the door was answered he would explain he was new to the neighborhood and was trumping up business. If there was no answer, he would pick the lock and enter the building. Anything of value would be taken, leaving anything that wasn't easily transportable.

Many local residents had a safe installed. Due to most homes' interior walls being made of drywall, any safe was usually found bolted to the floor in one of the closets. Using the skills he had been taught by Spencer Turner, most of the safes were child's play to open.

Careful of where he committed his burglaries, he referred to his "precinct map", making sure never to commit more than one robbery in the same precinct in any two-week period. With precincts not sharing information with each other over small things like a minor isolated burglary, no attention was drawn to him. He was not a greedy burglar, and he made a good living from the proceeds of his robberies

Early October in 2020, Lawrence had been casing properties in the 1600 block of East 53rd Street in Brooklyn. A quiet street with houses slightly offset from the road, perfect for unobtrusive observation. He had not been active in the area before; the nearest police station was the 63rd precinct; he had not burgled anyone in that precinct's area before. The neighborhood was slightly upper middle class, usually a fairly rich environment for his line of work.

October 9, 2020, was a Friday, with Columbus Day on Monday October 12. His guess was that there was a good possibility that some residents would be going away for a long weekend. Parked in the middle of the 1600 block he caught sight of two adults and two young children leaving 1661 East 53rd Street. Leaving the house, they were wheeling two suitcases towards a Honda SUV parked directly in front of their property. He watched as they packed the children and suitcases into the car. It looked to him like they were leaving on a trip, hopefully for the long weekend.

As the family drove away, he gave them half an hour, just in case they had forgotten something and came back. He pulled on his latex gloves and walked up to the front door and knocked, no reply, he tried ringing the doorbell with the same result. Without bending down he reached for the first of the two locks, inserted his lock picks, and had the lock opened in under ten seconds. Reaching up for the second lock it also proved no problem, he opened the door and stepped into the house.

His first check was for an alarm system, they were normally located within a few feet of the front door. No alarm was found so he made his way down the hall and up the stairs to the bedrooms. A systematic search resulted in a small amount of jewelry, two rings, a few bracelets and three watches; one men's watch and two women's.

Moving on to the closet he found the safe bolted to the floor, partially hidden by hanging clothes. It was a very common model and proved no problem to him, so he opened it. In it was a Glock 19, three magazines and a box of fifty rounds, $1,500 cash, and some slightly more valuable jewelry. Leaving the gun, he pocketed the valuables.

Satisfied that there was nothing of value left in the bedrooms, he headed back down the stairs and into the living room. He scanned the room looking for small portable items that he could sell off. Along the left side wall was a sideboard full of photographs, trophies, and medals, he decided to check them out. It appeared that the man of the house was something of a sportsman.

Glancing at the photographs he saw a good looking, blond thirty-something year old man whose sporting claim to fame was athletics; he was a runner. Just as he was turning away a large photograph hanging on the wall caught his attention. It was a picture of two men, on the left a younger version of the owner of the house, but the picture of the man on the right made him stare in disbelief.

Staring back at him was an identical younger version of himself. Both men were dressed in police uniforms, the caption under the photo reading 'New York Police Academy class 1452, September 2012'. How was this possible? He leaned closer to read the names printed below – right Howard A. Friend – left Ethan L. O'Connell.

Chapter 29
Louise Martin

Mills and Hayes arrived at Wentworth Hospital, parked in one of the "Doctor's Only" spots, put their "Police Business" card on the windscreen and entered the Emergency Room area. Mills flashed her detective's shield and asked the whereabouts of Louise Martin. They were directed to examination room 13B.

Without ceremony the two detectives walked up to the room and opened the door. Inside were a nurse, a doctor and Louise Martin. The doctor looked up to see who was interrupting her examination. The two detectives flashed their shields.

'I don't care who the hell you are, but you are not permitted in this room until I am done with my examination. Get out immediately! I will let you know when you can see the patient.' The doctor barked at them, standing between them and her patient.

Mills looked at Hayes who just shrugged her shoulders, they did an about turn and left the room. They had barely left the room when Hayes' cellphone rang, she noted the call was from O'Connell. She answered, and after chastising him, she brought him up to date with the news of the Zodiac Rapist's latest attack.

They were kept waiting by the doctor for twenty minutes until she exited the examination room and walked over to them.

'I am done with my examination you can go in now. I will have a written report and a full rape kit will be available to you within the hour. Maybe next time, knock on the door before rushing into an examination room. You'd think the NYPD would know better,' she walked off, handing the chart to the nurse and continued her rounds.

Taking the rebuff on the chin, Mills and Hayes headed into the room. Louise Martin was sitting on the edge of the examination table, she was fully dressed and accompanied by a nurse.

'Hello Ms. Martin, I am Detective Linda Mills, and this is my partner June Hayes. If you are up to it, we would like to ask you some questions and maybe get a statement. The sooner we know exactly what happened and who we are looking for, the sooner we can catch the man who did this to you.'

'I am fine, so ask any questions you want,' Louise Martin replied, her voice a bit shaky.

'Tell us exactly what you remember about earlier today,' Mills took out her notebook, ready to record her responses.

'I worked the early shift at Target, the one West 45th street and went directly home to my apartment just four blocks away. I was carrying two parcels, so it was a bit of a struggle to get my keys out and open the two door locks. I pushed the door open and kinda backed into the apartment.

Before I knew what was happening, I felt an arm around my neck and a voice telling me he would kill me if I made any sound. I dropped my parcels, and he turned me around. He was holding a large knife in his hand; he was very tall and was wearing a black balaclava. I noticed he had very blue eyes.'

'When he spoke, did he have a very Bronx accent?' Mills asked.

'No, he was very well spoken; no real New York accent.'

Hayes and Mills looked at each slightly surprised. According to all the previous victims, the Zodiac Rapist definitely had a strong Bronx accent.

'Then he pushed me into the bedroom and forced me to undress and lie down on the bed on my back. He then stuffed my panties in my mouth and tied my bra around my head, I couldn't talk or cry out. He then took two pairs of my pantyhose and tied my hands to the headboard.

He unzipped his pants and took out his penis, it was almost fully erect, he put on a condom, forced my legs apart and stuck it in me. It hurt like hell. I think he enjoyed hurting me; it seemed to get him even more excited. I was petrified he was going to kill me but the minute he came he rolled off and just went into the bathroom and flushed the condom.

When he came back to the bed, I was crying which I think annoyed him. He must have punched me as I don't remember anything else until your doctor woke me up. I have a very sore jaw the doctor here said I have a big bruise on the left side of my face.' Her hand moved to touch the bruise on her face, as if to convince herself that it was real.

'Can you describe any of the physical attributes of your attacker?'

asked Mills.

'Not really except he had a very big penis. I have never seen one that size.'

'Did you see if he was circumcised or not?'

'I couldn't tell, I had my eyes closed. The doctor here told me I had some bruising around my privates but other than that and the smack on the jaw, I am fine. Do you know who did this?' Her eyes were tearing up, and they could see how much she needed them to tell her they'd get the guy.

'Not yet. We are following some leads. I am sorry for your experience; we will catch this man and punish him to the full extent of the law. We are leaving now; can we give you a ride home?' Mills put her hand on Louise's shoulder to offer her reassurance.

'Thank you but my sister is on her way over, I will stay at her house tonight.'

'Good idea. When you feel up to it, can you come down to the 35th precinct and give us a formal statement?' Louise nodded and Mills handed her a card.

'If you remember anything, or need anything, please don't hesitate to call me, ok?'

In the meantime, O'Connell had arrived back at the precinct finding the situation room empty. Muttering to himself, he walked down the stairs to the first floor and into interview room #2 where he found Shaw and Garcia.

Garcia: 'Nice of you to join us, where the fuck have you been and why were you not answering your cellphone?'

'Boss, I had the day off today, you agreed to it. As for my cellphone being off, I had to switch it off as they are not allowed in the building where I was.' Ethan explained.

'Where were you?'

'I was attending to some personal business,' he answered vaguely.

'Well, we have another Zodiac rape. He must be escalating because he has totally changed his schedule and direction. This time after raping her he attacked his victim, rendering her unconscious. Not like any of the others.

Barry Hughes made an interesting discovery. He found one of your credit cards shoved up her vagina along with the Gemini card. There were also some hairs, maybe from his head or chest and a single pubic hair. They have been sent for DNA testing. I suggest you give Barry a call and supply your DNA, so we can eliminate you in case the DNA on the credit card is yours.'

'Okay Boss, I will do that right now. Why are we not back in the situation room? He probably knows we have found the bugs as we have not spoken about anything in the room for a couple of days now. We should just remove them as they serve no purpose at this stage. He's beaten us at our game, fucking up our plans for April 1.'

'You are right about the bugs. I will remove them immediately so we can stop pussy footing around and get back down to business. Come up to the situation room as soon as you are done with Barry. Mills and Hayes should be back soon, we can then consolidate what we have.'

O'Connell left the room while Garcia and Shaw gathered up their belongings and headed back up to the situation room. Hayes and Mills had both arrived back from the hospital.

Garcia walked over to the situation room telephone, picked it up, unscrewed the mouth piece, shouted '*Fuck you, you pervert! I am coming for you, please resist arrest so I can put a bullet in your fucking head!*' He then ripped out the bug, threw it onto the floor and crushed it with his foot.

Hayes and Mills stared at him wide-eyed, not sure what was going on. He stomped over to his office and repeated the performance on his office phone. He returned to the general office somewhat more composed.

'Okay, let's get after this bastard, the press is going to be all over us. You can be sure the news of this latest rape will hit the airwaves within hours. The Mayor will call Captain Andrews, who will shit all over the Lieutenant and as we all know, shit rolls downhill, and that is us,' Garcia took a swig of coffee and slammed his mug back down on the desk. Some things never changed.

Watching from the security of his apartment, the man chuckled to himself. Detective Garcia, your troubles are just beginning. You may think you are secure, but I still have eyes on you. I think it is time to stir the pot.

'He is escalating and with the knowledge that we had him pinned for April 1, he had to change his plans. Now that the bugs are gone, he can no longer hear us, he is now working blind. What next, team? Where do we look for his next victim?' Garcia tossed the question out to the room.

Mills: 'He still stuck to a familiar theme: attacked on the New Moon, still in a 400 block, but going north not south.'

Hayes: 'I think we can assume he will stay in the same vicinity. What I want to know is how does he select his victims? So far there is no discernible connection to any of them. All are white, maybe he just mistook Lola Estes, she looks white. All of them are single, with no children and living alone. He must have access to the housing records of the area. Maybe we can find out if anyone has been making inquiries?'

Shaw: 'I think what he does is case an area looking for women, observes them and their movements. Once he has a potential victim, he concentrates on her, makes sure she lives alone and in a building he can access. He has three months to put together his next victim.'

Mills: 'What about Louise Martin, he did her in one month?'

The conversation was interrupted by the situation room phone ringing. Shaw was the closest, he picked up the receiver and hit the speaker button.

'This is Detective Shaw.'

'Ah Detective Shaw, it sounds like I am on speaker phone, good. Then the lot of you will get this message loud and clear.

I noticed you disconnected the two bugs on the phones, very clever of you. Never mind. I have other means of getting the latest updates on your attempts of catching me.'

Interrupting the call. Garcia shouted, 'You smug bastard! I am coming for you; I will personally put a bullet in your head.'

'Now now, Detective, take a deep breath and listen carefully. I am pissed off with you and your team. I seriously object to your pinning today's attack on me. You know I do not beat up my ladies, so you are barking up the wrong tree here.

Someone is copying my methods and not doing a very good job, I might add. A little birdie tells me one of your team is not present. Where was he when this attack occurred? I suggest you look a bit closer to home. Make sure you let the people know that this dastardly crime was not committed by me.

Like the great Arnold Schwarzenegger once said, *I'll be back.*'

Before any of the detectives could reply, the phone line went dead. At the same moment O'Connell walked back into the room. The other four detectives just stared at him.

'What's going on, why are you all staring at me with your mouths open? It looks like you have just seen a ghost.'

Garcia: 'No ghost, we have just heard from the Zodiac Rapist. That fucker claims that he did not rape Louise Martin. He was quite adamant that we should not accuse him of this one. He said to look nearer to home.'

Hayes: 'If he didn't do it, how the hell did he even know about it?'

Shaw: 'Good question. We didn't talk about it in this room before we ripped out the bugs.'

Garcia: 'He must have a contact of some sort, there is no way he could know the details unless he did it or someone from here told him about it. If there is a leak, we need to find it and shut it down real quick.

I doubt we will get DNA results from Barry before tomorrow, let's call it a day. Do not talk to the press, do I make myself clear?' Everyone nodded.

Hayes: 'You know, Boss, when I took the call telling us about the rape, he did not sound like our guy, no Bronx accent. Louise Martin also told us he did not have a typical New York accent. Maybe he really didn't do this one.'

Before anyone could reply, Garcia's office phone rang. Expecting the worst, he hurried across the room and picked up the receiver. His four detectives observed from afar. Judging by his body language they could make out that the call was from above. He hung up the call and walked back into the office.

'That was the Lieutenant, like I said shit rolls downhill. Can you believe our perp called the Mayor's office and told him what he told us. He said if anything connecting him to Martin's rape appears in the press, he will call CNN and give them the story. And we know how CNN loves drama,' Garcia rolled his eyes.

'So, Johnston has put the onus on me, and that includes you, that this story does not leave the precinct. I think tomorrow's going to be a shit show, so be ready for it. I'll see you all bright and early,' he waved the others out of the room.

Leaving Garcia behind, the other four detectives packed up and headed downstairs. Shaw broke the silence.

'Are any of you up for a few drinks at the pub?'

Hayes: 'Not me for me, thanks, I am driving. O'Connell, we can go. I will just have a Coke or something.'

O'Connell: 'No thanks, I am good. I have stuff to do at home.'

Mills turned to Shaw: 'It looks like it's just you and me, buster.'

Hayes drove home with her usual aggression, making it back to O'Connell's apartment in record time. She hit the brakes, put the car in park and turned to her passenger.

'So where were you? Why didn't you answer my calls? I was concerned about you.'

'I told you before, I couldn't answer as I was in City Hall and all cellphones are to be switched off while in the building.'

'Did you find what you were looking for?'

'Not totally, but I do have a starting point. Look, thanks for keeping this to yourself. I am going to have an early night. I will pick you up in the morning.'

He leaned over and pecked her on the cheek, opened the car door and walked up the steps to his apartment. With a slight wave he entered the building and shut the door.

'That's not like him, he's hiding something,' thought Hayes as she drove away.

Chapter 30
DNA

Driving away June Hayes contemplated the changes she had noticed in O'Connell over the past few days. He seemed detached, distant not just to her but to everyone. She put it down to the shock of finding out that he was adopted after all these years. She wondered how she would react if she had found out that her parents had given her up for adoption.

Back in the confines of his apartment, O'Connell was going through similar thoughts. Who were his biological parents? What were the circumstances that they found themselves in that would lead them into giving up a child? Although he thought of Dennis and Mary as his parents, he knew he had to find out who he really was.

Was there any connection to his parents and the staged murder of Colin and Christine Marx? Now that he knew he had been adopted, it raised the question: was a member of his biological family somehow involved?

The day spent trying to track down the circumstances of his birth and his subsequent adoption had provided very little clarity. He had traced the names of the owners or occupants of 81 Prospect Place but tracking them down and finding out what had occurred at those premises on June 15, 1990 promised to be a whole lot more difficult. It was with these thoughts rolling around in his head that he eventually fell asleep.

The following morning his body clock woke him at the normal time, he rose, showered, and dressed. Still on temporary suspension, he figured he could spend part of the day tracking down the people who had brokered his adoption. It would have to be done surreptitiously; he was still not ready to make it public knowledge.

Hayes was waiting as usual, dressed in her normal dark blue jeans and white blouse. She was well wrapped up to combat the cold. She opened the car door, slid into the passenger seat, and buckled up in one smooth action.

'So, how are you this cold morning?'

'I am good thank you. Sorry about last night. I have been a bit distracted with this whole being adopted thing. I will try and put it to the back of my mind until I can track down who was present and what the circumstances were.'

'What do you think about our perp claiming he did not rape Louise Martin? The person who called it in did not sound like our guy. He had a more neutral accent, a bit like yours, no Bronx in that voice,' she adjusted the heater in her direction.

'A bit like my voice? Why would you say that?' Ethan glanced at her and then back to the road in front of him.

'Don't take offense. All I am saying is our perp is so Bronx in the way he talks, your accent is completely neutral, not even New York. That's all I meant. So, let's drop it.' They drove the rest of the way in silence.

As usual, they were first to arrive followed ten minutes later by Mills and Shaw. Strangely, Garcia was nowhere to be seen. Not sure what the next step was, they decided to wait for their boss to show up. He duly arrived at 9.10 am at least forty minutes later than usual.

He walked straight into his office, put down his briefcase and returned to the general office.

'Don't give me the eyeball. Johnston called me and told me to meet him in his office – first thing before speaking to anyone. As you know, it would take an act of God to get him in before 9.00 am.

He told me we have orders from above: no mention of the Martin rape and the claims of Zodiac man that he is not responsible. We are to follow up based on the theory that he is responsible but also in a parallel investigation that he could be telling the truth.

Our first hope is that Barry Hughes and his team come up with some positive DNA results. It does seem a bit strange that our perp did make some basic mistakes and leave DNA. Hopefully it leads to his capture.'

'Speak of the devil and he appears,' said Mills as Barry Hughes entered the situation room.

Garcia: 'Barry, please tell me you have the silver bullet, so we can put this bastard away for good.'

Watching from the comfort of his apartment, the man chuckled. It was all going to plan, this should be fun, well maybe not fun for all but at least for himself.

'I have some good news and some bad news,' Barry began.

Garcia: 'Give us the good news first.'

'We did the full DNA tests. We found DNA on the credit card obviously left by the rapist when he inserted it into Martin's vagina. The hairs found on her chest were from the perp's head and matched that on the credit card. The single pubic hair was also an exact match to the other two samples. I can categorically state that all three samples were from the same person.'

'So, what's the bad news?' inquired Shaw.

'No match of this DNA could be found on any of our databases. This person has never been arrested for any crime. We also did not find any fingerprints other than those of Ms. Martin.

So, if we ever apprehend the culprit, we can place him at the scene of the crime. Other than that, we are screwed,' Barry handed the report to Garcia.

Just as he finished speaking his cellphone rang and he answered it. Listening intently, his facial expressions changed from one of interest to one of shocked disbelief.

'That was the lab. We have found an exact match. The DNA found on Ms. Martin belongs to Detective Ethan O'Connell.'

There was a stunned silence as everyone turned to O'Connell, who looked as shocked as the rest of them.

'How is that possible? I was nowhere near that address yesterday. There must be some mistake!'

Hughes: 'No mistake. When they found your DNA matched, they double and triple checked.'

Hayes: 'Let's all calm down, there must be an explanation. There is no way Ethan did this.'

Shaw: 'Now it's Ethan? If you two are involved, it is better you are removed from this investigation. We can't have emotions clouding your judgment.'

Garcia: 'O'Connell, Hayes, is this true? You do know that this goes against department protocol.'

Hayes looked over at O'Connell, who just nodded. 'Yes Boss, we are sort of, but nothing serious. I will excuse myself from this investigation if you insist, but you know Ethan couldn't have done this.'

Garcia: 'You can stay on the investigation, but you need to look at the facts we have, not at the person you know. I find it hard to believe

O'Connell is involved but the DNA does not lie and it places him at the crime scene.

Let's get Ms. Martin up on the timeline and go through the process. What do we know?' Ethan slumped into the nearest chair and rubbed his hands over his face.

Mills: 'We know Martin left her shift at Target at 12.30, it is a four-block walk to her apartment. She estimates she got home at or just before 1.00. She was then attacked and raped. She remembers the rapist as being very tall, white with blue eyes, he also had a very large penis.'

Shaw: 'It's funny how they all remember the perp had a big dick. No facial features, just a huge schlong.'

Mills: 'Getting some penis envy there, Dave? She also states that it was over very quickly, maybe a couple of minutes. So, maybe he's done by 1.05, he then takes off the condom, flushes it and for some reason clocks her one on the jaw and leaves.'

Hayes: 'I took the call from the perp at 1.22, it was traced back to a payphone at the Port Authority Bus Terminal on 42nd Street. A seven-block walk could be done quite easily in around fifteen minutes.'

Garcia: 'Okay, that seems clear enough. Now seeing we found your DNA at the crime scene, O'Connell, can you account for your whereabouts yesterday up to the time you checked into the office? This is informal now, we just need to account for your movements. Do you want a lawyer present?'

Before O'Connell could answer, the office telephone rang and Mills answered it.

'Boss, Louise Martin is downstairs. She has come in to give a formal statement.'

'Good, Hayes can you go and collect her and get her written statement? Keep her there until we have finished with O'Connell, I will talk to her then.'

O'Connell; 'As you know, I had a personal day yesterday, with your approval of course. I had some personal business at City Hall. I took public transport and arrived there in time for opening at 9.00 am. It was a zoo, it took me over two hours to eventually get to the Inquiry window.

I filled in the required form and was told to go and pay $20, that took me until just after midday. I was then directed to another room where I was given a number and told to wait. They eventually called my number just after 1.00 pm and was told to go another room. I got up to the room only to find they are closed for lunch from 1 to 2 pm.

When I eventually got into the room at 2 pm, there were two people in front of me. I spent the next hour conducting my business. When I was done, I walked out of the building and switched on my cellphone, that's when I saw the messages from Hayes. I called her and heard about the attack on Martin so I came directly into the precinct.'

Garcia: 'Can anyone verify your whereabouts at the times you mentioned?'

'I assume I will be on their CCTV if they have one. I am sure they have a record of my payment of $20, that probably has a time stamp on it.'

Garcia: 'So, from approximately 12 noon until just after 2 pm, have you anything or anyone who can corroborate your whereabouts?'

'No, not really, as I said maybe on CCTV.'

'City Hall to 426 West 49th street is about twenty-five minutes by the subway. From the apartment to Port Authority Bus Terminal is what, about half a mile, an easy ten-minute walk. I am not jumping to conclusions here, but you are going to have to account for your time for that period,' Garcia said.

'Boss, somebody is setting me up here! It must go back to when I was mugged. The DNA on my credit card is understandable, but I have no answer to the hair. I will take a lie detector test to prove I am not involved.'

From afar the whole scenario was being observed. "This is going even better than I had hoped. Him having no alibi is a bit of unexpected luck; this is going to clinch the deal."

'Okay, let's cover all bases. Shaw, take Mills with you and go down to City Hall and see what they have covered by CCTV. O'Connell, I am going to get you in a lineup and see if Ms. Martin can identify you. No, don't object. It's just to cover all bases. I will organize a lie detector test but that will take time to get done, probably only tomorrow.

I am going down to the interview room to see Martin and ask her if she is up for an identity lineup. You hang around here and keep out of trouble. I believe you had nothing to do with this but let's do this by the book.'

Garcia walked down to the ground floor where he met Hayes who was on the way back. He turned her around and the two of them went back into the room to speak to Louise Martin.

'Ms. Martin, thank you for coming in and giving us your statement. I have a request that I hope you will agree to. We have a suspect and with your permission I would like you to try and identify him in a lineup. You will be behind a one-way mirror so you will be able to see him but he will not be able to see you. What do you say?'

'Yes, I will do it. He was well covered up and was wearing a balaclava but maybe I could pick him out.'

'Great. You wait here with detective Hayes while I set things up.'

Leaving the two women, Garcia went over to the desk sergeant and put in his request for a minimum of seven tall men six foot plus. Dress them up wearing a balaclava and covering all their features except for their eyes. Without explanation to the sergeant, Garcia went back up to the situation room.

He explained the situation to O'Connell, left him sitting at his desk and went into his office to make the call to arrange the lie detector test. He was informed the earliest that could be done was the following day at 10.00 am. It took three quarters of an hour to round up eight men for the lineup.

O'Connell, suitably dressed, joined the other eight and was handed the number six card. Garcia, Hayes and Louise Martin congregated in the observation room. Garcia pressed the intercom button and instructed the nine men to enter the room.

'Alright, Ms. Martin, take your time. If you think you have spotted your assailant, just tell us the number. I will call him out and get him to step forward so you can get a closer look.'

Louise Martin took a deep breath and started scanning the men from number one on the left. Of the nine men present number four was the closest in size to O'Connell. Martin stopped at #4 giving him a long serious look but she continued. She stopped again at #6, O'Connell, spending even more time examining him, before continuing. Seven through nine she skimmed over.

'Detective Garcia, I am not sure between #4 and #6.'

'Numbers four and six take one step forward the rest of you may leave by the same door you entered,' Garcia instructed via the intercom. He turned to Louise Martin. 'Take your time, go back to when you were apprehended, see if something jogs your memory.'

'Is it possible that they can say something? I might recognize his voice. If they could say the line "Cry out and I will slash your throat". That is what he said to me,' Louise crossed her arms, as if to shield herself from them.

Garcia pressed the intercom button and said, 'Number four say the line "Cry out and I will slash your throat".' He complied; Louise shook her head. 'Number six, your turn to say the line.'

O'Connell repeated the line and Louise Martin went stiff and started shaking. She cried out. 'That's him, that's the man who attacked and raped me! I recognize the bright blue eyes and that voice I will never forget.'

Garcia turned to Hayes, both looked shocked. *Could it really be O'Connell who committed this crime?* Why didn't it make sense? His DNA was at the crime scene, he was so far unaccounted for over the period the rape was committed, and now he was pulled out of a lineup.

'Ms. Martin, thank you for your help, you may have just taken a very dangerous man off the streets. Please keep this information to yourself as we want to make sure that we have crossed the T's and dotted the I's before we make the news available to the public. Detective Hayes will arrange for someone to give you a ride home. Thank you again.' June led Louise out of the room and Garcia stared through the mirror at the two men left in the room.

As soon as June and Louise had left the room, Garcia pressed the intercom button and called out, 'Number four you can leave. Six, stay where you are.'

As soon as number four had left the room, Garcia opened the inter leading door and entered the room. 'You can take off the balaclava, O'Connell, she fingered you as the rapist. This was an unofficial lineup as there was no IA rep present, but I can't let you leave the precinct.

I am not going to charge you for the rape at this time, I will wait until we see what Mills and Shaw find out at City Hall. Let's hope the CCTV can place you there and if not, hopefully the lie detector test clears you. Unfortunately, tonight you sleep in the holding cell. I will lock you in once the Lieutenant has left for the day and the shift has changed, no point in drawing any more attention to you. We still can't rule out that someone in this place is leaking information and the last thing I need in my life right now is someone leaking it that a cop is the Zodiac rapist.'

'Boss, like I said before, this is a setup, I was nowhere near 49th

Street today!' Ethan felt like his life was collapsing around him. *How was this even possible?*

'Then tell me what you were doing at City Hall that is so secretive?' Garcia challenged.

'I cannot say at this point, there are a few things in my past that have come up that I need answers to before I can make them public.'

'Seriously? You've been picked out of a lineup as a rapist and you're seriously not going to tell me what was so damn important at City Hall?' Ethan shook his head and Garcia sighed in frustration.

'I must be a fucking idiot but I'm going to trust you. You better not let me down, O'Connell. I'll rip you a new asshole if you do.'

Chapter 31
Exposed

The phone in Garcia's office broke the conversation cycle. He got up and walked over to his office, leaving Hayes and O'Connell in the situation room.

He barked into the receiver, 'Garcia.'

'It's me, Boss, we are just about ready to leave City Hall. There is not much to report as we are not getting any cooperation from the staff here. Their response is all the same, "Do you have a search warrant?" Jesus, you'd think we were all on the same side here. Can you see if you can get the necessary warrant? Mills and I are coming back to the precinct.'

'Okay Dave, I should have expected that City Hall is useless on a good day. The current anti-cop sentiment probably isn't helping either. I will go and see the Lieutenant. This is not good news for O'Connell, it looks like he spends tonight in lockup.'

Garcia hung up the phone and returned to the two waiting detectives. 'Bad news, O'Connell. Shaw and Mills weren't given any access to the CCTV at City Hall, so we are going to need a warrant. That's going to take hours, so we won't get it before they close at City Hall. This means at least tonight in lockup for you.'

'Shit, Boss, I had nothing to do with Louise Martin! This is a set up and I'm fucked if I know why someone would want to do this,' Ethan replied in frustration.

Watching remotely, the man smiled. This is better than I hoped for, I will have unrestricted access and enough time for what I must do.

'Sorry, but it can't be helped. If you were an ordinary citizen, I'd have enough to charge you with rape and robbery. Your DNA at the crime scene, the victim picking you out of a lineup and no verifiable alibi. For the record, I know you are not responsible but should this get out and the press find out that we let you walk, the shit would truly hit the fan. This isn't personal, O'Connell.

I am going to see Sergeant Dooley to explain the situation, hopefully he can put you in a holding cell on your own.'

'Okay Boss, I understand.'

Garcia made the short walk down to the ground floor where he caught Dooley's attention and indicated he wanted to talk in private. Dooley left the front desk and followed Garcia to a private office at the rear of the building.

'Mick, I have a favor to ask. I need somewhere secure for one of my detectives to spend the night. I would rather that fewer people know where he is, it's just for tonight hopefully.'

'I can put him up in the back holding cell with a *do not disturb* instruction. This is a bit unusual, who is the detective?'

'It's O'Connell. He needs to be kept from any press and any inquisitive cops. I will fill you in on the details tomorrow. Thanks for the help, pal, I owe you one,' Garcia patted his shoulder and left the room.

Garcia trudged his way back up to the third floor and entered the situation room to find Shaw and Mills had returned. He addressed the four detectives.

'I spoke with Dooley; he doesn't know the details, but he agreed you could spend the night in the back holding cell. He assured me you will not be disturbed. I will get the warrant for City Hall and hopefully early tomorrow we can verify your movements and get done with this.'

'I understand, thanks Boss. June, seeing how I won't be driving you home tonight, do you want to take my car?'

'I am not sure that is a good idea, insurance, and all that. I'll just take a cab.'

'No, you won't. I'll get you a ride home with one of the patrol cars. Back to work, any theories as to why our perp is denying this attack? Could there be a copycat out there?' asked Garcia.

'I can't see a copycat; there is no way he could know the exact details of each rape. The New Moon thing, the four hundred block addresses, the inserting of the zodiac card into the victims' vagina,' offered Hayes.

'If someone is following the rapes, they could easily work out the New Moon thing, the addresses, and the zodiac connections. I don't think we ever released information on where the cards were found. I think this bastard did do Martin; he is just fucking with us,' replied Mills.

Garcia: 'Let's work on the premise he did do Martin. O'Connell, you have the lie detector test tomorrow at 10 am. You've got to hope that goes well for you. Have you any scenario where you can explain the hair DNA found at the scene?'

'I reckon the person who mugged me is our perp. The credit card is easy, I would have touched it many times. I carry a comb in the same pocket as my wallet so the hairs found on her chest could have been caught up in my wallet. The pubic hair, I have no clue,' Ethan replied, still trying to wrap his brain around what had happened. *How did it come to this?*

Shaw: 'Maybe you were like the cops you see on the TV or the movies, you know, tucking your weapon in your pants waistband. Maybe it snagged one of your pubes, either from the nut sack or butt crack.'

Garcia: 'Enough joking, this is a serious matter. Let's wait for the search at City Hall and the results of the lie detector test. In the meantime, we have done all we can for today, I suggest we get down to the Pub and have a drink on me and get something to eat. I will bring O'Connell back here after the afternoon shift change, just less conspicuous.'

Secure in the knowledge that O'Connell was not going to be home before sometime tomorrow at the earliest, the man made ready to put the next phase of his plan into action.

He arrived at 595 Morgan Avenue at 6.45 pm, it was dark enough to obscure his detailed features and there was virtually no foot traffic. He was wearing a large backpack and carrying a heavy canvas bag. He walked up to the front door and had it open in seconds. Turning around, he checked for anyone observing him, and finding none he entered the building, closed the door, and locked it.

Switching lights on as he went, he opened the door to the basement and descended the one flight of stairs. He placed the large canvas bag on the floor and removed his backpack. From the backpack he extracted a power drill, already fitted with a quarter inch drill bit. Taking a tape measure and a marking pencil he walked over to the right-hand wall.

The basement was constructed with drywall covering raw concrete. Starting at the point of the toilet door he measured ten feet towards the middle of the wall and made a mark. He then measured ten feet to the left of that point and made a mark. Fixing the tape measure at ten feet he walked to the mark in the middle of the wall. Walking out at ninety degrees, when reached the ten-foot mark, he first went left and then returned and walked right. He ensured that there were no power plugs, light fittings or furniture within the semi-circle, nothing that could be used.

Returning to the center point of the wall he made two marks six inches from the floor and three inches apart. He plugged his extension cord into a power outlet and then connected it to his drill. From his canvas bag he extracted two large heavy metal brackets. Carefully lining them up on the edge of each marker he drilled two holes for each bracket. Next, he picked out a tube of strong fast drying adhesive, he cemented the two brackets directly over the drilled holes. Four large bolts were produced, he changed the drill bit for the correct size socket. He covered the bolts with the same adhesive and proceeded to screw them into the wall.

After waiting for thirty minutes to ensure the brackets were secure, he then retrieved a twenty-foot heavy link metal chain from his canvas bag. The chain was threaded through the eyes on the two brackets. Once securely threaded, he attached a wrist clamp at each end of the chain using a link secured by a heavy bolt. The clamps themselves functioned much like handcuffs, once closed only a special key could reopen them. Only these shackles would be secured around the captive's ankles, not his wrists.

Satisfied that everything was in place, he left the basement and went up to the second bedroom. Here he stripped the single bed and removed the mattress which he then carried down to the basement. On a return journey he collected two blankets and a pillow which he deposited on the mattress that was now positioned on the floor directly under the two wall brackets.

He stood back and surveyed his handiwork, satisfied, he smiled, everything was now in place. All he had to do was wait. Secure in the knowledge that O'Connell was safely out of the way, he would spend the night sleeping in his bed. Tomorrow was going to be interesting.

O'Connell was woken at 8.00 am by Garcia.

'I hope you had a pleasant night. I have decent coffee and donuts upstairs so let's go and prepare you for your polygraph test.'

'Surprisingly, I slept very well, I did have some weird dreams though.'

Garcia didn't care.

The two of them were met in the situation room by June Hayes. She hurried over and handed him a small wash bag.

'I put together some toiletries for you. Just a toothbrush and toothpaste, there is also[a small soap and some deodorant. I can't imagine you feel too fresh after a night in lockup,' Ethan smiled gratefully.

'Thanks June, I will go and clean up but first some coffee and a donut. Hopefully Shaw and Mills can find something to back up my City Hall alibi. I am confident I can pass the polygraph test. I didn't do this.'

By the time Shaw and Mills arrived at 8.30 am the search warrant had been delivered. Garcia handed it over and told them to be on their way. Shaw refused to leave before he had coffee and a donut. Garcia handed him and Mills each a cup and a paper bag containing four donuts and pointed them towards the door.

It was a nervy ninety-five-minute wait until Garcia was called informing him that the polygraph equipment was set up in interview room #2. He was instructed to bring O'Connell down immediately. O'Connell had given permission to Garcia, Hayes and Lieutenant Johnston to allow them to observe the test from the viewing room attached to interview room #2.

Johnston met them at the door to the interview room, he motioned Garcia and Hayes toward the viewing room and waved O'Connell into the interview room. Standing next to the polygraph was a petite, forty-something dark haired woman who walked towards O'Connell and extended her hand.

'Good morning, I am Officer Gillian Barker. I will be conducting your test today. I want you to relax and breathe normally. If you will sit down in the chair next to the equipment, we can get started.'

She motioned to the chair and O'Connell sat down resting his arms on the armrests, he took a deep breath and then relaxed.

'I am going to hook you up to the machine, so please roll up your right shirt sleeve just up you elbow so that it doesn't get caught up in any of the wires. Thank you. If you could lean forward slightly, I can start to hook you up.'

She produced two corrugated tubes that were gently attached to his upper and lower chest areas. These were used to measure the breathing of the subject. Next a blood pressure cuff was attached to his arm. This was only slightly inflated to a light pressure as it is used to collect constant data to detect any changes that occur in the heart rate and the pulse rate during the test.

Two finger cuffs were attached to two adjoining fingers on the same hand. These were used to measure skin conductivity which relates to sweat gland activity. Then another clip called a plethysmograph was attached to another finger. This was a medical device that measures blood rate volume.

A motion sensor in the form of a movement mat was placed under the arm, this is used to detect any motion which may be used to try and influence the testing process.

All the data collected was recorded which allowed the tester to ensure that there were no anomalies or errors included along with the actual testing results. This was to prevent false results or the subject purposely trying to influence the detector test.

Satisfied that everything was correctly connected, she addressed O'Connell.

'Detective, I am going to ask you a series of questions; please only answer yes or no. The first ones are obvious questions and will be used to set a base line. Are you feeling relaxed and ready to start?'

'Yes.'

'Is your name Ethan O'Connell?'

'Yes'

'Are you a detective at this precinct?'

'Yes.'

'Are you married?'

'No.'

'Are you in a relationship?'

'Um um, yes.' Aware that June was watching, he wasn't sure of the right answer.

'Just a yes or no please. Try and answer without any hesitation.' Ethan nodded.

'Have you ever committed any crime?'

'No.'

'Have you ever cheated on a test?'

'No.'

'Were you at City Hall between 9 am and 2 pm on February 1, this year?'

'Yes.'

'Did you break into the apartment 426 West 49th Street on February 1, this year.'

'No.'

'Did you attack and rape Louise Martin?'

'No.'

'Have you ever sexually assaulted any person, male or female?'

'No.'

Officer Barker flipped a switch on the recording equipment and addressed O'Connell. 'I have enough data to make a definite judgment. I thank you for your time, I am now going to disconnect you so please just relax this will only take a few minutes.'

Working quickly and efficiently, Barker first removed the two corrugated tubes, then the two finger cuffs and the blood pressure machine and finally the plethysmograph.

'Okay Detective, we are all done you may leave us now. I will discuss the results with Lieutenant Johnston. When we are done, I am sure he will speak to you. Thank you again.'

She extended her hand, O'Connell shook it, turned and left the room without any comment. As he stepped out of the interview room he was met by Shaw, Hayes and Johnston.

'I will talk to Officer Barker; please don't leave the building. I will call you as soon as I have the validated results.' Ethan acknowledged his request and left with the others.

Garcia, Hayes and O'Connell left Johnston and headed back up the third floor in silence. Nothing was said until they were in the confines of the situation room.

'That seemed to go quite well. Hopefully Shaw and Mills will come back confirming your whereabouts. In the meantime, I am going to catch up on some paperwork in my office. You two just take it easy.'

'I noticed you stumbled on one of her questions, why was that?' June asked.

'I knew you, Garcia and Johnston were watching so I wasn't sure what would happen if I said yes or how you would feel if I said no.' he answered, honestly.

'If you were referring to me then you gave the right answer, if you were referring to someone else then you gave the wrong answer.'

'I gave the right answer.'

'Maybe we can spend the night together, work off some of the tensions.'

'I'd love to but hopefully when Shaw and Mills get back and corroborate my alibi, Garcia will let me leave for the day. I need to get properly cleaned up and I have some stuff to take care of, so I'll take a rain check but tomorrow night definitely.'

That works out perfectly for me, he will be on his own. Only one to deal with.

At exactly 11.45 am, Shaw and Mills arrived back in the situation room. Garcia saw them arrive and left his office to join the others.

'Okay Dave, what news? Let it be good,' Garcia crossed his arms, waiting for the update.

'Really good, Boss. We managed to establish O'Connell's movements; the key ones were at 12.15 pm when he paid a $20 fee in room 100 to conduct a property search. The next point we verified was that at 1.08 pm he presented the $20 receipt to the clerk in room 107 and the completed form for a property search. The property records are in room 202, we confirmed they are closed between 1 and 2 pm.

We timed the walk from room 107 to 202, it took two minutes, so he would have arrived there at around 1.12 pm. We know that Martin was raped before 1.22 pm, Hayes took the call and confirmed the time. So, unless O'Connell is a combination of Superman and The Flash, he couldn't have done Martin.'

'Jesus, thank God for that. I was sure you couldn't have done it. We have to wait and see the results of your polygraph, they can sometimes come up false but as your alibi checks out, you are free and clear as far as I am concerned.'

They had barely finished congratulating each other when a wheezing Johnston walked into the room.

'Man, we gotta get that elevator fixed. I knew I should have just called you but I wanted to do this in person. Barker evaluated your polygraph results; she tells me she has never seen an absolutely perfect score before, but she has now. You aced the test and are no longer a suspect. I am sorry we had to hold you overnight, but now that we have done it by the book, there can be no doubts or suspicions.

Mike, I suggest you give the man the rest of the day off and let him go home and take it easy. It's all hands to the pump, I want this bastard put away once and for all. Good day folks,' Johnston waddled out of the room and they collectively breathed a sigh of relief.

Garcia confirmed Johnston's request for O'Connell, who decided to leave immediately. He turned to Hayes and confirmed that he would pick her up at the normal time tomorrow.

O'Connell arrived home just after 2.00 pm, parked his car right outside his front door, locked it and walked up the stairs. He unlocked the front door and stepped into the house then turned around to close and lock the door. Before he could turn back around, he felt a sharp pain in his neck. It was the last thing he felt before collapsing to the floor.

Standing over him was a tall man wearing a full-face balaclava. He placed the empty ketamine syringe on the floor next to O'Connell's prone body. He then turned O'Connell onto his back and dragged him by his feet towards the basement door.

Once at the door he pulled O'Connell feet first down to the third step and then propped him up to a sitting position. Taking his right arm, he hoisted the body onto his left shoulder and backed carefully down the remaining steps. At the bottom of the stairs, he walked over to where the mattress was located and lowered the body. He placed a shackle on each ankle and secured the bolts locking them in place.

He knew it would take a few minutes for the ketamine to wear off so he walked over to the small fridge and opened a can of Miller Light. Taking a long swig, he walked over to the closest Lazy Boy chair and made himself comfortable. It took just seven minutes for O'Connell to start coming around. Still wearing the balaclava, he walked over to the mattress to watch O'Connell surface.

O'Connell, still groggy and disoriented, sat up and shook his head. He looked around at his surroundings, confused about why he was sitting on a mattress in his basement. He glanced up to see a very tall man wearing a balaclava standing over him. He tried to stand up but instantly realized his legs were shackled.

Finding his voice, he shouted out, 'Who the fuck are you and what are you doing in my basement? Why am I chained up? I am a New York cop and you are going to be in one huge pile of shit.'

'So many questions and so angry. I am your worst nightmare; your problems are only just beginning.'

'Who are you? What's with the balaclava, why don't you show your face?'

'Oh, you want to see who I am? Well, okay then, seeing as you asked so nicely and all.'

The man turned around, put his beer can on the nearest table and with his back turned to O'Connell, he removed his balaclava. He ran his fingers through his hair and turned around.

O'Connell looked the man in the face and gasped, 'No, it's not possible,' It felt like he'd been punched in the gut.

'Oh, but it is,' was the answer.

Chapter 32
June 15, 1990 5.30 am

No sooner had Dennis O'Connell left the building when the three remaining men began dismantling any trace of them having been in the building. The $100,000 had been checked and split into two. They had contemplated leaving the building and not paying the father his share but did not want to draw any further attention to themselves.

The final step before vacating the premises would be to pay off the parents and remove any trace evidence in the birthing room. The man in charge bundled up the $50,000 and made his way to the birthing room. He had barely entered the room when he was blocked by the frantic father.

'Where is the doctor? There is another baby coming!'

'What do you mean *another baby coming*?'

'My wife is in agony; there is another one almost out, the doctor must come!' The man yelled.

Fuck it, this was not part of the plan, he thought, but we cannot leave now or there could be consequences. 'Okay, I will get him wait here. Take this money in the meantime,' he pushed the pile of money into the man's hands.

He left the room muttering, this was a situation that could turn into a major problem. He called out to the "doctor." 'Brother, there is a second baby coming. Should we leave and let them get on with it?'

'No, if there is a problem and either or both die, we could end up in real shit. I will check her out and deliver the child. You make sure everything else is cleaned.'

By the time the doctor got to the women, she had crowned and the baby was on the way. How did he not see there was a second baby?

'Okay, all looks good, just push when you feel the next contraction. Your baby is almost there.'

'Hey doctor, has the buyer left already? Maybe he will take this other one as well. We can offer him a cut rate,' the father bargained; the panic forgotten as he saw a way to get more money.

'The buyer has left the building and we have no way of contacting him. You must take this child with you when you leave. It may be a blessing in disguise. Anyone knowing you and your wife must have known she was pregnant. This way there should be no questions. Now leave me. I need to bring your baby into the world.'

The father, Jack Livingstone, moved away from the doctor and his common law wife, Elizabeth "Lizzy" Barnes. Livingstone, who had just turned twenty-two, was a middle school dropout. Uneducated, with no job skills and no future, was a mean son of a bitch. He had been with twenty-one-year-old Lizzy for the past year and a half.

Between the two of them they managed to scrape through month by month. Lizzy's pregnancy came at an inopportune time, his first suggestion was for her to have an abortion, which she outright refused. An overheard conversation in his local bar gave Jake an idea to make a profit on Lizzy's condition. The narrator was sounding off on the subject of rich people buying newborn children and paying silly money for the privilege. The wheels in his brain started turning; abortions cost money but selling the kid could set them up nicely. His mind was made up.

Jake went about finding out all he could about "Baby Brokers". He asked around all the low life contacts he had and was led down many dead ends. But what he did find out was that the price being paid for a newborn baby far exceeded that of one more than one week old. His determination finally led him to an address in the Little Egypt area in Astoria Queens. There he made contact with a man only known as Mohammad.

He was led to a one room 'office' where he was told to take a seat. The office was only furnished with two chairs and a desk. There were no windows and only the single door through which he had just entered. Mohammad said he would be back shortly, and Jake should wait.

He was kept waiting almost fifteen minutes before the door opened and Mohammad and two similar looking men entered the room. No introductions were made and no other names provided.

The taller of the three men addressed him, 'What is your name and what is your business with us?'

'My name is Jake Livingstone and I am looking to use your services in placing a baby for adoption.'

'What makes you think we can help you with that? There are government agencies that perform those tasks.'

'Yes, I know that, but there is no money in that for us. We want to use a "baby broker" such as yourself to place the baby.'

'Mohammad, search him for any recording devices,' one of the men instructed.

Mohammad instructed Jake to lift his arms in the air and spread his legs, Jake complied. He was subjected to a thorough search, his shirt was unbuttoned, nothing suspicious was found. He was told to drop his trousers and lower his underpants; his butt cheeks were spread and his anus inspected. Finding nothing, Mohammad indicated all was clear.

'It seems that you are not a police plant, so let's get down to business. If the baby is already born and more than one week old, it is possible to place the child but is very difficult and a big risk.'

'My wife is about three months pregnant.'

'Excellent. That gives us a very good possibility of placing the child at a good price. What I need from you is an exact date or close as possible of when the child will be born. Mohammad will give you exact instructions on what to do and how to contact us. You will only make contact twice, once when you have the expected date of birth, which you must do within forty-eight hours of today, and secondly once your wife's contractions start. Is that clear? Any infringement of these rules will invalidate our agreement.'

'No Sir, I fully understand. How much money can we expect?'

'It is difficult to say, but providing the child is healthy, up to around $50,000. That is provided I can find the right buyer. I am leaving now; Mohammad will take care of you. Goodbye.'

The second the door closed Mohammad turned to Jake. I am giving you this phone number. Within the next three days you make a call to this number and tell us of the planned date of birth of the child.

The second and last call you make will be when your wife's water breaks. You will then be given instructions on what to do. If you do not follow these instructions and make any other calls to this phone number our agreement will be canceled, is this clear?'

'Yes, it is clear, thank you very much,' Jake noted the number and committed it to memory.

Getting no further response, Jake left the room and exited the building. He had to get to Lizzy with the news and to ensure that she kept their arrangement secret. He walked down the street and hopped aboard the first bus that passed by. He alighted the bus at the corner of Lexington Avenue and 59th Street. Across the street he entered the subway and made his way to the northbound Number 6 platform.

The 35-minute trip to Hunt's Point in the Bronx gave him time to contemplate how he would convey the news to Lizzy. He decided on the direct approach, to give her no time to weigh up the consequences, just the positives. By the time he reached their squalid Bryant Avenue apartment it was just after 5 pm, she was sure to be home.

As usual, the elevator wasn't working but being in the mood he was in, he didn't bother cursing. Taking the stairs two at a time he bounded up to the third floor, turned right and stopped outside the door of 3B. He tried the door and it opened, she had forgotten to lock it behind her, but he was in a good mood and wouldn't berate her this time.

'Lizzy, where are you? I've got great news! All our problems will be solved, come here,' he called out.

Lizzy hadn't been home for more than a few minutes, still dressed in her "Fat Arnie's Diner" uniform where she worked as a waitress, she looked exhausted. She could use some good news and the fact that Jake was in a good mood was a bonus.

'Lizzy, I have managed to organize someone to adopt our baby when it is born. They will pay us up to $5,000 to take the child off our hands. Great news, hey.'

'Why would you want me to give up our baby?' Lizzy asked, her hand protectively moving down to her belly.

'You know we can't afford a child and the money will help us get out of debt. We can always have another child later,' Jake reasoned.

'But $5,000?'

Realizing he may have underestimated her by trying to shortchange her, he replied, 'That was the bottom line they said, it could be more, maybe up to ten grand. Anyway, we are going to do it, end of discussion. Now, you must work out when the baby will be born.'

'I already have. I think it will be in the middle of June. Are you sure there is no other way?'

'There is no other way. Now, you have to take care of yourself, and we need to stay away from doctors and do not tell that shithead boss of yours, Fat Arnie, about your condition.'

The following day Jake made the first call confirming a date around the middle of June. For the next six months Lizzy had the calmest time of their relationship. No more beatings, even when Jake had tried one on, he was always considerate. Maybe giving the baby up for adoption was the best choice.

Lizzie's contractions began right on cue, 10 pm on the night of June 14. Jake made the second phone call which was answered on the second ring. He was given an address in Prospect Heights and told to get there immediately.

Packing only a change of clothing for Lizzy, the couple made their way downstairs. Jake, in the meantime, had called the number for a local mini-cab company. The cab arrived within minutes, Jake gave the address, and they were on their way. The $25 fee was an expense that would be well worth it in his eyes, and unavoidable.

They were met by the same three men from the first meeting. Lizzy was ushered into a side room where there was a bed, wash basin and two chairs. Jake was told to take one of the chairs, sit down and shut up. Lizzy was directed to the bed and told to lie down and remove her underwear, which she did. The doctor performed a perfunctory examination and called for Mohammad.

'Mohammad, make the call, I estimate this baby will be born in the next five or six hours. It's 11.40 pm now so call the number around 3.45 am to be sure that they do not arrive too much before the child is born. Timing is very important; the child must not spend any time with the mother.'

By 3.30 am it was clear the baby was on its way and Mohammad dialed the number. The call was answered immediately. He indicated to the doctor that the buyer was on the way. At exactly 4.35 am, Lizzy produced a healthy baby boy.

The doctor tied and snipped the umbilical cord and immediately handed him off to the third man. Despite Lizzy's pleas to at least hold the child one time, he was wrapped up in a birthing blanket and taken from the room. The afterbirth was gathered up and dumped into a bag for disposal. He gave Lizzy a cursory examination, finding no tears, he cleaned her up.

With perfect timing, the child was handed off to the buyers and the money exchange completed. All in all, a satisfactory transaction. Time to clean up any evidence and leave the building. That was until he heard Jake's shout for help.

Fifty-five minutes after the first child, at 5.30 am the second baby boy was born. This time Lizzy was handed the baby and immediately she burst into tears. She knew the first baby was gone but she still had a child. Jake consoled himself with the fact that he was $50,000 better off; he was pretty sure he could convince Lizzy to give the child up for adoption through normal channels.

The doctor performed the second examination, which included ensuring there wasn't a third baby, cleaned Lizzy up and turned to Jake.

'You must take your wife and the child to the nearest facility which is the Center for Community Health Hospital. Tell them she gave birth before you could get to the hospital. Do not involve anyone else as we, and that includes you, will end up being arrested. Also, if we hear anything about this transaction through the grapevine, we have people who will take care of you. Now leave the building, your wife is young and strong and will have little discomfort in walking.'

Jake understood the implied threat, helped Lizzy to her feet and with the baby wrapped in a stained white towel, left the building. The short two and a half block walk to the hospital was accomplished without incident. Lizzy struggled to walk so it was a slow journey, with Jake helping her. They arrived at the Emergency Room where a nurse spotted them and immediately whisked them into a consulting room. A doctor was called and she examined the mother and child, finding both in satisfactory condition.

On questioning them, both had the same story. Lizzy felt her water breaking and, not understanding what was happening, they made their way by bus to the hospital. They had alighted the bus four blocks away and began walking. Lizzy had felt the baby coming so they found shelter in an alcove. When the baby came, Jake knew how to tie the umbilical cord and cut it. The nurse and doctor were both skeptical as Jake hardly looked like he could open a pickle jar, let alone cut an umbilical cord, but as mother and child were well, they dropped the subject.

Once formalities were complete, they were issued a record of birth showing Elizabeth Barnes as mother and Jake Livingstone as the father. The baby's name was recorded as Matthew Livingstone.

Matthew Livingstone would lead a very different life to that of his twin brother Ethan O'Connell.

Chapter 33
Matthew Livingstone

With baby Matthew wrapped up in a hospital birthing blanket the new parents were free to leave the hospital. Being totally unprepared to take home a newly born child, Lizzy and Jake had no clue what to do next. The orderly manning the front door of the hospital noticed the confused couple.

'What seems to be the issue? Can I be of help?'

Lizzy answered, 'I have just given birth to my baby boy, we are quite a distance from home, and I don't have anything prepared and don't really know what I need.'

'My girlfriend Theresa works at the CVS on 9th street about half a mile away. Why don't you take a cab over there and ask for her, tell her I sent you. She will fix you up with what you need.'

Lizzy thanked the man and she and her little family took a short cab ride to the CVS on 9th Street. Jake was feeling generous just this one time. True to the orderly's word, Theresa set them up with all that they would need for the first few days. Lizzy had decided that she would breastfeed Matthew, but Theresa suggested she take some baby formula just in case.

Jake paid for the supplies in cash and they left the store. Loaded down with nearly $100 worth of goods for Matthew, there was no way they could make it home using public transport. Jake still feeling flush with cash hailed a passing taxi. The trip home to apartment 3B, 1130 Bryant Avenue in the Hunt's Point area of the Bronx would take the best part of one hour and set him back $43.00, the most he had ever paid for a cab.

The first few months of Matthew's life went by without incident. Jake told Lizzy that the $5.000 they had received for selling the other boy would tide them over until she could get back to work. He, on the other hand, seemed to have no intention of resuming work or even looking for new employment. Lizzy was just happy that there were no more beatings and that she had the baby she had always wanted.

Neither of them wasted any thought on the fact that Matthew had a twin brother somewhere out there.

At Jake's insistence, Lizzy went back to work at Fat Arnie's Diner by August 1, Matthew was seven weeks old. Fat Arnie was not happy with Lizzy bringing the baby into the diner but at $8.00 per hour plus tips, Lizzy couldn't afford childcare.

Jake on the other hand was living large, not seeing the need to find work as he had plenty of cash. He had started drinking heavily again and when drunk he began berating Lizzy over anything and everything he could think of. She knew better than to talk back to him, so she just accepted her fate.

By Matthew's first birthday, Jake's money had virtually run out. Lizzy, still unaware that their payment was $50,000, was under the impression that Jake had been doing work of some kind. Now that the funds had been depleted, Jake no longer gave her his weekly "pay". They could not live on her income alone.

When she asked a visibly drunk Jake where his weekly wages were, he became belligerent. Against her better judgment, she continued to press him about his paycheck. Feeling cornered in his lie, he responded in the only way he knew how. It was the first of many beatings she would suffer.

Jake remembered the easy money they had made selling their baby and decided *why not do it again*? Try as he might, he could not get Lizzy pregnant again. A visit to the local doctor resulted in several tests, which finally concluded that Lizzy would be unable to have another child. Something to do with damage done giving birth to Matthew.

Despite the family hardships, young Matthew, known to everyone as Matty, thrived. He was a friendly child, always with a ready smile. By the time he started school in the fall of 1996, he was big for his age. It was difficult to see where he got his size and looks from, the only trait he had from his parents were his mother's blue eyes.

By the time Matty was due to start school, the family had relocated to 605 Costner Street in The Bronx. It was a big step down from one squalid apartment to another. Jake was still unemployed and scrounged money wherever he could find it, day jobs, a bit of petty thievery and panhandling.

Matty started at the George Washington School, Public School #47 on August 19, 1996. As far as public schools went, this one was one of the rougher schools in the Bronx area. Being white in a predominately black school he came in for a lot of bullying. After returning home on the first day in a tearful state, his father questioned him on why he was crying. He told his father that a group of seven-year-old black kids had teased him and pushed him around.

Jake grabbed him by the collar and slapped him twice across the face, 'Don't you ever come crying to me again about being bullied. Stand up for yourself and don't take any shit from any other kid. Fight back, don't be a wimp!'

Matty took his father's advice literally. The next day at first recess, he marched over to the group who had picked on him the previous day. He walked over to the biggest kid in the group and without any warning punched him on the nose. The kid dropped to the ground holding his bleeding nose. His friends stood back in awe.

'What did you do that for?' the boy cried out, blood dripping through his fingers.

'That is just a warning, do not fuck around with me or I will hurt you. Now stay the fuck away from me,' Matty may have been six years old, but he'd heard his father cussing his entire life.

Matty was an instant hero to the minority white kids of his age. They gravitated towards him for their own protection. Matty and his little gang of white kids never had any further problems while at PS47.

As far as his schoolwork went, he did above average but only enough to stay out of the teachers' bad books. Physical activities were where he excelled. Being the youngest in the class was offset by him being the biggest and strongest. Other kids looked up to him and all knew not to mess with him.

His elementary school years passed with no further incidents but also with no real achievements. Home life existed on two planes; there was peace and enough food to go around when Jake managed to "score" some money and absolute terror when the opposite occurred.

When Jake had drink in him, he was a mean bastard. He would erupt for no reason and anyone in his path bore the brunt of his anger. Lizzy was fiercely protective of her son and took the brunt of that anger to keep Jake from hurting Matty.

Matty started his middle school year on August 16, 2000, at (X286) Fannie Lou Harmer. He was ten years and two months old. His commute to and from school was by the free school bus service. He was again in a school system that was predominately African

American and Hispanic kids.

On Monday August 30, he was called from his classroom and told to report to the front office. Waiting there for him was a uniformed police officer, who with no explanation told him to follow him to the waiting police cruiser. Not a word was spoken on the trip back to Costner Street.

Fifteen minutes later the cruiser pulled up outside number 605. The scene was one of complete chaos, he spotted his father standing next to an ambulance talking to a paramedic and a uniformed police officer. Breaking away from the cop that had brought him home, he ran to his father fearing the worst.

'Dad, what's happening? Where's Mom?' Matty was looking around frantically, trying to find his mom.

'Son, there has been an accident. Mom was cleaning the outside windows when she slipped and fell. She is gone, she died instantly by hitting her head on the sidewalk. There was nothing I could do,' Jake said, feigning emotional distress. Matty knew better. His father had never felt bad about anything that happened to his mom.

Matty looked around and saw the gurney, the unmistakable shape of a body under the sheet. He ran towards it calling for his mother while attempting to remove the sheet. He was held back by one of the paramedics.

Turning to his father, he screamed at the top of his voice, 'You did this, you killed her!'

'Why would he say that?' asked the cop, standing next to Jake.

'He is just shocked and is lashing out, he doesn't mean it,' Jake explained calmly, his rage building on the inside. That little fucker was going to have his head smacked in just as soon as these cops left.

'I do mean it, you must have beaten her again, you killed her!' shouted Matty at the top of his voice.

The cop turned to the female paramedic, 'Can you look after the boy until we can get him to calm down? Mr. Livingstone, you need to come down to the station and give a statement. Do you need a ride?'

Jake nodded and followed the cop to the police cruiser. He was concerned that his outburst might lead to the police investigating his claims. Through all of her beatings, Lizzy had never once called the cops or laid a charge against him. He knew she had some old bruises and scars that might show up if someone was looking for them.

At the station house, Matty was led away to a waiting room, and given a Mountain Dew and a packet of Cheetos. Jake was escorted to an interview room and told to wait. They kept him waiting for almost half an hour before a detective entered the room. He was accompanied by a uniformed officer.

'Mr. Livingstone, I am sorry for your loss, but I must ask you some questions. Do you want a lawyer present?'

'Why do I need a lawyer? Am I being accused of something?'

'No, it is just police procedure where the cause of a death may be in question. Again, do you want a lawyer present? The court will provide one if you cannot afford representation.'

'No Sir, I have nothing to hide,' Jake had been lying his whole life. He was sure he could lie his way out of this problem.

'Right, my name is Detective Robert Fowler, badge 12785. Are you Jake Livingstone, the husband of Elizabeth, the deceased?'

'No, we never married. She is Elizabeth Barnes. I am the father of the boy, Matthew Livingstone.'

'So, you are the Common Law husband?'

'Yes.'

'Can you tell me what occurred this morning at 605 Costner Street here in The Bronx?'

'I was sitting in the front room watching television, Lizzy was cleaning up. I said to her it was about time she did something about cleaning the windows as you could hardly see out of them. She told me to fuck off and clean them myself.

Well, as any other self-respecting man, I would not take that from her and told her if she didn't do the job to my satisfaction there would be trouble. A man has to assert his authority, right? She knows better than to push me, so she got a bucket of water and some cleaning liquid and got to work.'

'You say 'if she didn't do the job right there would be trouble,' what exactly do you mean by that? Would you have physically abused her?'

'No Sir, you have it wrong. I just implied there would be trouble, it always works. Anyway, she started to wash the inside of the windows, took her about twenty minutes and then she starts packing up. I said to her *"what about the outside?"*. She looks at me like I am an idiot. The dirt is on the outside, I mean how stupid is she? I tell her she must clean the outside as well.'

'Then what happened?' Detective Fowler was starting to loathe this sack of shit sitting in front of him but had to remain impartial.

'She gets on the ledge but forgets to take the bucket and asks me to hand it to her. I get up from the sofa, pick up the bucket and hand it to her through the window. The stupid woman takes the bucket in both hands, leans back and falls off the ledge. The rest is history she fell and hit her head on the sidewalk. I rushed downstairs but she was dead when I got to her, there was nothing I could do. I called 911.'

'We didn't find a bucket on or near the sidewalk. Why is that?'

'Shit, you saw the neighborhood, some asshole probably stole it, Jake waved his hand to indicate the answer was obvious.

'Okay Mr. Livingston, write down exactly what you have told me and sign it as your statement. You do write, don't you?' Fowler couldn't resist getting a dig in at this arrogant son of a bitch.

'Of course, I do, Jake answered defensively, irritated at having his intelligence called into question.

Detective Fowler left Jake to complete his statement and went looking for Matthew. He found him silently crying on a chair in the corner.

'Hello Matthew, I am Detective Fowler. I am really sorry for your loss, I am going to ask you a few questions, is that OK?' Detective Fowler crouched down in front of him to get to his eye level.

'Yes Sir.'

Going strictly against police protocol, Fowler just jumped in.

'Did your father beat your mother?'

'Yes Sir.'

'Many times, or just a few?'

'Many times, mostly when he was drunk.'

'Did your father beat you?'

'Yes, but most times he tried my mother would try and stop him and then he would beat her instead.'

'Did she ever call the police?'

'No, she was too scared, Matty sniffed, wiping his nose on his sleeve.

'Thank you, you have been a great help, Detective Fowler patted him on the shoulder.

Fowler left Matty and went looking for his Lieutenant, whom he found in his office.

'Boss, we have a dead woman. Elizabeth Barnes fell from a third-floor apartment window, hit head her on the sidewalk and died instantly. We have her common law husband, Jake Livingston, in interview room #1. I have spoken with his son Matthew who confirms his father regularly beat the deceased. I want to hold him on suspicion of pushing her out of the said window.'

'You interviewed the son? Was the father present or did he give his permission?'

'Neither Boss. He did it. I can just tell, mean little bastard.'

'You dumb son of a bitch, you know you can't interview a minor without the proper process in place. If, and this is a big if, this gets to court they will throw it out. You know this, what is wrong with you?' the Lieutenant slapped his palm against his desk.

'Boss, the autopsy will show bruising, I guarantee it.'

'It may very well be but there could be any reason for old bruises. You interviewing the kid without the proper process negates his testimony. Get Livingston's statement and cut him loose.'

'But Boss,' Fowler started to disagree.

'No buts, just do it. Now.'

Jake finished and signed his statement and retrieved Matthew from the waiting room. With a smirk on his face, he left the precinct and returned home. Once safely inside the apartment he turned to Matthew.

'Your dumb bitch mother is dead; you need to get over it. If I have any crap from you, you may just go the same way as her. You don't talk to the cops without me being there. Got it?'

It was at that moment that Matty was convinced that his father had killed his mother. He just nodded; he knew there was nothing he could do about it now but his time would come.

For his middle school years Matty went with the flow. He never stood out, just did what he had to, never looking for trouble. His home life was a day-to-day existence. Some days there was food and other days not. All depended on Jake making some money and whether he was willing to spend any of it on feeding his kid.

Jake's inability to find regular employment had led him to affiliate himself with the local gang – Point Crowns. Being a white man in a predominately Hispanic gang, he was used mainly as a gofer. His jobs consisted of collecting debts, running small amounts of drugs, mainly heroin and cocaine.

Fourteen-year-old Matthew Livingston entered high school in the fall of 2004. He was already 5'10" and a solid 145lb. Good looking with piercing blue eyes and a shock of brown hair, he was popular with the girls. Very well endowed, he had lost his virginity to one of the neighborhood wives.

He had a part time job delivering groceries and was seduced by one of the ladies he was delivering to. Aside from teaching him the art of sex, she also gave him a huge tip. Word got around and Matty found himself a regular delivery route, more sex than any teenage boy would wish for and great tips. Wise beyond his years, he always made sure that there was never any chance of him being caught by an angry husband or boyfriend.

When he wasn't making deliveries, he was casing the area for opportunities. Aware that one day he would either break away from his father or somehow be let down by him, it drove him to squirrel away as much cash as he could.

He started his junior year of high school in the fall of 2006. Now a strapping 6'3" he stood out from the crowd. Having little or no interest in school or after-hours curricular activities, his only mission was survival.

On Friday September 22, 2006, it finally happened. Jake was still involved with the Point Crowns gang and had just finished a debt collection. On his way back to hand in the cash, he stopped for a drink at a local bar where he overheard a conversation. The two men involved were well known for being connected to a horse race betting syndicate. They were quietly discussing an upcoming race where they knew that it was being fixed, an insignificant race at a local track. It was a sure thing at 5-1 odds, they were stood to make a small killing.

Jake was never one to miss an opportunity and decided to "borrow" two grand from his cash collections and lay a bet on the race. At 5-1 he would clear ten grand which would set him up. He went to the nearest off-course tote and he laid the bet on horse #8 Lucky for Some. Somewhere there was a disconnect and the horse came in second. What he hadn't heard was that the race was fixed to ensure that #8 was backed for a place but not a win.

Jake was fully aware of what would happen if he pitched up two grand short; he wouldn't make it out of the door alive. He wasn't family, he was just a gofer, they would make an example of him. He took the only action he could think of; he would leave the area and take the remaining proceeds with him. He had collected $7,450, less the $2,000 bet, it left him enough to disappear.

11.30 pm there was a knock on the apartment door. Matty answered the door only to be confronted by three large heavily tattooed Hispanic men.

'Where is that cocksucker, Jake Livingston?'

'He is not home. I don't know where he is.'

Matty was pushed aside as the three men forced themselves into the apartment. It didn't take them long to search a two-room apartment to find he wasn't home.

'You tell that fucker if he doesn't show up with our money by the morning, he is a dead man. And don't think we won't take it out on you as well.'

Matty realized that the threat was real; he was sure his father had somehow ripped these gangsters off and done a runner. If that was the case, there was no way he would be paying back their money by the morning. It meant one thing for sure; they would be coming around to see him the next day. A message had to be sent *don't steal from the Point Crowners.*

Sixteen-year-old Matthew Livingston made an immediate decision that day that probably saved his life. He collected his life's savings, packed a bag, and left the apartment. He headed for the Port Authority where he booked a one-way ticket to San Francisco. It would be several years before he returned to New York.

Jake Livingston's body was found two weeks later in a dark alley. Both his hands had been chopped off and his throat cut, a clear message that nobody steals from the Point Crowns gang. Nobody was ever prosecuted for the murder.

Chapter 34
Taken

Ethan stared at the man who was hovering over him, it was like looking into a mirror. He was an exact copy of himself, right down to the same haircut.

'Who the hell are you?'

'I am your twin brother, O'Connell. I don't know how the hell that happened, but it did and here we are.'

As Ethan attempted to stand up and face his twin, he became aware that he had shackles on each ankle. He turned around to face the wall to see that he had been secured by a very stout chain.

'What is going on here? Why am I chained up, what do you want?'

'What do I want? It's payback time.'

'Payback for what? I don't understand, up until this minute I didn't even know you existed,' Ethan tugged on the chain, realization setting in.

'I am taking over your life as it seems a whole lot better than the one I was subjected to. We are identical twins; we have the same birthday. My parents are your parents, I know you found out you were adopted and are trying to track down your biological parents. Well, over the next few hours I will introduce you to them.'

'How do you know that I am trying to track down my biological parents?'

'I know everything about you, I have your whole house bugged. There are cameras in your bedroom, three of them down here, I have been monitoring your every move.'

'Jesus, how long has this been going on?' Ethan looked around his basement, trying to see where a camera could possibly have been hidden.

'Long enough. I know your every nuance, how you speak. I have watched you with June Hayes and I am looking forward to having my way with her,' Matthew chuckled, envisioning his plan.

'You have no chance! The minute you open your mouth everyone will know it is not me.'

In his best Bronx accent, he replied, 'My bro, that June you can see she's not a slide' Changing his voice, he lost the accent and repeated the comment, 'My brother, that June you can see she's not promiscuous.'

Shocked by the perfect imitation of his voice, Ethan just stared at him. 'They will still get you. How do you hope to fool them back at the precinct? You don't know the layout of the place, who sits where, what discussions we have had. Someone will ask you something or you will say or do something that will give you away.'

'How wrong you are brother. I know everything about your so called "Situation Room". I have had the place bugged for a while now,' Matthew sat down in the Lazy-Boy, kicked up the footrest and took a swig of beer.

'Two bugged telephones won't tell you anything about the place,' Ethan countered.

'I really suckered the whole lot of you with those. The telephone bugs were just a decoy, the situation room and Garcia's office are both covered by cameras. Here, take a look, I saw and listened to every discussion,' he whipped out his tablet and tapped on the screen.

He selected the cameras and turned the tablet towards Ethan. There in high definition was the complete view of Shaw, Hayes and Mills in the situation room and of Garcia sitting behind his desk in his office. Ethan was stunned, he could hear and see everything.

'Jesus, no wonder you knew what we were doing and what reactions we had when you called. We had the techies sweep the rooms for bugs, but they only found the ones on the phones.'

'I figured you would eventually find the phone bugs, so I watched your techies arrive and sweep the two phones. The minute I heard they would check both offices for further bugs I disabled the cameras. As there was no signal being sent when they were disabled, they never found anything. You were all so predictable,' Matthew mocked.

'So, you are obviously the Zodiac Rapist but why have you gone to so much trouble just to capture me?' *Stay calm, get him talking about himself. He thinks he's so smart. Trip him up, O'Connell, THINK!*

'It's a long story but what the hell, we have plenty of time so I will bring you up to date,' Matthew made himself comfortable, clearly enjoying Ethan's discomfort.

'So you are going to tell me why, but if this was your plan, why the fuck did you rape those women and then slaughter the Marx's'?'

'All in good time, dear brother, but let's start at the beginning, shall we? As you now know we were born on the same day, and we look exactly alike so we can assume we are twin brothers. My birth name is Matthew Livingstone, our parents are Jake Livingstone and Elizabeth Barnes, she was always called Lizzie. They were never married.'

'How do you know that they are our biological parents? Maybe you were also adopted.'

'I wasn't adopted but I'll get to that soon, just be patient. Our mother was a saint and our father a drunken bully and an absolute piece of shit. We both lived in fear of Jake, if he had a drink in him, he would come home and beat whichever one of us he laid eyes on first. If he tried to beat me, Mom would often intervene and take the beating instead of me.

There was never any money in the house. Mom worked as a waitress most of the time, Jake worked at whatever he could make money doing and with the least possible effort. We lived in a little shit-hole of an apartment in the Bronx. Life was what Mom and I made of it; we kept clear of Jake as much as possible.

I was ten years old when I started at middle school, I used to catch the school bus to and from home. Two weeks into my freshman year on August 30, 2010, a date I will never forget, a cop pitched up at the school and with no explanation took me home.

When we got there, I found that my Mom was dead. She supposedly fell out of the apartment window while cleaning the windows. I went crazy and accused Jake of pushing her. I told the cops about the beatings but she had never laid a charge against him, so the fucking bastard got away with it. He threatened me that I would go the same way if I spoke to the cops again.

The old man got himself involved with an Hispanic gang called the Point Crowns. I think he was just a bag man for them, doing collections, maybe running some drugs. Anyway, the beating had stopped as I was already taller than him.

In September 2006, I had just started my junior year in high school when the shit finally caught up with Jake. I am not too sure what happened, but it seemed like he had done a runner with a bag full of their cash. They came round and told me if he didn't pitch up with their cash by the next morning, they would be coming around again to see me.

I knew these gangsters liked to send a message when someone crossed them, so I collected up what cash I had and bought a one-way bus ticket to San Francisco. The cops found Jake's body a couple of weeks later, he had his throat cut and his hands chopped off. The Point Crowns don't fuck about, you steal from them you die. Nobody was ever caught,' Matthew recounted the events without emotion.

'Tell me how you know your parents were our biological parents.'

'Well, without any investigations it is blatantly obvious we are direct family. I will get to how I know shortly, but in the meantime, let me continue my journey.

I stayed in San Fran until around July 2009 before coming home. I was still worried that the Point Crowners may still be looking for me, so I kept a low profile. Took small cash-only jobs, then I got lucky for the first time in my life. In 2017 I got a job with a locksmith; he taught me everything you could ever know about locks and safes.

The old guy, Spencer Turner, had me doing all the call-outs as he was getting on a bit. Just two years after I joined his business, he put the company van and all its tools in my name. I think he knew he was dying, anyway shortly afterwards he did die. After a bit of crap from his son over the van, I was free and clear.

I had planned to continue with the business of fixing or changing locks but with no actual office, business was slow. Having seen how people just left shit lying around in their houses I decided that being a burglar was an easier and more profitable job. The van was a good cover.'

'So, you turned to life of crime just like Jake.'

'I had been stealing ever since I was a kid; this was just a whole lot more profitable. And don't you dare compare me to that sack of shit.'

'When did you add rape and murder to your list of things to do? It's a big leap from stealing to killing.'

'I had been casing the 1600 block of East 53rd Street. It was Columbus Day 2020. I saw the occupants of 1661 leaving for the weekend and decided to break into their house. The robbery went very well. I scored a Glock 19, three magazines of ammunition, about $1,500 cash and some slightly valuable jewelry. I saw it as a profitable hour's work.

It was when I went into the lounge that things changed. I saw a framed photograph of two graduating police officers. One was the occupant of the house – Howard A. Friend and the other was you, my dear brother.'

'I remember Howard Friend; we graduated on the same day. So, seeing that photo set you off?'

'It didn't set me off, but it did make me very curious. I had thought of contacting you, but I first wanted to find out all about you. I needed to know if we were twins and if so, why you were not part of my family growing up, so I decided to research everything I could find out about you before making contact.'

'I still don't get it, once you found out all about me, why didn't you make contact?' Ethan was trying to piece together how things had led to this moment.

'Hang on. You'll see why shortly. I looked up where my birth was first recorded - Center for Community Health Hospital. According to their records, my parents arrived with me already born. There was some suspicion that the birth had been carried out by someone with medical knowledge, but the staff didn't pursue it.

Using some of my "Street" contacts, I managed to find out that there were Baby Brokers operating out of the Little Egypt area in Astoria Queens during the 1990's. I tracked down one of the people possibly involved and got lucky. His name was Mohammad. On pain of death, he admitted he knew of the transaction, it was the one and only time that a second baby was born. They had no idea she was carrying twins.

The first baby, you, had been born, paid for and the new parents had left the building. He told me your father had paid $100,000 for you, half to Mohammad and half to Jake. By the time I was being born you and your parents were long gone. Jake and my Mom were left with me, in hindsight it was probably why Jake hated me so much.

For the sake of half an hour or so, you end up with a life of privilege and I was left behind.'

'I am sure if my folks knew there was a second baby, they would have taken you as well, no matter the cost. Shit happens, that's life.'

'You are right, shit does happen as you are going to find out. Once I had this information I dug into your life. The internet is a wonderful tool, I traced your success at those quality schools you attended. Great sportsman, excellent student you were living the perfect life.

When I found the story on how your parents were murdered it got me thinking, maybe it was time to contact you and form a relationship with my cop brother.'

'So why didn't you? You're my brother.'

'While I was doing all this research, I continued my life as a burglar. The bills don't pay themselves, you know. It was a single incident that changed everything. I always made sure that any place I robbed was unoccupied. Well, that changed on October 31, 2021. I had broken into an apartment in the 400 block of West 84th street on the Upper West Side.

I normally stay away from that area as many of the places up there have good security. I tried this particular apartment posing as a locksmith. If anyone had answered the door, I would just say I had a call out to this address. They would deny having called me out and I would have just faked irritation at someone wasting my time and walked away.

I got no response, so I used my lock picking skills to enter the apartment. I was busy collecting some good stuff to fence when I heard the front door opening. I panicked slightly, I put on my balaclava and hid in the bedroom walk-in closet. Well, this attractive woman walks into the bedroom and starts undressing.

Something clicked with me, maybe it was seeing a half-naked woman or just the thrill of being there without her knowing. The next thing I know is I have my arm around her neck and my hand over her mouth. She started to struggle and the more she did, the more turned on I got.

I ripped off her bra and panties and got her on the bed still with my hand over her mouth. I told her if she made any noise, I would kill her. She stopped struggling, I spread her legs, took out my dick and fucked her.' Matthew shrugged at the memory of it and took another swig of his beer.

'When you started this spree of rapes and robbery, we checked all reported incidents for the past two years. There was no record of this one,' Ethan replied.

'I know and that kind of made me angry. When I was done with her, I gave her a smack on the jaw and left. I expected it to be reported, but nothing. I don't know why she chose not to report.'

'You didn't say whether you used a condom or not.'

'I did not use one, it was a spur of the moment thing.'

'What changed with the others?' *Get him talking so you can nail his ass to the wall just as soon as you get out of here.*

'Although this one wasn't planned, it really excited me, and I had the urge to do it again. I decided future escapades would be more organized and planned. I also wanted to be acknowledged.'

'Hence the zodiac cards, the New Moon thing etcetera. Why only Gemini and Sagittarius cards?'

'Gemini is obvious, the twins. Sagittarius is half man, half beast, describes me to a "T". I thought it would be cool to establish the persona of a serial criminal, keep you boys on your toes and guessing.'

'So again, why did you murder the Marxs' and in such a way as to mirror what happened to my folks?'

'I am not one hundred percent sure why I started on that path. I think I got the idea after Sandra Williamson. There was quite a bit of excitement at the 35th precinct. All of a sudden there was something different going on in the city, but it still felt like it was just a ripple. It was then that I got the idea to make a statement that would get your attention.

Having read all I could about the murder of your parents, I figured there would be things that were not reported in the papers. I decided to see if I could get hold of the whole file on the murders, so I went in person to the 94th. I got myself a fake ID and a detective's shield, just walked in flashed the shield and the old guy just handed over the complete file on your parents' case. That old guy was dumber than fuck.'

'That was taking a big chance, what would have happened if he had challenged you?'

'I am of the opinion that if you walk confidently into a place like you know what is going on, nobody ever doubts that you aren't who you say you are. Anyway, I took the evidence box and just walked out of the building, nobody so much as gave me a second glance.

I studied the case for the best part of a week, noting every detail, especially those not reported in the press. I kept the single pubic hair that was found at the site of the murder. I figured it would throw the investigators off, just confuse them when I did my victims.'

'What was the point of that? I thought you said you wanted the infamy.'

'Oh yes, I did, but I knew the person who killed your parents has never been caught so I wanted you to think their murderer had resurfaced. The addition of the zodiac cards was to link the murders to the rapes and get you all running around in circles. Purely for my entertainment, of course.

I started planning the murders in May; all I had to do was select my victims and wait until the tenth anniversary of the murder of your family. I intended doing it in the precinct jurisdiction that you were assigned to – the 10th, I wanted you to be directly involved in the case.

Luckily, I had someone in your precinct who provided me with the information that you were going to be transferred to homicide at the 35th. A couple of weeks before D-day I was told you would be moving over on the exact day I had planned on replicating the murder. It was almost symbolic, don't you think?

I changed my plans and began the search for a husband and wife in your soon-to-be home precinct. I would love to tell the two who were my original choice just how close they came to being killed. Maybe they would send you a thank you note.

While I was planning the murders, I continued with the Zodiac Rapist trend. I wanted to create fear and tension in the public. I worked to a fixed pattern, not because voices in my head told me to but just to setup the whole "serial" thing. Nothing scares people more than the possibility of a serial rapist/killer on the loose.'

'You ARE a serial rapist! How did you know I was being transferred to the 35th on that exact day when I was only told three weeks earlier?'

'I have a lady friend in the police HR department; she told me of your transfer. I had told her that I was interested in white collar crimes and the detectives who work on them. The 10th precinct, your home base, was the center for those investigations. Your transfer worked perfectly for my plan.'

'So, your plan was to make me relive my folks murder, for what purpose?'

'To make you suffer and to confuse you, isn't that obvious? I thought it might send your team down the path that the original murderer had resurfaced ten years later. Other than your suffering, it would muddy the waters, so it seems like both goals were achieved.

Once I knew your team had worked out my sequence and planned to take me out on April 1, I moved my plan to further confuse you. Who's the April Fool now? Louise Martin was selected with all the same pattern, single white female, living alone, living in a 400 block, the New Moon but I added a twist. Instead of going three blocks south each time I went three blocks north of the first rape.

On the face of it, it had to look like it was the work of the Serial Rapist but for me to make it look like a copycat I made slight modifications. I knocked her out and I left some DNA. The hairs were yours. I got them out of your bathroom. The DNA on the credit card was mine. The fact that your DNA experts confirmed they were all from the same person proves we are identical.'

'You knew they would have to take my DNA to eliminate me from the crime.'

'Yep! The fact that you couldn't immediately provide an alibi was a bonus, it made my task so much easier. Your night in the cells gave me all the time I needed to set up your basement. Funny how things work out, isn't it?'

'If you think locking me up in my basement is going let you assume my identity, I think you are out of your goddamn mind. If you are going to kill me, how the hell do you propose to get rid of my body?'

'All in good time, brother. It's almost 2.00 pm and I have a surprise for you. I have hooked up my tablet to the big screen TV so watch what happens next.'

Livingstone walked over the TV, switched it on and then turned it towards O'Connell. He tapped a few keys on his tablet which transferred the images to the TV.

'I am going to walk over to the far end of the room so as not to interrupt the show. Watch carefully and you will see how easily I can assume your identity.'

Livingstone walked over to the far end of the basement and turned his back to O'Connell. In the situation room Garcia's telephone rang, he answered it, listened for a few seconds then ended the call. He walked out of his office into the situation room.

'That was Mick Dooley from the front desk you are never gonna believe this. Some kid just walked into the precinct and dropped a brown paper bag on the desk, he then turned and ran. The bag contained O'Connell's shield, weapon and wallet.'

'They couldn't catch the kid?' asked Shaw.

'No, he was out of there like a scalded cat. The bag and its contents are on the way up here. What the hell is going on, why would the mugger return these items?'

'I wonder if it is because he has no further use for the stuff and is making a point.' offered Hayes.

A uniformed cop brought the bag in and gave it to Garcia. He pulled on a pair of latex gloves and inspected the contents.

'Yes, it's O'Connell's stuff. I am going to bag the stuff in an evidence bag and send it in for prints. Hayes, can you give O'Connell the news? I'm sure he will be relieved.'

Watching from the basement, Livingstone turned back towards the incredulous O'Connell and smiled. The cellphone he was holding rang, he let it ring three times and answered it.

'O'Connell.'

'Ethan, it's June, I have some good news; your shield, weapon and wallet have been handed in at the precinct.'

'Wow, how about that, really good news! Who handed them in?' Matthew asked, smiling at Ethan.

'Just some street kid, he dropped it on the reception desk and did a runner.'

'Hopefully they can be dusted for prints. Maybe they will now lift my suspension and I can get to proper detective work. Thanks for the call, I will pick you up as usual tomorrow. Should I bring my toothbrush?' He shot Ethan a wink.

'Yes please.'

Livingstone ended the call and smiled at O'Connell, 'See that? She was fooled. Tomorrow night, I will sample the delicious fruits of June Hayes. I know all your moves and I will throw in a few new ones that she hasn't seen before. They're better than your moves, by the way.

My only regret is that I haven't bugged her apartment so you will be unable to observe. Don't worry, I will give all the intimate details when I get home.'

'Fuck you! She will know it's not me. Are you just going to keep me chained up like this and starve me to death?'

'Don't worry, Brother. I will make sure you're comfortable and fed before I leave. I have no intention of starving you to death. Relax. I will bring you down some refreshments a little later as I have a few things to get ready for tomorrow.'

Chapter 35
Deception

Ethan watched Livingstone leave the room. He evaluated his situation, and it was plain to see that there was no way he could free himself from the shackles. He would have to try and entice Livingstone to come closer to him and hope he could overpower him.

The shackles around his ankles were loose but not loose enough for him to pull them over his feet. They were each secured by a bolt so there was no lock to try and pick. The chain that secured him to the bracket in the wall was too thick to hope he could somehow break one of the links. The bracket in the wall was also heavy duty and did not look like it could be removed. On top of that he had no access to a tool that he could use to try and free himself.

His thoughts were interrupted by Matthew's return; he was carrying a large cooler box. He deposited it just out of Ethan's reach. He smiled and left the basement. A few minutes later he returned carrying a case of sixty bottles of water, these were placed alongside the cooler box. Again, he left only to return minutes later carrying a large plastic bucket and an equally large garbage bin.

He dug into the bucket and extracted a packet of paper plates and plastic knives, forks and spoons. He then moved the bucket to the left edge of the mattress where Ethan was sitting. The garbage bin was placed on the right edge of the mattress.

'Ok brother, you are all set up. You have a bucket for you to relieve yourself, not ideal, I know, but it's the best I can do. The cooler box contains meals, I ordered them from Nutritious Meals. They promised that they are all healthy and good for you. You have plenty of water and enough food to last for five days. See, I'm concerned about your well-being.'

'What the fuck are you trying to do? You can't keep me locked up like this for five days,' Ethan pulled the chain; this was his one shot to get his brother before he was left alone to live or die.

'But I can, and I am going to. I need at least five days to implement the next stage of my plan.'

'What is your plan?'

'All in good time. Now I am going to leave you. The TV is on, my tablet is connected to it so you can enjoy the experience. I only wish I had put cameras in June's apartment, but unfortunately you will have to take my word for it.'

'You bastard! If you have a grudge against me, why don't you leave her out of it? She hasn't done anything to you.'

'A grudge? You think this is a simple grudge? It's way beyond that, brother. I want the full Ethan O'Connell experience and she is part of that. I am leaving you now, here is the TV remote in case you get bored watching the fun at the precinct. I will check in with you in the morning before I leave to pick up June.'

He tossed the remote to Ethan and left the basement without so much as a backward glance. Unknown to Ethan, he locked the basement door. Ethan spent a miserable night, most of which was contemplating his fate. He could see no way that this would end well for him. His only hope was that Livingstone would be caught out and then someone would come looking for him.

He must have fallen asleep as he was awakened by Matthew making an appearance, dressed and ready to leave for work. Ethan could only look on in horror, it was like looking into a mirror. On appearances alone, there was no way anyone would be able to tell that it wasn't him that they were looking at.

'What do you think, brother, reckon I pass muster?' he did a girly twirl around, to infuriate Ethan.

'Yes, you do, you sick bastard, but you will make a slip up and will be exposed.'

'I doubt it. I will not be home tonight as I will be pleasuring June. I wish you were able to see me perform. I will see you tomorrow morning, enjoy your day. There is plenty of sustenance, so you won't go hungry but don't overeat. When the food is done, so will you be.'

On his way out, Livingstone kicked the cooler box towards the mattress giving Ethan access. Ethan heard him lock the basement door as he left.

Livingstone knew where June Hayes lived but what he didn't know was the protocol. Should he lean in and kiss her, if so, where? On the mouth, the cheek? If he didn't kiss her, would she wonder why, or if he did would she also wonder why?

He pulled up outside her apartment building, she was waiting, looking at her watch. As she walked towards the car, he leaned over and popped open the passenger side door, at the same time he purposefully dropped his cellphone between the two front seats. She moved to enter the car.

'Dammit, I dropped my cellphone, it's down between the seats, can you check your side? Good morning, by the way.'

'Good morning to you too. It so annoying when that happens, let me have a look.'

It only took her a few seconds to extract the cellphone from under her seat. She handed it over to Livingstone and slid onto the seat. At the same time, she leaned over and kissed him on the cheek. The first test passed and he was on his way.

'It's great that you will get your shield, ID and weapon back, I am sure they will reinstate you to active duty. What do you think the bastard will do next?'

'I don't know, the man seems to be always a couple of steps ahead of us. We need to find out what motivates him if we have any hope of catching him.'

He smiled to himself as he pulled into a parking spot at the precinct. The two of them walked into the precinct and were greeted by Sergeant Mick Dooley.

'Jesus, O'Connell you are one lucky bastard to get your stuff back. We should get the results of any fingerprints this morning. Knowing you, I will find evidence that will lead directly to the Zodiac Rapist.'

'I doubt it, Sarge the man seems way too smart to make a mistake like that. I reckon that he is just fucking with us.'

The two detectives made their way up to the situation room, they were the first to arrive. Livingstone walked over to his desk and sat down. He turned towards the middle camera, formed his index finger and thumb into the shape of a gun. He smiled and made a shooting motion towards the camera; he knew O'Connell would be watching and it would annoy him no end.

He was correct. Ethan was watching and fuming; he watched as Garcia, Shaw and Mills arrived. There wasn't a single moment that the arrivals reacted to Livingstone other than they would have if it was him sitting there. Unless he did something totally out of character, he would get away with his deception.

At 10.15 am Dooley called Garcia with the news that no fingerprints or DNA had been found on O'Connell's returned possessions; he was free to pick them up at the front desk. He removed the three credit cards all of which had been blocked and theatrically cut them into pieces. He then opened his "new" wallet and removed two of the replacement cards, turning to the hidden camera he flashed the cards, kissed them and inserted them into his wallet.

Ethan spent a frustrating day watching the proceedings in the situation room. Livingstone played his part perfectly, never making the slightest misstep. He made frequent trips to the men's bathroom where he checked up on Ethan, everything was going to plan. At 5.30 pm the team were all getting ready to leave, Livingstone motioned to June to come over. He led her directly in front of the left-hand side camera.

Talking softly but loud enough for his voice to be picked up on the camera, 'June, are you still okay that I stay over at your place tonight?' She smiled and nodded. 'I think we could probably go out for meal before going to your place as a celebration on me returning to active duty. We need to make sure we have the sustenance and energy for what I hope will be a special night.'

June nodded in agreement, this was a different Ethan, more romantic, she liked it. Ethan watching and listening caught June's reaction, he was sure she saw something different in the person before her. There was hope that the impostor would be exposed.

Livingstone knew that June's favorite local eatery was Amaranto Mexican Restaurant, one block southeast from her apartment. Without asking her, he drove directly to the restaurant and found a parking spot almost in front of the entrance.

'Wow, how did you pick this place? It is my all-time favorite place!' she gushed, enthusiastically.

'I am a detective, you know. Let's get in there, it's on me,' he winked at her. This was going to be a great evening.

'Why? We should split the bill.'

'Absolutely not. This is thanks for you standing by me and believing in me.'

For the next two and a half hours, they ate their fill and drank two pitchers of margaritas and one of red sangria. They finished off with a flaming sambuka. Livingstone settled the bill, leaving a more than generous tip, after all O'Connell was paying. Having drunk more than the legal limit, they decided to leave the car where it was and take the four-minute walk to June's apartment.

They made their way northeast up Hart Street, stopping at the corner of Wyckoff Avenue. June threw her arms around Livingstone's neck, drew his face down to her level and passionately kissed him.

In a husky whisper she said, 'Take me back to my apartment and show me what you've got, I am as horny as hell so be quick, otherwise I am going have my way with you right here, right now.'

Needing no second invitation, Livingstone grabbed her by the hand, looked left and right, and seeing the road was clear he pulled her across the street. They arrived at her apartment breathless, June fumbled for her keys and managed to get the front door opened before Livingstone finished pulling his overcoat off.

Once inside there was a frantic scramble to remove clothing while heading for the bedroom. By the time they made it into the room, June was naked apart from her tiny thong panties, Livingstone still had on his socks and his underpants. No standing to ceremony, June threw back the bedclothes, divested herself of her thong and jumped on the bed laying on her back.

'Come on, lover, get naked and get over here,' she beckoned, and Matthew grinned down at her.

Livingstone kicked off his socks and underpants. With the lights off, he could barely make June out on the bed. Fully erect, he crawled onto the bed, conscious of the O'Connell playbook as far as sex was concerned and he made his first move.

He started by gently kissing her neck, he felt her groan with pleasure, he knew she loved this. Next, he moved his head down to her right breast, caressing it gently as he took her swollen nipple between his lips and sucked, again she groaned. He knew he was on track so onto the next phase, He knelt up and straddled his legs each side of her, moving downwards across her stomach gently dragging his tongue across her belly.

He reached her pubic area, lying on his stomach he parted her legs. With his head now firmly between her thighs he searched for her clitoris with his tongue. Finding the right spot, he gently began massaging it. June tensed up raising her knees slightly.

'Oh my God as much as I love this, I wish he would get a move on, be a bit less vanilla.'

Unable to wait any longer, she pushed him away, rolled him onto his back and in one motion she straddled him. With his penis deep inside her, she began a frantic motion thrusting her pelvis backwards and forwards. Livingstone was slightly startled as this was a big deviation from her normal lovemaking. He decided to go with the flow as she was doing all the driving.

It didn't take her long to reach an explosive orgasm. She fell forward with her face buried into his chest; she was struggling for breath.

'Wow, I really needed that, now let me take care of you,' she kissed his chest and lightly ran her fingers over his belly.

'Oh no you don't, I am just getting started.'

He lifted her off his still very erect penis and turned her over onto her stomach. He knelt over her with his knees on either side of her body, gripping her by the waist he pulled her roughly to her knees. Pushing her head into the bed he exposed her buttocks, grabbing her by the hips he pulled her towards him.

He entered her and began pounding her hard. She went rigid for a few seconds before relaxing and forcing herself closer to him by pushing herself backwards. In less than two minutes her whole body started shuddering as she began her second orgasm. Matthew didn't stop or slow down and very soon June reached another climax. She was ready to collapse but he just continued.

He could feel her beginning to shudder again; this time he relaxed and let nature take its course and they both came together. June, totally satiated, collapsed onto her stomach, pulling him down with her. They both lay still trying to catch their breath. Matthew was first to react as he lifted his huge frame off her inert body and rolled onto the bed next to her.

She raised her head and looked at him, 'Oh my God, Ethan, where did all that come from? You have totally worn me out,' she rolled onto her back and stared up at the ceiling.

'It was your own fault. When you pushed me away from you then rolled me over and jumped on me, it was a bit of a shock, but man what a turn on. I have always been a bit reluctant to go crazy with you; when you took control like that, I figured fuck it why not let go. I loved it.'

'Me too. I doubt if I'll be able to walk for a week, I have never had multiple orgasms before but now I am dead,' she rolled over, turned her back to him and was asleep in seconds.

I thought it was the man's job to roll over and sleep immediately after sex. Ethan, buddy, it's sad that you never fucked her properly and now you'll never know what you are missing. Maybe I'll get her back to your place and let you watch on the TV.'

He looked across at June, sleeping naked beside him and shook his head. *'It will be a pity to waste this lovely creature, but she made herself part of his life. He wanted O'Connell to feel real mental pain before the physical pain. It can't be helped but I will enjoy her for the next few days.'*

He looked at the clock on the bedside table – 11.25 pm, it was time for him to leave. Careful not to disturb her, he slipped off the bed and started retrieving his discarded clothes. Once he had dressed, he decided it would be best to leave her a note. "I've gone home. Thank you for an amazing time. Great food and the most amazing sex I have ever had. See you in the morning."

It was almost midnight when he arrived back at Morgan Avenue, he unlocked the basement door and went straight down the stairs. The TV was off, and Ethan was asleep on the mattress. He switched on the main light.

'Wake up, Bro! I'm home after a hectic day and night. I hope you enjoyed your day. What did you think of my performance at the precinct, seeing as you couldn't see the one at June's apartment?'

'Fuck off. You are going to get caught, you will slip up. What you do with June makes no difference to me; she's just someone I work with,' Ethan lied. The idea that he had slept with June destroyed him, but he couldn't give Matthew the satisfaction.

'No slip ups, Pal. I aced it. Seriously, June is not just a colleague, I have watched the two of you. Her reaction tonight thinking I was you showed me this is more than just a casual thing with her. She did say it was the best sex she has ever had and will struggle to walk tomorrow.'

Ethan's anger got the better of him and he lunged at Livingstone, only to be pulled back by the chains and shackles around his feet. Livingstone just laughed at him.

'Easy there, Tiger, you will hurt yourself carrying on like that. Did you enjoy your meals? I did try and get the best in for you, you are paying for them anyway. I am going to bed now. I will look in on you tomorrow before June arrives to pick me up.'

Chapter 36
Taunting

Ethan, angry at being so helpless, spent another frustrating and uncomfortable night alone in the basement. Based on what Livingstone had said about the food running out in five days and that being the end of him, he estimated he had three days of food left; more if he rationed his meals. He couldn't just sit around contemplating his eventual demise, there had to be something he could do.

New York building and safety codes require that a smoke detector be installed in every room of a building apart from bathrooms. Whoever had finished the basement of this building had not complied, there was no smoke detector. Even if there had been one and he managed to start a fire and set off the alarm, the only person to respond would be Livingstone.

The HVAC (Heating, ventilation, and cooling) system only had outlet vents in the basement but one of the outlets was within his reach. If he could remove the vent coverings he could try and force his blanket into the system and block off the heating to the rest of the apartment. Maybe that would get Livingstone down into the basement and give him a chance to overpower him.

With all these thoughts going through his head, he realized he was becoming desperate. Even if he could somehow overpower Livingstone, he was still limited in his movement because of the shackles around his ankles. Being totally identical in all physical aspects, he estimated that they were probably equal in strength too. He would have to hope that June would realize that Livingstone was not him and raise the alarm.

Turning to the television, he watched as Livingstone awoke, it was 6.30 am. He stretched, sat up in the bed and looked directly into the camera, with a huge grin on his face. He addressed Ethan. 'Good morning, brother, I hope you had a comfortable night, I must say I did. This bed of yours, now mine, is perfect, I think I will give it a whirl tonight with June. I will be down shortly maybe we can have breakfast together.'

Ethan watched as his twin brother stood up with his back to the camera, he was naked. He strolled casually toward the bathroom fully aware Ethan would be watching him. He emerged seven minutes later, showered, dressed only in pair of red briefs, Ethan realized there was no way anyone could tell the difference between the two of them. It would have to be a slip up on Livingstone's part for him to fail.

Livingstone joined Ethan in the basement at 6.55 am, he walked in full of the joys of life. 'Sorry brother, but I won't be joining you for breakfast. I am running a bit late and don't want to be late for June. No point in giving her anything to think about. You enjoy your day and we'll both be back this evening. I am going to show you how you should have been performing in bed, just a pity you won't ever get to put my moves into action. Laters!'

'Fuck you, Livingstone. I promise you this will not end well for you. I cannot believe we came from the same parents. You might look like me, but you will never be me, you are too sick in the head.'

He could see that he had hit a nerve in his brother, and he got the desired reaction.

'The only thing you got over me is that you were born first. Your adoptive parents secured you a proper life. Me, I got the father from hell. For the sake of half an hour, our lives could have been different. Soon, thirty-one years later, I will have the life I should have had.'

'You are not smart enough to take over my life. You are nothing but a bitter killer and rapist. June will see through you soon enough.'

'Yes, she may very well do that, but you won't be around to see it. I gotta go and pick up our morning coffee, can't be late. You know what a punctual creature June is.'

Livingstone turned and started walking towards the door, Ethan watched him go and came to the realization that he was screwed. No one was going to see that Matthew Livingstone wasn't Ethan O'Connell.

Right on cue, June Hayes arrived outside the O'Connell apartment, she popped open the passenger door and smiled.

'Morning Ethan, you are looking very spiffy this morning. I was surprised to see you had left last night. I was looking forward to waking up next to you and having a repeat session. Maybe not as intense as the previous one, just a gentle reminder,' she smiled, seductively.

'Morning to you, pretty lady. I was tempted but you might just have killed me off, so I decided to come home and get some rest. Where did that passion come from last night? It was a few notches up on our normal sex. I hope to be in tip top shape for a repeat performance tonight.'

'I think all the built-up tension of the last two days just spilled over. I may have started it but you sure as hell took it up another level, I loved it. Don't you think maybe we should cool it? You know, company regs?'

'Screw the regs. I can't get enough of you. Anyway, I think Shaw and Mills are doing it too, so if they can we sure can.'

'Hopefully we nail this Zodiac Rapist soon and I can get posted back to the 94th then it is moot.'

'That may take some time. So far, he has made us look a bit stupid. Anyway, even if you do catch him, I think Garcia will want to keep you on at the 35th.'

'What do you mean "if *you* catch him" don't you mean when *we* catch him?' June looked at him curiously.

Livingstone flinched. 'Yes of course, when *we* catch him,' he would have to be more careful, a silly slip like that could sink him.

Ethan June and Livingstone arrived at the precinct, followed shortly thereafter by Garcia. Shaw and Mills arrived together carrying coffee and donuts. He watched the interpersonal interactions; it was like watching a recording of himself. Livingstone fitted in seamlessly, not a hint of suspicion.

With the whole team assembled, Garcia called a meeting.

'Folks, we need to formulate a plan going forward. We don't know what his next move is likely to be.'

Mills: 'The next New Moon is on Wednesday March 2. If he has accelerated to one per month, then that should be his next attack.'

Shaw: 'Yes, but where the hell will he strike? The last one was 49th Street, will the next be 52nd Street?'

Garcia: 'The last one was a deviation, instead of continuing the pattern of three blocks south each time he went three blocks north of the original.'

Mills: 'If it is the 400 block of West 52nd we have a huge problem. That block is packed solid with houses and apartments, there is no way we can cover that area.'

Hayes: 'How do we know if he will strike again and if he does then surely, he won't stick to his normal pattern as he knows we have worked that out?'

Livingstone turned slightly towards the nearest camera, 'I am sure he will strike again. He is very clever, but I think he may stick to his normal pattern.'

Ethan, watching from the basement, could see how Livingstone was going to muddy the waters. What he couldn't work out was what he hoped to achieve. Was he going to continue raping women every New Moon? He realized that he'd be dead by March 2 if Livingstone's plan to deal with him worked. If his plan was to assume Ethan's life, would he stop the rapes and just become Ethan? He decided to confront Livingstone the next time he saw him.

With Livingston seamlessly moving into his O'Connell persona, Ethan's only hope was for him to make a mistake. Bored with watching the developments at the 35th, he put his mind to trying to find some way to free himself from his shackles. What he needed was a MacGyver moment (from the old hit TV show of the same name – starring Richard Dean Andersen). He looked around to see what, if anything, he could use to free himself.

The ankle chain was made of welded links, there being no breaks in each link. The links were 5/16 unplated steel, strong enough that they could not be broken through without being cut. He would need a hacksaw or a bolt cutter neither of which he had to hand.

Restricted by the length of the chain, the only thing he could reach that may be of use was the air conditioner vent. The metal vent covering was 18inches in length and 6 inches in height, it was slatted and clipped into the dry wall. He easily removed the vent and looked inside the hole. Beyond the drywall was the raw concrete of the basement shell. He was able to easily stick both his hands into the hole.

Gripping the chain in both hands he maneuvered his right hand into the hole. He held the chain hard against the concrete and tried to move it backwards and forwards scuffing it against the hard concrete. Given the size of the opening and him holding the chain he estimated the forward movement was no more than six inches. After moving the chain forwards and backwards for a few minutes he removed his right hand. Looking at the link he had been rubbing across the concrete there was barely any damage to its surface. This would take forever.

The amount of effort he had put in for so little success left him disheartened. There was some promise, but it was going to take a very long time to work though the link to such an extent that he could un-link the chain. Time was something he didn't have enough of if Livingston's implied threat was to be carried out.

He was also fully aware that Livingston could be observing at any time. He would have to watch the TV to judge when his brother was out of the precinct, traveling home after work, at June's apartment or at night when he was sleeping.

Livingston was confident that Ethan was secure in the basement and had not spent any time checking up on him via the tablet. In his opinion, there was no way Ethan could free himself from the chains so why risk himself being seen by someone in the precinct.

Shortly after 6.00 pm, Ethan watched as Livingston called June over to his desk. Facing the camera he whispered to June, 'I hope you remembered to pack your toothbrush, you won't need pajamas though as you are going to spend the night naked.'

'Yes, the toothbrush is my glove box, right next to my can of Red Bull. I am ready for an encore. Let's blow this joint and get the show on the road.'

Ethan, seething with anger and frustration, lashed out at the object nearest to him which just happened to be his ablution bucket. The kick sent the bucket tumbling across the floor, leaving its contents splattered everywhere. The bucket ended up against the far wall, well out of his reach. Not only was there nowhere to relive himself but the stench would only get worse.

Chapter 37
Suspicion

Both Livingstone and Hayes turned down Garcia's suggestion that the team have a couple of drinks after work, Hayes' excuse was that she was driving, and Livingstone's excuse was that he was her passenger.

During the drive back towards Morgan Avenue, Livingstone could feel the heat emanating from June's body, and he knew she was primed for action. He calculated they would reach the apartment around 6.45 pm, it was too early. He didn't want her walking around the apartment and if they went directly to the bedroom the sex might be all over before 9.00 pm. He needed a distraction.

June pulled up and parked around a hundred feet from the apartment's front door, she reached into the glove box to retrieve her toothbrush and can of Red Bull.

'Leave those. We can get them on the way back, I know a nice little pub nearby, what say we have a couple of beverages and something to eat before we turn in. It's only a short walk and I am sure you'll like it.'

They both got out of the car, June locked it and joined Livingston on the sidewalk. Hand in hand they started walking north towards Nassau Avenue. They reached the corner, crossed the street, and turned right. Reaching Goldie's Bar, Livingstone pulled open the door and stepped back to let June enter.

'The beers are cold and the food is the best in the neighborhood, or so they say. Enter madam, and let's find us a nice private booth.'

June glanced at him with a puzzled look on her face, *has he forgotten we were here last Saturday?* She made no comment but made her way into the Bar. She found an empty booth and the two of them sat down. Before either of them could say anything, a waitress came over.

'Hi, I am Samantha, I will be your server tonight. Can I start you with something to drink? Our beer special is Goldie's Lager.'

Livingstone looked up at the girl and answered her. 'That sounds great. I would like to try that, what about you. June?' June nodded in agreement. *We had this last weekend; why is he acting like he's never tried them?*

'Oh, it's you, Ethan. I didn't recognize you at first,' and looking across at June, 'you two do make a lovely couple. I will get those drafts started and give you some time to peruse the food menu.'

June stared at Livingstone with a worried look on her face; he in turn realized he had made a major slip and was panicked.

'Ethan, what's going on? We were here last Saturday. You told me this was your local Pub, but you're acting like it's your first visit here.'

Composing himself to the best of his ability, Livingstone answered, 'Sorry, June, with all that has been going on this week, I must have forgotten that we have been here before. It is my local Pub but I didn't want you to think I spend too much time in here drinking. I find that I can't even remember what I had for breakfast each morning, maybe I need help.'

'I think I understand; your brain must be going around and around with all that has happened to you. The trauma of finding out you were adopted, being mugged, and being placed on desk duty by IA. You have my sympathies, let's get loaded and fed then take me back to your place and I will do my best to clear your mind.'

'Jesus, I dodged a bullet there. I am going to have to be very careful not going into areas where O'Connell may have been with her. I don't want her to be in doubt about me and damn sure I don't want her creeping around the apartment tonight. The basement is locked, O'Connell is secure even if he makes a noise, she won't hear it in the bedroom.'

It was 9.30 pm by the time they had eaten and consumed a good few drinks. They split the check; June insisted. Livingstone left a generous tip, and they staggered out of the bar headed for O'Connell's apartment.

They passed June's parked car where she insisted on grabbing her toothbrush and Red Bull. Giggling, the two of them staggered up the stairs to the apartment's front door. Livingstone made a big deal out of trying to unlock the door, much to June's amusement. Once through the door, laughing raucously, they divested themselves of their overcoats leaving them where they fell.

With June leading the way, they ran for the stairs heading for the bedroom. The minute she crossed the threshold of the bedroom she started undressing. Livingstone excused himself and headed for the bathroom with the pretext of having to relieve himself.

Once in the bathroom, he reached for the tablet he had left to keep an eye on O'Connell. With no cameras in the bathroom, he was able to observe his brother without him being aware he was being watched. He could see his prisoner avidly watching the TV screen where he had a good view of June rapidly removing the last of her clothing.

He scanned the basement area to see if anything was amiss. The first thing that caught his attention was the overturned ablution bucket. He noticed the excrement spread over the floor and chuckled to himself; it was obvious O'Connell had kicked it over in a fit of anger. Well, bad luck for him, he would have to live out the last few days of his life shitting and pissing where he lay.

Satisfied everything was in order, he switched off the tablet and stored it in the drawer under the washbasin. It was password protected; in the unlikely event of June finding it he was safe in the knowledge she wouldn't be able to use it. He heard June calling from the bedroom.

'What's taking you so long, you haven't fallen asleep in there have you?'

'Nope. I'm on my way, prepare yourself for the night of your life. You have unlocked the beast in me.'

He stripped down to his red briefs and pranced from the bathroom into the bedroom. Swinging his hips seductively he approached the bed, June was completely naked waiting in anticipation. He turned his back to her and slowly slipped his briefs down to around his ankles. Once divested of his briefs he spun around to face her, he was fully erect.

June gasped, 'Bring that gorgeous cock of yours over here. I am ready and waiting.'

'Patience dear, tonight you get the total Ethan treatment, you unleashed the beast in me and now it's time to take it up another level,' he looked towards the hidden camera, certain that O'Connell would be watching and grinned maliciously.

Ethan was watching; he had been diligently sawing away at the chain link, making some progress but surely not enough to be break out in time. The moment he saw Livingstone and June arrive in the bedroom he focused his total attention on them. He watched as June removed her clothes, admiring her body he felt like he was there with her. The illusion swiftly shattered when Livingstone emerged from the bathroom. He wanted to shout out to June that it wasn't him there in the bedroom, but he could do nothing but watch.

For the next two hours, Livingstone put June through every conceivable sexual position imaginable. His staying power was immense, which belied the claim of the rape victims that he needed them to show fear before he could perform and even then, it was all over in minutes.

Livingstone made sure that Ethan would be able to see everything, his moves and positioning June were geared towards the cameras. Ethan watched, drawn to it almost like watching a car crash. He despised what was going on but couldn't take his eyes off the screen.

He watched the expressions on their faces, June's was one of extreme pleasure, but Livingstone seemed detached. He was driving June to all levels yet the look on his face was not one of pleasure, this performance was solely to taunt Ethan.

Finally, just before midnight Livingstone turned June over onto her stomach and lifted her into a kneeling position. With her facing the camera he lifted her into the "doggie" position and mounted from the rear. Staring directly into the camera, he proceeded to pound June into one final explosive orgasm. As she was nearing exhaustion, he also reached a shuddering climax, smiling at Ethan he pushed June down on the bed, she lay there without moving or saying a word.

'I hope the encore was to your satisfaction, my Lady.'

'Good God, Ethan. I have never experienced anything like this. I don't think I am able to move right now, roll me over, put a fork in me, I am well and truly done,' she rolled onto her back, completely spent and exhausted.

Ethan watched from the basement, wanting to scream out at her, *'it's not me!'*

He felt like he had been watching a porn film, starring himself yet not physically taking part. He was sure that Livingstone would have somehow recorded the whole thing and would probably use it to his benefit sometime in the future.

He was helpless; there was nothing he could do about the situation. If this continued, he would be dead in the next few weeks. What was Livingstone's plan? Was he going to assume his identity permanently and take over his whole life? What about June? It didn't look like he had any real interest in her other than to taunt him.

'We better get some sleep as you need to be up in a couple of hours.'

'What do you mean I've gotta be up in a couple of hours? It's only midnight. I was hoping you would make me breakfast in the morning.'

'You are out of luck there, lady. I am driving tomorrow, and you need to get your car back to your place, get all cleaned up and be ready for me when I pick you up. 5.00 am is probably a good time, I'll set the alarm.'

'You are kicking me out in the middle of the night?' June asked, incredulously.

'Come on, June 5.00 am is hardly the middle of the night. It just makes sense. I am done and ready for the sack, move over and pull back the covers,'

June just gave him a frosty look but didn't argue as she complied and pulled aside the bed covers. She turned to her right side with her back towards Livingstone. Even though she was annoyed, she fell asleep in an instant. Ethan watched as Livingstone just shrugged his shoulders, he waved at Ethan, turned his back to June and was asleep within minutes.

At 5.00 am Livingstone's alarm sounded, waking not only himself and June but Ethan as well. June, still naked, sat up in the bed, stretched once then stood up and began looking for her previously discarded clothing. Ethan and Livingstone both watched her. She was clearly still annoyed but she never uttered a word.

As soon as she was fully dressed, she turned to leave.

'What? No goodbye kiss? That's not very nice of you.' Matthew said.

'Fuck you, Ethan, I feel like I have been used by you, kicking me out at this ungodly hour. I'll see you later,' she grabbed her belongings and left without another word.

Ethan took note of June's disposition, his hope rising. Maybe she will see through Livingstone, this could be the first crack. Livingstone, on the other hand, just rolled over in bed and was asleep before June left the building.

Livingstone's second alarm sounded loudly, bringing Ethan back to reality. Livingstone sat up in bed and without glancing towards the camera headed off towards the bathroom. Ethan watched him go, realizing he was one day closer to his possible demise and unlikely to have managed to cut through the chain link in time to escape.

Fifteen minutes later, Livingstone emerged from the bathroom fully dressed ready for work. Ethan still found it difficult looking at a carbon-copy of himself, dressed in his clothes and taking over his life. Even if he didn't make it, he had to hope that Livingstone would be found out and put away for good.

He watched as Livingstone walked over to where the bedroom camera was positioned, stopping directly in front of it.

'So, Ethan, what did you think of our performance last night? June seemed to love it. I was a bit bored after a while. I don't see any long-term relationship between us, I'll probably cut her loose after I have dealt with you.

I was going to pay you a visit this morning but after seeing what you did to your living quarters, I think I'll give it a miss. Kicking shit all over the place seems a bit childish to me, but that's your choice though. You will spend your last few days living in a stinking mess.

Well, enjoy your day. I am off to pick June up and then spend the day trying to work out where the Zodiac Rapist will strike next. I think he will have a real surprise for them, dumb bastards.'

Ethan watched him leave the bedroom. As soon as he was out of sight, he returned to his task of trying to saw his way through the chain link. To avoid the monotony of the task at hand, he replayed the previous night's action in his mind. He had to find something that might give Livingstone away. If he could find it, then maybe June would as well.

As he replayed last night's scenes in his mind, nothing jumped out at him. For all intents and purposes, it was him who was fucking June. There was no lovemaking, just pure sex. Livingstone was an exact duplicate of himself, no discernible physical differences that he could find.

As he went through the final scene where Livingstone climaxed and then pushed June away from him and onto the bed, he finally saw it. How the hell did he miss that and how did June not notice?

Chapter 38
In the Wind

June was ready and waiting standing on the sidewalk when Livingstone drove up. He stopped his car next to her Mini Cooper and popped open the passenger door. She walked over with a fixed angry look on her face, slipped into the passenger seat, reached over for the seat-belt and clicked it into place. Staring ahead, she made no comment.

'What's with you? No greeting and it looks like someone killed your dog or something,' Matthew greeted her, completely oblivious to the reason she was fuming.

'What's with me, you ask? Jesus, how dumb are you? You virtually kicked me out of your bed with a poor excuse. What are you trying to tell me without saying it? What am I to you? Just a casual fuck? The other night you snuck out of my place leaving like a thief in the night.'

'So many questions, let me answer all of them or at least try to. Firstly, you are more to me than just a fuck. We are just starting out together and I am feeling my way into a possible relationship. I don't know why I fear getting involved. I am just not used to it.

You need to give me time and some space and if that works, I will get used to the close intimacy that I am having difficulty with. I am sorry you feel I kicked you out of my bed. I just figured you would need time to drive back to your place and get ready before I picked you up.

We can't be doing this every night, not only are we breaking police protocols but working on only a couple of hours sleep is not a good idea. Why don't we limit this to one or two nights and maybe the whole weekend? We take a complete change of clothing on weeknights, which will eliminate the need to rush home in the middle of the night.

Maybe we can try this weekend, pack a bag, and get away somewhere. Give us both a chance to get used to waking up together in the morning. I am sorry to have offended you, what do you say?'

This schmoozing up to a woman was not his usual style; maybe it was Ethan's.

'I'm sorry I'm grumpy. This weekend sounds like a great idea. I just felt I was being used but as you have explained that is not the case.'

'Okay, let's put this aside for the time being and put on our professional faces.'

'Good idea, it's time we caught this rapist bastard. I just wish I knew how he always seems one step ahead of us,' June looked out the window at the traffic, trying to collect her thoughts.

'I think he is probably highly intelligent; unless he makes a slip up, I'm starting to wonder if he will ever be caught,' Matthew faked concern.

'Don't worry, Ethan, we will get him.'

Livingstone just smiled to himself; he knew they had no hope of catching him. His next one will throw them completely off track.

June sat back in the passenger seat contemplating how she and Ethan were so compatible sexually; *all we now need is to get to totally trusting each other*, she thought. She replayed the previous night in her mind.

The sex was mind blowing, she couldn't believe how far they had come since the first few times. She knew Ethan was troubled about finding out about being adopted but he did seem a bit out of kilter. The incident at the Pub troubled her, he seemed to have no memory of them being there just a few days before.

She put it down to all that had happened in the last week. She smiled to herself, visualizing their final coupling, she on her knees totally vulnerable and totally at his mercy. She lost count of how many times she had an orgasm. He was so in control; he knew exactly which buttons to push. Her thoughts were interrupted by their arrival at the precinct.

As usual they were first to arrive. Strangely Mills arrived on her own and there was no sign of Garcia nor Shaw. By 9.00 am the three of them figured something was up.

'Hey O'Connell, you heard anything from Garcia and Shaw?' asked Mills.

'Nothing. I would have thought that if anyone knew something was going on with Shaw, it would be you,' Matthew replied, grateful to have inside knowledge about Shaw and Mills.

'Why would you think I know what's going on with Shaw?' Linda challenged.

'The two of you always seem to arrive together. I just thought he may have said something.'

'What are you implying? You do know it is against police regulations for officers of the same precinct to hook up. Unlike you and Hayes, I respect the rule.'

'Hold it, Linda, there is nothing going on between O'Connell and me, we know the rules. We always arrive and leave together because we share a ride, nothing else,' June clarified.

'You must think we're stupid, it's written all over your face. O'Connell on the other hand, doesn't give anything away. I've seen how you look at him,' Linda shot back.

'Okay, you two ladies chatter away, I'm going to see if I can find out where Garcia and Shaw are.'

Livingstone left the office and headed downstairs to chat to the desk sergeant.

Mills turned to Hayes and said, 'You and I need to talk in private, let's go to the ladies' locker room.'

They reached the locker room and did a quick check to see they were alone, finding no one else there, they sat down facing the door.

'This conversation is just between the two of us; it will go no further. Do you agree?' Said Mills.

'Yes Linda, of course it will stay in this room,' June promised.

'Good. O'Connell was right in his assumption that Dave and I hook up on a regular basis. As you have also probably found out, when a potential boyfriend finds out you are a cop, it tends to end quickly. Maybe they are scared off by the fact that we are armed most of the time, who the fuck knows. It is just easier hooking up with another cop.

We don't live together and are not exclusive, but I don't think either of us sleeps around. Now with you and O'Connell, when I look at you, I see you are committed. I thought he looked the same but recently not so much. There seems to be a bit of a change in him.

All I am saying is be careful and discreet. I doubt if Dave knows as he is not the most observant, strange that for a detective. With Garcia, I don't know, and I don't think he would make an issue of it if he did know.

If you are hoping to get reassigned back to the 94th to continue your relationship in the open, I reckon you will be out of luck. Garcia wants to make your temporary assignment permanent.'

'Ethan said the same about me staying on here. We will take our relationship to wherever it leads us. You said you saw a change in Ethan, that he seemed less interested. I have noticed a few things about him that seem different,' June confided.

'What do you mean?' Linda looked at her, cocking her head to one side.

'He forgot that we had been to his local pub just a few days ago. We put it down to the recent mugging and the related stress.

I know that this may be getting a bit personal, but our lovemaking has completely changed. He was very vanilla but the last couple of times he has become a sex machine. I am not complaining but he turned one eighty degrees.'

'Well, that can't be bad. Seeing as we are getting personal, please answer me the question that all women want to know. He is six three at least, size fifteen shoes and the common consensus would be that he is large in the pants.'

'Yes, he is a big boy, and he sure knows how to use it,' she smiled as she remembered their final orgasm of the previous night.

'No wonder you are grinning,' Linda mused.

June was going to reply when she suddenly stopped and gasped. She closed her eyes visualizing that final moment.

'Oh my God, it's surely not possible, I must be mistaken,' June shook her head, trying to organize her train of thought.

'Mistaken about what?'

'This is going to sound stupid, but I am one hundred percent sure that Ethan is circumcised, yet after our last sexual act he went to the bathroom to clean up. When he returned to the bedroom his erection was gone and his penis had shrunk back to a normal size. I swear he had a full foreskin, how is that possible?' June stared at Linda, all concern about oversharing gone.

'You've gotta be mistaken.'

'No. Most of the time when we've got naked, he has had a full-on erection. I slept over one night and saw him in a less aroused state, he was definitely circumcised. I didn't think anything of it but last night I was admiring his naked body as he returned to the bed, he had a full foreskin.'

'It's not possible to be mistaken. I've had my fair share of male penises, all shapes, and sizes. The difference between a circumcised penis and one that hasn't been chopped is clear. Once they have an erection is more difficult to differentiate, but flaccid they are completely different. You must be mistaken.'

'No, Linda, I am not. Thinking about it now, I am convinced Ethan was circumcised but somehow now he is not. What do I do?'

'Well, you can't very well walk up to him and ask him, he'll think you're nuts.'

'You remember when we interviewed the five rape victims and what they said about the rapist's penis being uncircumcised or not, we need to review those notes.' June stood up quickly.

The two detectives left the ladies locker room and returned to the situation room; Livingstone had not returned. Garcia and Shaw were still missing. Mills pulled up the interview file and saved it to her laptop.

'I think given the circumstances we should find a place to review the file without being disturbed. Let's try one of the interview rooms,' said Mills.

Interview room #2 was free, Hayes flipped the switch to "Occupied" and followed Mills into the room. They took up the two seats which would have been used by the interviewers, Mills booted up her laptop and called up the interview file.

Mills: 'The first victim, Sandra Williamson, said that he was fully erect, but she was certain he was uncircumcised. Lola Estes said she couldn't be sure, Heather Smith thought he was uncircumcised. Denise Todd was adamant he was uncircumcised; Shirley Richardson wasn't sure.

Hayes: 'So, that's two not sure, two definitely and one probably. Not totally conclusive but under the circumstances I am sure that Estes and Richardson weren't looking to see the finer details of the rapist's penis. What about Louise Martin? Let's pull up her file.'

Mills loaded the Martin file and checked her version of the rape. 'She said she had her eyes tightly closed and couldn't tell whether he was or not. Okay, so what's our next move?'

'I am one hundred percent sure that the man I was with last night and the man who is somewhere in this building is Ethan O'Connell. Yes, he has been a little off for the last few days, but it is him, definitely.'

'Then I have no explanation. No man can be circumcised one day and the uncircumcised the next,' replied Mills, sitting back in her chair looking at June.

'Louise Martin identified Ethan as the rapist when he spoke. It's far easier to change your voice than to change your body parts. Maybe the man upstairs is not Ethan O'Connell, but a doppelganger.'

'No way, that man is O'Connell, there is no chance of a perfect doppelganger, there has to be some other explanation.

I think maybe there is an explanation, but you have to keep this to yourself. Ethan O'Connell was adopted at birth, what if he had a twin?' whispered Hayes.

'Jesus, that could be it, but how do we find out?' Linda sat bolt upright.

'He told me he had made some progress in tracking down his birth parents. We spent a whole weekend going through various documents his parents left. They are in his basement, I have a key to his apartment, I think we should go and take a look.'

'Good idea, I'll call Garcia and tell him we are following a lead. You stay here, I'll go up to the situation room and get my car keys and your purse and meet you outside at my car.'

June nodded in agreement as she watched Linda Mills dial Garcia's cellphone number, it went straight to voicemail.

'Boss, Mills here, just to let you know we have received a lead in the case. Hayes and I are going to follow up on it, I will brief you when we have something concrete.'

Mills ran up the two flights of stairs into the situation room, O'Connell was the only one present.

'Hey, I was wondering where everyone was, Garcia and Shaw are in court with their cellphones switched off. Any idea where Hayes is? I can't seem to find her anywhere,' Matthew asked, continuing the charade of a concerned boyfriend.

'We've just been given a hot lead on the rapist case, so we are going to interview Shirley Richardson. She says she may have remembered something. Hopefully it leads somewhere, I have left a message for Garcia, we'll give an update if there is anything to report.'

'Shouldn't I come with you?' *The last thing I need is some dumb broad remembering something that could fuck with my plans.*

'No, she says it's very intimate and wants to talk to female cops. You look after the home office. I'll call you if we find anything.'

Not waiting for an answer, she grabbed hers and Hayes' purses and dashed for the door. Hayes was waiting at the car; Mills beeped the doors open and they got in. The drive to Morgan Avenue was done in record time, twice Mills activated the police siren to get through traffic.

Livingstone, all alone in the office, decided to spend the time observing O'Connell. He watched as his captive lay on the mattress with his back to the cameras, his body tight against the back wall. It appeared that he had his hands inserted in the air conditioner duct and seemed to be moving back and forward. *'Was he trying to grind through the chain links? Poor fool, he doesn't have the time to get through one of those, he'll be dead long before that happens.'*

Mills pulled up outside of O'Connell's apartment and double parked, she placed her "Police Business" card on the dashboard. They ran up the steps to the front door, Hayes unlocked the door and they both stepped in.

'All of his adoption stuff is in filing cabinets in the basement, so I think we should start there.' She tried the door only to find it locked. 'That's strange. I didn't think he ever locked the door, maybe he is worried that someone will find out about his situation. Do you think we should try and pick the lock?'

'No time for subtleties, step back sister, we can always apologize later.'

She drew her service weapon and without thinking twice put a single bullet into the door lock. The noise was deafening, but the door burst open.

Downstairs O'Connell heard the noise; he was confused, why was there gunfire? Back in the precinct, Livingstone also heard the sound. The next thing he saw was Mills and Hayes appear in the basement. He knew his game was up; he had to get out of the precinct immediately. He grabbed his coat and tablet and headed for the stairs. In his haste he forgot to deactivate the cameras. He made it out of the building without encountering Garcia and Shaw.

By the time Hayes and Mills reached the basement, O'Connell had turned around to face them, the two detectives stopped in their tracks, stunned at what they were witnessing.

'Ethan is that you?' cried Hayes. 'What is going on?'

'Jesus, thank God you are here! I thought I'd eventually die down here. Where is Livingstone? Have you got him in custody?'

'Who the hell is Livingstone?' inquired Mills.

'My twin brother, Matthew Livingstone. He is the Zodiac Rapist and he killed the Marx's too. He has had me shackled here for the last three days, at least I think it's three days. I don't even know anymore.'

'We had reason to believe that the person who we thought was you might not be you. I dunno if that makes sense, to avoid embarrassment I'll let June explain later. We need to get hold of Garcia and let him know what's going on.

I tried calling him earlier, but it went straight to voicemail. I think him and Shaw are in court.'

O'Connell looked over at the TV set, 'No, they are both back at the precinct, Garcia is in his office, Shaw at his desk.'

'How do you know that?' asked Mills.

'Livingstone has the whole office bugged with cameras, look over there on the TV screen. He also has my apartment bugged, down here, upstairs and in my bedroom. That's why he knew exactly what was going on, he heard every word we said and followed everything we have on the timeline. He kept an eye on me via his tablet.'

'No wonder he was always a few steps ahead. Why did he also put it up on the TV down here?' asked Hayes.

'To taunt me, he wanted me to see just how clever he is, the sick bastard.'

'You said he also bugged your bedroom, then you must have seen everything, or did he switch off those cameras at night?' June asked, realization dawning on her that she had slept with the Zodiac rapist.

'No June, he made sure I saw everything; he wanted me to suffer,' Ethan shut his eyes at the memory of it.

'Oh Ethan, I thought I was with you. I think I'm going to throw up. I slept with a rapist!' June turned her back on him, unable to see the pain on his face.

'I realize that June, it was pure hell being chained up here and not being able to do anything about it. It doesn't change my feelings for you.'

Their conversation was interrupted by Garcia's phone ringing on the TV.

'Boss, it's Mills, you are never going to believe what's happened. The person we thought was O'Connell is actually his identical twin brother, Mathew Livingstone. I am here at O'Connell's apartment with Hayes, we found him chained up in the basement. We are going to a need serious bolt cutter to free him, can you send someone over, quick, fast and in a hurry?

In the meantime, you need to put out a BOLO on Livingstone. We will bring you completely up to date when we get back to the precinct,' Mills rambled through the details as quickly as she could.

'Are you shitting me?! That wasn't O'Connell but a twin brother? I will say nothing to the lieutenant until I have a full explanation from the three of you. I will get someone over with a bolt cutter. Fuck me, what next?' They watched Garcia slam his trademark mug into the desk. That really was the best gift anyone could have gotten him.

'Sorry about the mess and smell. I kicked over my waste bucket in a fit of frustrated rage. I must stink a bit too. Other than being able to brush my teeth, I haven't washed in days. Jesus, am I glad to see you two! I thought I would see my last days shackled to my basement wall. He said I had food for five days as that was the amount of time he needed to fully implement the next stage of his plan. We have to catch this bastard and bring him to justice before he kills or rapes again.' Ethan jangled his chains to emphasize his frustration.

Livingstone, armed with O'Connell's weapon, shield, identity and car was on his way out of New York City, heading west on the 495 to hook up with the I95 South. With no clear plan in place, he figured getting out of New York was the first step. He planned to find a cheap, no questions asked motel somewhere near Philadelphia.

To throw any pursuers off his scent, he took the I95 North off ramp near Secaucus, New Jersey. Driving in a northerly direction he took the first off ramp and pulled into the first gas station he found. He filled up the car using O'Connell's visa card. Next, he went across the road to an ATM and drew out the maximum cash amount allowable - $1,000 from O'Connell's bank account.

Rejoining the I95 southbound, he headed for Philly, some ninety miles away. He figured he had at least an hour's head start and hopefully anyone looking for him would assume he was heading north.

Angry that his plans had been foiled, he vowed to take revenge on both O'Connell and Hayes. He racked his brain trying to think just how they had realized that he wasn't O'Connell. He was positive he hadn't made a slip up. Yes, he had screwed up slightly over the Pub but she seemed to believe his story. He would find out what gave him away before he killed her.

Chapter 39
Rescued

'The smell is getting to me. I think I'll clean the place while we wait for the bolt cutter to arrive. Where is your cleaning stuff?' Mills asked.

'Up in the kitchen, you'll find everything under the kitchen sink. Thanks for doing this, I'm embarrassed enough by being shackled in my own basement without people having to clean up the mess I have made.' Ethan had the good sense to look embarrassed, but Mills couldn't have cared less.

'It's no problem. I'll go and get a bucket, mop, and some air freshener. June, I think you need to tell him what led us here.'

Realizing Mills was giving her a chance to speak to Ethan alone, she just nodded. As soon as Mills had left the basement, she turned to Ethan.

'Ethan, I am so sorry all this has happened. I was one hundred percent sure it was you; I had no reason to think otherwise. He did seem a bit distracted and confused about having been to Goldie's Bar before. I put it down to all to the trauma you had experienced over the last weeks. He is identical to you, he even had your voice down pat, how did he do that?' June tried to recall everything he had ever said to her to find any mistake that she might have missed.

'He has been studying me ever since he found out I was his twin brother. He set up the Marx murders to get my attention. Once he had the precinct and my place bugged, he learned and copied all my mannerisms and my voice.'

'Well, he made a good job of it, but why the need to destroy you, why not be happy he had a twin brother?'

'We were separated at birth; my folks paid a lot of money for me on the baby black market and were unaware that there was a second baby. I got taken into a great and loving family, he got the shit end of the stick. He stayed with his biological parents. His father was, according to him, an absolute bastard who probably killed his mother. He wanted my life and felt the only way to get that was to eliminate me but to make me suffer first.

Watching him with you was one of the hardest things I have ever witnessed. I saw how he could move into my life and take it over. It was only watching you last night that I realized you may see he wasn't me.'

'I sort of came to that last night. Today when I went through what we had done last night, reliving everything, I came to the shocking conclusion that something was wrong.

This is very embarrassing to tell you. Last night was the first time I had seen him fully naked with his penis slack and rested. I saw he was uncircumcised, and I was positive that you were circumcised. I talked to Linda about my concern, as it didn't make sense. She agreed it wasn't possible so there must be something wrong.

We decided to come here and see if we could find anything. We thought maybe you had found something in your search for your biological parents. So here we are. How did you end up down here?'

Before O'Connell could answer, Mills arrived carrying a mop, a bucket filled with a strong disinfectant and aerosol air freshener. Before starting the cleanup, she listened to O'Connell recount what had happened to him landing up shackled in his own basement.

'Jesus, Ethan, if he had wanted to take over your life why didn't he just kill you when he had the chance? It seems like a hell of an effort when it would have been a simple solution to kill you,' Mills said.

'I know, Linda, but he made it clear to me that he wanted me to suffer and see him moving so easily into my life. This was to be payback for all the shitty things he had compared to my idyllic life. I did suffer watching him take my place but thanks to you two, it is over.

We have to apprehend him; I don't think he is going to take the current situation very well. If he disappears, I am sure he will rape and maybe kill again.'

The loud shrill of the doorbell caught their attention. Mills reacted, dropping the mop and drew her weapon. Indicating that the other two should remain silent, she moved quickly up the stairs and out of the basement. Looking through the peephole on the front door, she recognized Jimmy Wilson armed with a large bolt cutter. She opened the door and told him to follow her as she led him down into the basement.

Wilson blanched at the smell that hit him, he recognized Hayes but barely recognized O'Connell.

'Shit, what the hell happened here?'

'Shit happened, Jimmy. Actual shit. We'll get into the details later, Jimmy. Can you free him from the chains and shackles?'

Wilson inspected the chains and ankle shackle, 'I can cut the chain but the shackles on his ankles will need to be cut with an angle grinder or a circular saw. I can do that back at the precinct. In the meantime, let's get him free of the chain so he can move about.'

It took ten seconds for Wilson to cut through one of the chain links. O'Connell pulled the loose chain through the ankle brackets, finally able to move around freely.

'Thanks Jimmy, you don't know how happy I am able to move around. I am going to go upstairs, take a shower and put on clean clothes, then we can head back to the precinct.'

With his work complete, Jimmy left the basement and headed back to the precinct. Hayes and Mills went up to the ground floor, leaving the clean-up of the basement to someone else. O'Connell appeared twenty minutes later, clean and dressed, the scraggly beard would have to wait. With Mills driving, they headed back to the 35th.

Livingstone, in the meantime, had taken the I95 South towards Philadelphia. One hour and forty-five minutes later, he took Exit 22. Taking a left turn on 4th Street then a left on Market Street, he finally took a right on Bank Street. He stopped in front of the Moonlight Motel. The rundown motel would be the perfect place to hole up for a few days. The desk clerk was more than happy to take a cash payment for two days, no registration required.

Once settled into his room, Livingstone set the next part of his plan into action. He climbed into O'Connell's car and drove it south on Bank Street. Turning left into Chestnut Street he pulled into the parking lot for Viva Pizzas. Inside the store he ordered a large pepperoni and mushroom pizza to go. When the pizza was ready, he paid in cash and left the store. Leaving the keys in the ignition, he walked back to the motel. With any luck the car would be gone by morning.

O'Connell, Hayes, and Mills arrived back at the 35th and were greeted by Garcia and Shaw. The next twenty minutes were taken up by O'Connell being grilled by the other two detectives. Both admitted that they were completely taken in by Livingstone.

'The BOLO is out but it's going to be difficult to catch him, this is a huge area. He has all your credentials, your weapon and probably your car. I think you should start by contacting your bank and credit card companies and put block on those accounts.'

'No Boss, I think he may be a bit desperate and try and use them. It will give us an idea of his movements if he does. Let me go online and check if there has been any activity on my cards.'

He logged on to his checking account first. 'He has drawn out the maximum for a single day $1,000. It was at an ATM located at a gas station on Mill Creek Road, Secaucus New Jersey. That's just off the I95 going north. Let me check my Visa card.' Logging off the bank account he called up his Bank of America Visa card. 'Yes, it looks like he filled up at the Exxon gas station at the same place. He's gotta be heading north.'

Shaw: 'Where the hell would he be going? Canada? He's got a good few hours' start on us.'

Garcia: 'Man, he could be going anywhere, but at least we have him moving north. I am going to see the Lieutenant and bring him up to date. At least we know the identity of the Zodiac Rapist and who murdered the Marx husband and wife. I am sure Johnston is going to want to release this information up the line to his boss.'

As Garcia left the office, Jimmy Wilson arrived armed with a circular saw.

'Okay boys and girls, stand back while I cut through these shackles. Hopefully I don't end up cutting off his leg as well. Sit back and put your right leg up on the desk and keep it still. The sparks may be hot but hold tight and I'll have you shackle-free in no time.' Jimmy pulled on his safety goggles and handed a pair to Ethan.

True to his word, Wilson had both shackles off in under five minutes, no accidents, and no burns.

Garcia returned to the office and called his detectives together.

'I have brought the Lieutenant up to date and the plan is to hold off any press releases until we have a better idea which way Livingstone was heading. He didn't want to create a wholesale panic that the Zodiac Rapist was on the run.

He was surprised that Livingstone managed to get into the precinct unnoticed and then plant hidden cameras in the room. He has called the Techies from 1PP to come over and dismantle the cameras, they should be here any minute. I just wonder why they never found them the first time.'

The same two Techies who found the telephone bugs arrived to search and remove all cameras. The detectives, offering no comment, watched as they set up their equipment.

Once set up, they began a sweep of the wall facing the time line, immediately the sensor began beeping. The NYPD career poster was taken down from the wall and inspected, the first of the cameras had been located. Leaving the camera in the poster, they continued the sweep. The second camera was in the picture of the President, it too was taken down.

After finding no more cameras in the general office, they moved over to Garcia's room. The sensor reacted immediately, and the camera was traced to Garcia's twenty-year service award. Three cameras had been located which tied in with O'Connell's observations seen from his basement.

'Looks like we have them all detectives. They are all still transmitting we should be able to locate where they are sending their signals to. As soon as I can triangulate the signals, I should have a location.'

Garcia: 'So how come you missed these the first time around? That sensor device went off almost immediately.'

'The cameras had to have been deactivated last time. The person observing you must have seen us beginning the scan and remotely deactivated them. I am getting the co-ordinates of their source – 2952 Fenton Avenue in the East Bronx. The controller there is still recording.'

'So, put the cameras back in place, if someone does look at them, I don't want to let them know they have been found. O'Connell, you, Hayes, and Mills get around to this address; you need to locate the controller. Before you enter the premises, wait for backup, I will send additional bodies. If Livingstone is there, try and take him alive, if not take him out. Go.'

The three detectives donned their bulletproof vests, checked their weapons, and headed down to the parking garage, Mills pulled rank and took the wheel. The 17-mile trip to the Bronx would take them almost an hour. They decided against using the police siren as they didn't want to give warning to Livingstone if he was at home.

Backup in the form of an additional six well-armed officers arrived five minutes after the detectives. Mills took charge of the operation and pulled the team together.

'O'Connell and I will go in first, Hayes, you position yourself at the bottom of the fire escape, Jones, you go with her. If he comes out and does not surrender take him down. There is only one way in and no back door. The rest of you follow us in, he is armed and dangerous, but I would prefer to take him alive. Follow me his apartment is on the second floor.'

With Mills leading the way, followed by O'Connell and five well-armed officers, they reached the door of Livingstone's apartment. Mills banged on the door.

'Open up, it's the police! Livingstone, we know you are in there, come out with your hands up and you will not be harmed.'

Receiving no reply, she indicated to the leading officer to break the door down. Using his heavy battering ram, it only took one swing and the door crashed open. Gun drawn, Mills stepped into the apartment followed similarly by O'Connell and then the five police officers.

The apartment only had three rooms, one bedroom, a bathroom, and a kitchen/living room. All were empty, Mills gave the "All Clear". She turned to the leading officer.

'Jimbo, thanks for your help, we'll take over from here. Can you cordon off the apartment as a crime scene and have one of your team stand guard?'

Jimbo nodded and pressed his intercom radio switch, 'Jonesy, can you bring Detective Hayes up to the apartment with you. We are going back to the precinct; you mark the apartment as a crime scene and stay behind keep any onlookers away.'

In the far corner of the living room to the left of a large flat screen TV was a desk covered in computer equipment. A console was attached to the TV via an HDMI cable, O'Connell picked up the TV remote and switched it on. The TV screen burst into life; it showed six separate views. One for each of the cameras Livingstone had hidden.

A USB cable ran from the console to a laptop. Hayes opened the laptop and switched it on, it booted up to display a screen the same as the TV. At the bottom of the screen was a command function 'F1 for menu' she pressed the function key.

The first thing that caught her eye was "Option #4 – Archive.", she took the option. The six cameras were listed by location, she chose "Bedroom"; a list of dates was displayed, so she picked the latest one.

It showed O'Connell entering the bedroom and begin divesting himself of his clothes. Fortunately, he went out of view before he was completely naked. The screen went blank for a few seconds only to refresh showing a rear view of him coming out of the bathroom, a date and time was displayed at the bottom of the screen. She watched him dress and leave the room, and the screen went blank again.

Hayes realized the consequences of the archived data and pressed the "Escape Key" returning the screen to the main menu. *'Oh my God everything thing that has happened in these six areas has been recorded and can be replayed. Someone is going to see me having sex with Ethan and his twin brother. I have to have that removed.'* she thought in a blind panic.

She looked over her shoulder only to see both Ethan and Mills looking at her. Mills took the initiative, 'June, unplug those two devices. We will need to get them back to the precinct as I am sure we will find there is evidence on them.'

Not needing a second invitation, she bundled up the laptop and the controller, determined not to let them out of her sight. With nothing left to do, the three detectives handed over custody of the apartment to Officer Jones and made ready to return to the precinct. Hayes climbed into the rear seat of the car with O'Connell in the front passenger seat and Mills driving.

'Ethan, this laptop contains everything that any camera recorded. It has all of your bedroom activity; we cannot let anyone see this. If nothing else, we must delete that particular archive.'

'June, we are the only ones who know what is on that laptop other than Livingstone. I suggest we go back to the precinct via my apartment. We can remove the camera from my bedroom, then copy the archive for the camera onto a thumb drive before deleting the archive file. It should only take a few minutes. Are you okay with that, Linda?'

'Only if I can watch a replay. I might pick up a few tips. Just joking, sure I am okay,' June closed her eyes in relief.

By the time they began the return journey to the precinct from Ethan's apartment, they found themselves in late afternoon traffic. Having completed the backup and deletion of the bedroom camera archive from the laptop, Ethan removed all traces of the camera. For all intents and purposes, it had never existed.

The three detectives arrived back at the precinct and handed over the controller and laptop to the desk sergeant with the instructions they be entered into evidence under the Zodiac Rapist case. Up on the third floor they found Garcia and Shaw waiting for them.

'Boss, we found the controller and laptop that monitored and recorded everything from the five cameras that Livingstone had hidden. I have handed the equipment into evidence. I think you can have the technical guys remove the cameras as well.'

'Thanks Mills, good job the three of you. We have not had any sightings of Livingstone, but we will leave the BOLO in place. O'Connell, if you can monitor your credit and debit cards and call in any activity you find, that would be helpful. I reckon we call it a day, anyone for a few drinks?'

Mills and Shaw both agreed but O'Connell said he needed to get home and start something of a clean-up. Hayes was driving so she also declined.

On the ride back home, the conversation centered around their relationship and if the events of recent days would change it.

'Ethan, I think we should talk about what has happened over the last three or four days. Like I said, as far as I was concerned, I was with you. There were one or two things that I felt were slightly off, but I put that down to stress. Are we going to be okay?'

'June, the hardest thing for me to see was Livingstone and you having sex. It was like watching myself in a porn movie, I was extremely angry at the time, not because of you and him but him knowing I was watching, He wanted me to suffer, and I did. It is very hard to get that image out of my mind.

As far as we are concerned my feelings towards you remain the same. I am just sorry you got caught up in his disgusting plan. I don't blame you for any of it. You were as much a victim as anyone else this bastard has messed with, and I am so very sorry.'

'Do you want me to come in and stay over tonight?'

'I think I need to make some effort to clean up the basement and clear my mind over what has happened. Please don't take this the wrong way, but I think I need tonight to recover.

I have no car so can you pick me up tomorrow? I will make it up to you, just give me some time. He will be caught soon, and we can get back to normal.'

June pulled up outside the apartment and turned towards Ethan, he leaned in and kissed her passionately on the lips, she responded in kind.

'Go home and double lock your doors, it's unlikely that he will try and get into your apartment. He is a skilled lock picker, so also jam a chair under the inside doorknob. I will do the same here.

Tomorrow we should get the Boss to organize some police presence at both our places. I don't know how crazy he is but so far, his plan has come off the rails so who knows what he will do.'

'I will be careful, see you tomorrow same time.'

Chapter 40
The Return

Livingstone awoke early the next day, he showered and having no change of clothes, dressed in the same attire as he wore the previous day. He put the remains of last night's pizza in the microwave and while that was reheating, he made use of the free coffee.

Making sure that he had left nothing behind, he dropped the room key card on the dresser table then hung the "Do not Disturb" sign on the front doorknob and closed the door behind him. He was sure that if, by chance, the police came calling looking for him, the desk clerk would deny he had ever been there. There was no registration and if he did confirm he had been there he would have to give back the $100.

Next, he retraced his steps to the Viva Pizza's parking lot. As expected, the car was gone, hopefully to some chop shop. Wrapped up against the cold weather, he made the short journey on foot to the Greyhound Bus Station at Filbert Street, less than one mile away.

It was early morning, so the station was crowded and the ticket counters busy. He looked up at the departures schedule. There was a bus leaving for Chicago, Illinois in just over an hour. There was also a bus departing for 42nd Street Port Authority in New York leaving ten minutes after the Chicago departure.

There were four ticket windows operating and six automated terminals. He decided on booking the Chicago ticket using the automated system, if O'Connell had blocked all his credit cards it would be rejected but there was no other human intervention. He inserted the Visa credit card, keyed in his name and destination. Much to his surprise the transaction was accepted, and the ticket printed. The trip to Chicago would take around twenty-one hours.

Next, he then joined the line to purchase his ticket for New York, which he paid for in cash. The short trip would be around two hours as there were numerous stops on the way. He estimated he would arrive at the Port Authority around 10.15 am.

He assumed that a BOLO had been put out on him giving

O'Connell's car details. He wanted the police to think he was in Philadelphia and concentrate their search there. There was a good chance the BOLO would pick up whoever was driving O'Connell's car. The ticket to Chicago would lead them on a wild goose chase and give him more time to disappear into the underworld of New York City.

He watched as the passengers boarded the bus to Chicago. As each person climbed aboard, their ticket was inspected for the correct destination, but it was not marked off against any list. The departure time arrived, and the ticket inspector checked his watch, he shrugged his shoulders and turned to the driver. They were obviously discussing that there was at least one passenger missing. Five minutes later the inspector stepped off the bus, the driver closed the doors and reversed the bus out of the parking bay.

Livingstone watched the bus depart, satisfied it had left the station, he walked over to bay 35, showed his ticket and boarded the bus to New York. Four minutes later the driver closed the doors, put the bus in reverse and pulled out of the parking bay. They were on their way to New York.

He found two seats at the very rear of the bus right next to the bathroom, the least popular seats on the bus. The bus wasn't full, so he had both seats to himself, giving him space to contemplate his next move. He hadn't totally given up on his plan for O'Connell. He decided to add June Hayes to his final solution though he still hadn't figured out how she had discovered he wasn't O'Connell.

Hayes pulled up outside O'Connell's apartment right on time, she found him waiting with two cups of coffee. Still a little nervous that it might be Livingstone, she slowly opened the car door. O'Connell passed her the two cups of coffee and realizing her concern he pulled up his trouser leg to expose his right ankle.

'See, it's me, it's easier to show you my damaged ankle rather than the other distinct difference. I understand your concern. I think Livingstone is well in the wind, probably in Canada. We should check with the border checkpoints when we get into the office. I checked my accounts when I got up this morning, as of 7.00 am no more transactions.

I have set email alerts to inform me if there are any purchases on credit cards or bank debit card. I will check again for emails when we get into the office.

I spent most of yesterday evening cleaning up the basement. I so regret kicking over that bucket in a fit of rage, but I had the best sleep I have had in days. I am ready to track down that bastard.'

'Oh Ethan, I am so glad you are okay. I can't imagine what it would have been like if he had got away with it. I would never have known he wasn't you,' her eyes teared up and she looked out of the driver's window to hide them from Ethan. He pretended not to notice but reached for her hand.

'I think he may have had plans for you as well as me. Watching him with you, I could see there was no pleasure in it for him. He is a mixture of a sociopath and a psychopath. We both dodged a bullet here, so let's catch him and put him away for good.' She squeezed his hand in acknowledgment.

They arrived at the precinct to find the rest of the team in place, Shaw had brought coffee and donuts. Garcia, with his whole team in place, proceeded to give a status report.

'The BOLO hasn't turned up anything yet. If he was heading up the I95 he would have been picked up. If he was making a direct run to Canada, he could have taken the I87, the I90 or any combination. Either he beat us to it, or he has gone off into the countryside.

If he tries to cross at any of the normal border checkpoints, he will be identified but if he chooses to go over off-road, we may never find him. You got any updates on your bank accounts, O'Connell?'

'There was nothing on my cell first thing this morning. If there are any transactions, I will get an email. I am going to check that again right now.'

On his way to his desk, he grabbed a cup of coffee and a donut. He booted up his desktop and logged on. He checked his Yahoo mail account and there among the slew of the usual meaningless emails, was one from his Bank of America Visa account. He clicked on it; it was for $104.50 purchase made at Philadelphia Bus Terminal.

'Boss, he has purchased a Greyhound Bus ticket in Philly – one way to Chicago. If the bus left on time, then it is already on the road to Chicago.'

'Right, I'll get the BOLO redirected to Philly, you get on the phone and call the Greyhound office in Philly and see if they can confirm that he is on the bus, also get the stops that it will make on the way. That bastard could get off at any of those stops.'

O'Connell dialed the appropriate number and identified himself and asked to speak to a supervisor. After a short wait he was connected to a lady who identified herself as the ticket office supervisor. He explained he was a detective with the NYPD and was trying to track down someone who had bought a one-way ticket from Philadelphia to Chicago.

In the meantime, Garcia was on a call to Philadelphia Police Headquarters. He was put through to Captain Edward "Buzz" Foley. He identified himself and explained the situation.

'We have reason to believe that the Zodiac Rapist may be in your area. His name is Matthew Livingstone, but is using an ID belonging to Ethan O'Connell, who is one of my detectives. He is the identical twin brother of O'Connell.

We have a BOLO out on him which I have updated to include Philadelphia. He is armed and has the detective's shield and driver's license. I would class him as extremely dangerous. We need him apprehended, alive, if possible, but rather dead than him escaping.'

Garcia provided a detailed description of Livingstone and promised to send copies of all of O'Connell's ID documents. Foley in turn promised to have his cops on the lookout for both the car and Livingstone.

O'Connell completed his call and addressed his colleagues.

'The lady I spoke to was very helpful, but she couldn't confirm that Livingstone actually boarded the bus. Company policy states that the dispatcher and the driver are supposed to identify each ticket holder and check them off against the passenger list. She knew for a fact that this was not happening; all they were doing was count the number of passengers boarding against the number of tickets sold.

If the ticket was for correct destination with the correct departure date and time, the ticket holder was allowed onboard without showing any identification. If the number sold is not matched by the number boarding, the driver will wait five minutes before departing.

I didn't tell her why we were looking for Livingstone. She told me that the major stops the bus would make were Harrisburg PA, Pittsburgh PA, Columbus OH, Indianapolis IN, Gary IN and finally Chicago, approximately twenty-one hours on the road.'

'I have updated Captain Buzz Foley of Philadelphia PD; he will get the BOLO out in his area and hopefully find your car. I think the best plan is to have a police presence at each of the major stops to see if Livingstone tries to disembark. If he does, we take him. We cannot risk trying to board the bus and apprehend him, he is armed and too many civilians could get hurt.'

Shaw placed a call into the Harrisburg PD and put them in the picture. Being firm with them just being there and do not board. 'Mills, you take Pittsburgh, Hayes, you call Columbus, O'Connell, call Indianapolis and I'll call Gary. We can't let him disembark unchecked in Chicago.'

While the detectives were busy calling the various Police Departments across the Midwest, Livingstone arrived at New York Port Authority. He was the last person off the bus, disembarking slowly, carefully checking his surroundings for any police presence. Finding none, he merged in with the departing crowd as they left the bus terminal.

He made his way to Grand Central on 42nd Street where he took the IRT Lexington Avenue line #5 to Gun Hill Road. He figured that his apartment had probably been found and searched, but if not, he could recover some of his belongings.

Ten stops later and after a short walk, Livingstone arrived outside of his apartment building. Watching from across the road he noticed that there was a police officer standing guard outside his apartment door. He checked his watch and it showed 1.02 pm, he contemplated just walking up to the cop and identifying himself as O'Connell.

While debating with himself about whether to proceed, the cop on duty solved the problem for him. The cop left his post and Livingstone watched as he reappeared outside of the building and walked over to Gun Hill Gourmet Deli. Livingstone took his chance, and the second the cop entered the eatery, he crossed the road ran up to the second floor, unlocked the apartment door, entered, and closed the door behind him making sure he locked it.

A quick search of his apartment confirmed that all his surveillance equipment was missing. He headed into the bedroom and packed a backpack with three changes of clothing and a pair of New Balance sneakers. From the bathroom he loaded in his toothbrush and toothpaste, his electric shaver and deodorant.

Moving his remaining clothes aside in his closet he reached into the rear and using a small screwdriver he opened a panel in the floor. Secured under the floorboards was a solid metal lock-box which he retrieved and carried out into the bedroom.

The box contained nearly $2,000 in cash, a driver's license and two credit cards all in the name of Brian M. Wellens. Always knowing that at some point in his existence he would have to disappear for a while, this was his escape plan.

Satisfied that he had everything he needed, he walked up to the front door of his apartment and peered through the spyglass. The cop was back, he was busy eating a sub, obviously bought at the Deli. Frustrated, Livingstone had no other option than to leave via the rear apartment window.

He opened the window and stuck his head out. His apartment on the second floor was the end unit on the south side of the building. To his right was the intersection with Fenton Avenue and Gun Hill Road. At 1.15 pm on a cold New York day the traffic was busy at the intersection. Looking left down Fenton Avenue there were only three people visible. Two of them were walking south away from his building. A single woman was walking her dog on the opposite side of the road coming towards the apartment building.

Realizing he had to take a chance, he climbed out of the window and, holding on to the frame, he pulled the window down as far as he could. Gripping on the very bottom of the window ledge he lowered himself over the edge. Fully extended he released his grip and took the twelve-foot drop to the pavement. He landed safely and immediately assumed a crouching position.

Making out that he was tying his shoelaces, he glanced over at the woman walking her dog. She glanced in his direction but had no reaction towards him. He stood up, turned around and headed toward Gun Hill Road where he turned left and made his way towards the nearby subway station.

In the meantime, the Harrisburg police had arrived at the bus depot too late. They were able to confirm that nobody alighted or disembarked from the bus. The Pittsburgh PD confirmed that they were onsite to meet the bus. They checked with the ticket office that there were seats available and requested that one ticket be issued for boarding.

The Philadelphia police pulled over a car for running a stop sign. When the cop approached the vehicle the driver and his passenger both made a bolt for it. The cop checked the car's license plate and identified it as O'Connell's car. He immediately called it in to headquarters, who then informed Garcia.

Twenty-five minutes later the Greyhound bus pulled into the

Pittsburgh depot, where the two PPD cops were waiting. Three people disembarked and one new passenger boarded. Checking that none of the leaving passengers were Livingstone, one of the cops showed his ticket and climbed aboard.

He made his way to the rear of the bus checking each passenger as he went, none of them matched Livingstone's description. He checked that the bathroom at the rear was empty. Certain that Livingstone was not onboard, he returned to the front of the bus and instructed the driver to open the door. He told his partner that the bus was clear, and he should inform headquarters immediately.

Buzz Foley called Garcia with the news that Livingstone wasn't on the bus but given his car was found in Philadelphia, he may very well be still in the area. Garcia thanked him and agreed that the BOLO should stay in place.

'Well folks, it looks like Livingstone is leading us a merry dance. He is not on the way to Canada or Chicago. O'Connell, your car has been found in one piece. I will get it back to you as soon as the Philadelphia PD releases it. He may still be in Philly or the surrounding area. You got any thoughts?'

'Boss, I think he set up this elaborate scheme to buy himself time. He has been gone a day and a half, but he must have slept over somewhere,' said Mills.

'I reckon he will come back to New York; he knows the area. He knew that we would eventually find out that his plan was to lead us astray, but I think Mills is right he will come back to New York. By the way, will the department reimburse me for what he has run up on my credit card and the cash from my bank account, given that you asked me not to block them?'

'I assume you have now put a block on the credit cards, you will have to put in a claim for reimbursement, but that may take a while.

Okay, let's assume he is back in town. We have his apartment under surveillance, so he is unlikely to try and go back there. O'Connell, you, and Hayes take a trip down there, check with the cop on duty and also see if anything inside the apartment has been disturbed.'

The two detectives arrived at Livingstone's apartment to find Officer Jones on duty, Hayes addressed him. 'Hey Jonesy, I see you pulled this duty as well, must be your unlucky day. How are you doing, any action?'

'Nope, not a thing, it's freezing cold standing out here. I don't know why I can't be on guard from the inside.'

'Why don't you come on in with us? I'll let them know back at the precinct that we authorized you to move inside. You got the keys?'

Jones nodded and opened the door; he stepped back to let Hayes and O'Connell into the apartment. A quick check showed nothing seemed out of place, the bedroom was left exactly as they remembered it. They were just about to leave when Hayes spotted a slightly open window.

'Hey Ethan, do you remember that window over there being slightly open?'

'No, I am positive all windows were securely shut,' he walked over to the window to inspect it. 'Look, I am pretty sure there are fingerprints on the window frame, almost like someone was hanging on it from the outside.

Put in a call to the Boss and see if we can get some prints lifted from here. We should be able to match them to other prints of Livingstone's found around the place. I bet you he's been here. Hey Jonesy, have you been here all the time today?'

'Yes, apart from about five minutes when I went to the corner deli for something to eat. I think they have forgotten about me; about time they sent some relief.' Ethan cursed under his breath at that slip in procedure.

'Boss, it's Hayes here, we are at Livingstone's apartment. It looks like he may have been here as we found a partially opened window. Can you get someone over to check for prints? Okay thanks, also can you send someone to relieve Jones? Good I'll tell him,' she ended the call.

'The Boss will send someone over to do the prints. Jonesy, you will get some relief. Garcia says you should stay in the apartment with the door locked.'

It took over an hour for the fingerprint cop to arrive, he was accompanied by Jones' relief. O'Connell directed the cop over to the open window. After dusting the whole window area, he turned his attention to the bottom frame and the outside ledge. Ten minutes later he announced his findings.

'I have an excellent set of prints on the bottom window frame, they look fresh. I would estimate less than twelve hours old. Eight fingers on the inside and two thumb and two palm prints on the outside. I would say he was hanging on the frame outside the window. I doubt we have his prints on file, so I will take more prints from other areas as a comparison. If they match, it should give us proof that he has been here recently.'

'Thanks, we will leave you to do your job. We are heading back to the precinct. Hey Jonesy, want a ride back?'

'I sure do thanks, June.'

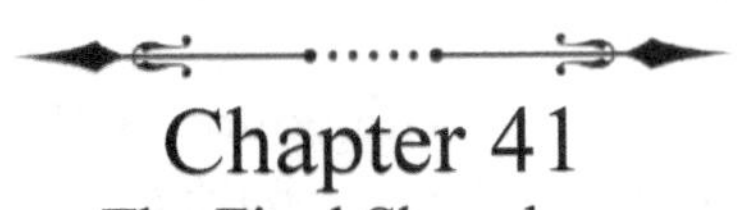

Chapter 41
The Final Showdown

O'Connell, Hayes, and Jones returned to the precinct to report their findings to Garcia. By the time they dropped Jones off and got up to the situation room, the results of the fingerprinting had been reported to Garcia.

'Welcome back, you took your time. I have some news for you all. I have the results of the fingerprinting at Livingstone's apartment.

The prints found on the window frame were made within the last twenty-four hours. They were matched against prints found elsewhere in the apartment. We can safely assume that they all belong to Livingstone, which means he is back in the city.

He somehow managed to get into the apartment despite us having a cop guarding the front door. Any idea how that was possible?'

'The cop on duty was told to stay outside of the apartment in the cold. He had had no relief and left his post to grab food. He said he was away for no more than five minutes; he went to the Deli on the same corner as the apartment block.

We can only assume Livingstone was watching the apartment and when Jones left for the Deli, he saw his chance and got into the apartment,' said O'Connell.

'Well, he obviously took a risk getting into his apartment, especially after the trouble he went to misdirecting us. There must have been a good reason for him taking the chance, any ideas?' asked Garcia.

Shaw: 'I reckon he probably had cash stashed there, maybe even other identity documents. But then again, we searched that place thoroughly and didn't find anything like that, so maybe he had it hidden in a secret spot?'

'You could be right, but he still has my shield, gun and driver's license. I don't think he will try and leave the city; he will hole up somewhere where he can move about without attracting attention.'

'Why do you think he came back to New York?' asked Mills,

directing her question to O'Connell.

'I think he has unfinished business with me, maybe with Hayes as well. The trouble he went to to set this whole thing up, just to punish me, he is not going to let it go.'

Garcia: 'I think we should put additional police protection on both of you.

Off the record, I know the two of you are involved, against police protocol I may add, but the best way to protect you both is for you to stay together until we catch this bastard. What do you say?'

'Boss, that would be up to Hayes but I have no problem. I think it is a good idea but for how long? Livingstone has already proved he can play the long game. What do you say, June?'

'Of course, I agree. It makes sense that it's easier to protect us both if we are in the same place. I would prefer it to be my apartment, not that I have anything against your place.'

Mills: 'Maybe we should split them up. O'Connell could stay with me, and Hayes can move in with Shaw. What do you say, Boss?'

'The poor man has had enough trauma in recent days so I couldn't possibly subject him to anymore. I am sure he appreciates the offer though. Okay, enough joking around, what do we have in the way of suggestions on putting Livingstone away once and for all?'

O'Connell: 'Well, he no longer has his cameras in the office nor at my place so he cannot be one step ahead of us anymore. Now that he missed out on killing me, I am sure he will plan something and try again. I just wonder if he might return to robbery and raping.'

Hayes: 'If he stays true to his MO, the next New Moon is March 2, but last time he deviated by going three blocks north. Do we need to get a profiler in from the Feds?'

Garcia: 'Hell no, they will take over the whole case, we've put in too much work to give this over now. Anyway, we know exactly what he is doing. He gets off on power and control, we saw it with the six rape cases and the way he had control over O'Connell.'

'Jesus and the absolute control he had over me. I hope there is no viewing of those recordings,' thought Hayes.

Mills: 'I think he will do something on March 2 just to get our attention. Where and what, I have no clue. Three blocks north would be 52nd Street or if he goes back south then it could be 31st Street. If he does something he will revert to his normal MO. What could a shrink tell us about him that we don't already know?'

Shaw: 'We better hope it's not 52nd Street; that area is packed solid with apartments. We have already cased 31st Street as we thought that's where he would strike last time.'

Mills: 'If he does go back to rape and robbery then I think he will change where he strikes next just to mess with us. What does the Lieutenant think we should do?'

Garcia: 'Lieutenant Johnston just wants it to be one day before his retirement. I have suggested that he circulate Livingstone's description to every NYPD cop. It might make it tough for you though, O'Connell. You won't be able to move without being accosted by some overzealous beat cop.

We decided to give it one more week before doing that, also we don't want to cause a citywide panic. These things usually end up with every nut job in the area calling in a sighting. It's just counterproductive and we don't have the bodies to spare to deal with that.

We keep on following up on leads. It's two and a half weeks before the next New Moon. We now know exactly who we are looking for, so my plan is to put as many plain clothes cops around the 400 blocks of 52nd and 31st Streets as we have available. Put them there, maybe from the 28th through March 2. Hopefully he stays on his tried and trusted path. Anyone got any better ideas?'

Livingstone, in the meantime, had found himself a cheap hotel room in the Little Italy area of the city. He checked in under the name of Brian Wellens and paid for three weeks in advance using a credit card in the same name. His plan was to spend the next two weeks breaking into houses in the greater New York City environs.

Using his old contacts for disposing of his stolen goods, he began accumulating what he felt was sufficient cash to fund his disappearance from New York once he had completed his final tasks.

O'Connell moved in with Hayes as planned. They both turned down the offer of around-the-clock police protection as they felt that Livingstone wouldn't risk trying to attack them again. Both felt he had left the area and was laying low somewhere. They were also certain he planned to find another victim and it would happen on March 1.

Garcia had gotten approval from Lieutenant Johnston to post undercover cops in and around the 400 blocks of both 31st and 52nd Streets. The surveillance would start on Sunday February 27 and continue through March 1. The cops all knew exactly who they were looking for, their instructions were to apprehend Livingstone, failing that if he resisted or attempted to flee, they had orders to shoot to kill.

Morning broke on March 1, a chilly 43F, overcast with a slight drizzle. The two sets of cops at each site were relieved with nothing to report. The full team of detectives in the situation room at the 35th precinct was present and had been since 6.00 am. There was an air of expectation that this would be the day the five of them were on edge.

Livingstone had anticipated that the cops were expecting him at one of the two logical sites, but he had other plans. He had spent three days observing his selected victim's routine and decided the best time to confront her would be just after she returned from work, 6.15 pm.

Back at the precinct, time passed slowly and frustratingly. Had they totally miscalculated Livingstone's plans? Maybe he would strike early evening, they decided to keep the surveillance going through to midnight. At 6.00 pm Garcia authorized supper for the team, and Mills and Shaw were sent out to pick up the food.

Livingstone watched from his vantage point as his intended victim appeared. She was walking confidently along the sidewalk, right on schedule, it was 6.02 pm. He watched as she entered her building, she unlocked the door and without so much as look in any direction she entered her apartment and closed the door.

He waited ten minutes, giving her enough time to settle in. He could see her kitchen lights from his vantage point; he saw them come on, so it was time for him to make his move. He crossed the road and entered the apartment building, walked up to her front door, and rang the bell.

A few seconds later he heard footsteps, there was a pause and a voice said, 'Who is this? What do you want?'

Livingstone held the detective's shield and ID up to the peephole in the front door.

'It's Detective O'Connell, ma'am. I have some information regarding your attacker, may I come in?'

Sandra Williamson peered through the peephole and identified Ethan O'Connell.

'Yes Detective, I will unlock the door' which she did, 'Please come in. I hope it's good news, have you caught him?' she asked, hopefully.

Livingstone smiled, 'Not exactly caught him, but we know who he is, so I am here to give you the details.'

'Have you told the other victims yet? We have created a support group. I am sure they are going to be pleased.'

'The other detectives on the team have been tasked with that.'

'Great. Can I offer you a drink, coffee, tea or maybe a beer?' she said, showing him through to the lounge.

'Coffee would be good, thank you.'

'I'll just spark up the Keurig, Colombian dark okay for you?' Livingstone nodded. 'It won't take a minute. Do you have a photograph of my attacker?'

'I sure do. Here he is, quite a good-looking man, I must admit.'

He walked over to Williamson, flipped open his Police ID and showed it to her. She looked at him confused, not quite comprehending what he was showing her.

'But that's a photo of you, what's going on?' she asked, fear creeping into her voice.

Reverting to his natural Bronx accent he answered her, 'That's not strictly true; it is in fact a photo of my twin brother, Ethan O'Connell. Let me introduce myself. I am Matthew Livingstone, your worst nightmare.'

Before she could comprehend what was happening, he produced a large Bowie knife and held it to her throat. She opened her mouth to scream, before she could utter a sound, his left hand clamped her mouth closed.

'Now don't be silly, Sandra, screaming will just annoy me. I thought that you never got the chance to see what I looked like at our last meeting. That was bad form on my part, so now I am here to correct that. Open your mouth.'

Terrified, she complied; Livingstone stuffed a cloth in her mouth, effectively gagging her. With the knife held to her throat he guided her towards the bedroom.

'Take off your clothes and don't do anything stupid.' He watched as she fearfully disrobed, admiring her firm well-proportioned body. Naked, she faced him, not sure what to do next, so he made that decision for her by roughly pushing her backwards onto the bed. She shut her eyes tightly, tears rolling down her cheeks; *not again, please.*

Still holding the knife in his right hand, he unbuckled his belt and dropped his trousers, freeing his already erect penis. Forcing her legs apart he knelt above her and without ceremony rammed his huge member into her. He felt her stiffen with pain, which was key to him, and begin pounding into her. He looked at the fear on her face, her eyes tightly closed, he felt the absolute power and control he craved.

As he was about to ejaculate, he leaned over to his right, lowered his head to her left breast and without warning bit off her nipple. Her muffled scream put him over the edge and gave him the orgasmic relief he craved. Swallowing the nipple, he lifted his head and reached for the pillow next to her head.

Covering her face with the pillow and holding it firmly in place, he reached under it and with his right hand slit her throat. She convulsed once and was then still. Holding the pillow over her head he waited until the blood ceased to flow. Once satisfied that she was dead, he lifted himself off her body, stood up and pulled up his trousers.

Examining his handiwork, he smiled. *Perfect.* The only blood on him was a small amount on his right hand where he had cut her throat, easily washed off. He walked over to the bathroom and washed off the blood not bothering to try and remove any fingerprints. He wanted them to know who it was this time.

Satisfied, he returned to the bedroom and removed the pillow covering her face. Opening his wallet, he removed a Sagittarius Zodiac card and inserted it into her vagina. Taking a black permanent marker, he left a message on her chest for the cops. He had thought of making a call in to Garcia but decided it would be more effective if she was discovered by someone else.

He left the apartment, leaving the front door wide open, walked down the stairs unobserved, and turned right on 46th street. Within minutes he was on the subway.

By leaving the apartment door open, he knew it wouldn't take long for a curious neighbor to investigate. He was right. At 6.35 pm Williamson's next-door neighbor returned from work and noticed her door open. He knew this was unusual; ever since her attack she never ever had the door open unattended.

He put his head through the doorway and called out her name. Getting no response, he carefully entered the apartment. Finding no one in the lounge or kitchen, he finally checked her bedroom. He almost threw up at the sight of her bloodied naked body on the bed.

He ran from the building and called 911. He was instructed not to touch anything and to wait outside until the police arrived. The 911 dispatcher put out the call and at the same time called the 35th precinct. The address set off alarms with Sergeant Mick Dooley and he immediately called Garcia.

'Mike, it's Dooley. There has been a murder at Sandra Williamson's address, it looks like she could be the victim. Her neighbor found her door open and went in to find a body. A patrol car is on its way over, I will call Barry Hughes at CSI. I suggest you get your team over there pronto. It could be Livingstone's work, the bastard!'

Garcia hung up the phone and addressed his team. 'It looks like Livingstone has attacked and killed Sandra Williamson. Dave, you're with me. Mills, you take O'Connell and Hayes. We need to get to her apartment like yesterday, we'll probably meet Barry Hughes and his team there.'

Garcia stopped at the front desk and spoke to Sergeant Dooley.

'Mick, we need to send cops to all the other women who were Livingstone's victims. I don't know if he plans to kill off the rest of them but better safe than sorry. Make sure the cops you send do not leave those women's side, no exceptions! Thanks.'

The team of detectives made the nine-block drive in record time. They arrived with sirens blaring. An ever-increasing crowd had gathered and there were already two news vans onsite. *How the fuck did they get there so fast?* With Mills in the lead, they pushed their way through the throng of people, reaching the yellow police demarcation tape, where they were stopped by two beat cops. Garcia flashed his shield and ID card.

'Who is in charge here?' asked Garcia.

'Not sure sir, we were told to hold back members of the public. The CSI team have arrived, they are inside on the second floor.'

Garcia lifted the tape and followed by his four detectives entered the building and rushed up the stairs. They found another cop standing guard at the apartment door.

Mills recognized him, 'Jonesy, you keep turning up, where you the one who found the victim?'

'Yeah, we picked up the 911 call, came over and found the neighbor. That's him over there, he could barely speak. I was first in followed by my partner. We found her in the bedroom, I have never seen so much blood in my life. The CSI team are in there now.'

Garcia led his team into the apartment, it wasn't difficult to see where the bedroom was. He walked up to the door and poked his head into the room where he spotted Barry Hughes. He called out to him.

'What have we got here, Barry?'

'Jesus, Mike, it's a mess. I can confirm the victim is Sandra Williamson; I remember her from the rape case, she was the first victim. She died from a severed carotid artery, probably dead within a few seconds. There is semen in her vagina she has had intercourse within the last hour. It was forced there is bruising around the area.

But wait for it, her left nipple is missing, bitten off while she was still alive. He must have taken it with him as there is no sign of it here. I found a Sagittarius Zodiac card in her vagina, it looks like your boy is at it again, only this time he has added murder.

The lack of blood splatter is because he held the pillow over her face when he slit her throat. I would imagine there would have been some blood on his hands and obviously the knife but not enough to be noticed if seen by someone. Come and take a look at this.'

Garcia followed Hughes over to the bed, he was directed to the writing on Williamson's chest. In black permanent marker were written the words – *'This one is on you, O'Connell'*.

'Jesus, O'Connell, he really has it in for you. This is not your fault; he is just goading you. By the looks of it, he has lost his fucking mind. Mills, can you call Mick Dooley and check that he has the other five women protected as there is no telling where the fucking monster will attack next?' Mills shot him a thumbs up to acknowledge the request.

'I hope we track him down and he resists or tries to flee. It will save everyone a lot of time and effort to just shoot the fucker instead of trying this in court. There is always the chance he will be declared insane or some other reason not to lock him up forever.'

With nothing else for them to do at the crime scene, Garcia suggested they head back to the precinct as it was already after 7.00 pm. Barry Hughes promised to have a full report by first thing tomorrow. The Medical Examiner hadn't arrived on the scene yet but other than to confirm the method and time of death, there was nothing new he would be able to tell them.

The drive back to the precinct was a more sedate journey. The talk in both cars was about what to expect next from Livingstone. The consensus was that he was not going away quietly but the question was would he stick to the New Moon timeline or had he totally accelerated?

As the team were walking past the front desk, Mick Dooley called out to O'Connell.

'Hey O'Connell, good news, the Philly PD released your car. They shipped it up to the vehicle pound in Brooklyn. You can pick it up any time.'

'Thanks Sarge.'

Up on the third floor, Garcia addressed his team.

'Folks, it's been a long day, there is nothing for us to do in what remains of the day. We know who it is and if he was hoping to kill off the other women, we have it covered. Let's call it quits. Go home get some sleep and we hit it again tomorrow.'

'June, can you give me a ride to the Brooklyn pound? It's kind of on the way home. I'll pick up my car and drive around to your place. I need to pick up a few things from my apartment first,' asked O'Connell.

'Sure, I can.'

Hayes dropped O'Connell off at the pound, leaving him to fill in the necessary paperwork. Typical bureaucratic red tape took up the next twenty minutes. By the time his car was released to him, Hayes was already home. She got out of her work clothes and jumped into the shower. Feeling refreshed and clean, she slipped into T-shirt and sweatpants, not bothering with underwear.

No sooner had she walked into the living room when the front doorbell rang. She wondered who it was, she walked up to the door and peered through the peephole. She recognized Ethan, without stopping to question why he didn't use his key, she opened the door.

'That was quick, normally they take forever to release a vehicle. It probably helped that you were a cop. I have just showered. Do you want to shower first or are you ready for a drink?'

Adopting his normal Bronx accent, he replied. 'No. I think better without booze.'

Startled, she took a step backwards, momentarily confused. Livingstone stepped forward and punched her squarely on the jaw, she crumpled and unconscious she dropped to the floor. He rolled her over onto her stomach, pulled both her arms behind her back and handcuffed her.

Still groggy she was pulled to her feet. Livingstone stood behind her, supporting her in the standing position.

'Wakey wakey, June, you want to be alert for your final part in my plan. I am sure Ethan will be here shortly.'

She turned her head to face him, 'What are doing? This has gone way too far; you will be caught. When you kill a cop, we never stop until you are dead or in custody with the former as the preferred conclusion.'

'That may very well be, but neither of you will be around to witness it. When I am done here, I will disappear and won't ever be found,' he breathed against the side of her face, relishing the fear she must be feeling.

Cupping her mouth with his left hand he reached around to her front with his Bowie knife. In one deft movement, he sliced open the front of her T-shirt exposing her breasts. He felt her gasp as he slipped the knife under the waistband of her sweatpants. With one violent movement, he cut open the sweatpants from the crotch to the waist causing them to drop to her ankles. She was now totally exposed facing the front door some twelve feet away.

'Now we wait for your boyfriend. Don't do anything silly. I don't want to have to kill you before he gets here.'

The words were barely out of his mouth when they heard movement at the front door. Using his key, Ethan opened the door, pushing it with his backside as he was carrying a large box. Once inside, he turned around to put the box down and close the door. At first, he didn't notice June and Livingstone, only when straightened up did he become aware of June's naked form in front of him.

'Hello, brother, stay exactly where you are and don't make any dumb moves, otherwise June here will lose her head – literally. This is not the way I wanted this to end, you haven't suffered nearly enough for my liking. I wanted you to be awake when I took your girlfriend to her final resting place.'

He looked up to see June naked with her arms secured behind her back. Livingstone was standing behind her, he had a large Bowie knife at her throat. In his right hand he held Ethan's police-issue gun.

'Livingstone, this is between the two of us, let her go she has done nothing to you. It's me that you want. I will drop my weapon on the floor. I am at your mercy.'

'Not gonna happen. I had planned to have you watch as I fucked her then cut her throat. I wanted you to feel real pain before I killed you. You and your cop buddies have screwed that up. How did they know I wasn't you?'

'I am circumcised, you are not. June realized it and the rest is now history. Come on, let her go,' Ethan held up his hands, in a feeble attempt to reason with the psycho in front of him.

Livingstone shook his head and stared Ethan straight in the eye. He lifted his right hand and without warning fired two shots, hitting Ethan squarely in the chest. The impact of the bullets knocked him backwards, he hit the floor and never moved. June watched in horror then sprang into action. She bit into Livingstone's left hand, the one holding the knife. He dropped the knife and shouted out in pain.

'You bitch! I was going to take my time with you but now you have fucked that up. Get down on your knees,' he ordered.

June did not react to his demand, so Livingstone pushed her violently forward. Unable to brace her fall, she fell face first onto the carpeted floor. Livingstone leaned down and grabbed her handcuffed hands and pulled her to her knees.

Keeping her in that position he undid the belt holding up his trousers. He unbuttoned the waistband and unzipped the fly. The violence of the moment and June's fear had turned him on, he was fully erect. He positioned himself behind her, upset that O'Connell was not going to see his plan come to fruition.

Just as he was about to penetrate June, two shots rang out, the first hit him in the chest, the second right between the eyes. The last thing he saw before he died was Ethan O'Connell, sitting on the floor gun in hand. He fell forward onto June, his dead weight pushing her face forward onto the floor, breaking her nose.

Ethan staggered up and walked over to where Livingstone was lying on top of June. He rolled his twin's inert body off June, and using his key he unlocked the handcuffs freeing her arms. She rolled over onto her back, with blood pouring from her broken nose, she threw her arms around him and buried her head in his chest.

'I thought he had killed you and I would be next. I didn't want to live if you were dead. How are you still alive?'

'I had so much crap to carry over that I decided rather than carry this thing, I would just wear it.'

He unbuttoned his shirt to expose his NYPD issue bulletproof vest. There were two flattened bullets right in the middle of the vest.

'It's good to know that these things work, I will never complain about wearing one in the future. When the bullets hit me, I thought I was dead, I couldn't breathe, couldn't move. Thank God, he didn't aim for the head. Are you OK?' He ran his hands over her face, careful not to hurt her any more than she was already hurt.

'My face feels like the Hulk just hit me, she turned to look at the body bleeding out on her carpet. 'He is dead, isn't he? Jesus, that was some shooting. We've gotta call this in, can you do it? I need to put some clothes on and clean up this bleeding, it feels like it might be broken,' her hands were trembling from the adrenaline rushing through her body and Ethan steadied her hands with his own. They sat there for a few minutes longer, both grateful to be alive, both knowing how easily things could have gone the other way in a blink.

June went off to change while Ethan called 911, he asked for an ambulance for June and reported the shooting and death of Matthew Livingstone. He hung up and called Garcia's cellphone.

'Boss, it's O'Connell, just to let you know the Zodiac Rapist is no longer a threat. He is lying stone dead in Hayes' hallway with two bullets in him. Yes, I plugged him. Self-defense. I called it in on 911 but I think you better get over here. No, June is okay, but I think her nose may be broken. I have called for a bus.'

The ambulance arrived first and despite her protestations, June Hayes was loaded up and taken to nearby Woodhull Hospital. Garcia arrived as the ambulance was leaving, he was followed by Shaw and Hayes. Working by the book, CSI had been called out and Barry Hughes arrived a further five minutes later.

The four detectives watched as CSI took photographs from all possible angles. Once done, Hughes dismissed his team and handed over Livingstone's body to the waiting Medical Examiner who declared Livingstone dead by way of a bullet to the brain; he then gave custody of the body to the coroner.

With the apartment cleared of all but the four detectives and Barry Hughes, O'Connell suggested that they retreat into the sitting room, and he would open up beers for those who wanted them. It was a unanimous yes. With everyone seated and a beer in their hand, O'Connell went through the sequence of events. When he finished the questions started.

Mills: 'How did he get in?'

'I think he must have knocked, and June would have recognized him as me. She let him in. It looks like she took a whack on the jaw, so he overpowered her, handcuffed her, and then stuck a knife to her throat.'

Shaw: 'So, you stumbled into this,' he shook his head, incredulous at the turn of events.

'Yeah, I was carrying a suitcase and a couple of other things, so I backed into the hallway. I turned around and there they were. June had been stripped naked and he was behind her with a knife at her throat and my service weapon in his right hand.'

Mills: 'What was he hoping to do? Kill you both?'

'He said we had ruined his plan so now he would have to kill me, then he was going to rape and kill June and it would be on my conscience. He then raised the gun and put two rounds into my chest. Not sure when it would have been on my conscience if I was dead on the floor. Shit for brains, I guess.'

Garcia: 'And you just happened to be wearing your bulletproof vest? Luckily, he didn't shoot your head. What made you wear your vest?'

'I thought that if he was going to target June and me, that I should bring it with me. It was just easier to wear it than carry it.'

Mills: 'You lucky bastard. So, the shots put you on your back, must have hurt like crazy.'

'It sure as hell did, I think I might have cracked a rib or two. I came to and saw him forcing June down onto her knees, he had his dick out and was ready to rape her. I never gave him a chance, one in the chest and one between the eyes. Even though he was my brother, I never felt any remorse.'

'Shaw: 'Well, at least we know the vests work. Good riddance to the bastard. You saved us and the taxpayer a whole lot of time and money.'

Garcia: 'Good job, O'Connell, you will need to make a full statement as will Hayes. IA will also probably interview you; you know what they are like with officer-involved shootings. Let's pack it in for now, I suggest you get yourself off to the hospital and get those ribs checked out, look in and see how Hayes is doing. I hope to see you both in the office tomorrow but seriously, take some time if you need to, ok? Same goes for Hayes; you've both been through the wringer in the past few days. Make sure this place is locked up when you leave. Good night'

Chapter 42
The Aftermath

By the time Ethan arrived at the hospital, the word was out about what had gone down. One of the typical ambulance chaser reporters had spotted June Hayes arriving in an ambulance. He asked one of the attending paramedics what was going on and all he heard was "Zodiac Rapist."

Another reporter who was monitoring the police radio communications picked up the report of Sandra Williamson's murder and also the connection with the Zodiac Rapist. Both of them, putting one and one together, assumed the Zodiac Rapist had struck again. The crowds outside Williamson's apartment caused a minor panic as the word spread.

Back at the precinct, Garcia was busy briefing Lieutenant Grover Johnston on the whole situation. He had barely finished when Johnston's phone rang; it was Captain Bruce Andrews, who had been made aware that something major was going on. He was brought up to date and immediately called Mayor Rodney Harmon. The Mayor, who was never one to miss an opportunity to put himself front and center, had already called a press conference.

Ethan was recognized as he attempted to enter the hospital and was immediately surrounded by various members of the press and television reporters. He was bombarded with questions, microphones were thrust into his face, there was a frenzy. Fighting his way through the crowd without comment he made it to the Emergency room front door. Confronted by security blocking his way, he flashed his shield and ID and was allowed entry.

Inside the ER he asked where he could find Detective June Hayes and he was guided to a curtained cubicle. He pulled back the curtain to find June sitting up on the bed being attended to by a young doctor. The doctor was putting finishing touches to an aluminum brace on the bridge of her nose. It was secured in place with two strips of tape, one across her forehead and the other across her cheeks.

'Hi June, how are you feeling? You look like you've gone ten rounds with Mike Tyson,' he joked, trying to lighten the tension after a rough day.

'I feel like it too, but I am okay; just a broken nose and aching jaw bone. Just another day at the office, right?' she tried to smile and flinched at the pain in her jaw.

'I have recommended she stay in overnight for observation, just in case but she won't listen. Maybe you can convince her?' the doctor cocked an eyebrow in Ethan's direction, and he shrugged.

'Sorry Doc, she's a stubborn one, but I will keep an eye on her. Is she free to go?'

'Yes, she just needs to checkout at the nurse's station. I want to thank you both for taking that vile Zodiac Rapist off the streets. Now, take her home and make sure she rests.'

Ethan watched as June checked herself out. They were then given the option of leaving by the rear exit, which they gratefully accepted. Avoiding the press and the TV cameras, they made it back to Ethan's apartment. Safely inside he poured them each a stiff whiskey and they settled down to watch the latest news on TV. June put her legs over his and he absently rubbed her foot, never taking his eyes from the TV screen.

Tuning into to ABC7NY they saw Mayor Rodney Harmon flanked by Commissioner Malcom Rodgers and Captain Bruce Andrews. Harmon, putting himself front and center on TV, was busy extolling the wonderful work of Captain Andrews and his team of detectives from the 35th Precinct.

Andrews, to his credit, handed out the praise directly to Detective Mike Garcia. The TV cameras panned across to Mike, who was looking distinctly uncomfortable. Lieutenant Grover Johnston was conspicuous by his absence. Mike was questioned on how his team went about capturing the infamous Zodiac Rapist, and he immediately mentioned the great teamwork of his detectives, whom he named individually.

As he went about detailing the sequence of events, photos of Detective Ethan O'Connell on the right of the screen and Matthew Livingstone on the left were displayed. Apart from the different clothes, they were mirror images. It was easy to see why the whole saga would capture the public's imagination. No mention was made of the demise of Sandra Williamson; that would come later.

Tired of all the hoopla and exhaustion finally catching up with them, June and Ethan decided it was time for bed. June had been given some painkillers and that, mixed with the stiff shot of whiskey, put her lights out the minute her head hit the pillow. Ethan, having originally thought he may have broken a couple of ribs, felt that it was probably only bruising, the evidence of which was clearly visible.

The following morning, they both woke early at 6.30 am just as the sun was trying to peak out over the horizon. Another bleak rainy day in the forecast. June was first out of the bed; she hurried over to the bathroom to check herself out in the mirror. She was shocked to see two huge red bloodshot eyes surrounded by deep black bruising. The point where Livingstone had struck her on the jaw was also deeply bruised. She looked like a beaten-up Panda bear.

Neither of them felt like eating so they decided to get showered and head for the precinct, hopefully to avoid any waiting press or TV cameras. It was just after 7.00 am when Ethan pulled up outside the precinct, and the press were already waiting. He decided that it might be better to answer a few questions rather than to keep avoiding them. Maybe that would get rid of them.

With their backs to the front door of the precinct, the two detectives turned to face the press. To their surprise, the first order of business was an ovation for their heroic actions in taking down the Zodiac Rapist.

Ethan fielded questions about his and his twin brother's relationship. He answered them, making it quite clear that until a few weeks ago he never knew Livingstone had existed. He was sad to find he had a brother who was determined to kill him and those close to him. He put off further questions by saying he was sure full details of the case would be released in due course.

June was almost ignored, until one TV reporter asked her what her relationship was to Ethan. Caught on the back foot, she didn't deny or confirm and just said they were detective partners. They took the opportunity to end the questioning by making a quick about turn and disappeared into the precinct.

As they passed the front desk, the cops on duty burst into spontaneous applause. There was also a lot of banter about June's new look. A couple of the male cops offered to date her, even though she looked pretty scary, all-in good fun. June took the jests in stride; it made her feel normal again.

Garcia, Shaw, and Mills were already in the situation room, busy dismantling the "timeline"; it was old news now. A few minutes later Johnston came wheezing into the room, which was a first for him.

The next hour was spent reliving the previous day's events, making sure everyone had the same memories of what went down. Each of the five detectives were required to make a written statement. The happy gathering was interrupted by the arrival of four IA detectives; they certainly weren't waiting for the ink to dry.

Ethan and June were summoned separately to be interviewed. It was police policy to go through the process in the event of a fatal shooting. None of the cops felt comfortable going through the process; they always felt IA were looking for a reason to find them guilty of something.

Most of the rest of the day was taken up with writing statements and interviews with IA. By 3.00 pm, IA were finished with Ethan and June; their recommendation was that both were to be suspended from duty for a minimum of two weeks on full pay until all reports and investigations were completed.

IA had barely left the building when a contingent of big brass arrived. The Mayor, the Police Commissioner, the precinct Captain, and the Police Union Representative. Accompanying them were an ABC7NY TV anchor and cameraman; so as not to show favoritism, the party included a CNN anchor and her cameraman.

The five detectives were ushered into the situation room and asked to stand up against the right-hand wall next to Garcia's office. Once all were satisfactorily positioned, the Mayor took over. With the cameras firmly on him and the Police Commissioner, he began his customary long-winded speech.

For the next ten minutes, he extolled the excellence of the 35th precinct's Homicide Detectives. Calling out each one individually, starting with Garcia, then Shaw and Mills. Hayes was called forward where she was awarded 'The Police Commendation Medal for Bravery'.

Finally, it was the perceived hero in bringing down The Zodiac Rapist, Detective Ethan O'Connell. He was awarded 'The New York City Police Department Medal of Valor'. He was asked to say a few words.

'Thank you, Mayor Harmon, it is a great honor, but this medal shouldn't be for me. Without my colleagues, we would not have caught Livingstone. If Linda Mills and June Hayes had not worked out that Livingstone was not me, I would now be dead. They saved my life and for that I will be eternally grateful. We are all just happy that an evil man is no longer roaming the streets of our city. Thank you all.'

Harmon could have ended the news conference there and then, but he spent the next five minutes extolling how his new Police procedures were taking effect and would continue after his reelection.

The party broke up and the five detectives plus Lieutenant Johnston took the rest of the day off and headed for the Pub. They were joined by all the off-duty cops, and a copious amount of liquor was consumed.

The following day Ethan and June left for the warmer climes of Cozumel in Mexico for two weeks at an all-inclusive resort.

The story ran for the next few days, the public couldn't get enough of the handsome twins who had such different lives. How could two people, identical in every physical way, be so different physiologically?

Ethan and Jane were cleared by IA and the whole saga was consigned to history.

That is until Sandra Williamson's estranged sister, who was living in Aurora, Illinois, read how her sister's death was tied into the Zodiac Rapist. She contacted a lawyer, and they launched a civil case against the New York Police Department. The suit cited police negligence in not protecting her 'beloved' sister. The suit was for $5,000,000 in damages.

As with many inmates of the New York prison system the inmates of Green Haven Correctional Facility Route 216 Stormville New York followed the case of the Zodiac Rapist with great interest.

Career criminal and Serial offender Nicholas "Nasty Nick" Barkus who was doing a ten year stretch for robbery and sexual assault was no different. He followed the daily news updates and when the final outcome was detailed he couldn't contain himself any longer.

He bragged to his cell mate that he knew details about the murder of the O'Connell's that the news reports did not release. He said the cops never found the Japanese Tanto sword that was used in the murder and they never would as he knew what had happened to it.

His cell mate seeing an opportunity to get his sentence reduced requested to speak to the warden. He related Barkus' story to the warden who passed the details on to the Captain at the 94th precinct. The information was quickly escalated and the DNA samples from the O'Connell murders was compared to a sample extracted from Barkus.

The match was perfect and Barkus was officially charged with the robbery and murder of Dennis and Mary O'Connell. He was found guilty and sentenced to life without the possibility of parole.

The End

About the Author

James "Jim" Bellis was born in Johannesburg. He spent his formative years in South Africa, Rhodesia and England. After a short stint as a bank clerk he found his niche as a computer programmer. His professional career was spent designing and writing computer software.

Now retired he lives in Conway, South Carolina with his wife Philippa, with whom he shares five children and nine grandchildren.

Be Afraid is his third published book, following:

Wildfire

Wildfire: The Revenge

Contact me via email I will personally answer all.

jimbellis@yahoo.com